A VEIL FOR A CAPITAL

A VEIL FOR A CAPITAL

William Shaw

The Book Guild Ltd
Sussex, England

First published in Great Britain in 2003 by
The Book Guild Ltd
25 High Street,
Lewes, East Sussex
BN7 2LU

Typesetting in Baskerville by
Keyboard Services, Luton, Bedfordshire

Printed in Great Britain by
Antony Rowe Ltd, Chippenham, Wiltshire

A catalogue record for this book is available from
The British Library

ISBN 1 85776 674 1

PART ONE

1

Curiosity killed the cat, his mother always told him. She might as well have saved her breath. He was in the curiosity business and he was curious now.

The woman sitting a few rows ahead of him on the opposite side of the aisle of the 757 was certainly worth more than a passing thought. He was first attracted to her in the lounge at Heathrow. Poised, leggy and blonde, in a way not normally given to people who aren't either movie stars or pretending to be, she wore a yellow dress of the simple kind only money can buy, together with accessories by Gucci.

She was preoccupied, perhaps unhappy. She leafed listlessly through a copy of *Vogue* as if it were a travel brochure for Kamchatka. Her husband, if it was he, not quite portly but, at fiftyish, starting to head that way, was a pin-striped affair with tufts of silvery hair teasing each ear. He always seemed to be getting up for something. Once or twice she looked up at him, annoyed. Now, on the plane, Paul regretted that the man was sitting on the aisle-side. The woman's blonde hair was just about visible above the back of her window-seat. Was she gazing sadly out the window? The presumed husband had an open briefcase on his lap and he was going through his papers as avidly as if they were a TV dinner.

Come off it, lad, just because a woman is beautiful doesn't mean she's unfulfilled – even if she ought to be. Paul had a professional stake in not mixing fantasies with observation.

Flight BA430 to Schipol Airport was a short journey and wouldn't last much longer. Paul turned his mind away from the damsel in possible distress to a brown envelope he'd brought out from his inside breast pocket, labelled 'Top Secret'. Here we go. Thank God there are still some secrets left. Inside this envelope there were three others. At the top left-hand corner of one was typed: '662 – To Be Read First'. The second was marked 'Personal', while the third was stamped – this time in red – with 'Not To Be Opened Except In An Emergency'.

He opened the 662 envelope. No more envelopes inside this one, so at least it wasn't a game. It contained a memo from Head of Department to 662, otherwise himself:

> You have been briefed on the purpose of your assignment in Amsterdam. This note gives you authority to commit the Department as required by circumstances. The name of your contact is contained in the envelope marked 'Not To Be Opened Except In An Emergency'. Only this person is aware of the reason for your visit. I trust your meeting will be successful. Good luck.
>
> C.
>
> P.S. Read and destroy this communication and the one marked 'Personal'.

Paul wondered why they bothered. He'd been through the whole thing with 'C' the previous night. He knew whom he was to see, he knew what it was all about. True, every bureaucracy needs all the details in triplicate ('for the files'), but Paul was a legman by instinct and profession and had never really come to terms with the pen-pushers and the red tape. That made promotion difficult.

He looked out the window, down at the tiny ships plying their trade like radio-controlled models on the Serpentine. Daily business-as-usual on the North Sea. Whose world is the more real? Theirs or mine? he asked himself. He'd never made up his mind about that one. Sometimes one, sometimes the other seemed realler. The lulling vibration of the aircraft merged the two into one in his mind.

Paul felt a *frisson* of surprise when he flipped over the envelope marked 'Personal'. On the back was printed 'Office of the Prime Minister'. He knew his assignment was a little unusual but this seemed to be taking it a bit far. He tore it open with a shade more curiosity. It contained the photocopy of a note from the Prime Minister's secretary to 'C':

> The P.M. has asked me to convey to you the gravity with which she views the destabilising possibilities of the situation you discussed with her today. Notwithstanding the lack of solid evidence for immediate action at top level, the indicators - we agree - are sufficiently ominous for you to be authorised to seek the co-operation of the Intelligence Community globally, to take preventative action against terrorist groupings with high-risk targets in mind, and to report back to her for regular briefings on the situation.
>
> M.J. Grossmith

Thank you, M.J. Grossmith. You've made my day. What's this, then? 'C' didn't say anything about the Prime Minister last night. What has caused her to have a bee in her bonnet (not for the first time) that we don't already know about? 'C' had had to put up with a fair amount of Prime Ministerial interference during the present administration, and not always with a good grace. Was the P.M. on the prowl for new enemies now that the Reds-under-the-bed syndrome was no longer feasible, due to a certain impatience of the citizens in the streets of a number of Eastern European countries, including the Big One? Was she looking for a new mast-head for her particular brand of patriotism? Was it paranoia? Or was the Intelligence Service required to find new pretexts for the maintenance of high defence spending levels?

Paul liked all these subversive ideas but sensed that it was something more.

Terrorism.

And then he recalled the joint resolution on international terrorism signed by the leaders of the recent O.E.C.D. summit. The P.M.'s discussion with 'C' was obviously a follow-through on the chit-chat she'd picked up in Ottawa. So – to the battle-stations, lads.

Now Paul knew why 'C', who normally gave the impression of sleep-walking, had been almost animated in last evening's chat about 'indicators'. Indicators. Oh yes, there are always plenty of those if that's what you're looking for. That is, if you see a villain in every seaweed-munching crank.

Where was the substance to the fear, expressed darkly by 'C', that a terrorist group might well be hatching a plan to hold a capital city like Paris or London to ransom? It sounded a bit Fu Manchuish. Or even shades of Professor Moriarty. The suspicion that 'C' might be indulging in a little collective madness – whose source was a fairly excitable Prime Minister – came over Paul. He had asked for more to go on but 'C' had snapped that it was Paul's job to find that.

So, where do we start? Unlike dealing with a time-honoured and well-established adversary like Moscow (those dear, dead days of 'Smersh'), messing about with terrorist groups was far trickier. Far more own-goals were scored. Never mind the P.L.O., Red Brigade, Iranians of various persuasions – we hadn't even been particularly successful, intelligence-wise, against the Irish. Well, we had, of course, but it was funny how they always managed to pop up somewhere else. We had been dealing the 'final, devastating blow' to the I.R.A. for nearly twenty years. It was all very well to sign declarations against terrorists. The job was to catch the buggers. And catch them *before*, not *after* some supermarket or military barracks got blown up.

But what was being talked about wasn't a supermarket, or a barracks, or another Lockerbie. What was being suggested was a whole damned megalopolis. Come off it. How? With what? Why?

He would have to pick up some kind of lead in Amsterdam.

Stately city of junkies, prosties, graffiti: half money and half carnival. Already the city spread out somewhere below, a vast seventeenth-century landscape, thousands of houses built by thousands of old Dutch masters. The Cousins would tell him where to take it from here, 'C' had said.

No smiling eyes greeted Paul as he filed through with his collected luggage at Schipol, some time after landing at 11.35. The glass wall separating returning passengers from welcomers contained the latter like some kind of huge, human aquarium.

Nor were there any fish in that aquarium making a bee-line for, or more appropriately rising to the bait of, the blonde in the yellow dress and her seemingly important husband. Paul fancied he'd seen the man somewhere before: he had a celebrity-look about him. And didn't she shake him off petulantly, just then, when he'd offered to carry her hand-luggage? Paul caught a glimpse of what looked like a tiny scene. Maybe life with her wasn't all daffodils.

As he was getting into a taxi Paul saw that the couple had been met by a chauffeur, whose placard was no longer on display – so who they were remained a mystery to him. The chauffeur was now guiding them to an opulent limo, parked illegally, no doubt, and without fear of retribution.

The service frowned on agents meeting each other joyfully at airports: it made for such lovely snapshots. At least by getting into a taxi you could be anyone, bound for anywhere. It was standard procedure. As standard as flushing Top Secret communications down airplane loos. While they were still in the air, Paul had got another look at the blonde on the way back from his phoney ablutions. She didn't like him looking at her, that was obvious. And a bit hoity-toity. Why shouldn't he look at her? She was something to look at, and she must have picked up that concept by now. He wondered if it was mere haughtiness. He wondered if it was fear.

The real rendezvous-point for him was one of the gates into Vondel Park. He peeled off the luncheon-voucher-type notes until the driver seemed reasonably satisfied. Then he saw the hire-car across the road, complete with driver. I'll miss all this efficiency when I retire, he thought. The figure got out and unfolded as a heavily built man in a suit, about thirty-three. He might have been Dutch. By the warmth of their handshake it was obvious they were complete strangers to one another.

The driver kept the silence of a discreet servant as they rode over Vondel Bridge and past the Rijksmuseum. Paul was always promising himself a visit whenever he came this way but decided once again that the Night Watch would have to wait a little longer.

After crossing the Amstel at the end of Utrechtstraat,

they turned shortly into Joden Breestraat, pulling up a short distance away from the Rembrandthuis where You-Know-Who had fought his losing battle with mortgage repayments.

Paul got out of the car and went up the front steps to the door of the house. He waved goodbye to the man as the hire-car drove off. Not a barrel of laughs, any of those boys.

The dark and heavy atmosphere of the tall house enveloped him as the girl led him into the drawing-room. Not a girl, exactly; more a woman in her thirties, black hair, attractive in a heavy-ankled sort of way. She and the house seemed to go together.

'You're Anna?' he asked. They really briefed you in London.

'Yes, Mr Finningham,' she replied. Golly, they'd briefed her, too.

The drawing-room fireplace was flanked on either side by bookshelves filled with leather-bound volumes. Anna selected a Shakespeare which she might have been about to read aloud from, only the book didn't quite come off the shelf. It was a lever which swung the entire left-hand bookcase round, to reveal a slightly cosier room within – cosy except for its strip-lighting and the fact that it had no windows. She shut the secret door, which was an oak wall-panel on this side of the 'books', and bade Paul make himself comfortable in one of the three armchairs.

'Would you like something? We have coffee and sandwiches.'

'Yes both, thanks,' said Paul, who'd had little breakfast. The sideboard looked like a drinks cabinet but he was pretty sure there wasn't any of the hard stuff around – not in one of Her Majesty's safe houses. Anna's little domestic touches were somewhat de-cosified by the cellophane wrapping around the plate of sandwiches she handed him, but the ham went down well enough. So did the coffee. Thank God flavour-granules stopped at Dover. Chief reason for going abroad.

Anna, a sleeper 'reawakened' for this occasion, sat down in another chair and folded her hands in her lap, *hausfrau*-like. Silence pervaded. Being of wildly different grades they didn't have a lot to talk about. And being foreign to each other they didn't even share the weather.

Nearly twenty minutes dragged by like this. They both jumped slightly when a buzzer attached to the front doorbell rasped out. Anna excused herself and opened the wall-panel with a control-button, taking care to shut it behind her.

In a moment or two the panel opened again and in loped a fair-haired, blue-eyed and lanky Jimmy-Stewart-type American, unaccompanied this time by Anna. As the door closed behind him he held out a very long hand to Paul.

'Hi Paul, how are you?'

'Fine. How's it going?' They shook hands.

'That's some password: "yes, but the clouds will pass". Pure poetry, maybe John Greenleaf Whittier or somebody. A little old-fashioned, don't you think?' Andy Hartford from the C.I.A., fresh from Langley, Virginia, sank down in one of the armchairs as if he owned the place – which perhaps by now the C.I.A. did.

'I'll take it up with the Literature Section,' said Paul. 'I think I've eaten all the sandwiches.'

'That's all right, I ate on the way over. Funny herring-things I grabbed off a fish-stall. Dunno about them, really. So. What brings you here?'

'Very funny,' said Paul. 'I was going to ask you.'

'Thereby hangs a tale, "old chap".'

Andy thought he was a whiz at a British accent, which

he was always pulling out from God-knew-where. In reality it was execrable.

'First, I want some of that coffee.'

Paul let him forage for himself. 'Look,' he said, 'my chief's jumping up and down with stuff about a major threat to one of the capitals, maybe London, we don't know. The question is who, why, how?'

'That's three questions,' replied Andy, sitting down with his coffee.

'Ha-ha. Right then, why not go for four? Question One: Who are they? Question Two: How are they going to do it? Three: Where? And Four: Why? What's the motive? The angle?'

'You like getting to the point, oh boy. Well, it seems to me Question One and Question Four are the same. If we knew the answer to the one we'd know the answer to the other.' Andy Hartford made a face. 'This crap's cold.'

'Get Mata Hari out there to warm it up for you.'

'Hey, wasn't Mata Hari Dutch?'

'If I didn't know you better I'd say you were being a little evasive,' snapped Paul. 'The point is, I've been sent over here because "C" says you can tell me what's going on. Are you going to, or what?'

'Come on, Paul, give me time. It's a little complicated. I've still got fucking jet-lag.'

Excuses. 'What have we got, then? Sons of the Ayatollah pouring stuff into our drinking water?'

'Didn't think you needed their help with that,' said Andy, grimacing as he parted company with his half-imbibed coffee.

'Is it Arabs at all? Or the Red Brigade? What kind of resources do they have?'

'Give us a break!' Andy held up his hand. 'We don't know that much, I can say that right now. What we have is what we have, that's all.'

'I think this is a wild-goose chase,' muttered Paul.

'I didn't say that,' said Andy. 'You just have to listen and see what you make of it.' Paul had first come across Andy Hartford during joint covert operations in the Caribbean, where the C.I.A. man had initiated him into the mysteries of rum-based cocktails – forget your *pina colada* rubbish. Apart from his skill with the shaker Andy generally had something worth knowing, even if it took a while to prise it out of him.

'Did you have a good trip over?'

'Wrong direction. West to east is always the wrong direction, doesn't matter how many times you do it.'

'Why Amsterdam?'

Andy sat forward in his chair. 'Because that's the one solid piece of info we have. Whatever it is is based in this country, so here's where we start. I said it's complicated, and I mean it. If how we know what we know gets out, the shit will hit the fan in Moscow.'

Paul's eyebrows raised. 'It's come from a mole of yours in the K.G.B.' he said.

'Got it. That's what's so delicate about all this. The source. It's different from how it used to be. In the old days, you exposed one of your own by mistake or whatever, all that happened was that he got caught and eventually exchanged for one of theirs. The stakes are higher now. The Russian President's staking everything on good relations with us. So the Russkies find we're still working operatives over there and he's discredited in the eyes of his own people. Policy is: we don't embarrass the Russian President at any cost. That's straight from Langley.'

'What has your operative come across?'

Andy shrugged. 'Not a hell of a lot. Maybe as much as the whole K.G.B. knows, maybe less. What there is is definite, it's hard and horny, but kind of a jigsaw with most of the big bits missing. Or like a dream where you've got her legs open and then you wake up. Hell, our guy's only a filing-clerk at the Lubianka. Maybe I've said too much already.'

'So far you haven't said anything at all!' cried Paul. 'My chief told me all this, more or less, last night, except for your Lubianka clerk.'

'He didn't know about that – we wouldn't even put it through the cipher,' said Andy. 'I'm supposed to be able to trust you. And I do – honestly, Paul. But I don't trust your outfit. You're the only one outside the Company who knows about our clerk. It's not going to get out, is it?' he stared meaningly – and maddeningly – into Paul's eyes.

Paul shifted in his chair, thinking all this somewhat juvenile. 'I'm going to have to make my full report to "C",' he said. 'I don't have any choice about that and anyway, he has the right to know everything.'

'Langley told him the substance of the plot as we picked it up – damned well had to since London may be the target. But we're not giving away our sources for your de-coders to tattle. Talk to your Control face-to-face on that angle but don't write anything down about it till all this is in the archives.'

'Langley sounds pretty paranoid about this if you ask me,' said Paul.

'If those Kremlin hard-liners or some military strongmen get in we could all be up the creek *sans* paddle. It just needs one guy somewhere along the intelligence network to louse things up over a bunch of crackpot terrorists.'

'Seems to me it would be simpler to pull up stakes in Moscow altogether.'

Andy smiled. 'You cannot be serious,' he said.

'Anyhow, I won't be the one to "louse things up", if that's what you're worried about.' Paul would dearly like to have defended his Department. It was about as cleaned-up and watertight as any agency could be, but he knew this would only make Andy suspect special pleading on his part. He needed Andy's personal trust to get as much out of him as he could. This was confirmed when Andy next told him that Langley had sent him off with the strict instruction not to reveal the existence of the clerk, even to Paul. He was taking a lot on board, but he knew his man. So, Andy had him down as the British Agent Most Likely to Keep His Trap Shut. Paul was keeping it shut now. In fact he was grinding his teeth.

'So there we are.' Andy was winding up. 'Through our operative in Moscow the Company has reason to believe an organisation's been set up to terrorise the West by holding some major capital, probably either London or Paris, to ransom. Its size and strength are unknown. We think probably London because a high-up civil servant or politician there is believed to be involved.'

'Nobody told me that,' said Paul.

'Well, now you know,' said Andy levelly. 'Don't worry, it's not all British. There seems to be an ex-officer from one of the United States armed services in there somewhere too.'

'How do you know that without knowing who it is?'

'I told you the info was frustrating. Bits and pieces. Anyway, what we have says Mercenaries. It's got to be. I mean with an ex-military and some politician and Christ knows who else, it's not your classical *jihad,* is it?'

'Isn't that a bit of an assumption?'

'Computer projection on what we know,' said Andy, as if that clinched it. 'Amsterdam came into it, so it makes sense. Central, sort of neutral ground. Lot of oddballs around for local camouflage.'

'Not fanatical,' mused Paul, thoughtfully. 'Not fanatics, not a holy war. Does that rule out Arabs? Or are they still in the running? As a backer, perhaps? Bound to be an Arab country in there somewhere. Proximity to Europe says something.'

'Could be.'

'So which Arab country wants to hold a European capital to ransom?'

'Probably all of them.' Andy stroked his chin. 'Libya and Iran are up front, of course, but it's bloody hard hacking into their machinations.'

'Especially since your entire Middle Eastern operation went up the spout,' said Paul, working out some of his irritation about the C.I.A. in general. He had touched a nerve. The C.I.A.'s Middle Eastern organisation had been blown in Egypt the previous year – something not to be quickly repaired. It would take at least three to five years to get it up and running again, in the fully operational sense. That was somewhat late to be of assistance in this particular caper, which might be imminent for all they knew. Unfortunately, British Intelligence had been relying largely on American in the Middle Eastern sphere.

'Hell, it might not even be a country involved,' said Andy. 'It could be one of those groups they shelter here, there and everywhere. Fucking mess.'

'And it all came from your boy in the K.G.B.,' said Paul. 'How do *they* know? Could be because they still *do* have a Middle Eastern operation worthy of the name. Bound to be, now that they've got their Muslim problem erupting in their faces.'

Andy's tubular limbs craved exercise. He pulled himself out of his deep armchair and began wandering about. Paul wondered if he could stop him in his tracks.

'So why don't we go to them?' He succeeded. Andy stopped dead.

'Go to the K.G.B.?'

'Makes sense,' Paul shrugged innocently. 'Your man

only knows so much. Perhaps the official version will reveal more.'

'I don't know if I'm hearing you right. We go to them with this and they'll know where it came from.'

'Not necessarily,' said Paul. 'Good God, don't you chaps know anything about bluff after all these years? I thought poker was your game. You run the biggest intelligence-gathering organisation in the world – well, the most sophisticated. The K.G.B. got lucky in this particular instance. Who's to say you didn't as well? Tell them your vast computer network's come up with something you'd like to check out with them.'

Andy stared into space for a moment. 'What reason do we give them for wanting to rope them into this?'

'I should have thought it was obvious. A joint effort to halt the Menace of Terrorism throughout the world, which includes them with a vengeance!'

'They weren't signatories to the O.E.C.D. declaration.'

'I hardly think that's relevant,' said Paul exasperatedly.

'No, what I mean is, so far as Russia's concerned they're specifically excluded from these big joint-intelligence deals. Langley policy is not to get into direct contact with the K.G.B. I suppose if I put it in triplicate to the Director I just might be able to exchange cookie recipes. The security stinks. And back home it's still political dynamite. We've still got a Vice President jerking off over the Soviet Menace, you know.'

Andy was sounding off too much. Paul could see he was interested. Wait for it, he thought. He was right. After getting his breath back, Andy resumed, in a quieter vein:

'Have you got authority to go to the K.G.B.?'

'I could get it.'

Andy scratched his head, looking more like Jimmy Stewart than ever; a Jimmy Stewart wondering if he should run Dietrich in. In reality his mind was turning over all sorts of possibilities, wondering if these things shouldn't be being tossed back and forth at a higher level in his organisation – instead of just between him and an agent who didn't even work for the same country. But there was no denying the fascination of it. There must be a way out. He couldn't go back to Washington with all this now; his mission had scarcely begun. 'If we were to make this a British Intelligence initiative, then all I'd have to do would be to sit in on an informal basis. And I guess Washington could find out about it later – if at all,' said Andy hopefully.

Great, thought Paul. The bastard was happy enough to cast aspersions on British Intelligence when it suited him to be paranoid, and then just as happy to let it carry the can. Oh well, it *had* been Paul's idea.

Paul sighed. 'I'll get "C" on the blower, then.' He excused himself.

'Well, I suppose you're right,' said 'C' over the telephone. 'I don't imagine we need go to a higher authority over this. Anyhow I can't keep ringing the P.M. every five minutes.'

'She does say to seek co-operation from the intelligence community globally,' Paul pointed out helpfully.

'Yes, I suppose that clears us. You're certain this is absolutely necessary?'

'It's a lead we have to follow,' said Paul.

'You'll be meeting in Amsterdam?'

'That's where the action is.'

'I'll notify Joint Operations to set it up, then. How are you getting on with Jack Buchanan?'

'Who?'

'Andy Hartford. For some reason or other he always reminds me of Jack Buchanan. An American Jack Buchanan if you can imagine such a thing.'

'Never heard of him.'

'You're too young. Never mind. Report back to me after your meeting with "G", won't you? And give him my regards.'

Another twenty-four hours elapsed during which the K.G.B. presumably hummed and hawed on their side before duly coughing up Georgi Arbatov, known in the trade as 'G'. A three-cornered meeting, which included Andy Hartford, was set up on neutral ground in a hotel-room in the centre of Amsterdam. The Russians knew all about the safe house at Joden Breestraat and had known of it for years, but decorum dictated that they not actually be invited there.

When they shook hands Paul noticed what he couldn't help feel was a genially wicked gleam in the Russian's slightly bulgy eyes, a wickedness all the more emphasised by heavy Cossack eyebrows. Arbatov's tie was askew and he wore one of those penetratingly blue double-breasted Russian suits that are tailored for Siberian bears.

'You won't have met Andy Hartford, I don't think,' said Paul to Georgi as the latter strode into the room with arm outstretched. Hardly.

'I know you only by reputation, Mr Hartford,' he said, shaking the American's hand vigorously. 'Though I suppose that is not exactly a compliment in our trade, is it?' He seemed to be enjoying himself. Andy was transfixed by the former mortal enemy. For a while it looked as if it might be love at first sight.

'Would you like some tea, Mr Arbatov?' asked Paul.

'I wonder. Have you by chance any vodka?'

By chance, Paul had. The Service overlooked nothing. Andy was already drinking bourbon. 'Not the proper sort, I expect, Mr Arbatov,' said Paul, pouring the most he could into a tiny glass.

'Please, call me Georgi,' said Arbatov. 'And I'll call you Paul. And I'll call *you* Andy. Much better!' The American raised his glass in silent acknowledgement. 'Well! This is good! The three of us meeting here! Like the Berlin Wall coming down!' He downed the colourless firewater in one gulp.

' "C" sends his regards,' said Paul, primly sipping his tea. The Russian burst into laughter, in that sudden, alarming way they have. Perhaps he recalled the days of their youth, interrogating Nazi war-criminals together. He dried his eyes and asked for another vodka. Paul poured him one and then gave him the bottle. The conversation went on to the subject of angling, solely between Georgi and Andy. Paul wondered whether Andy pulled all this instant knowledge of flies out of a lifelong hobby or had got it up during the twenty-four hours they'd waited. Either way, he was something a little more or a little less than the freshman callowness he gave off. Maybe it had been the same with the cocktails. Had they spotted Paul as an alcoholic? It was worrying.

The superpowers were getting along fine. Paul, who was feeling left out, decided it was time to get down to business.

'My Department has been following certain lines of investigation concerning irregular activities in the United Kingdom and elsewhere,' he began tentatively, hoping his nose wouldn't grow or sprout twigs, like Pinocchio's. 'We've, um, stumbled across information that has been put together from various sources and cross-checked.'

'And you think this information might be of interest to us?' Georgi asked, pouring a third vodka.

Paul and Andy exchanged quick glances. 'Potentially,' said Paul, 'we think it might be of great interest to you. And you might be able to help us.'

Georgi's eyebrows raised about twenty degrees. 'If you want our help, then it must be terrorism.'

'Got it in one,' said Andy.

Georgi shrugged. 'I don't know if we can help you in the West. We have our own problems but I do not think they are connected. Unless you believe in big conspiracy theories. The day for that is past.'

Paul pressed on. 'We are reasoning that the connection could be Islamic. If that's the case they could be operating on either side' (of the Iron Curtain, he had been about to add, but stopped himself just in time. Old habits died hard).

'And have you more definite proof that the source is Islamic?' asked Georgi pointedly. Well might he ask.

'That's just it,' confessed Paul. 'We haven't. We know that whatever it is is based here in Amsterdam for convenience to strike at a major western European capital, and the strongest bet is London. But who it is, who's financing it, or why, we haven't a clue.'

The old gleam came back into Georgi's eyes. 'How do you know it isn't us?' he asked.

'Is it?' Andy asked, poker-faced.

'Not so far as I'm aware,' chortled Georgi. 'Of course we are a very large organisation and I cannot be expected to keep up with the whole range of our activities!' Once again tears accompanied the laughter.

'I kind of think you'd know about this one,' said Andy drily. Paul reflected briefly on the irony of the situation: here we are, telling the Russian information he already knows, pretending it comes from our own sources, while he's pretending he doesn't know anything about it. 'Just *because* you are such a large organisation,' continued Andy, 'you might have come across something that could correspond to what the British have found. And we'd want to get in on the act, too.'

'It would have to be considered,' said Georgi, reverting to solemnity.

Paul realised he and Andy were offering the Russian a horse-trade without any horses on view for inspection. He decided to say so. 'You mean that we don't seem to be offering you anything concrete?' Georgi Arbatov shrugged but made no comment. 'The truth is that any trade of information is bound to be uneven just at the moment.'

'That seems to mean that you think we have something to offer you,' said the K.G.B. man. 'But I can assure you, so far as I am aware we know nothing of such plots in the West.'

Andy stepped in. 'Terrorist activity is having an internationally destabilising effect. Our leaders weren't fooling around when they signed the joint declaration on terrorism. And I can't think your leadership wants it, either – airports blown up, planes hi-jacked, shopping centres bombed – it's the last thing you need. Maybe nailing this thing will benefit all of us for future world peace and understanding.'

'That is all very well, my friend, but if I can't help you, I can't help you.'

'You must have operatives in the Middle East,' protested Paul. Andy gave him a sharp look. And so did Georgi. 'I mean, if we think that's where it's emanating from you might be the first people to know!'

Georgi Arbatov suddenly stood up, putting his glass down on the side-table by his chair. 'I'm sorry, but we have no information.' *Nyet.*

'I don't believe you, Georgi,' said Andy, venturing forth where before he'd dared not tread. Both westerners were hungry for some word from this man.

Georgi looked a little downcast. 'I suppose after all these bitter years, I couldn't expect you to,' he sighed. Then he was suddenly brisk. 'Is that everything? If it is, then I think I must leave you.'

Paul said: 'Could you at least check back with your people to see if there's anything at all? It's desperately important to us: London may be on the line. But more than that, even, it could have implications for you as well. We're not talking liberation groups here or causes you have traditionally supported. We're talking about a malignant force, working only for money – and money can finance villainy in the East as well as in the West!'

'I'm sorry gentlemen, there is nothing I can do for you.' An arm shot out from Georgi's side. 'A pleasure to meet you both,' he said. 'Perhaps if you come up with anything more solid, that might be of use to the Soviet Union, you would contact me through the proper channels? In the interests of international co-operation,' he added, offering a last, brief twinkle of his old merry self.

Andy held Georgi's hand long enough to reply: 'And the same goes if you hear anything, okay?'

'Of course, of course. Thank you for the vodka. Not so bad.'

He was gone. Andy stood looking at the closed door for a few moments.

'Well, I hope I didn't chance our arm too far on that one,' sighed Paul.

'He's got something,' said Andy.

'What do you mean?'

'He knows what's going on. He wasn't prepared for a dialogue because they're working along these lines and they don't want us to queer their pitch. I know these guys. If they want to share something they'll be all over you. If not, then it means they've got something they don't want anyone to have. I think they've got a line on this and I'd work on that assumption if I were you.'

'You make it sound like a breakthrough,' said Paul mournfully. 'Let's face it, we didn't get much change out of him. I'm sorry I've wasted your time.'

'Don't look at it like that' said Andy, who seemed to have been newly-galvanised by the meeting with Arbatov. 'He wasn't even prepared to refer back to his people! Doesn't that in itself tell you something about what's going on? It tells me a whole lot!'

American optimism was good sometimes, like a breath of much-needed oxygen. Paul became half-convinced by Andy that the dear old K.G.B. still had a few teeth and might well hold the key to the elusive mystery. The meeting had been essential for establishing suspicions of this: they did, after all, know more than the clerk planted amongst them by the C.I.A. So at least one of the meeting's objectives had been met, even if the other – finding out what exactly they *did* know – had proved to be beyond reach.

Paul and Andy agreed to meet up again in due course as the joint operation was put together. Paul was to return to England for the time being and pursue things from his end. The fancy international stuff was over – now, time for the foot-slog back home. Andy would co-ordinate in Amsterdam, tracking down leads to the Dutch H.Q. of the terrorists, wherever it might be. But sooner or later there'd have to be results or he'd be recalled to Langley.

'It's your pigeon, really,' said Andy.

'Thanks a million, mate,' murmured Paul.

'Christ, don't worry – we'll lick this thing. And I'll get to work on the American connection, whatever it is. We'll put the Washington computers on to it.'

'Well, that's something,' said Paul, feeling suddenly drab and hopeless. Something in Georgi's manner convinced him now as never before that a plot was indeed afoot. But his questions were still unanswered as he left for Schipol: who? how? where? when? and why? Every single one.

*   *   *

You don't usually expect anything exciting on a return journey, especially out of the old newspapers you pick up for a bit of escapism on the way. But there it was. Boxed in black, front-page-right of the *Mail*: 'Murder of Minister's Wife'.

And there was the picture.

It was taken perhaps during a summer gone by: she was wearing a wide-brimmed hat, her face glowing in the cool light thrown up from below. Perhaps she'd got herself up for a local fête.

The glamorous lady, more recently seen in the yellow dress and the Gucci shoes. The one Paul would like to have rescued, if she'd needed him.

Apparently she had, after all. And right there in little old Amsterdam.

2

The dress was brown now – perhaps it was a different one. It clung to what remained of Sarah Parris, dripping obscenely as she was pulled out of the Amstel, not too far upstream from the Central Station. Her once-slim body was bloated, her once-coiffured blonde head stoved in on one side. It took an autopsy to prove that she hadn't simply bumped against the prow of some passing barge. In fact it had all the hallmarks of a professional job.

Sarah Parris. Deceased wife of Clive Parris, M.P., the Minister for Nuclear Energy in the British government.

Not in the inner cabinet, of course. Only a fairly junior minister. But important enough for his wife's murder to hit all the front pages – the cheaper the tabloid, the blacker the print. Clive Parris wouldn't have been used to this sort of publicity. He got a bit of a splash during the Chernobyl disaster, reassuring all and sundry that Nothing Like That Could Happen Here. Otherwise he had been dull copy so far as the Press generally were concerned.

Now, of course, it was different. The papers said Sarah had been accompanying her husband to a conference with other nuclear ministers from the E.E.C. in Amsterdam. No explanation was put forward by the police or other sources for her murder. As her handbag was missing it was possible to establish robbery as a motive. The British Press rattled on about the tide of junkeyism in Amsterdam – so unlike our own dear old innocent London. Paul seemed to remember hearing somewhere that the Dutch had pretty well got their heroin problem under some control. But of course a drug-related killing was always possible. Amsterdam could be a pretty violent town. But why *her* of all people? An unhappy woman he'd seen on the plane?

He thought he had sensed fear then. Was he just getting sentimental? It really would be a whole new ball game if he had been witness to her betrayal of fear. Robbery, certainly of the mugging kind, would have to be ruled out if Paul truly believed what he had seen. His memory struggled with those few, brief, fleeting glimpses of her. Could he be sure that was what he had seen, or was he simply reading into it the horror of subsequent events?

The coincidence with other things that might be going on in Holland nagged at him, too. There was no obvious connection. On the face of it there was no connection at all.

He decided to take it to 'C'. 'Frankly, it's nothing more than intuition at this stage,' he confessed to the old man.

'Clive Parris, eh?' mused 'C'. 'Is he your British high-up suspect?'

'I'm not jumping to any conclusions,' said Paul cautiously.

'C' was warming to the idea. The civil servant in him thought that Prime Ministers needed taking down a peg from time to time, especially this one, whose comeuppance was a bit overdue. Clive Parris was her appointee to the sensitive post of governing Britain's nuclear energy. It was rumoured she had her eye on him for better things one day. 'To hell with intuition,' he told Paul, and ordered up Parris's file for close inspection. 'I think your sighting of her on the plane only a couple of days prior to her death was very timely, if I may say so,' he cackled. It was a little unseemly, this behaviour on the part of his boss, Paul felt, hardened agent though he was supposed to be. The combination of the woman's beauty and tragic end had got to him. He shied away from being the instrument by which 'C' could make a little extra-curricular political capital.

Still, 'C' *was* boss, so Paul got down to the file. There was a fresh supplement from Special Branch, who kept files on all cases of luminaries such as cabinet ministers or their wives getting nobbled abroad. Special Branch's report merely echoed the later post-autopsy press reports confirming that Sarah's death was well and truly violent murder. Special Branch were maintaining a close liaison with the Dutch police on the ensuing investigation. And that was it.

Apart from a little hastily compiled internal correspondence on the Parris's security arrangements while in Amsterdam. Although officially the responsibility of the host country, Clive Parris himself had apparently been unobtrusively accompanied by a plain-clothes-man from London. The same nominal protection, however, did not extend to his wife. He was not of a sufficiently high level for that. On such bureaucratic niceties are the fates of people decided. But the important thing about this correspondence was that it established Parris to have been under constant observation. Or was he, thought Paul. He was neither a Royal nor a crook; surely attention to him could have been lax enough for him to duck out for the odd half-hour now and then? It would have been relatively easy for him to slip out of the conference hall on the pretext of going for a pee or something, or out of the back of his hotel, if he'd wanted to shake off his minder for a while. That is, if he were entertaining the murder of his wife. Why should he want to do that? After all, if he *were* implicated or involved in a big plot of some kind, surely the last thing he'd do at a time like this would be to draw attention to himself. Attention! He was on every front page from the *Sun* to the *Financial Times*!

So, ironically, his wife's death in Amsterdam made Clive Parris even less of a suspect in Paul's eyes. Unless he was the murderer – in which case the crime was one for the police, not for Paul, 'C', or anyone to do with Intelligence.

Yet there was this coincidence: everything suddenly happening in Amsterdam. Even logic couldn't shake it from Paul's mind.

Clive Parris had professed to the Press (through a 'spokesman') his complete stupefaction and deep sadness at his wife's death. He apparently couldn't understand why anyone would have done such a thing, unless the motive were robbery of some sort. Nice one, that last tag, thought Paul. Keep the idea of robbery alive, even in your most harrowing moments of grief.

Still, Paul had to admit to himself that he didn't have any better ideas than the one proffered so publicly by Clive Parris.

Parris said to the police that he and she had gone their separate ways while in Amsterdam, apart from the opening E.E.C. function. He attended meetings and luncheons; she went shopping or sightseeing, had a coffee morning with the other ministerial wives. On the fatal night, Parris was late from a meeting which had overrun and so had not had occasion to miss her until about midnight. Well, so much for him, then. He surely had an alibi. Depending on when she was actually killed. Depending on whether or not he had done it himself or hired somebody else. The latter seemed more plausible: would a British minister knock his wife on the head on some street in a foreign country? On a street, anywhere – it seemed bizarre. Until one remembered John

Stonehouse. (Does *anyone* remember John Stonehouse, the Labour minister who skilfully finessed a counterfeit Lord Lucan scenario all those years ago?)

Paul wanted badly to question Clive Parris for himself.

'Out of the question at this stage, Paul,' said 'C'. 'He's already had a going-over from both the Dutch police and Special Branch when he got back home. Another lot of questioning from us and he'll be off, complaining to *her* about persecution. Can't do it. Not yet.' Actually, 'C' was now so hot for Parris to be implicated that he didn't want anything clumsy to gum up the chance, such as getting the P.M.'s dander up over her bereaved minister being bullied. Besides, if the man truly had something to hide, he would only be forewarned if he thought Intelligence were after him.

So Paul had to content himself with the boring details of Parris's potted biography. Never mind. Great oaks from little acorns grow. Grandfather a milling tycoon; home at Baythorne Manor, the ancient baronial towers of a not-so-baronial family; public school (Rugby); National Service; Trinity, Cambridge. Too late for the Cambridge Apostles or any of that gay-bolshie crowd, no radical tendencies noted while a student. Just a plodding, hard worker, gaining an honours degree in physics of all things. How mundane, for a family like his who had long since eschewed Grandfather's earthy practicality, and thought the law to be the very *least* of proper callings. Maybe Clive was a throwback. At any rate, he had shown more perspicacity than he may have been given credit for: the physics degree held him in good stead for the upward climb, post-Wilsonian era. After postgraduate work and research, Clive had begun to rise in the nuclear industry while starting to dabble in local constituency affairs for the party. After a couple of tries in a couple of impossible seats, he was elected to the safe seat of

Ramshurst and Bewlay in 1979. Six years later he was a government minister.

In 1984 he had married Sarah Illingworth, daughter of a naval officer. There were no children. Significant? Ah well, that's for you to find out! Paul searched long and hard for any whiff of scandal on these yellowing pages: nothing. No apparent extra-marital affairs, no bun in some other oven, no boyfriends – nothing. Zilch, as Andy would say.

'He's incredibly boring, isn't he?' said 'C', looking in. Paul made a despairing gesture. 'In fact,' continued 'C', 'something of a cold fish altogether, or so they say. Never done anything wrong, never a hair out of place, not so much as an overdue library book. Doesn't seem natural to me.'

'Come on,' expostulated Paul, 'don't be so unfair. He never did anything to blot his copybook so immediately he comes under suspicion. Hardly an incentive to be sober and law-abiding, is it?'

'Maybe he has a hobby,' hinted 'C' ambiguously.

'Tennis, swimming and collecting stamps,' said Paul with finality.

'I don't believe it,' said 'C'. 'What kind of a Prime Minister would he make? I can just see the likes of *him* trudging up to Lockerbie or Hillsborough to dispense compassion among the humble.'

'Is he in the running?' asked Paul, surprised.

'Could be. Safe and steady, young enough, but old enough to replace *her*, or even her successor, when the time comes. Not been in the rut of the junior ranks *too* long, but could be a dark horse when all the seniors go down, if he himself can get some senior experience first.'

Paul was inclined to doubt it, but he lacked 'C''s political savvy. Clive Parris as future Prime Minister? Stranger things happened at sea.

'We might be doing this country a positive service for once in our lives if we could nail him,' said 'C', who seemed to be working up a positive hatred for the man.

'I can't see how we're going to do that,' said Paul.

'*Something's* not right about him,' persisted 'C'. 'Nobody really likes him much, not even his own P.P.S., Brixdale. He's a member of the usual clubs and all that but he doesn't exactly glitter. Secretive – that's what he is, secretive.'

'About what?'

'He's got to be into something. On the fiddle? Ambitious? Hiding a habit? Writing a diary?'

'I'm going to talk to Jane Illingworth,' said Paul, slapping Parris's file down on the desk.

'Who's she?'

But Jane Illingworth wasn't at home. The newspaper office where she worked as an assistant features editor informed Paul that she was in Amsterdam on a private matter and was expected back at the paper in a day or two.

You always remember the day when the greatest catastrophe of your life befell. Jane Illingworth was tidying up yet another article in the Green Revolution series, removing split infinitives from her Amstrad the very moment when the phone rang in her office. On that day.

'British Embassy in Amsterdam for you, Jane – they won't say what it's about,' said Suzie on the line.

'That's all right. Put them through.'

'Hello? Is that Miss Illingworth?'

'Yes.'

'Miss *Jane* Illingworth?'

That's when Jane knew something was wrong. Something like the San Andreas Fault opening up at her feet.

They were very sorry to have to inform her that her sister had been killed in an accident in Amsterdam during the night. Her brother-in-law Mr Parris had asked them to telephone her to convey the news as soon as possible. They would give her all the assistance they could if she required it at any time.

Thank you. Thank you. Goodbye.

Sarah's summer school uniform dress, spread out around her on the lawn as she read aloud a letter she'd had from that boy who'd written to her near the end of term – Greg, his name was. Mummy wouldn't mind: how could she object? Not to a shared holiday with lots of others, not *nowadays*! The violet checks of the pattern didn't suit Sarah's colouring at all, not that those wretched uniforms suited any of the girls. Sarah was going to change out of the horrid thing in a minute and get into some real clothes at last! The ankles flattened against the grass, the white socks, the intermittent giggling at what Greg said in his letter, or what he *meant* to say, or what he *would* have said if he could write decently or find some time to himself. What did it matter? He was a boy, wasn't he? A boy was worth ten girls who could write letters. Little sister suspected something, suspected that Sarah would really *do it* this summer of all summers – little sister gazing at big one, envious but admiring, deliciously resentful, hating but loving – no, not loving, don't be loving, don't dredge all *that* up now!

Jane was back in her office again. Everything was as it had been; she herself was as she had been. She heard the traffic in the street below as if for the first time. And then Humphrey stuck his head round the door and asked if she was thinking of a bite of lunch later? He had to ask now because he was just off.

'What is it? You look pissed-off about something.'

'My sister's been killed.'

Humphrey smiled even as the penny dropped, but in a moment he was holding her and she sobbed and sobbed out of an endless reservoir. 'It's all right, love, it's all right.' It wasn't all right. Jane couldn't get that horrid school dress out of her mind...

She buried her face into his chest, into the male coarseness of his jacket. She felt his body tensing, edging away, seeking release. 'I'm sorry, darling, I've got to go. This damned... I'll be back lunchtime. Try to get through the morning. I don't think you should be alone...' That's right, run away. It's not your problem anyhow. Go back to your wife in Norwich.

He was gone. Humphrey wasn't that bad, he was all right.

Commissaris Sweelinck at the Central Police Station in Amsterdam was also sympathetic, though he didn't take her in his arms. He told Jane in his rough-sounding English what had happened to her sister, matter-of-factly, step-by-step. Jane grew almost detached in her admiration for the way the ageing policeman spelled it out as honestly as he could to her. Late in the afternoon of the fatal day, Sarah Parris had left the Hotel Erasmus where she and her husband were staying and had not returned. Her body had been discovered and fished out of the Amstel early the following morning.

'Did Mr Parris report her disappearance?' asked Jane.

'Why, yes, he did,' said Commissaris Sweelinck, slightly taken aback at the suddenly brisk, reporterish tone. 'But not until very late. After his late meeting he had drinks and had not returned to the hotel until much later than he had intended. He waited an hour, and then at midnight had contacted us.'

'Why did he wait an hour?'

Sweelinck shrugged. 'Ask him that yourself if you want to. He is still here in Amsterdam. Did your people book you a room to stay?'

Yes, they had done all that. A clean little room with a single bed and all mod-cons, and now a visit from Clive Parris thrown in.

'My dear Jane.'

'Clive.'

'They told me at the embassy you'd arrived. I'm sorry. I can't tell you how sorry I am. I know you and she were close.'

That damned dress...

He was sitting on the side of the bed now with his head in his hands. Junior statesman in despair. Jane felt herself a bitch for thinking that just then.

Miraculously, he recovered himself. 'I've told the embassy here to pull out all the stops. We can't let these monsters get away with it. I won't rest until there's been a proper and thorough investigation and a conviction.'

'Was there more than one, then?' Jane asked.

'What?'

'More than one killer?'

'Oh well, I don't know. These sorts of characters run in gangs, don't they?'

'Do you think she was killed by a gang?'

'I don't want to rush to any conclusions, but that's my guess, yes. Did the police offer you any thoughts?'

'No, they didn't share their thoughts with me. I don't suppose they feel under any obligation to do that. The inquest is tomorrow?'

'Yes, and then I'm returning to London. I can't stay here. Not after... The conference will have to go on without me. I might even resign, you know. There doesn't seem to be much point...'

'You should think first before you do that,' said Jane. 'It's your career. It's the thing that will keep you going.' Inwardly she felt not the slightest shred of concern for him.

'Yes, you're right,' he said.

'*Why* did she die, Clive?'

'If I knew the answer to that I'd have done something about it myself by now!' Done what? Massacred the culprit or culprits with his own bare hands?

'Did she bring anything valuable with her to Amsterdam?' asked Jane.

'What? Oh. She might have – I don't remember. She didn't show me everything she brought with her.'

'They said you and she went to a function on the first night. Was she wearing any valuable jewellery then?'

'Dear Jane, you sound just like a reporter. Darling girl, the police asked me all these things before–'

'I'm asking you now, Clive.'

'You're upset. Perfectly understandable. No, nothing much. Some smallish emeralds, I think.'

'Do you still have the emeralds?'

'Yes. Yes, I think so.'

'They would have gone through everything with you afterwards, wouldn't they? To establish whether or not anything had been stolen from her?'

'Yes, of course they did. The emeralds certainly aren't missing. Whether she had anything else or not–'

'That she would have taken out with her? On a walk or something?'

'It doesn't sound very likely, does it?'

'Robbery has to be ruled out, then,' said Jane.

'I suppose so.'

'Why else should she be killed, Clive?'

'I don't know! Surely you can imagine how many times I've asked myself that? I don't know. It's beyond belief!'

'Is it possible she had a lover? Here in Amsterdam?'

'Jane, please.'

'I'm sorry.'

'The idea's ridiculous. I don't think she'd ever been here before in her life.'

'So perhaps she'd made a rendezvous? On neutral ground?'

'With a lover? It's absurd!'

'I'm sorry to bring such an idea up, Clive, at a time like this.'

'No, it's all right. We have to turn over every stone. Perhaps it's possible. I don't mean to impugn your sister's reputation but can any husband be sure that his wife doesn't have a lover? Even in a marriage as close and as loving as ours was?'

This was getting interesting. Jane let him go on.

'Good God, now isn't the time for me to be suggesting any such thing! But what can one say? Anything might have been possible. Who can say otherwise, after a violent death?'

At least the idea wasn't so intolerable for Clive in his time of grief and bereavement that he couldn't spell it out: sowing the seed, perhaps?

All right, she was just taking it out on her sister's husband because of her own shock. But there was something *horribly posed* about him. Do politicians ever relax? Or become themselves? Or was it something more sinister than occupational habits?

And a little while before, it had not been a *crime passionel* but a gang killing. Either he was very receptive to Jane's suggestions or he was trying to deflect all avenues of suspicion away from himself. Later, Jane read in the paper that he had suggested robbery as a motive – even after going through her things with the police! He certainly wasn't at a loss for reasons why she should die, whatever 'stupefaction' he had professed! The man was positively creative.

And as for thinking that he and Sarah had a happy marriage – well, that was news to her. Sarah hadn't been a happy woman from the day of her wedding, or so it seemed to Jane, though Jane had to admit to seeing her only intermittently after that. Yet Sarah seemed to wrap herself in a brittle kind of chic, which contrasted sharply with her natural and mainly grave schoolgirl poise. As young girls, the two sisters had been inseparable, at least in the holidays outside of boarding-school. Jane was seven years younger and to Sarah she was like her living doll, but a doll who grew into an intimate friend. Until later on – when Clive Parris came along. Had Jane ever got over a certain latent jealousy about that? Had that coloured her feelings about Clive all this time, intensifying them now that Sarah had been murdered? Jane couldn't but suspect her own feelings. At the same time, even on purely objective grounds, her sister's marriage intrigued her.

Clive and Sarah had met at a dinner party given by the local archdeacon, who was Clive's cousin. What the attraction was for Sarah, Jane couldn't imagine. Clive Parris wasn't quite old enough to be her father but he was getting on. It was difficult to imagine him ever having been young, climbing trees and getting scrapes on his knees, ever having done anything for the pure joy of doing it. He was outwardly urbane and charming, trying not to talk like the Tory stick he looked. It wasn't just that he was dull: there was an underlying nervousness, a calculation, an eye on the next moment, a constant anticipation of what the next move should be. He was never wholly 'there', never wholly sharing in spontaneous amusement, never really candid about himself. Yet Sarah seemed taken with him; perhaps the untimely death of their own father had steered her towards mature men as a kind of security. Jane never managed to get up the courage to ask Sarah why she was going through with it.

Within six months of that dinner party they were married. Jane didn't expect to hear from Sarah for a while.

She didn't hear from her at all. At the very least Jane might have expected Sarah to take her aside now and then to confide over hubby's foibles, how stupid he could be and so on; she'd always done that before over previous boyfriends. But no such girls-together talk ever resumed. Had Sarah got sucked into the ambition of the rising M.P.? Jane couldn't conceive of her sister drowning out her own youthful hopes and dreams in the tawdry rise of the mediocre Clive Parris.

What was *unhealthy* about Clive? Was he a secret homosexual? Nothing 'unhealthy' about that in itself – Jane considered herself broadminded on that score, insofar as she'd ever thought about homosexuality. But if that was the reason for a certain strain and pretence, couldn't it be interpreted as unhealthy in the long run? As for physical activity: Clive certainly always looked a little unwholesomely pink around the gills. He took no exercise – 'tennis' consisted mainly of watching it and officiating at club functions, no doubt for political reasons. Work seemed to be his all-consuming passion. But was work a cover-up for something else?

Had that 'something else' burst out in murder?

At about the same time that Paul was once more revising his view of Clive's innocence in any big, subversive plot – hazarding that perhaps Sarah had made a discovery and so had had to be removed from the scene in Amsterdam, regardless of the consequences – Jane was doing some reflecting on Clive herself, particularly his odd behaviour at their meeting after Sarah's death.

There was something, well, *gutless* about the way he was taking it. The very genuineness of his bereavement seemed doubtful, even the stabs at grief which he had manifested in front of Jane. She couldn't decide if he was merely distracted or deliberately trying to cover his tracks.

Jane politely turned down his invitation to dinner for that evening of their meeting, saying she was too tired – by implication too distraught. Though he might wonder why she had rejected the opportunity to offer *him* a little comfort – after all, as the spouse he was the one with the strongest reason for being upset. Let him be suspicious, thought Jane. If you cut him, he would pour out not blood but a well-chilled hock, perhaps a Bernkasteler. She'd see the sweating, long-necked bottle there and would puke all over the hors d'oeuvres, no thank you.

Now she realised why she had instinctively gone to Amsterdam. Clive, who had merely intended to let her know what had happened, was clearly surprised at her arrival. She should perhaps have waited in London for his report. After all, Sarah was beyond any help from her. No. Jane had gone to Amsterdam to find things out for herself because she didn't trust her brother-in-law – on what grounds exactly, she couldn't say. Even if it kept her away from work for two or three days she would glean information from the authorities herself. If what she heard seemed unsatisfactory she might even indulge in a little detective-work. These dark thoughts somehow kept Jane going, but they weren't powerful enough to hold back the inevitable. She found tears shortly before dawn, and cried herself to sleep.

After learning the result of the post-mortem, Jane was not surprised to pick up a note from Clive saying that he had decided to return to London. Well, she might as well, too. With the departure both of Clive and of her sister's body for England, there was nothing more for Jane to do in Amsterdam. Her heart wasn't any longer in tracing Sarah's movements around the streets of the Dutch city, of reconstructing the crime for herself, of duplicating all the things the police had already done. And deep down she felt the answers to her not-entirely-articulated questions lay back in England, not here on the streets of Amsterdam.

A male voice on the answering machine in her flat back at Maida Vale, giving a telephone number and a possible time to call, put Jane in some turmoil. The voice sounded plausibly official when it spoke of the matter as being 'to do with the death of your sister'. Jane didn't want the thing dredged up. Or at least one part of her wanted Sarah well and truly buried, with quiet dignity at Baythorne churchyard: buried and remembered for what she had been, when they were real sisters to one another, the best of sisters, the brightest, the most thoughtful, the most beautiful. But another part of Jane wasn't entirely content with the idea of the past being left alone, wasn't satisfied with the proffered explanations. Sarah was dead: where was justice?

It was that side of her which made her ring the number she'd been given.

He didn't sound quite so stilted and official in a live telephone conversation, this Paul Finningham. They agreed that her newspaper office wasn't the proper place and arranged that he should come up to her flat.

The man she met at the door was blue-eyed and fair-haired, about thirty-five or thirty-eight say, with a handsome, squarish sort of face. Punctiliously he showed her his identification to leave no room for doubt right from the start. Jane looked at the card but didn't really take it in. It was the hour when a drink would be quite respectable. Paul Finningham showed no hesitation about accepting a gin and tonic. If he was on duty it wasn't very policeman-like.

Paul held up the glass to her in a sort of half-toast. 'As I said on the phone, we're not police, in case you're wondering about this. I'm afraid we do sometimes drink on the job.'

'All right by me,' said Jane, sitting opposite him before a fireplace, which was obscured by a large vase of dried reeds. 'I don't know if I can help you. I told the police in Holland everything I knew, which wasn't very much. I was only her sister – we hadn't seen each other for some time.' She paused, then spoke again. 'I have to be honest and say that I really don't know why you should want to interview me. I wasn't anywhere near Amsterdam at the time and if you're looking for someone to give you the low-down on her marriage or anything else, I'm afraid you've come to the wrong person.'

Tension had made her say too much in one go. He seemed to understand that. Uncannily, too, he was taking it in, as if everything she was saying was additional evidence of some sort. There is something a little disturbing about professional listeners, whoever they are. We spend our whole lives with people whom we assume aren't really listening to us; when you suddenly find yourself face-to-face with a policeman or a psychiatrist – with or without notepad – it's unsettling. Especially when they do *nothing* but listen.

His lack of verbal reaction irritated Jane. It made her want to throw a spoke in the works. 'I'd be grateful,' she said, 'if we could get this over with as soon as possible. I've had a tiring week and I don't know how much more of this I can bear.'

'Yes, I understand. I won't take up more of your time than I have to.' He then began probing into Sarah's past life, her state of mind, their relationship as sisters, and her marriage to Clive. Although Jane had been dwelling on these things herself, it nettled her to find some stranger suddenly weighing in on the very questions she had been tortuously formulating in her own mind. Why couldn't he ask straightforward, police-like questions, like 'where were you on the night of?' What was this presumptuous, pseudo-psychology stuff?

'I told you I couldn't shed any light on their marriage,' Jane said.

'But they had been married for more than six years,' said Paul.

'Yes, I know that.'

'Doesn't it strike you as a little odd? I'm sorry, I mean to say that it strikes me as a little odd – you're not knowing anything about their relationship.'

'It wasn't any of my business, was it?'

'But you've just told me you were very close as sisters.'

'Did I say that? No, all right, I said that.' Jane was annoyed with herself for getting tied up in stupid little knots of her own making. He seemed to try to help: 'Do you have any reason to believe Sarah might have been keeping something about her marriage from you?'

Jane began to cry. Paul looked down at his drink and left her to it. It was cruel. He should have sprung forth, in true Victorian fashion, grasping her hand and whipping out his handkerchief. Instead he sat there like a stone. She found that her tears were embarrassing them both, so she dried her own eyes. She even managed to carry on the conversation. 'I don't know that they were especially close. They probably were in the early days, like all newly-weds, so I'm told. Sarah didn't confide in me about him. It's true we had been confidants as kids. I thought it was probably because she was all wrapped up in him at the time.'

'But later?'

'I don't know. Of course he was much older than she was. And not very exciting.' Jane wondered if she should spell this out. 'As a man, I mean.'

A ghost of a smile appeared on Paul's face. 'Is that a feminine judgement?'

'No, I don't think so especially,' retorted Jane primly. 'I don't think anyone of either sex finds Clive a ball of fire.'

'They say sometimes such men prove the opposite in their more intimate moments,' said Paul.

'I don't think that's for either of us to speculate on.'

'I'm sorry, I thought you had brought it up?'

'I was only trying to answer your questions,' snapped Jane, 'which I have to say I find a bit beside the point. If you're so interested in Clive why don't you talk to him yourself? I'm sure he knows more about his own marriage than I do.'

Touché, thought Paul. Why do you suppose I'm talking to you instead, darling?

'*Have* you spoken to him?' she persisted.

'I myself haven't, but he has been questioned. I daresay he and I will be meeting in due course. Can I ask you something about your own relationship with him?'

'We're not lovers, if that's what you're implying,' flared up Jane again. *Really!* 'I resent your insinuation that we are.'

'I said nothing about you're being lovers, Miss Illingworth. You brought it up.' Jane blushed in spite of herself. Damn him, he *was* a policeman.

'Well, we weren't. I'd have thought that was obvious from the way I've talked about him. I can't say we had any sort of relationship at all.'

'You mean "have"?'

'What did I just say?'

'You said "had". I think you mean "have".'

'Are you trying to trap me?'

'I just want the record to be straight. You seemed to imply that you had some kind of relationship with Clive

Parris that now no longer exists. I wanted to make sure that wasn't what you meant to say.'

'It sounds to me as if you're trying to establish a motive for Clive and me to do away with Sarah. Perhaps I shouldn't have seen you at all without my solicitor! If you have any more questions; I really don't think I should answer them without my solicitor being present. I see I was wrong to let you in in the first place. Anyhow there's nothing you can use in evidence against me – you didn't even give me a warning!'

Paul put his empty glass down on the coffee-table. He assumed an air of extreme patience. 'The word "relationship" implies nothing more than some kind of situation between you, some kind of attitude, which is ongoing because you are both still alive and in communication. So let's get rid of that particular hare. And I have to say again that I am not a policeman and this is not a murder investigation. I don't regard anything you've said to me as material evidence, and I certainly wouldn't use it against you. I'm sorry we have to pursue these things when you are feeling as you do, quite naturally. But I'm afraid, Miss Illingworth, that we haven't enough time for you to get over your feelings. I only wish we had.' Unexpectedly his eyes twinkled. 'It would make my job easier, for a start.'

Anger in Jane gave way to curiosity. Up to now she really hadn't considered why Paul Finningham was here at all. Not a murder investigation? Then what was all this about? 'Are you investigating my sister's death?' she asked, tentatively.

'We are working with the police,' replied Paul.

'That doesn't answer my question. The police usually handle such things by themselves.'

Paul was firm. By way of bringing the conversation to a close he stood up. 'I can't discuss it with you, Miss

Illingworth. And I'd be grateful if you would keep all this to yourself.'

He pulled out a card. 'If anything occurs to you, perhaps you'd be good enough to give me a ring on this number?'

The card showed nothing but his name and a telephone number. 'Like what, for instance?' she asked.

Paul looked meaningly into her eyes. 'Anything,' he said.

Letting him out of the flat, Jane was more in the dark than ever. It must be something to do with national security, whatever that is, she thought. The implications made her shiver. Did the authorities suspect that someone was out to get Clive and had killed poor Sarah for some reason instead? Was Clive himself under suspicion – for this murder, or for something else? What made Jane feel a little sick, was that her suspicion of 'something going on' was no longer a mere fantasy or prejudice of her own. The interview had been distinctly unsettling.

But Jane couldn't bring herself to conclude that the experience of being interviewed by Paul Finningham had been altogether unpleasant.

3

Anatoly Lavitzsky sighed in the knowledge that he was unsuited to this way of life, which fate had suddenly twisted into being. He poured himself another jenever: filthy stuff, not purifying like the fiery vodka of the motherland, which ran down the throat like ignited glycerine. Not that he could take too much vodka; he'd never had the stomach for all that drinking, and he was drinking too much now. Natalia knew him well and would be ticking him off for it if she were here. Lavitzsky wondered what she was doing. Probably queuing up outside the shops, or vacuuming with that preposterously noisy machine whose nozzle kept falling out, or cooking the old standby, *bortsch*. They hadn't lived so regally, not the way it was made out by the papers back home. As assistant director at the establishment he had just about ticked over money-wise. Better than some. They had a house; they had a car that mostly worked, and a log hut overgrown with weeds and creepers grandly referred to by the family as the *dacha*. Natalia was never resentful. She got on with life in her own placid way. She had his children; she sighed over some new shortage or other. She got on. The whole world was carried on the backs of such women.

Lavitzsky pushed the filmy glass away from him and buried his face in his arms on the table. God, he missed her. Her homely, round moon-face and hair done up in a bun, the bosom into which so many troubles had been buried, the thighs that uncomplainingly opened to provide the only real pleasure in life. How he'd taken it all for granted! How much he needed her now – far more even than she ever needed him! At least she still had the children with her. He had nothing, no one. A man of his education and abilities: Assistant Director of the Weapons Establishment at Novoronezh, up from nothing, nothing at all. From nothing – to nothing. Here he was in a derelict hunting-lodge in the woods not far from s'Hertogenbosch, in the Netherlands of all places. It would be winter soon; he didn't think the place suitable. He would die of hypothermia if they didn't see about getting him moved.

They weren't friendly now. Perhaps facing the police back home would have been better after all. Cynical men, they wouldn't have taken it out personally on him. It was just the law, and breaking the law didn't make them angry unless you refused to co-operate. Or so he imagined. He'd heard what they had been like to other people. If it wasn't political, they weren't too bad. Was *this* political? If only he knew!

Anatoly Lavitzsky stopped crying. He was such an emotional dilettante, he couldn't even keep that up for long. 'I'm just a cork in the stream,' he said aloud. 'Let me bob where the waves toss me.' Somehow that made him feel better. He wondered if it was from Pushkin. Perhaps it was from the Bible. He didn't think the Bible had much to say about corks in bottles. His grandmother had possessed a much-decorated old Bible – weighed a tonne. He wondered what had happened to it, as he wondered what had happened to her – after Stalin's purge of the Old Believers.

Lavitzsky supposed it must soon be time to open a box of the powdered stuff that swelled up into the mashed potato with green bits in it that the Dutch were so fond of with their sausage. Only there was no sausage – the people looking after him were getting a little slack these days; there had been mutterings about funds 'running short'. He had become greatly in need of his usual ration of sausage, even more so than the cheap, yellowish jenever they brought from time to time. He wondered if he might put in a request for more sausage on Monday? Save me from teetotallers and vegetarians!

Lavitzsky thought of all sorts of ways to cut down, to be less trouble. But it was difficult. A man needs so many calories a day, and if not, then at least he should be able to starve to death on some tobacco and something to drink. And a man needs company at least of a sort, if he is not to become inhuman with loneliness. Their visits were sparser and briefer – when they came at all. One had promised to bring a cribbage-board. The board never arrived. Well, the man hadn't come any more either, so perhaps it didn't matter.

He was going nuts! His brain was running round and round things. This wouldn't do, he must keep his head above everything else. It was his brain that had got him so far, and it was his brain that would have to get him out of the pickle he was in. Think, man! A clear head...

It was entirely his brother Vassily's fault. Wretched spiv. Ever since he was a little boy at school Vassily had been in on some scam or other. While Anatoly beavered away at physics and got his hard-earned marks, Vassily went round with a supercilious smile on his face handing out goodies from the black market, goodies as insubstantial as the caviar which melted too quickly on the tongue and was gone. With Vassily everything melted as soon as it was conjured up. Like the supposed 'benefits' from those reactor-building contracts. If only Anatoly had been more of a man of the world he would have seen it coming. But all good things come to an end: any half-way sober adult should have realised that, and Anatoly hadn't. The sable-fur for Natalia had been his undoing – but her eyes had glistened so. He would go to prison-camp for a hundred years just to see his wife's eyes shine like that for once in her unhappy life.

Anyhow, Vassily had been snared under the new *perestroika* – well, new for Novoronezh, even if it had been rampant everywhere else. The local anti-corruption drive had shaken him from the tree like an overripe pear. Everyone knew it had been going on; *perestroika* simply brought the denouncers and the envious to the top, like scum. After the denouncers, the investigators. Investigating a trail of under-the-table contracts and pilfered building materials which led to his office at the Weapons Establishment. Ironically, this train of events coincided with what turned out to be the peak of Anatoly's career: to go as delegate to a symposium in Stockholm on the peaceful uses of atomic energy. The buzz of excitement in preparing for his first trip to the West was punctuated by frantic telephone calls from Vassily, which reached such a pitch that Anatoly ordered Natalia to keep the phone off the hook.

Once he'd arrived in Stockholm, Anatoly knew in his bones that there was no going back. He couldn't face the idea of the Gulag. It was virtually certain, even allowing for his brother being overly hysterical. They would all be caught in the net. Examples had to be made! Anatoly was high enough up to be made an example of, and at the same time not too high to discredit the system. Such crises always resulted in the sacrifice of middle-management! Anatoly had been around long enough to realise *that*.

His brain had worked overtime. He could hardly go to the Swedish authorities and ask for asylum. Sweden professed neutrality in such matters unless the humanitarian need was dire. In his case there'd be an enquiry and he would be shipped home for trial. But the West had other possibilities, and one of these which Anatoly had heard of he pursued now. He set his sights on the Peace Without Fear movement.

P.W.F. had been started some twenty years previously in France as a protest against that country's rapid development of atomic weaponry. There, *Paix sans Peur* became a thorn in the flesh of the authorities and some of its members were jailed, which gave the movement worldwide publicity. Soon it was established in Scandinavia and the Low Countries – and was particularly strongly-supported in the latter. Overnight, however, P.W.F. took on an aura of respectability in the West when its small underground organisation in the U.S.S.R. staged a demonstration in the Uspensky Sobor, one of the cathedrals in the Kremlin (now a museum) where during a religious service a banner of the P.W.F. was unfurled. This was in the days when such demonstrations were unheard-of, certainly in Moscow itself. The demonstrators were severely punished. In the West P.W.F. was seen as an organisation campaigning against atomic weapons inside the Soviet Union. It was this anti-Soviet strain inside P.W.F. that attracted Lavitzsky. Not long after arriving with his champagne-guzzling colleagues, who were oblivious to the cost of such frivolities in Sweden, Lavitzsky made contact with the Stockholm branch of P.W.F. He told them he was disillusioned with the Soviet system and wanted to offer his services to the cause of peace and disarmament.

With all the publicity attending the arrival of the Soviet delegation to Sweden, the P.W.F. were delighted to have him. Anatoly found himself holed up in luxury in a weekend chalet near Södertälje, receiving a constant stream of well-wishers, including a reporter with a little tape-recorder from Radio Free Europe. With tongue loosened by liquid hospitality, Lavitzsky denounced Soviet nuclear missile production and gave some details of its capacity.

The furious Soviet reaction was predictable. Moscow Radio and *Pravda* demanded Lavitzsky's immediate return so that he could face charges of corruption alongside his brother. Lavitzsky was easily able to persuade his new friends at P.W.F. that these smears only indicated how important he was. They decided he should be removed from neutral Sweden as soon as possible and sent to a safer asylum. He was shipped from Landskrona to Den Helder in the north of Holland, and then to the suburbs of Amsterdam.

But the trial of Vassily back in Russia attracted a certain notoriety abroad, enough to convince even the most sceptical anti-Soviet Westerner that there was some substance to the case against Anatoly. It was becoming apparent that Anatoly was no true defector at all, but a crook on the run – at the very least an accomplice in his brother's doings. His estimation in the P.W.F. sank. Before long he was bundled out of his reasonably comfortable bolt-hole in Amsterdam and sequestered here, in this tumbledown lodge in the woods, while P.W.F. decided what to do with him.

It was something of a predicament. If they handed him straight back to the Soviets P.W.F. would alienate their underground Russian brethren, who held the Communist authorities in such deep contempt that they would never approve such a co-operative action. But P.W.F. had to do something. Lavitzsky was now an embarrassment.

He was, however, not without value. Compared to what some poorer countries had by way of expertise, Anatoly was way out in front. Word was getting out that he was available.

A C.I.A. agent made himself known to P.W.F. headquarters in Amsterdam. He told them that he knew the Dutch authorities were ready to pounce on the organisation, in certain knowledge that they were harbouring Lavitzsky illegally. The result would be the loss of their Dutch base. He said the Central Intelligence Agency were searching for the Russian and were willing to relieve P.W.F., quietly, of all responsibility for him. They havered and wavered, but in the end the committee agreed that the agent should be told Lavitzsky's whereabouts and be allowed to remove him. The danger they were in prompted them not to ask too many questions.

A decision was taken before anyone tried to think too hard about the consequences: that Lavitzsky might be put to work with the American nuclear war machine. One more or less in that behemoth couldn't make as much difference as the loss of the P.W.F.'s very legality in Holland!

Lavitzsky was told only to expect to receive a friendly visitor.

The car headlamps flared across the unlit room. Lavitzsky fished in the wall-cupboard for a clean glass. The bottle contained a quarter of the jenever; it was still just possible to be hospitable. He then switched on the porch light. Every little gesture counted.

He opened the door to a large shadow.

He could see nothing but a square-headed outline. Cigar-smoke curled away from it.

'Hi,' said the silhouette.

'You are the man who was to come?'

'That's me,' said the figure, softly. Lavitzsky felt a sudden and instinctive tremor of fear.

'Come in, come in,' he said, regardless. 'Sorry it is so dark in here.' He turned on the light. In the room with him was a man of fairly handsome appearance: fifteen or twenty years earlier he might have been described by some as 'beautiful'. He had a still-boyish face, slightly turned-up nose, and what looked to be a fair musculature under the light jacket – certainly no suggestion of going to seed, and if anything, quite the reverse. His head was greying and shorn in the American military crew cut style. Somehow he didn't look right in civilian clothes. But what struck Lavitzsky most were his eyes: very light, pale blue. As they caught the light they were almost white, like an albino's. The man was carrying a brief-case.

Lavitzsky held out his hand. It wasn't taken up. 'Let's sit down, okay?' said the stranger. They sat down. The man put his brief-case on the floor beside him. Lavitzsky offered him a drink but he refused.

'They told me you were coming,' said Lavitzsky.

'What did they say about me?' asked the man, eyeing him through his cigar-smoke.

'Nothing, nothing at all.'

The man smiled. 'Good,' he said. 'You might only have been misled if they had.'

There was a pause. 'Do you mind if I–?' Lavitzsky asked, indicating the jenever. He didn't know why he felt he had to ask the man's permission, but he did. The American gestured to go ahead. Lavitzsky didn't enjoy his first swallow as much as usual. He nearly jumped when the man spoke again.

'Your friends don't like you so much any more, do they? Well, that *is* a shame. Looks like you've kind of dug yourself a hole, doesn't it?' He ended each statement with a question, as if he were a policeman. But who was he? What was he?

'How would you like to go to South America?' the man asked.

'S-South America?'

'Yeah. South America. Brazil or somewhere like that?'

'For a particular reason?'

'For good.'

'What do you mean, for good?'

The man crushed the remains of his cigar in a nearby ashtray. 'Somewhere where you can live without worrying that anybody's going to catch up with you, with enough money for living better than you've ever lived before in your life. Miss your wife?'

'What?'

'Miss your wife?'

Lavitzsky gulped and said yes.

'She could join you. And your kids. They're getting quite good nowadays about these things, the Russkies.'

'Yes,' said the 'Russkie'. With so many encouraging things being thrown at him all of a sudden, why did Lavitzsky still feel fear in the pit of his stomach? 'Would I be going there to do work of some kind?' he asked.

The man slowly shook his head. 'No. Not there. That place is for afterwards. I want you to do a job for me first.'

'Is it – an illegal job?'

The man smiled a crooked sort of grin. 'You don't think something legal would be enough to allow you to live in luxury in South America for the rest of your life, do you? Of course it's illegal. And the way I see it, you don't have much choice. Those people who are keeping you now want to ditch you, and I mean p.d.q.'

P.d.q.? What was this p.d.q.? It sounded ominous. Naturally Lavitzsky knew one didn't get something for nothing. He also knew that the decline of his lifestyle indicated an imminent downturn in his fortunes, one way or another. But – something illegal. Sounded big, too. Anatoly was tired of doing illegal things. He wanted somewhere quiet to rest, somewhere to gather up the shreds of his respectability and peace of mind.

'I can't,' he said. 'Not something like what you say.'

'How do you know, when you don't even know what it is?' said the American.

'What would it be?'

'I can't tell you that right now. You come along with me and you'll find out.'

Panic gripped the scientist. 'No! No! I can't leave here! I can't leave my friends!'

The American sneered. 'Friends? You haven't got any friends. It's the end of the line, Lavitzsky. Your so-called "friends" have sold you to me.'

'They can't have done that! What did you say? "Sold me?" Nobody sells anybody else! This is not slavery, slavery is not in the West! No! I won't go with you! I won't! I will ask–'

But he never got the chance to finish his tirade. The man suddenly lunged at him, grabbing his arm. Lavitzsky nearly had a heart-attack. He dropped his glass on the floor. The man brought himself nose-to-nose with him and grinned broadly. The grip was maintained, painfully.

'You are hurting. My arm–'

'Yeah, I know. It usually does.'

'Please – stop–'

'Will you reconsider? *Will you?*'

The American was going to break his arm, without compunction. Something illegal – it made sense, with such a man…

'Yes,' gasped Lavitzsky, almost without voice. The grip was released.

'Good. You do something for me, and I'll do something for you. That a deal?'

'Would it be – dangerous?' asked Lavitzsky.

'I said I'd tell you all about it when you came away with me.'

Lavitzsky's panic flared up again. He wasn't a physical type, he was a scientist, an intellectual. Why had he run away from Russia in the first place? Not because he was a hero – far from it!

'I can't come away with you! I can come away later – yes, I can come away after I've made some arrangements–'

'I think I've had about enough screwing around,' said the American. 'I told you you're finished here. If you don't come with me, you'll either be left here to starve and rot to death, or you'll be picked up and shipped back to a Siberian prison-camp. You know that as well as I do. Buddy, I'm your only hope.'

He picked up the brief-case.

'So, I'll give you the option. Two choices. Choice number one is: come with me now. Choice number two is in here.' He clicked open the brief-case.

What he brought out he held up and dangled in the Russian's face. It was a length of rope, the end of which was tied into a perfect hanging noose. Lavitzsky stared at the ghastly thing. It was like a nightmare.

The American threw down the brief-case, which had nothing else in it at all, and stood up with his rope, looking around him. 'I'll string this up for you before I leave, if you like.'

'You're crazy!' muttered the white-faced Lavitzsky, pressed back into his chair. But he could not keep his eyes off the noose.

'*I'm* crazy!' shouted the American harshly. 'Seems to me you're the crazy one if you don't go for what I'm offering you. But I'm a nice guy. I offer alternatives. And the alternative to my deal – the most painless one for you right now – is *this*.' He thrust the noose at him.

Lavitzsky shook. The American was now walking about, actually looking for somewhere to hang the rope. And Lavitzsky knew that he would hang himself, too, the way he was feeling, the way he was placed right now. The worst thing about it all was that the American was right: it *was* a realistic option.

'No,' he said weakly. 'No, don't bother about the rope.'

The American stopped hunting and looked at him, from the corner of the room. He returned and sat down, and grinned once more.

'That's better,' he said. He looked at the rope and then put it back into the case. 'I didn't know how well you would understand English,' he said.

Life had been complicated enough for Lavitzsky up to then.

It was about to become more so.

4

Humphrey Cathcart puckered his lips and blew a little kiss down the telephone.

'Seems to be a bad line,' said Jane. 'I can hear a sort of popping noise. You hear it too?'

'Okay, what can I do for you, darling?' asked Humphrey. 'Only don't push your luck. I'm not exactly flavour of the month around here at the moment.'

'What's happened?'

'Nothing, really, just a High Court injunction slapped on the paper. About a contracts story on the Seabreeze missile. I won't say it'll bring the government down but they aren't happy. Bob Stokes says he's standing firmly behind me on this thing, and we all know what that means. Doing time in the Scrubs until I've worked off a contempt of court rap.'

'It's that serious?'

'Woodward and Bernstein aren't in it. They talk big about freedom of the press in this country and all that happens is that the poor reporter ends up doing the slopping-out. Christ, I'm no martyr, Jane!'

'You'd better have your last meal with me, then.'

'It's not quite as far along as that, but I'd be delighted. Tonight?'

'When you've done something for me.'

'A trade-off?'

'I think you'd make a very good martyr,' said Jane. 'Anyhow, it just shows what a good reporter you are if you have them jumping.'

'Thanks for that. What is it, then?'

'It's to do with my brother-in-law.'

'Clive? What about him?'

'Keep it under your hat, for God's sake. It's just that I think there's something funny going on.'

'Over, er, your sister's death?' Humphrey was suddenly serious.

'I can't say – I wish I could.' He could sense anxiety underlying the outwardly brisk tone. 'I just don't know.'

'Darling, I'm not a sleuth – not that kind of sleuth anyway. Have you spoken to the police?'

'I can't do that, Humphrey – I haven't anything to go on!'

Humphrey braced himself to take what he knew her reaction was going to be. 'Jane, I know you must be feeling very upset–'

'That's got nothing to do with it! Well, perhaps it has, but – I need help on it, Humphrey.'

How she wanted to tell him that the visit from an intelligence agent more than substantiated her suspicions! But she bit her tongue and held back. Finningham had enjoined secrecy on her, after all.

'I'd like you to dig around if you could, Humphrey. You're in with all that crowd, it's your patch. There might be a story in it for you one day, you never know.'

Humphrey groaned. 'Why do you have to go on about a story? You know I can't refuse if that's true!'

Jane laughed. 'That's why I said it. Now we've settled that, what about supper this week?'

'Not tonight?'

'No, not tonight. I have to "wash my hair", as they say. Friday or Saturday perhaps?'

Humphrey hesitated. Jane sensed a blip of panic. 'Er – great. Could we make it Friday? I'm up in Norwich on Saturday. You know, usual visit with John and Timothy before the end of the hols. John's off to his new school next week.'

'Friday, then,' said Jane.

'That's okay, is it?'

'Of course it is.' Jane tried to sound as cordial as she could, but all the same, Felicity and her whelps were a pain in the ass.

While Paul Finningham was chasing up slender leads – usually dubious characters in various walks of life who turned out to have absolutely nothing for him at all – Jane was embarking on her own investigation. She could think of no one better-equipped to help than Humphrey, a shit-hot reporter, the expert in digging around. That's why he was in trouble now: obviously he'd dug a little too deeply over Seabreeze. Humphrey had one of those ferreting minds that wouldn't let anything go, no matter how obscured it was by deliberate obstructing. Sometimes it made him a bore, especially when he was on to something and wouldn't talk about anything else. In a lot of ways Humphrey was a bit of a nerd. Maybe it was his nerd-like way of persisting that got him results, whereas your more cynical and smooth bar-propper at El Vino's too easily remembered his place in the Fourth Estate when the going got rough. And there was even a kind of naivety about Humphrey that never left him, despite the wars and sordid stories he'd worked his way around. Jane had more than a soft spot for him and thought it might be love. They certainly got on easily enough. Perhaps a lot of it had to do with the fact that Humphrey took Jane as he found her, without a single hint of that snide sexism that permeates male-dominated offices and professions. He approached her at least as freshly as he would approach – a story.

Unlike Paul, he had no inkling that there was a race against time. Yet she too was impatient to learn what

Humphrey had tracked down, waiting through the next couple of days and resisting temptation to bother him for interim reports. She even suffered his marital problems over dinner.

'I'm pretty well resigned to the fact that whatever settlement there is will cost me an arm and a leg,' he said, wolfing down the moussaka. Had he been a little less wolfish he might have noticed that she was only playing with her food. 'But it's worth it if I can get things normalised and have decent access to the boys. They're reaching the ages where they need a father more than ever,' he added pompously. Why were men so pompous about fatherhood? And he really *must* be a nerd to go on talking to me about his wife! Even more than usual when he went on about Felicity, Jane was twitching with impatience. She wanted to hear about Clive.

'Anyhow, that's the least of my worries right now,' said Humphrey, scraping his plate clean.

'Doesn't seem to have affected your appetite.'

'They say anxiety can cause compulsive eating.'

'What's the difference between that and the other kind?'

He smiled. 'You mean you haven't noticed? Oh well, it can't be all that bad, then.'

'If you've got a little room for chocolate mousse with rum perhaps you'd like to tell me about Clive,' she said, clearing away.

'I was coming round to that,' said Humphrey, wiping his mouth. From the kitchen she heard him belch. He belonged to the old school which didn't burp in mixed company. She didn't know whether that appealed to her or not. 'It's hard to say what went wrong,' said Humphrey – he was still back on the old subject, not having quite worked Felicity out of his system. 'Felicity hated London – I think that must've been the start of it. She wouldn't live here and I was damned if I was going to commute from Norwich. So I stayed on in Town in the week, which only made the weekends worse. She said I was propping up the bar in the usual watering-hole, when what I was really doing was flogging my guts out to keep her in the style to which she was accustomed. Sorry, love,' he said, noticing at last Jane's knotted forehead. 'I do go on about it. Don't know why. Where were we?'

'Clive Parris.'

'Yes.' He drew breath, replete, and sat back in his chair. 'Whatever you do, don't for God's sake say that any of this came from me. Clive's involved in a lot of directorships and that's nothing earth-shaking. But I've dug out a shadowy sort of outfit that his name may be linked with. Sells sophisticated war hardware to underdeveloped nations, by which I mean to overdeveloped dictatorships of underdeveloped nations. Automatic weapons, Exocet missiles, that kind of thing. If he *is* active in it he's been doing very well at covering his tracks to date.'

'It could be the key!' exclaimed Jane.

'The key to what?'

'To what's going on! I don't know what it is, but it must have something to do with all that!' She suddenly sprang up. 'I've got something to show you,' she said, going over to her desk and fishing out an envelope. 'It was delivered to me this morning. I had to pay – there wasn't any postage on it.' From the envelope Jane drew out a piece of notepaper embossed at the top with the name Hotel Erasmus, Amsterdam. 'Obviously there's been some delay through the post because of the postage due.'

'Who's it from?'

'It's from Sarah.'

'My God.'

'I know,' said Jane. 'I feel like I'm in touch with the

dead. She must've stuffed this in an envelope and pushed it into the nearest post-box – it must've been about the last thing she ever did.'

'"Dear Podge." *Podge*?' He smiled in spite of himself. Such was not the stuff of thriller novels.

Jane too smiled, a little faraway. 'That's from when I was fat and fourteen.'

'Hardly how I'd describe you now.'

'She wanted to get through to me, Humphrey! She pulled that name out after all these years because for the first time in ages she wanted to talk!'

'"Dear Podge: When I get back on Wed. evening I must see you. It's so very important. I'll ring you at your flat." That's it?'

'Nothing about Amsterdam, or any mention of Clive. Just that. I hadn't had a note or a call from her in a year – not since my birthday, anyhow.'

'What does it mean, this sudden urge for a get-together?'

'It means that something was really wrong, and she had to confide in me about it. It's tied up with her death, Humph, it *must* be!'

'You ought to go to the authorities with this,' said Humphrey. 'It's material.'

'It was also meant to be something secret between her and me.'

'That can't matter now, can it?'

'Yes, I know. But somehow – well, it could mean something really bad, something that – if it got out, I mean, it would–'

'Drag her through the mud?' asked Humphrey gently.

'I owe it to poor Sarah to be discreet about this. It was something she wanted only me to know.'

'But if it will help the authorities solve her death?'

'Yes, and they will have it. But I must get more to go

on first. At this stage it just doesn't mean anything. At this stage they'd only be asking me endless questions over things I know nothing about.' Jane was recalling her questioning session with Paul Finningham and wondering what kind of a meal he'd make over this. Naturally she didn't know that Sarah's unhappiness or fear was the very thing he was trying to nail down, having otherwise only a dim memory of impressions to go by.

'You have your reasons,' said Humphrey, ceasing further objection. 'But if I were you I'd put it in the bank.'

'Bank?'

'Somewhere safe. There is such a thing as burglary, you know. If all this is some kind of sinister plot you might end up minus a piece of evidence. Or worse.'

'What do you mean, worse? You ought to be writing for the tabloids!'

Sarah's letter cast a pall over the remainder of the evening. Neither now thought seriously of getting into the hay with the other. But at least Humphrey came away with one consolation.

There certainly was the beginning of a story here. And it might turn out of such a proportion as to make Seabreeze look like a P.T.A. meeting.

He was a big boy, the blond leaning against the bar of the Hercules Club. Big in that raw-boned way of Dutch lads, a butch thing in his Tufboots with the little roll of sock around the top. He had nice legs, too, what Warren Booth could see under his skirt. Shapely, full calves, tanned and hairless. Down to his waist the boy was dressed like any young guy, wool sweater and leather jacket. Below the waist, his skirt was long and plaid like a rug, drawn tightly around him to show off his thighs and his butt. He looked sullen, but that kind often turned out to be the most good-natured if you worked up the balls to talk to them. Apart from the skirt, there was no hint of campness or even sophistication. Just a big, good-looking well-scrubbed Dutch farm-boy. In a skirt. Nineteen or twenty or thereabouts, I'd say, thought Warren. Kind of young to be so into it. That's nice!

Don't get too excited about it, though; it's sort of normal over here. Either it's tolerance or the Dutch must be the doziest people on earth. Warren felt a hand cover his on the table. He turned and looked into Piet's eyes. Earnest, studious Piet in the owl-glasses, pale from studying engineering. Piet, twenty-two, with whom Warren was now residing. They'd met in this same bar eighteen months before, so it had been going quite a long time. When you got to them they went in for long, deep friendships, these boys. Delicate, skinny Piet, ridding himself of the last vestiges of teenage acne, with his brown, dog-like eyes behind the spectacles. He was getting doggier by the day, more dependent than ever, and this brought out very bad things in Warren Booth, whose natural proclivity was for one-night stands.

'Okay, Piet,' he muttered, pulling his hand away.

'Maybe we should go home now?' said Piet.

'You go home if you want,' said Warren Booth, drowning his irritation at the singsong voice in a swig of potent light beer. God, that kid's got hair like a waving cornfield, he thought. He looked bored, not having a nice time, like himself. That's the trouble with being the most beautiful creature in the room: nobody else looks like being such a good time as oneself.

Warren Booth staggered up from his table, knocking his chair over. Piet got up, too. 'We should go home,' he called after the lurching American. Only fucking jealous, that was all that was the matter with him. Christ, that hair! Anywhere else in the world you'd swear it was dyed.

'Hey, listen,' he said, stumbling up to the bar. 'I couldn't help wondering, you know, when I saw you over here, I couldn't help wondering what it's like up that nice skirt of yours?'

The blond boy turned round. 'Yes?' he asked, coldly. And then Warren Booth saw that close up he wasn't nineteen or twenty, more like about twenty-nine, and that what had seemed like cow-licked freshness from afar was expertly applied make-up, just right for the light of a bar. Yeah, and he was a toughy, too. Warren Booth suddenly smelt Bad News.

'You want something to say to my friend?' asked another man sidling up. He was also pretty good-sized, older, pock-marked with dark curly hair. His ear-ring gleamed. Boyfriend, or pimp? Whatever he was, he grabbed Warren Booth by the lapel with one hand, nearly lifting the American's feet off the floor. Warren felt the heat of his breath on his face.

But he wasn't intimidated. He didn't even feel he was there, really. 'Get your fucking hands off of me, you pimp,' he said. The grip tightened. From his detached position somewhere up the slopes of Mount Olympus, Warren Booth wondered what would happen next.

Piet came up. He told the pock-marked man in Dutch to let Warren go. The man planted his free hand across Piet's face and pushed the boy backwards; Piet reeled across and over the nearest table, upsetting drinks to right and left of him. The whole place went silent. Then a gnarled-looking giant of past wars moved forward. The proprietor.

The blond boy tried a small smile and said to him in Dutch: 'We'll take him home. He's had too much to drink.' The gnarled man reflected for a moment and then nodded. Warren Booth found himself yoked between the 'boy' he'd accosted and his friend, his toes scudding across the floor as the three went outside. Piet tried to go after them but was held back by friendly hands.

Outside in the cold air, pushed against the wall round the side of the building, reality suddenly hit Warren Booth. Panic rose in him like bile. Somewhere a hundred miles away Piet was calling. Then Booth got it, full in the belly. He stopped breathing – it was more than pain, it was death. Then he sank to his knees and everything gushed out from his face – tears and beers. Dimly he saw the lower half of Pock-mark in front of him. He knew it was Pock-mark because the man was wearing trousers. Okay, it was all over. He looked a complete ass-hole and he would apologise. But when he was yanked up and pitted against the wall again he knew it wasn't all over. They were going to break a few bones.

He saw Pock-mark start to take a swing, to do a little softening-up before Pretty Boy got the chance to avenge his honour. He saw the swing, and waited numbly for the impact, but it didn't happen.

Have I died?

Then he couldn't see Pock-mark, either. With a yell the big man had leapt backwards into shadow. And then a grip on his shoulder that Booth hadn't noticed much was loosened and then gone. The youth reverted to girlhood and could be seen tripping down the street as lightly as if his big boots had been high-heels. His bum waggled and he didn't move as fast as he wanted because of the tightness of the skirt.

And into the light cast by the street-lamp, right there in front of Warren, stood Scottie Moore.

Piet was hovering about anxiously just beyond Scottie's left shoulder. Booth thought the blow was making him hallucinate.

'S-Scottie?'

The cigar shifted over to the corner of the mouth, making way for the grin.

'How are you, Kid?'

It was Scottie all right.

Scottie had always called him 'Kid', even though Booth had been thirty-four when they first met. Something in Booth warmed to being called 'Kid.' His Peter Pan instinct, maybe. Whatever it was, Scottie nailed it. No two men could be more different, yet unlike other machos of Warren's reluctant acquaintance, Scottie had never cast any aspersions on him for being gay. On the contrary, Scottie had always treated him as a friend, utterly without fear for his own masculinity. That was after he'd turned him down over the other – turned him down with such quiet and even menacing firmness that Warren Booth had never dared to make another pitch. Oddly, it seemed to draw them closer together rather than further apart. The original lust Booth felt for him mellowed into a kind of basking warmth in his company, made him feel more of a man because of such company.

Piet was shifting from one foot to the other, out of cold, out of excitement or frenzy cooling down. Scottie stood there, his arm loosely across Warren's shoulder. Warren began to cry.

'Long time, isn't it Kid? Long time,' whispered Scottie. 'Let's go back in. You need a drink.'

Piet moved forward. 'I don't think he should go back in there,' he protested.

'I saw you in there,' Scottie said to Piet. 'It takes guts to do what you tried to do. Kid your size.' He turned to Booth: 'You see that? He wasn't thinking of himself.'

Warren Booth nodded dumbly. Scottie was right. He felt like a selfish bastard.

'He'll be all right,' said Scottie to Piet. 'Hair of the dog.'

There was some hilarity in the Hercules Bar when

Warren Booth reappeared, flanked by two different men this time. The gnarled man's jaw dropped. He hadn't expected to see Warren Booth, alive, again. A few pairs of eyes lingered on Scottie Moore, the hunky unobtainable. He exuded difference in that milieu.

Piet stared at Scottie, almost mesmerised. These two Americans were suddenly deep in old memories from a world Piet would never know. The place they remembered – New York – was another country, and the time was another country too. Apparently Scottie had pulled Booth out of another bar in the Big Apple long ago and was now laughing about it Warren was laughing and half-coughing, but almost in a daze as if he hardly knew what Scottie was saying. He must've known, however, for he interjected his own contribution.

'That bitch,' he muttered.

'What bitch?' asked Scottie.

'You know. *Her*. Senator Freebody. Senator Hilda Freebody. Republican.'

'Oh, yeah.'

'How she made free with her body is anybody's guess. Tight old cunt! I was on that fucking stand *three days*! Senate fucking Subcommittee!'

'You made the papers in a big way.'

'So did she – that's what it was all about. Their careers on my back! Politicians! They had zilch on me, Scottie. Nothing except I was a god-damned faggot! Christ, I didn't even know the guy who was doing all the spying – he came from a different department! That didn't matter, did it? I was a faggot was all that mattered. So I get fired from my job because, goodness gracious me, you can't have fags in Sensitive Positions, can you? Embroidery or ballet-dancing, fine! But not guidance systems! Fags don't work on guidance systems! We're too "artistic" for that, aren't we?'

'Things have changed a bit over there.'

'Oh yeah? "Gay plague" and all that? Seems I heard the Lord is working out His vengeance on us!'

Scottie gave a nod to Piet. 'I think maybe it's time to go home, Kid,' he said softly to Warren Booth. It sounded almost like soliciting. It was merely the resumption of a familiarity that went back to the days when Warren Booth, down in the world after the witch-hunt that cost him his job at Neptune Telecommunications, was sharing a room in a boarding-house in Queens with Scottie. Scottie, too, had seemed to be down-and-out. Until the day when the ex-naval officer suddenly announced he was going to London on a cheap-rate night-flight ticket. 'You ought to get out too,' he said to Booth. 'There's nothing more in the U.S. of A. for you to do now, Kid.'

Warren Booth wasn't much trouble in the taxi. Even drunk he was a pussy-cat with Scottie Moore around. Piet felt a tinge of resentment. Not jealousy exactly, but the resentment of youth against the natural command of age. Whenever Warren Booth was drunk usually, Piet couldn't handle him at all. He was so different when sober, it was like schizophrenia.

It was no easy matter getting Booth up six flights of stairs. Doors opened as the three passed and then quickly closed again. They weren't the police: that was all that mattered.

Now Warren Booth was sitting over a basin on the side of his bed. Scottie suggested to Piet that he make some coffee.

'So what happened to you, Kid?' he asked, lighting up a fresh cigar after Warren had recovered himself. 'How did you get to Amsterdam?'

'Don't you know? I can't believe you showed up at the Hercules just by chance. Not your kind of scene, I'd have said.'

Scottie chuckled. 'You're fucking right. No, somebody told me you were around. Fill me in on how you got here.'

After Scottie left New York, Booth had gone to Thailand. Basically it was for the boys: those creamy-skinned, doe-eyed gentle boys for whom sex and a good berth for the night were all one. They surveyed the tacky club-land scene as they swivelled their narrow hips to the boogie. But man does not live by boys alone. By one means or another, Booth got himself into the drugs trade, doing reasonably well until expelled by the Thai authorities as an undesirable alien. He then heard that white South Africa was crying out for brains in his field. Unfortunately that episode came to a sorry end. Sharing a bed with a vibrantly uninhibited black boy, he was apprehended in embarrassing circumstances and somewhat brusquely informed by the South African police one afternoon that the boy was a courier for the Pan African Congress. (He had 'confessed', it seemed.) With all that taken into account, along with mixed-race sex *and* buggery, Warren Booth found he'd broken a fair number of South Africa's laws all at once. After being held in detention for a while, he was informed that the Ministry of the Interior had decided to deport him back to the States. He wasn't too keen to return to the land of his birth and asked one of those who visited him in prison (he being unaccountably thought of as a useful white friend to the cause of African nationalism) if he could be sprung. The result was that instead of landing at Kennedy Airport New York, he surfaced mysteriously in Mozambique. Unfortunately, foreigners in Mozambique were universally suspect. Booth decided to move on after being told that the alternative was to be served up as a McDonald's to the cockroaches in Maputo jail.

Amsterdam was at the other end of the drugs trade

from the Golden Triangle in the Far East; Booth knew he could find all the agents here from his knowledge at the 'grass'-roots there. He got into things and endured. Well, sort of. Living in a single room, divided from a kitchen with a sink full of dishes and broken eggshells, by a plastic curtain festooned with goldfish, wasn't even Warren's idea of luxury.

'Fuck me,' said Scottie Moore. 'You get around, don't you, Kid?'

'Long way from South Bend, Indiana,' said Booth.

Scottie pointed to Piet. 'Is he in on your business too?'

'Piet's a student,' said Warren, a shade protectively.

Piet made a shrugging gesture. 'It's all the same to me,' he said. 'I'm not a user, it's not my business.'

Warren swallowed a mouthful of coffee. It was reviving. 'Son of a bitch. You're here for something, aren't you, Scottie?'

Scottie just grinned.

'You want me for something, don't you?'

Scottie kept on grinning until Warren got the message.

'Piet,' he said, fishing out some crinkled notes, 'you wouldn't like to go out and get us something to eat, would you? Indonesian – they do good Indonesian here, you know, Scottie; they used to own the country. Treat's on me!'

Piet looked at them both, shrugged, and was gone. He would give them twenty minutes – that was all.

'Is it a big one, Scottie?'

Scottie nodded, slowly.

'Drugs?'

'No, not drugs.'

'What is it?'

Scottie took a long drag on the remains of his cigar. 'I can't tell you too much right now,' he said. 'But I want you to think back in time, Kid. Think back to the days when you were using your brains the way you were meant to.'

Booth looked down at the floor. 'That was a long time ago.'

'Before they started shouting "faggot", eh, Kid?'

5

Most people were twats. Ex-sergeant Maxton had kicked a few heads in from time to time, like niggers and little screaming yellow men. He'd kicked around a few spotty-faced little white gits in his time as well. Because they snivelled and wanted to go home to Mum. Twats. Then he got kicked out of the service. Sergeants of Her Majesty don't kick privates, and certainly not *in* the privates. Prior to the enquiry Maxton had been known as a stout disciplinarian, respected (if not feared) by the chinless wonders from Sandhurst who pretended to be in command. In truth he wasn't a disciplinarian at all. He just kicked people. His father in Yorkshire had beaten him at the drop of a hat from the time he was a tyke. He was usually drunk at the time. That's how Maxton came to understand a truth so rarely recognised by most: you get beaten not because you've done something wrong but because whoever beats you feels like it. Maxton's father had done it to him, and Maxton didn't see why he shouldn't carry on the tradition.

Once his old man had overstepped the mark, and he had nearly knocked his yellow false teeth down his scrawny throat. That was when Maxton was already a big boy – but his father hadn't noticed how he'd grown and went for him out of habit. It was the last time, and the old man never touched him again, or even so much as told him off. Maxton forever enjoyed reliving that triumph. That day when the old man stumbled and cursed, blood streaming out of his mouth, into the outside bog where he locked himself in for two hours while Mum fussed and thought he was dead. Maxton went off to the pictures and beat up a tramp out the back afterwards.

He couldn't take to civilian life in Barnsley after his dismissal from the army. A strange world where people said Hello and How Are You and Excuse Me and Thanks and were too scared to lay a fucking finger on each other. It drove him nuts, just like his wife drove him nuts. She took a fair number of cuts and bruises from him – he blacked her eye a few times and broke her arm once – before running off to Mother. There was no fun in women that way. They fell down at the lightest touch. But she was all the family he'd had, so when she left him he went to see someone he'd read about in the paper, an agent recruiting mercenaries to go to Zaire.

Zaire was mosquito-ridden and entirely without any action going on. Maxton wanted action. But whatever unrest there had been, was no more. So he and some of the lads drifted off to Angola and there they found plenty of action. It was a no-holds-barred war and he loved it. He liked dealing with Cuban captives. He strung one up by the heels once and beat the shit out of him. Later Maxton went on to El Salvador to fight guerillas, and found himself under Scottie's command.

There was something goading about this ex-Navy poofter. Maxton had always made it a rule never to mess with officers, but this was different: Scottie Moore got to him in a bad way. So one Saturday night he ambushed Moore coming out of the local cantina and they had a scrap. Moore beat him to within an inch of his life. And then, when Maxton was down, Moore got out a rubber-hose and worked him over again. Maxton lost all his front teeth and his nose was broken – nobody'd ever broken his nose. Moore broke some ribs as well. He left Maxton in the mud for dead.

There had been no pity, no 'sense of fair play', which Maxton despised. Scottie was a psycho, like himself, as it turned out. Only he was stronger than Maxton. Like a good psycho, Scottie visited him later in the makeshift hospital, with flowers and fruit. He said he was getting out of El Salvador because the money was lousy, and he advised Maxton – when he had recovered – to do the same. He said he was going to Europe for one reason or another, and gave Maxton a box-number to contact in London. If Maxton ever found himself at a loose end, he could do worse than make the effort to get in touch.

Scottie was the first bloke in Maxton's life who didn't qualify as a twat.

Scottie Moore recruited others as well as Maxton, with names showing they came from all over the place: Schiele, the bank-robber from Stuttgart, Hakayama, the mystical Mishima-follower from Japan, Figac, Waleski, and nearly half-a-dozen others. Now, in Holland, it was Maxton's job to whip them all into shape as a tight, new hit-squad. But there would be no rough stuff this time, warned Scottie. 'I know you and I know your record, Maxton. These are hand-picked boys and I've gone to a lot of trouble to find them. I catch you putting your hand to them and I'll do you over again. Only this time it'll be for good. It's not as if you'd be missed, would you?' Maxton took heed: Scottie was a psycho, and psychos never joke about violence.

They worked away in the woods of an estate, training in armed combat, exhausting themselves on an assault-course Maxton and Scottie had devised. The air was clean, the food plentiful if not over-exciting. No booze. No women on the premises. They were allowed the odd night off in the local town as a treat. It was wise to give them treats because they were a private army after all and could bugger off when they liked, really. That's what frustrated Maxton. He was really a bully who operated under authority; he didn't like having to manufacture his own. It was strenuous and sometimes required more finesse in relationships than Maxton had thought about in a lifetime. Maybe he was growing old. Anyhow, something in him was beginning to mellow, or be worn down, whichever it was. He became more focused on the job for its own sake than he would ever have done before. Kicking heads in wasn't everything. For Maxton, that was some turn-up.

But what was the job? Scottie Moore hadn't told him yet. Maxton knew it was about six weeks or so away, but he still didn't know what it was.

Sitting on the steps of the memorial in Dam Square in Amsterdam, surrounded by hippies, idlers and tourists, not much distinguished Maxton and Scottie from the others except their straighter casualness, their not-quite-focused-on-the-sights look. Today was Maxton's 'treat'. But he was beginning to think he now had the right to a bit of knowledge.

'You going to get round to telling us what this is all about, Mr Moore?' he asked.

'You'll know soon enough. Just keep doing the workouts. You know it's for an assault of some kind, and that's all you need to know at the moment. Now, what else is bugging you?'

'That twat Figac.'

'Oh yeah? What about him?'

'He's no use to you, Mr Moore. He thinks he's God Almighty. Any more of his fucking tantrums and I'll break his bleeding neck.'

'No you won't,' said Scottie with a rubber-hose note in his voice. 'Unhealthy idea. And bad for morale. Morale was never your strong point, was it?'

'He's off to the local knocking-shop whenever he gets

half a chance,' muttered Maxton. 'You talk about morale? Screws himself silly, it's disgusting.'

'He's French,' said Scottie drily, pondering Maxton's own standards with regard to morality. More likely it was envy.

'Fucking Frogs.'

It perplexed Maxton as to why Scottie Moore had recruited Figac, who seemed to believe he should be in charge, and wasted no opportunity to undermine Maxton's authority.

True, his credentials were as good as, if not better than, Maxton's own. Figac had been a corporal in the French Foreign Legion, based more recently in Corsica after the loss of France's North African colonies. As a very young man, a teenager in fact, Figac had seen bloody service in Algeria. He gained a reputation as *Le Bourreau*, the Executioner, though such a functionary as an executioner would have shown more consideration for his victims than did this Billy the Kid of a sadist in uniform. Figac had served under General Massu and was lucky not to have been shot when the general's *coup* against the authorities failed. No wonder Corsica offered little excitement afterwards.

He made it obvious that he thought the Yorkshireman slow-witted. Dimly Maxton perceived why Figac had been installed as 'corporal' under him. It was to ensure that Maxton himself didn't get too big for his boots or try to knock the boys around again. Figac kept Maxton wary, always conscious that the Frenchman would go to Scottie behind his back. Of course Scottie was too good a leader not to back Maxton to the hilt; nevertheless, Figac was there to stay.

'Has Steenkerke fixed up the barge?' asked Scottie, in Dam Square.

'Yeah, he's got it moored in the river. Don't worry, it

doesn't look like much on the outside. But it's good and thick enough, all right. The shooting-gallery's below decks and we can practise without waking up the whole countryside.'

'Good. Keep up the pressure. Don't let things slacken. Now, let's get plastered.'

They wouldn't get plastered, of course. Maxton wasn't really a drinking man and he'd never seen Scottie Moore pie-eyed, either.

What he didn't know was that he was being softened-up to be informed about the recruitment of Lavitzsky and Warren Booth, soon to join the strike-force at the camp.

'I've got some news,' said Scottie when they had a refill of their frothy steins.

'What's that, then?' asked Maxton. Maybe now he'd find out about the job.

'I've got us someone who will be taking care of the electronics side – a communications expert. And someone else who'll deal with the nuclear warheads.'

'Who are they?'

'You'll love 'em, Maxy. One's a Russian and the other's a fag.'

'Jesus Christ,' mumbled Maxton and took another swallow of piss-beer.

'I need them as much as I need you. And that's because they got more brains in their heads than the rest of you have in your balls, understand? They have a job to do same as you have, so I don't want any disrespectful treatment. You can teach them discipline without that shit. You'd better, anyway.'

'Whatever you say – you're the boss-man.'

'I'm going to let you be boss-man for a little while. I've got to go over to England for a few days and I'm leaving you in charge of the operation.'

'What about Steenkerke?' asked Maxton, referring to the exiled Afrikaaner whose extra-curricular activities had become an embarrassment even to B.O.S.S., and who had invested his ill-gotten gains from an illegal uranium trade in Dutch real estate. 'Why doesn't he take over?'

'Steenkerke is strictly the sleeping partner, or as much as he can be,' said Scottie. 'He provides the land and the facilities. He wants no active part in the running, so don't expect to go charging off to him for help. His only concern is to keep everything under wraps, maintain a low profile. After all, he's the one who's got to stay behind here when the rest of us have gone. You just make life easy for him, that's all. Steenkerke's vital and if he chickens out for any reason the whole operation's up the spout, understand?'

'Right. What if Figac gets too big for himself again?'

'That's your problem. Give you more practice in handling men under stress. Yeah, I know you've had plenty of that before, but it was a long time ago. Remember this is a mercenary group. Until we go for the Big One, they can leave any time they want to, and they know it. It's a weakness with all mercenary groups. Hell, didn't you and I pull out of Salvador because of the money?'

'Nobody's complaining about the money on this one.'

'It's going to get better, too.'

Maxton looked up into Scottie's eyes. Was he about to tell him, at last? 'How much better?'

'I'm going to tell you what you're going to get out of it. What do you say to two million dollars?'

Maxton was inwardly amazed. Christ, what *was* this job they were going to pull? The Bank of England? But he didn't show his amazement. Instead he narrowed his eyes and asked: 'What currency?'

'No currency. Gold.'

'Gold blocks?'

'That's what I said: gold.'

'Jesus. I guess it's none of my business, Mr Moore, but what's your cut?'

'No it isn't, but I'll tell you. I get five million, for setting it all up and running the thing. The others get one each. The whole operation's costing about twenty million.'

'What's it worth?'

Scottie lit a cigar. 'Can't tell you that yet. Still classified.' He stood up. Maxton started to rise, but Scottie put his hand out. 'No, stay where you are. Have a good time on your night out and don't get into fights. Remember: two million, Maxy. Keep you in knuckle-dusters for the rest of your life. Now I'm off to sort out the British end of things. See you when I see you.'

Two million. The jackpot. Maxton felt a little dazed after Scottie left the bar, and not because of the drink. It was going to be much bigger big-time than even he had thought.

Jane Illingworth knew she was a bitch for thinking Baythorne Manor too good for Clive Parris because she had always fancied the place for herself. Perhaps it was a little over-manicured for her taste, but it would mellow nicely under the influence of her slatternly habits. Indeed Baythorne Manor felt more like a home to her than any of the many houses in which she and her sister had grown up. Anyone would call it Home. It wasn't particularly large or of great architectural merit: it was early 18th century, its classical front partially and seductively covered in off-the-shoulder ivy. Like Baby Bear's porridge, it was 'just right'; not too grand, not too poky.

Behind the façade was an older part, built round three

sides of a courtyard, containing what in earlier times had been the kitchens, bakery, pantry, stores and a harness-room.

But it was the trees that got to Jane's soul. In front of the house, almost blocking out the light from the sitting-room was a rare cork tree brought back from Portugal some time in the last century. On the lawn at the side of the house was a great cedar, grey in some lights, under which it was said John Wesley had preached two hundred years earlier. Nearby was a Judas tree. Judas Iscariot had hanged himself from one like this. All for thirty pieces of silver. It brought Jane back with a jolt. Was someone in this vicinity doing something similar for rather more? She shuddered in the breeze that swayed the tree's branches.

Beyond the outbuildings at Baythorne there was a disused tennis court (so much for Clive Parris's 'hobby' – strictly for the readership of *Who's Who*). Below that was an orchard which sloped steeply down to the river bank, brushed gently here and there by willow trees. Opposite the river, the water-meadows stretched away into the distance – lush, level and dotted with clumps of nettles and thistles. Not far from the manor to one side was the church, its stubby tower rising over a high brick wall with a lych-gate in it. The delphiniums and lupins were nearly over now, for it was September, but the dahlias would go on till the first frosts. That might be quite some time, for the summer was maintaining the full heat of its life and showed no sign of abating. It was a cheering prospect, more summer – greenhouse effect or no greenhouse effect.

The funeral was for 2.30.

Jane fled from the cocktail party, which was thinly-disguised as a sort of pre-funeral wake, going on in the house. The only difference from the everyday, happy sort of cocktail party was the relative sobriety of the drinks – and perhaps the chat. Polite little sherries were the order of the day; no spirits or martinis. One had to do something hospitable for county folk, even at a time like this.

More than county folk were in attendance, of course, this being the Clive Parris household. Jeremy Brixdale, the Parliamentary Private Secretary, was there with his wife Amelia. A don from Cambridge; some of Sarah's and Jane's obscurer relations (their own parents having been long deceased); the sprinkling of mandatory old ladies who seem to be rented out for all family occasions, their expressions much the same at funerals as at weddings and christenings; and a man whom Jane recognised as Clive's best man at his wedding six years before. She wondered if they had seen one another since.

Away from them all, Jane sat down on the low wall of the tennis court and gave herself over to – what? Grief? Would she have another chance simply to grieve for Sarah today? Grief or not, the tears wouldn't come. Only the realisation that with Sarah's passing she really was alone in the world now except for a smattering of cousins and uncles and aunts. Damn the sort of occasion that makes you realise the truth of the old *cliché* about blood being thicker than water! At such times you know that being smart and saying you're married to an Amstrad isn't as amusing as it seemed at the time. Entering her late twenties, Jane wondered if perhaps she already had one foot in the grave. The idea of reaching thirty without getting some of the central questions of her life resolved appalled her.

A big black labrador wandered up, wagging his tail and swivelling his body as he drew nearer. 'Hello,' said Jane. 'You're Onslow, aren't you?' Patronising name for these serious, brown eyes and lovely long muzzle that looked soulfully up at her as she stroked his head, feeling for the bump on top. The name had been a joke of Sarah's, naming a tiny puppy after their grandfather. But the fully grown dog wasn't 'Onslow'.

He seemed to be finding in Sarah's sister someone dimly remembered as being like her. 'What do you know, Onslow?' asked Jane, holding his soft muzzle in both hands. *What have you seen?* He jerked away, not sure of her.

Humphrey would be getting his divorce soon, and then something might begin to happen in her life. Did it really matter now? His freedom might make things more complicated rather than less. And above everything, like a huge, black bird of evil, Sarah's death cast a shadow. Nothing could go forward for Jane until the mystery of that was solved once and for all.

A tall young man without much chin, dressed in a dark suit, was crossing the tennis-court towards her. He was Clive's nephew Tony.

'I've been sent to find you,' he said. 'You're to come up to the house for lunch.' He was ill-at-ease with her grief. 'Sorry to interrupt, but Uncle Clive wondered where you'd got to and I volunteered.' The young man was probably hoping during the course of the day for a quick one with any willing female in the master bedroom.

At a quarter past two everyone started to leave the house, entering the churchyard through the gate in the wall. Others were already in the church: people from the village and round about. A photographer was waiting by the lych-gate and when he saw which way everyone was entering he ran towards them. Two of the party who hadn't been at lunch in the house sprinted across the gravestones and stopped him. Special Branch, thought Jane.

She wondered whether the murderer was present here, making a grisly occasion even grislier. Clive was the very model of dignified grief, comforting distressed aunties in black, keeping an eye peeled to see that all the arrangements were going as planned. Brixdale, his P.P.S., looked a little shell-shocked and just stared into space. Did he have some inkling of the truth, Jane wondered.

The church with its funerary monuments from down through the centuries and its box pews was more than half full, an unusual sight. The rector entered and commenced with the rolling phrases of the 1662 Prayer-book. I suppose there are worse places to be laid to rest, mused Jane, though she had to look away as her sister's coffin was borne past her to the bottom of the chancel steps.

Later, outside, Clive threw down a handful of earth upon the coffin with appropriate solemnity. He might have been at a tree-planting ceremony. It was unfair to think such things. But what else could Jane think? Sarah should never have married him. She might be alive now if she hadn't...

Most of those attending went straight to their cars afterwards, but the immediate family returned to the house through the little gate in the wall. Onslow came out to meet them. Clive turned to Jane.

'Would you like Onslow?' he asked. 'He seems to have taken to you. Mrs Banham has quite enough to do looking after the house and I'm hardly ever here these days. He needs proper company.'

'I'd love to take him on, but I can't,' replied Jane, wondering if he'd offered Onslow to her because she happened to be the person next to him when they were approaching the house. 'He'd be cooped up in a London flat all day. Surely there's some way he can be kept on here?'

Not answering her, Clive turned to one of his cousins. 'Can you give him a home?'

The cousin thought for a moment. 'Could do. Buster's

getting pretty old, poor chap. Can hardly see anything these days. Yes, I'll take Onslow if you like. If you fetch me his lead and all the necessaries before we go–'

'That's extremely good of you,' said Clive. 'You understand why I–'

The cousin understood. There had really been no need for Clive to make such an elaborate show of remorse for ditching his dog. The last Jane saw of Onslow was him pulling against the lead and whining as he was dragged into the back of a Range Rover. He twisted round and looked at her through the rear window as the car drove away down the drive – almost reproachfully, it seemed to Jane.

The last of the Baythorne animals. The horses had long since vanished from the stables – Clive not being a hunting man. Now the stables were garages housing Bentley, Porsche, Sarah's 2CV. The semi-circular opening cut into the top of one of the large wooden doors had been neatly boarded up, so that no longer could the swallows fly in and out at all times of the day. They made a mess on the cars, after all. So the birds were gone, too. A home free at last from anything four-legged and furry or two-taloned and feathery – fit for human habitation.

By half-past five those who had stayed for tea were gone. That left Jane, who was invited to stay the night. And Mrs Banham the housekeeper, the only servant at Baythorne who lived in.

Jane felt at a loss now it was all over. She would have preferred returning to London but it seemed churlish not to accept Clive's invitation. He was only doing the decent thing and they *were* family, of a sort. Besides, there was the indefinable lure of Baythorne itself. Jane resigned herself to an evening of polite and watchful conversation.

Dinner was still a couple of hours or so away as Jane lay curled up on a window seat in the drawing-room, leafing through an expensive and very old edition of *Gulliver's Travels*. Clive came in and asked what she was reading.

'The unexpurgated version's not exactly nursery fare, is it? Isn't there a bit somewhere in which Gulliver puts out the fire in the Lilliputian palace by somewhat unorthodox methods?'

'Yes,' said Jane. 'In fact I just came across an illustration of it.' She found the page.

Clive twisted his head round to have a look. 'Good God, a bit near the knuckle, isn't it? Shows you the antiquity of this edition. Obviously *very* pre-Victorian.' He was still a stick, but suddenly the atmosphere between them was lighter, easier. 'I say,' he said, 'I've had a sudden impulse. It's a lovely hot evening – we aren't going to see many more of these. What say we shake off our troubles and go for a swim?'

Jane was so surprised she looked at the revitalised Clive Parris with open-mouthed wonder.

'I only mean a quick dip. Down in the river. Sudden inspiration. It might be good for both of us.' It was the first 'unorthodox' thing Jane had ever heard Clive say, it seemed to come from out of the blue. Perhaps he was the genuine article of a human being after all. He seemed all the more genuine for wanting to do this on the night of his wife's funeral. Perhaps he *had* been really grieving and had found the burden too much.

'I didn't bring anything with me,' said Jane.

'Would you mind wearing one of Sarah's costumes? By the way, if there are things of hers you like – I meant to say this before, but there hasn't been a chance till now – clothes and things like that, I want you to have them. No hurry, but some time, if you want.'

Suddenly Jane felt herself warming to him. 'Thank you, Clive, it's kind of you. Perhaps when I come down again I could see. Yes, and I'll go for a swim with you if you like.'

'Great, thanks!' he exclaimed, as if she were his benefactress. For a second Jane wondered if he were making some insane play for her on the spur of the moment, but pushed it out of her mind. No, he was definitely bent on swimming.

It was as he said a beautiful evening. The sun was changing the water of the meandering river to molten silver.

'See over there,' said Clive, pointing beyond the water-meadows. 'That's the tower of Baythorne Abbey. Stands out clearly this time of day. Almost two miles as the crow flies.' He slipped off a flannel bathrobe and stood on the sloping bank. Jane removed her sister's dressing-gown and stretched out in the sun, closing her eyes.

'Just be a bit careful,' warned Clive. 'There's not much current to speak of but the bank drops down almost sheer. About ten feet I should say.' He raised his arms, tensed, and dived in. Jane decided the best policy was sudden action, and she did the same. Christ, it was cold! Her lungs worked overtime as the two surfaced, bobbing about like a couple of youngsters. 'Great, isn't it?' he shouted, and with a lunge dived under again, kicking his feet in the air before they were submerged.

Opening her eyes underneath the surface, Jane could see nothing but an opaque pea soup, nothing but green everywhere. She felt what she thought was a hand groping for her leg: it might have been a branch, or the caress of a water-plant. She came up for air again.

Suddenly, near her, Clive broke through the surface like a missile, throwing up his hands and shouting what sounded like 'cramp!' He disappeared. There were only bubbles where he had been. Jane waited for him to re-emerge, but he didn't surface. 'Clive! Clive!' Ridiculous to call above water. She fretted and didn't know what to do. Resolving to do something, she dived in the direction of where she'd seen him last. She felt violent currents of water against her skin and headed towards their source, the undoubtedly panicking Clive.

Suddenly she felt an arm around her neck, so powerful that she couldn't rise to the life-giving air. She struggled to free herself but now he had both hands gripping her shoulders, forcing her down, down.

She was desperate for breath. Seemingly far away but still gripping her with fury, it seemed, Clive was shouting, even screaming. Jane's lungs were at bursting-point – she needed air, air! She kicked out and twisted. Nothing was working. She panicked. In her panic she must have caught Clive in the groin with one of her knees, and at once he released his grip on her. Jane got to the surface at last and sucked in the sweet air, the most precious thing in the world.

She found Clive clinging to the root of a tree by the bank. She swam towards the bank herself, as he slowly climbed out and slumped down, his head between his knees, his chest heaving.

'What happened?' she gasped out as she herself climbed the bank and shiveringly sat down beside him.

'C-cramp. Stomach. The water was c-colder than I thought. You all right, Jane?'

They had only little towels to cover their shivering bodies, shivering from fright as well as shock.

'I'm an ass,' he said as they limped back across the lawn to the house. There was no more to be said on that score. It seemed to be the case. He had nearly succeeded in drowning both of them.

Later he had recovered sufficiently to apologise to her properly. He seemed to feel so badly about it that Jane was compelled to put him at his ease. Mrs Banham took charge of Jane, smearing her shoulders with ointment and covering the ointment with lint. For only then could it be seen that Jane had sustained quite severe scratches on both shoulders, and she had bled without knowing it. 'I've told Mr Parris before that it's safer by the bridge,' clucked Mrs Banham. 'None of us'll go in by the meadows. I've told him before, but he won't listen. Like the Trivett boy, last year that was. Three days before he came up in Brayford Pool. Ever so sad. It eddies there, see?'

Clive appeared at the bedroom door with two large brandies. That alone was almost enough to merit complete forgiveness. 'She saved my life, Mrs Banham, quite literally saved it.'

'Well, I won't say I told you so, sir, but – is that better, Miss Jane?'

'Much better, thanks, Mrs Banham,' said Jane as the brandy bored a warm little hole down into her.

Clive continued to apologise, one way or another, all evening *ad nauseam*. Jane locked her door before climbing into bed.

'Why didn't you show me this note before, Miss Illingworth?' asked Paul Finningham. Had ringing him on impulse been such a good idea?

His brusqueness irritated Jane. After all, she was the one who had nearly died, not him. 'I didn't know how it could help, because I had no notion of what she might have been referring to.'

'None?'

'Absolutely none. It took me completely by surprise.'

'Well, I'm glad you decided to show it to me now! I wish you wouldn't take the law into your own hands – you can have no idea whether this note might be taken into account along with other factors or not.'

'Do you have any idea of that?' she asked.

'It might interest you to know,' said Paul, who then told

Jane that he had flown on the same flight as her sister and had noticed her in an unhappy state, an impression he might have been able to confirm earlier if he had been aware of the existence of this note. And on that impression rested a good case for saying that the slaying had been premeditated. Jane was stunned at the news, but Paul kept up the barrage. 'If you were so sure Clive Parris was trying to murder you, why didn't you report him immediately to the police? Instead you went on to have dinner with him and even slept in his house!'

He had Jane on the defensive, and it showed. 'Why don't you say "his bed"?' she flung at him. 'Anyhow I wasn't *sure* he was trying to do it, and *do* allow me to have been somewhat shocked at the time!'

They both paused for breath. Jane looked down at her lap. 'I'm sorry,' she said. 'I should have showed you the note. I've held everything up.'

Paul smiled. 'It's not as bad as all that. At least now we know.'

'I'm sure Clive is guilty of something. The more I think about it the more I believe it. Can't you confront him with it?'

Paul shrugged. 'With what? Evidence? Miss Illingworth, he isn't your common or garden suspect. He's a government minister. Anything we try and pin on him has to stick. So far there's nothing but these disturbing indications. The note from your sister. His apparent – and I emphasise apparent – attempt to drown you. And the fact that she was murdered in Amsterdam.'

'What's that got to do with it?'

'I wish I could tell you, but I can't. Not yet.'

'Mr Finningham?'

'Yes?'

'There's something else I have to tell you.'

'What's that?'

Jane then told Paul about what Humphrey had discovered – the possible connection of Clive Parris with an armaments consortium. His eyes took on a gleam, which he hastily concealed. She hadn't specifically mentioned Humphrey in all this. 'You've been quite busy on your own account,' he said.

'I am a journalist, it was easy for me to track these things down.'

'Interesting. It looks as if we're going to have to put a tail on Mr Clive Parris.'

Clive followed? How exciting!

'And I've just one more question to ask you, Miss Illingworth.'

'Yes?'

'Would you have dinner with me this evening?'

6

It might not have been the biggest terrorist set-up in history, but they were going to pull the biggest job.

They were going to demand a ransom for London itself.

Scottie Moore had almost turned it down when it was put to him. His first reaction was that it was crazy. And then he had to ask himself why it was crazy. It was crazy because it was too big. But then, when you broke the operation down, step-by-step, taking everything into consideration as you went along, it began to make sense. It began to look as if it could work. And with some twenty million bucks worth of backing, it had to work. Even after investing twenty million dollars, a profit was still going to be turned.

London was reckoned worth 100 million in gold. Cheap at the price, really. A bargain. And before they were finished, the powers that be would be begging them to take it.

The hardware and the ammunition for the job had to come from inside Britain. Scottie wasn't risking searches even in out-of-the-way coves. Men could scatter; caches of arms couldn't.

He kept up with the papers. Usually when governments got wind of terrorist activities there was some big splash publicity-wise. Scottie had seen not a trace, not a whisper, that anyone knew anything was going on. That didn't mean there was no anti-terrorist activity going on. Something was always going on – you had to assume that.

Even if Scottie had known of Paul's efforts and enquiries it wouldn't have surprised him.

When Warren Booth and Lavitzsky were safely installed at Steenkerke's HQ in the woods, under the tender care of ex-Sergeant Maxton, Scottie Moore departed for London. He travelled under a false identity as John Jarvis Ferguson, a U.S. citizen permanently domiciled in New Haven, Connecticut. Ferguson was supposed to be an import–export agent specialising in hi-fi equipment and video recorders, with an office in Hilversum. Putting away his jacket and jeans for a dark suit, slim brief-case and overnight bag, Scottie, or Abel Scott Moore, returned to the respectable world for a rare visit. Walking unconcernedly through the Green area, with no worry of being picked up – because he had nothing on him – Moore experienced euphoria. Even if by some astounding chance he was recognised for who he was, he had no criminal record in the United Kingdom and nothing to fear. John Jarvis Ferguson was certainly boring, but there was a lot to be said for being him if you were ever in need of a rest.

Not that he was on a holiday. This trip was Phase Two. Scottie looked at all the people getting on and off the tube during the long journey to the centre of London. Going about their daily business with all the self-absorption of people who had no idea of what was on the cards for them. Walking along the great thoroughfares of the metropolis he exalted in the fact that before very long all this would probably be brought to a standstill. While he dictated the terms of survival for the twenty million inhabitants.

When all this is over, he thought, what do I do then?

Ostensibly he had his plan – a little place in South America he had lined up. A bolt-hole in a corrupt little country where only money counted, and nothing else ever would. After this job he would have his five million dollars in gold. But he would never be able to do anything else again. No one ransoming London could ever hope to walk into any western country again – without maybe a complete change of face, which Scottie wasn't that hot to have. As far as pulling some other job – it would be pushing your luck.

No, he would die a nice, long leisurely death by a swimming-pool somewhere. It was only one way to die. Another was to go quickly, by cyanide capsule before they got to you. Either way it was death, the fate of man and all creatures. Scottie wondered, really, which was the best? A long-anticipated death in the sun enfeebled by time, or instant departure in the heat of the moment, ablaze with all one's powers? When he balanced it up, Scottie couldn't really decide which was the best way to go. He knew which was the most *rational*. But then he no longer considered himself rational – not deep inside.

The truth was he no longer cared. Ordinary, day-to-day survival – that was one thing. Or grafting to get the biggest slice of the cake you could out of life. But what was it all for? What did it matter?

There were the history books to consider. What did it matter how one died if one also made one's mark on history? By ransoming London? Or even by destroying it? The idea of dying himself in the midst of that destruction bothered Scottie not at all. He would be immortalised.

The thought of destroying London was not an idle one. London's annihilation was fully within Scottie's power – or soon would be, if the next few days proceeded according to plan.

The Austrian Grenadier, on Ludgate Hill, wasn't one of the City's more *bijou* hostelries. It resolutely fell out of line with the prevailing trend to turn public houses into

Surbiton's idea of a Moroccan bordello. No doubt it was only a matter of time before falling profits, the new business-rate and new ownership would have the Victorian fittings ripped out and the general air of cosy dinginess replaced with muzak and subdued cocktail-bar lighting.

Scottie ordered a lager and a cheese sandwich, looking like a business man having a snack lunch between appointments. He cased the place for possible observers, mentally scrutinising each customer. As it filled up the clientele looked relentlessly typical of City folk – but you could never be sure about anyone. Scottie knew of enough boasts of being able to 'smell a pig a mile away' – frequently failed boasts. He didn't pretend to be clairvoyant where the Law was concerned. But he had a sharp eye for the seemingly premeditated action, the self-conscious leaning against the bar, the quick check on appearance, the drink being nursed a little too perfunctorily. Looking for everything he could think of, Scottie satisfied himself that so far the way was clear.

He knew his own tracks were pretty well covered, but you could never be sure of the other guy's. Someone always slipped up somewhere along the line. Scottie had a sort of Sod's Law view about such things. Of course you yourself dealt with professionals, but down the chain away from the professionals were the semi-professionals, and then the flunkies, the mediocre, the slipshod, the drunks, the druggies, the lazy, the amateurs. And the Law snapped where the link was weakest. Scottie had had some uncomfortable moments wondering how long the chain was that led away from the one he was about to deal with.

The hands of the yellow moon-faced clock on the wall with the Roman numerals were at 1.25. He ordered another lager and a pork-pie: waiting always made him hungry. At 1.35 a business-type came in clutching a black rolled umbrella. He ordered a double whisky. Scottie looked casually along the bar at another business-type who was sitting and contemplating a second gin and tonic. Hooked over the edge of the bar by him was another neatly rolled umbrella.

Scottie left the bar with his lager and pork-pie and found an empty table for two in a corner, which had just become vacant. The later of the business men picked up his whisky and came over and sat down beside him, hanging his umbrella on a hook just behind.

'Lucky I was told you had red hair or I might have tried doing business with that sonofabitch,' muttered Scottie, indicating Gin-and-Tonic at the bar. 'This rolled umbrella stuff is for the birds. Everybody and his brother carries a rolled umbrella in these parts. Christ, I'm a Canadian and even I knew that.' Scottie was annoyed at being kept waiting three-quarters of an hour. It smacked of unprofessionalism. Worse, it smacked of a seller's market.

'Canadian, eh?' said the business man, sipping his drink. 'I'm glad I didn't put my foot in it. I'd have said American for certain.'

'What should I call you?' asked Scottie. 'I always like to call a man something other than Hey You. I'm Philip.'

'Like the Duke of Edinburgh? Can I call you Phil?'

'My mother never liked diminutives, but it's okay by me.'

'Call me Arnie.'

'Okay, Arnie.'

'Have you brought your shopping-list with you?' asked Arnie.

Scottie pointed to his own head. 'It's all up here.'

'Wise man. Well, let's get down to business, then.' Arnie edged a little closer to Scottie in his seat. 'What do you want?'

'M35 sub-machine guns. RG34 grenades and smoke grenades. Fair amount of ammunition, we're in for a long job here, no smash-and-grab. I'll write down the quantities later.'

'No, it's all right. I'll keep them in *my* head. You say smoke grenades. What about the East German S32? Has a seven-second fuse. You're lucky we're not in short supply. Can't get them out of the East any more, you know.'

'Is that going to be your excuse for raising the price?' asked Scottie.

'All I can do is quote you and you see what you think. Times aren't what they were now that Honecker and that lot in Czechoslovakia aren't around any more.'

'I like the idea of the S32s, anyway,' said Scottie. 'And there's something else. I want a Carl Gustav Recoilless Anti-Tank Gun, using an armour-piercing shell containing a shaped charge.' It was a type of ammunition to cause a further explosion once it had pierced the armour. The shaped charge form of ammunition was not unlike the semtex used by the I.R.A. Scottie smiled. 'You think you can do that one for me, Arnie?'

'Fuck me,' said Arnie. 'What are you going to do with it?'

'You know better than to ask me that,' said Scottie.

'What about the Carl Gustav M2? Penetrates 400mm of armour plate.'

Scottie shook his head. He wasn't going to tell Arnie that the kind of armour-plating he had in mind came in a thickness anywhere from 760mm to 1200. No point in filling the lad's head with stories to tell. 'Sorry Arnie, no dice. You get me what I want or the whole deal's off.'

'You want this thing badly, don't you, Phil?' Arnie stared into his glass, sweating a little now in the London heat, looking as if all sorts of little calculations were going through his head. Then he looked up. 'It'll cost you,' he said.

'I know that. My principal is prepared to pay what it costs.'

'I mean for more than the gun itself. Have you any idea how many people we have to buy off to look the other way while we get you the latest thing in armour-piercing technology?'

'Spare me the difficulties,' said Scottie. 'You can do it, right?'

Arnie nodded.

'Okay, if it's possible, then we're on. That particular Carl Gustav's essential. As I said, the deal's off without it. And we know who to look for if you slip in something inferior.'

Arnie was sensing, uneasily, that he was dealing with a bigger mob than he'd been led to believe. Who needed a Carl Gustav of that magnitude to rob a bank? Or even blow a hole into a Marine barracks? 'It's going to take a little time,' he said.

'Don't stall,' said Scottie. 'We're paying well and we've got a deadline, which you are going to meet.'

'It may have to be more than the amount originally agreed. Inflation–'

'Inflation, my ass. What figure did you have in mind?'

Arnie asked for the quantities, which Scottie gave. He then whipped out a calculator and did some figuring. It ran to six figures, with £50,000 down straight away. 'For that kind of money,' observed Scottie, 'we can expect delivery in two weeks.'

'Three.'

'Okay, three. I'll give you details on that, too.' Which he proceeded to do, Arnie taking it in and committing it to memory.

'Well,' he then said, sitting back. 'This seems all right. I thought I was going to have to haggle.'

'Not in this business,' said Arnie. 'You seem to have plenty to burn, by the way.'

'We won't go into that,' said Scottie with finality.

'I can't settle the deal now. I've got to have a consultation with my people first. You can hand over the £50,000 later.'

'When?'

'Tomorrow. I don't foresee any problems.'

Scottie smiled. 'Good. Because I wasn't ready to hand anything over today anyway.'

'Hilton Hotel at 3.00 tomorrow. Foyer. We'll find you if you don't find us.'

Scottie then raised a separate issue that was dealt with and settled after some discussion between the two.

'Tomorrow at 3.00, then,' said Arnie, and left.

Later Scottie wondered if he'd have done better to whittle the price down a bit. He didn't think it mattered. His principal would pay to the hilt – there wasn't any point in inspiring grudges down the line. Pay well if you want people to be happy in their work. As for the hardware: you don't tool up for projects like this by going to Woolworths.

After leaving the Austrian Grenadier, Scottie Moore hailed a taxi which he took as far as the Merchant Navy Memorial on Tower Hill. There he got out and walked along the north side of the Tower, gazing at the bastions on the farther side of the dry moat.

It had been impregnable enough in its time, the Tower, but people escaped from you all the same, didn't they, you bastard? For more than half a thousand years the Tower had been the strongest bastion devised by the wit of man, but somebody was always clever enough to fool the system. In all sorts of ways. Like every security system ever devised by the wit of man, it proved as leaky as a sieve. There's a way out of everything, thought Scottie: look at Captain Blood, Houdini, the Wooden Horse of Troy, the Brinks Robbery, the computer hackers in high school getting into the Pentagon's 'foolproof' system. Human beings devise, and human beings dispose.

He turned the corner into Tower Bridge Road. Ahead stood the famous twin-towered bridge. First the squat structure like a gateway, leading on to the bridge, then the whole rising up to the two pinnacled Gothic towers, housing the machinery for raising and lowering the bascules so that large vessels could pass through, right into the Pool as far as London Bridge. They don't build babies like you any more, thought Scottie, allowing himself a little good old tourist sentiment.

He walked to the exact centre of Tower Bridge and leant on the parapet, staring out over the Pool. To his right the dome of St Paul's peeped round the high-rise Lego of commerce. Dead ahead lay the present London Bridge: more than 900 feet of river spanned by three elongated arches. On the south side were Victorian warehouses, some derelict and others recently virtually demolished. Scottie looked at them with more than passing interest, but he couldn't find them as fascinating as the cruiser, H.M.S. *Belfast*.

Belfast was of course a floating museum, moored some 150 yards from the south bank.

He would be going over the *Belfast* all in good time. First he had to get himself conveniently accommodated. He retraced his steps to the Tower Hotel, which overlooks the Thames and Tower Bridge. At the desk he asked for, and got, a room overlooking the Pool. It was a double, but he paid the extra without a murmur.

'That's quite a view,' he couldn't help remarking to the

porter when shown into his room. It was, too: the bridge looked close enough to touch.

From the literature provided Scottie learned that the hotel was part of a larger complex, which included a yacht marina in what was once St Katherine's Dock. He didn't know whether that particular fact was important for him just now or not, but he kept it at the back of his mind.

A visit to the *Belfast* had to wait till next day. Scottie had the more pressing business of cash-transfers to deal with. And what more respectable institution for all this than the Chase Manhattan Bank?

The following morning was fresh and grey as Scottie walked from the hotel up the steps on to Tower Bridge, then across the Thames and down into Tooley Street. Here was what he was looking for: a sign on a lamp-post pointing to the river: 'To H.M.S. *Belfast*.' Two hundred yards down an alley, through a gateway and on to a wharf. Ahead lay the cruiser, large and grey, grey like the day and the water.

The *Belfast* wasn't moored to the quay, but some 150 yards into the river, secured fore and aft by eight enormous anchor chains disappearing down into the turbid water. Scottie saw there was a permanent walkway connecting the quay with the quarterdeck. Even after all these years the *Belfast* still showed her battle scars from the Second World War. Her bow faced upstream so that her port side was parallel to the quay. In addition to the anchors she was held in place by two pontoons. Around one of these lay a number of small boats moored to Jacob's ladders over the side of the *Belfast*. These ladders might come in useful, mused Scottie. Like any tourist, he paid his admission fee and went on board by way of the catwalk to the quarterdeck.

He would check from the guidebook (because he liked

to be accurate about such things) that it was about 11,000 tons when laden and just under 600 feet long. At least that's what his experienced nautical eye told him. But the guidebook was principally to supply him with cut-away sections of the ship. No longer the bogus City gent, Scottie was now the old ex-naval officer familiarising himself with the general layout of a World War II British warship. Museum-piece though it was, *Belfast* was at the nub of his plan, the plan that he had worked out with others.

A young petty officer approached and asked if he could be of assistance (it was a little too early in the day for tourists *en masse*); he gave Scottie the opportunity to ramble away about an uncle of his who had served in World War II and had been involved in the handing over of those famous veteran destroyers to the Royal Navy by Roosevelt – big deal. America still had most of the former British bases, but where now were those destroyers? The petty officer wondered, too. He assured Scottie that he had only to ask if there was anything he wanted to know. Scottie was obliged.

Scottie then moved off along the quarterdeck, passing the rear turrets, each with their three six-inch guns. Almost amidships, near the aft funnel, he came to a watertight door. Descending to the deck below by a companion ladder, he went to the souvenir shop to pick up the guidebook and leaflets which would prove so useful to the whole enterprise. They had known in general what was to be done: not in detail, though, so far as *Belfast* was concerned.

The *Belfast* had seen honourable service in the Arctic and in the Far East. The fact that so much had been removed, including deck-clutter like hawzers, would make matters easier from the point of view of the strike-force. And in such a large, sprawling ship like *Belfast* it would be possible to locate somewhere to secrete a cache of arms. If an ordinary lady could bluff her way past the Beefeaters in the Tower of London two hundred years ago to get her husband out of his dungeon, it was surely possible for a smart character like Scottie to think of a way to smuggle weapons aboard the Belfast.

And another thing: he would have to check out the crew complement of the cruiser.

Scottie sat down on a bollard and gazed over the port side at the derelict warehouses. Would anyone suspect twelve men of being holed-up behind those grimy brick walls? After leaving the *Belfast* he would get into one or two of them somehow and have a look around.

Two Japanese, their faces wreathed in smiles, asked him affably if he would take their picture. It was a bore, but it made him look like part of the tourist scene. Scottie snapped them.

Then he resumed his examination of the blank walls of the warehouses. When coming up Abbots Lane he had noticed there were no openings on the street side except for the locked main doors. He would attempt entry from the area where the buildings had been demolished.

He stuck his tongue out at a small sticky child of indeterminate sex – the child ran off to Mother. Too many bloody visitors. During the attack they were bound to get in the way.

Passing through a watertight door he entered the operations room, then the bridge, then the admiral's day room, down past the main deck to number two deck. He remembered reading long ago that in most cruisers and such the number two deck had a clear passageway running from stem to stern, which the jolly British tars called 'the Burma Road'. With the sketch-plan he'd bought, Scottie followed this 'Burma Road' towards the bow, passing under 'B' and 'A' gun-turrets. Forward of

'A' turret he passed through another watertight bulkhead door into the capstan flat, which contained the mechanism for turning the capstans on the forecastle deck – used for lowering and raising the *Belfast*'s four bow anchors so long ago. Here were lockers where weapons could be stored. Some were un-padlocked and empty. Scottie sat down on a small shoe locker to study the scene. On the starboard side was a bulkhead, and beside it the ship's brig. Inside the brig was a dummy standing beside a piece of bread made of putty, a coy little display dating no doubt from 1971 when the ship was converted into the museum it now was.

Now Scottie was near the bow itself: there must be a paint or stores locker nearby, he thought. He was alone, which was good. Beside him was a loosely fastened small bulkhead door signposted 'No Admittance to the Public'. He turned the clamps slowly and the door swung open. Yes, it was the artic store with the paint locker to starboard and a low-voltage generator room to port. None of these rooms was locked, and there was probably no necessity for the crew to visit them: ideal for weapons concealment. Here also his party could shed some of their outer clothing. All Scottie had to do now was to find an exit to the main deck.

In the crew's quarters for 'A' turret was a ladder up to the main deck. Fine. Next he must check exactly where it came out. He soon located the exit under the starboard gun of 'A' turret. It was a small, watertight hatch-cover which could be opened easily. Better and better. He reckoned that a dozen men could be through it in about fifty seconds. He had found the route.

Retracing his steps, he acted the tourist once more and took flash photos of the various points along that route. He looked the very picture of a man simply fascinated by old warships.

Should the strike-force be split into two groups so that the objective could be attacked simultaneously from both bow and stern? Scottie decided this might be impractical because of the difficulty of concealing weapons anywhere on the *Belfast* aft of the forward funnel. But he would have ample time to consider this back in Holland.

Leaning over the rail he got to chatting with one of the crew. It must've been the cushiest number in the whole Royal Navy. With the end of the tourist season coming up (perhaps less visitors then, he hoped) only eight men were on duty, and for security reasons most of these were concentrated aft. No buffet was available for visitors, but the crew had a bar of their own on the bridge superstructure forward of the catapult deck on the starboard side. Thanking him, Scottie sidled along to have a gander at this bar. It would be simple to close its bulkhead door, he decided, sealing the whole crew inside. Our relaxed friend by the rail would soon be earning his Navy pay by the sweat of his fear.

When he had first come aboard Scottie had noticed a small wedding-party being photographed on the quarter-deck. Further along on his travels he saw what was probably the officers' wardroom laid out for a reception, with glasses of drink ready to be served in the ante-room opposite.

Then it struck him: how to get the weapons on to the *Belfast*. Brilliant. As funny as an Ealing comedy.

Light-heartedly he completed his survey of the old *Belfast*, returning down the catwalk to the quay, as he'd arrived. Now for those warehouses.

Working his way through the demolished section, Scottie was able to get into a warehouse, from the back, which was roughly level with *Belfast*. It was quite empty and derelict and he was pleasantly surprised to find no signs of use by meths drinkers or squatters. Vast open areas on several floors were reached by iron staircases and at the ends were smaller rooms, presumably once used as offices. He took more pictures. Later back at the hotel he would draw up a more elaborate sketch-map of the whole area. This would be put on a slide for the projector back at Steenkerke's, along with the snapshots. Later still he would calculate and refine the precise timings, going over the various routes again. So far he had made only rough timings on his preliminary reconnoitre.

That was the morning's work done. Time for lunch and the Hilton meeting after. Scottie Moore felt more buoyant than he usually allowed himself to be. For five million dollars in gold, this was going to be a piece of cake.

7

'That you, Paul?'

'Andy?'

'Yeah. Hey listen, Something's come up. Our embassy here was contacted about a guy named Lavitzsky. It could be the breakthrough you're looking for.'

'I'm all ears.'

'Not on the phone. Anyway, I've got some stuff coming through from Washington. Can we fix up a meeting?'

'Your place or mine?'

'Let's make it yours. I think maybe I ought to brief your Control direct.'

'Great! Listen, I've got a bed if you like.'

'All the better for the expenses. How about a slap-up meal on the Company?'

'Wouldn't say no. When?'

'Day after tomorrow?'

'Right.'

'I'll ring you when I'm arriving. "Pip, pip!"'

Andy Hartford's call was the first sign of something happening on this increasingly frustrating case. The only progress Paul had made so far was with Jane Illingworth. Even that had proved tentative. The dinner out had been a quiet success, but the lady wasn't in the mood for fast working. Oddly for him, that didn't suit Paul either. Not that he didn't fancy her like crazy, but she was connected with the case and he felt inhibited about taking it any further than dating. Something was inhibiting her, too. He felt it wasn't because she was over-moralistic or found him repellent in some way. His antennae sensed quite the opposite, which made it all the more exciting in a tense sort of a way.

In fact there was a feeling of destiny about this budding relationship and Paul wasn't going to spoil it by being untoward.

He wondered why she was still unhitched at twenty-seven – probably no stranger than the fact that he was the same, and ten years older. Had she looked at the marriage of Clive and her sister and decided that that kind of fate wasn't for her? As for himself, Paul just hadn't had the patience to find the woman to share his life for ever more. He'd never had any difficulty finding a partner for a night, or a weekend, and he had his own version of the 'little black book'. But it was becoming an unsatisfactory sort of a life, and he knew he wouldn't be able to go on trading on his youth for ever. Already he was beginning to be looked upon by the younger, perter secretaries as middle-aged, and the lives of some of his later partners seemed to be scarred with sorrow and littered with marital failure. He was entering the slags' market and it was time to get down to the task of assessing his domestic arrangements seriously! That didn't mean he rejected career-women as potential helpmates. If anything, he wanted to be spliced to a woman he could respect for her own professional attainments. That was one of the things – only one – drawing him nearer and nearer to Jane. It was indeed all very exciting.

More so than the case, which was worrying him now. Days went by and he had bugger-all to report to the vulturish 'C'.

But did the fact that he had nothing to report mean nothing was going on? Paul dreaded the opposite being the case. Something *was* afoot: but up till now they'd been clutching at straws trying to find it.

All the possible leads had petered out. A tail was on Clive Parris but they were just going through the motions with him so far. He went about his departmental, parliamentary and constituency rounds as if God were in His heaven and all was right, etc., etc. Paul wondered if he wouldn't have done better staying in Amsterdam with Andy, who seemed to be coming up with all the possibilities. Hell, the thing was in Britain's lap, whatever was targetted was more than likely to be in England, and here was Paul, playing second fiddle to the C.I.A. It was frustrating, to say the least.

There was nothing for it but to bide his time, get in a supply of Jack Daniels and wait for Andy to come up with the goods.

Slumping into one of Paul's two saggy armchairs, Andy asked him what he knew about Anatoly Lavitzsky.

'I ran a check on him after you called,' said Paul. 'Defector, eighteen months ago. Disappeared out of Sweden, not traced since. Curious sort of a case – I mean, not to have surfaced.'

'Not as odd as all that, considering that he was up on corruption charges in the Soviet Union. The Russians would dearly love to have him back to string him up alongside his brother Vassily, who's now doing time in one of their new, improved health-camps. No official establishment this side would touch Anatoly.'

'He was pretty highly qualified.'

Andy looked glum. 'I know. That's what's bothering me.' Then he brightened. 'But we found out where he's been.' Andy then told Paul about the P.W.F. movement, Anatoly's 'hosts'.

'Until recently,' said Andy. 'Then, what do you think? The C.I.A. came along and obligingly took Anatoly off their hands. Just when he was becoming a pain in the backside to them.'

Paul's eyebrows raised. 'You mean *you've* got him?'

'We should be so lucky. No. Not us. Somebody posing as us went right up to the P.W.F. in broad daylight and threatened them with exposure for holding Lavitzsky. They seem to be a gullible bunch of loonies and they handed him over, no questions asked.'

'To whom? for Christ's sake?'

'That's just it, Paul. I got a call from the American embassy the other day. They'd had a visit from a guy belonging to this P.W.F., a Dutch Professor van Something-or-other. He wanted to check that Lavitzsky had been properly handed over to us, making sure that he and his organisation weren't in trouble any more. Now as you can imagine, when somebody goes around posing as a C.I.A. agent it kind of makes us interested.

'I talked to this Professor van Huffinpuffer – fat old toad, he was – but he gave us a lead, after all. His description of the American phoney agent fits with the general idea of an ex-services type. In other words, Paul my friend, he could be the guy mentioned by our man in Moscow. I'm not jumping to conclusions on this thing, but there it is.'

'And we still haven't located Lavitzsky?'

Andy shook his head. 'Anyway, it's our man's first mistake. He should never have surfaced like that, whoever he is. He should have sent somebody in his place to collar Lavitzsky.'

'Maybe there wasn't anybody else,' said Paul. 'If this is recruitment on a high level. What do they want with a nuclear weapons expert?'

Andy shrugged. 'Search me. Anyway, we're sure now about a Dutch operation. We're combing the place. Funny how it's even harder in a small country than in a big one. What's up in the U.K.? I gather you're working the murdered wife angle. I've been following it, too, but the Dutch police haven't come up with anything so far.'

'I know,' said Paul gloomily. 'Neither have I.'

'Why don't you just confront the husband with it?'

'None of your head-on tactics here, mate,' said Paul. 'Anyway there's an embargo on questioning him at the moment. I'm having him followed but it's not got anywhere so far.' He told Andy about Sarah's desperate note to her sister Jane and about the curious attempted drowning incident at Baythorne Manor. 'I've been working on the sister – she has her suspicions.'

'Sounds good,' said Andy. 'She a nice looker, this sister?'

'She has a hare-lip, knock-knees, thyroid and halitosis, but otherwise she's not bad.'

Andy smiled. 'I get it. You didn't by any chance resort to unorthodox means to get information out of her?'

'If taking someone out to dinner is unorthodox,' said Paul, feeling pleased with himself for once.

'I thought Amsterdam was the place,' grumbled Andy. 'Anyway, when you get around to it, invite me to the wedding. Seriously: do you think there's anything to her story? The note sounds interesting.'

'Trouble is, no detail – just a general air of desperation. It could have meant anything, a breakdown of her marriage, a miscarriage, a lover, anything.'

'I'm not sure about this attempted drowning. How the hell did that happen?'

Paul relayed the gory details as he'd had them from Jane.

Andy shook his head. 'No, still not convincing. He wouldn't do it unless he had some reason to suspect your Jane knew what was going on, and why should he do that? No, she just hates his guts. Maybe she was drunk on the funeral sherry.'

'I don't think it can have been that,' said Paul. Something in his huffy reply made Andy laugh out loud.

'Bastard,' said Paul, reddening. 'Anyway, her suspicions are perfectly legitimate. After her sister died she turned up in Amsterdam and seems to have taken an overly active interest in the murder investigation. She told me over dinner that Clive had been a bit taken aback at the way she questioned him and she thought maybe she'd gone over the top.'

Andy still wasn't convinced. 'He wouldn't have murdered his wife with some big illegal deal coming up that involved him. He just *might* have got her out of the way by hiring somebody else to do it, if she had learned something she wasn't supposed to know. Then it's more difficult to pin on him – but it still puts him in the limelight. He *could've* taken that gamble, I guess.'

'Enough of all this theorising,' said Paul.

'Yes, enough!' Andy dived into his brief-case and pulled out masses of papers – computer print-outs.

'What's all that?' asked Paul, getting up to freshen their drinks.

'Science in action,' said Andy, spreading the papers across the floor in front of him. 'They've been busy back home while we've been nibbling at the edges. Our Director of Operations at Langley's been co-ordinating efforts with the F.B.I. We've got a man from M.I.T. called Aaron Levi – don't know if you've ever heard of him. He's just about the foremost criminal psychiatrist in the U.S.A. Ta very much, mate,' he said, as Paul placed another Jack Daniels by his elbow. The cockney accent hadn't improved. 'We've worked with Levi before. He's the one who came up with the idea of F.B.I. files being re-classified under specific headings: "Known Super Criminals", "Terrorist Activists", "Ex-convicts" with sub-classifications, "Fanatics" and one or two others, I forget.

Provides clearer computer leads for both detection and prevention. We decided to get Levi in again specially to deal with this case. He's extracted, uh, 4,362 names from all the relevant classes or types. With the help of supplementary information from state police forces Langley traced all the ones now living inside the United States. Turns out that, uh, 4,282 of them are resident Stateside at this present moment. Eighteen more are untraced, presumed dead. Then there are another 62 who have left the United States and not returned so far. A check on the emigration records shows they all had valid passports. Most of them are in Europe so far as anyone can tell – at least that's where they were originally headed.'

Paul sighed. 'Well, if it comes to a matter of lists, I've got one of 92 compiled from our own sources. Clive Parris is on it, but that doesn't mean much at this stage. As a high-up in the government and involved in nuclear power he's bound to be there.'

'Your list takes in people who haven't been to prison,' said Andy. 'Mine's ex-cons and Most Wanteds, or even the acquitted.'

'Which means that your ex-serviceman probably isn't down there,' said Paul.

'Maybe he is, maybe he isn't. Depends on if he ever committed an offence. Besides, there are more guys involved in this than just him. If they are Americans we'll find them. He's bound to recruit somebody sooner or later with a record.'

'Not if he's recruiting boffins.'

'Recruiting what?'

'Sorry, eggheads.'

'Oh, yeah. Thought you said "muffins". Well, forget about the ex-service guy a minute. I found something else that might be useful.'

'What's that?'

'I decided to run a check from the Dutch end of things, with the help of the Dutch immigration service. Their computer coughs up 16 American names that check against Levi's – 16 who appear to be still in the Netherlands, though you can never be sure nowadays with all these free borders.'

'It's beginning to sound interesting,' said Paul.

'Most of these seem to be druggies or perverts, paedophiles and characters like that. Including one man who had a small record of soliciting from time to time in New York City. Nothing big – Christ, in *New York*? But I got kind of interested in him.' Andy half-smiled. 'Don't get me wrong on that.'

'What about him?'

'His record in the States is so petty he might not have got on the Levi list at all, except that he was once brought before a Senate subcommittee investigating espionage in the Neptune Telecommunications case a few years back. He was found totally clean. But his homosexuality made him "sensitive" in the communications business and he was thrown out on his ear. After that he picked up the soliciting raps. Seems to have gone downhill.'

'And harbouring a pretty considerable grudge, I would have thought,' said Paul.

'You might think so. Here he is. Warren Booth. Mean anything to you?'

Paul shook his head. 'What's interesting about him?'

'That Neptune background. He's a communications expert in guidance systems. Doesn't that ring bells? Here are two guys, one Russian and one American, both experts in nuclear weapons, one way or another, both turfed out, both down and out or so we think, and both now fixed as being in Holland. One of them, Lavitzsky, has definitely been picked up to do a job. I want to know if Booth has been scooped up, too.'

'I gather you haven't located Booth yet?'

'Hell, he could have disappeared down a manhole in that Amsterdam underworld. We're working on it as fast as we can. I hope maybe he'll have surfaced by the time I get back tomorrow.'

'Can I come back with you? I'd like to be in on it. I've got one or two things to clear up first but I could get a night plane to Schipol tomorrow evening.'

'Sure, join the fun,' said Andy, 'if you're not getting enough here.'

Andy was due to see Paul's Control in the morning and report to him on the progress to date, accompanied by Paul. In view of Dutch developments, with the action switching to Amsterdam, Paul was confident of his superior's acquiescence in the matter of his dispatch to the Netherlands.

It was suggested in the West that Lavitzsky had worked on the Soviet SS25 missile, but nobody knew for sure. These missiles, installed and ready to fire, were fitted with independent warheads which could be separately targetted, each warhead with a destructive power thirty times that of the atomic bomb dropped on Hiroshima. *Glasnost* or no *glasnost*, they were still around – as British military chiefs insisted on reminding a government sorely pressed for new sources of revenue, pressured by an opposition making hay out of the possibility of a new 'social dividend' arising from their hoped-for missile bonfire.

It was apposite, therefore, for government ministers and officials to be invited along to Upper Heyford Base in East Anglia to view the West's answer to the SS25, code-named 'Glickum'. With them were Ministry of Defence chiefs, Service chiefs and NATO representatives.

Humphrey Cathcart found himself among the respectful members of the Press on this sumptuous outing. His whole instinct was against being fed handout fodder, pre-digested news, publicity sheets. He hated being manipulated. But digging around here was strictly *verboten*. You wrote as you were told, straight from the photocopied pages with the ministerial crest on the top. In view of his already-mounting legal problems, Humphrey's editor had to pull a few strings to get him invited.

Proceedings began with American karate-chop salutes answered by palm-exposed British salutes, followed by drinks and general *bonhomie* before getting down to the more serious business of killing.

The visitors were shown diagrams of the missiles' power and effectiveness and then taken on site to see the weapons in various stages of assembly. Humphrey edged nearer to Clive Parris, Minister for Nuclear Energy, who seemed to be asking so many questions: how was the weapon fired? What triggered the mechanism? Had the fall-out been tested for area spread? Were Russian and American warheads interchangeable? Of course he could ask what questions he liked. But they were detailed and many. His portfolio was peaceful uses, not military. Humphrey took in the publicity-fodder and concentrated his full attention on his quarry, Clive Parris. Unbeknown to him, another – unidentified – member of the party was keeping watch over the minister too.

Steenkerke's contacts in the human 'export' trade were good and finding the sort of man they needed turned out not to be as difficult as Scottie had thought it might be. They tracked Jordaan down to a fishermen's bar in Scheveningen harbour. It was small, overcrowded and reeking of stale cigar-smoke, but it was a reasonable-enough cover under which to do business.

Jordaan was another big Dutchman, with a face of rough stubble. He reminded Scottie of the villain in those Popeye cartoons who was always making off with Olive Oyl.

Steenkerke approached Jordaan first. He had a few words in Dutch with him before gesturing to Scottie to come over. A round of beers was set up.

'They call you the Body-snatcher,' said Scottie to Jordaan, 'or so I'm told.'

'Not so much now,' said Jordaan glumly into his drink.

'You work for yourself?'

'I'm my own boss. I do what I want to do,' replied Jordaan, tapping his own chest.

'Just the man we want,' said Scottie.

'Human cargo?' asked Jordaan. Scottie nodded. 'Pakis, Indians or what?'

'No,' said Scottie, 'white people, same as you and me. One-way trip, though.'

'How many?'

'Twelve.'

Jordaan shrugged. 'They'll be in luxury, then. I've packed them in twenty-five, thirty at a time, sometimes. Never had no complaints.' He chuckled at his own humour, then became glum again. 'Not so much business now like there was.' He drank half his glass of beer and set the mug down. 'Three thousand five hundred guilders a head,' he announced.

'That's just over a thousand pounds sterling,' said Scottie, starting to grin, with his cigar between his teeth. 'Twelve thousand pounds total. Must be the most expensive trip to England since the Armada.'

Steenkerke looked alarmed. Jordaan shrugged again.

Scottie continued. 'In sterling I don't go above £750 a head. That's more like two thousand three hundred guilders.'

Jordaan sneered. 'Why don't you take the ferry from Hook to Harwich? You're not thinking of the risk.'

Scottie stretched across the table and spoke very closely into Jordaan's ear. 'I'll give you risk, sonny-boy. I happen to know you need the work, Jordaan. The supply of little brown men has dried up. You said so yourself just now. And you're too fucking lazy to get off your ass and find yourself a proper job. Now are you going to stop fucking around and take us for two thousand three hundred a head?'

Jordaan may have been a touch bulkier than Scottie, but between his sagging burnt-out-case look and Scottie's deep and vicious drive there was no comparison.

'Two thousand five hundred,' murmured the big man with a sigh.

'Okay,' agreed Scottie, sitting back. 'I'll buy that. Just. Two thousand five hundred guilders a man.'

'When do we go?' asked Jordaan.

Scottie looked at Steenkerke. Steenkerke nodded.

'Look, you can trust me,' protested Jordaan. 'Anyway, I have to make plans, get the right crew.'

'I know I can trust you,' said Scottie. 'I can trust you not to sleep nights if you cheat on me and spread this around, can't I?'

Jordaan looked at him without saying anything.

'Okay then,' said Scottie. 'Night of the 4th and 5th November. No moon that night, we've checked. We reckon a good-sized fishing boat like yours could get us up into the Blackwater Estuary, then into Salcott Channel as far as the tide allows.'

'I've been there,' said Jordaan. Scottie already knew that.

Scottie clapped him on the shoulder, grinning again. 'Good boy. And you'll get us there nice and safe and sound, won't you?'

'I was never caught by the British in sixteen years,' boasted Jordaan. 'They won't get me now, either. You have my word on that.'

Scottie still grinned. 'For what that's worth,' he said.

'Why did you try to beat him down like that?' queried Steenkerke as they left the bar. 'Your people can pay what he asked and more.'

'I don't like it when a slob like that makes the rules, that's all.' Scottie smiled. 'My people *are* going to pay what he asked. Just thought I'd take a little extra commission.'

8

As she lay beside him at the decadent hour of three o'clock in the afternoon, Jane Illingworth couldn't quite believe what had hit her.

Paul rang her unexpectedly at the office asking if she was free for lunch; their dinner engagement for the evening was off. Jane had been going to stay in to tackle a backlog of work. But seeing Paul even for a brief flit in a Garfunkel's was more fun than work.

As it turned out, neither was particularly hungry and the food was toyed with on the plates. There was a different kind of hunger about. He had kissed her goodnight at the door of her flat on their first date, but now, when he took her arm and guided her out of the restaurant it was as if he was touching her for the first time. Something told them both that he wasn't just guiding her into the street.

'Do you have to go back straight away?' he asked on the pavement outside.

'I should, really,' she said, but there was hesitation in her voice, and that was enough.

'It's just that I have to go abroad for a bit and I don't have any idea when I'm getting back. Well, in terms of days, anyway.' He looked down at his feet like a schoolboy asking his first girl to a dance. But she knew he wasn't talking about a dance.

'We could go back to my flat for some coffee,' she said. 'But I can't be too long.' That addition was totally ridiculous. If they were going back to her flat there would be no way she'd be at work again that day, backlog or no backlog. 'Haven't you got anything to do?' she asked him.

He grinned. 'I've got plenty to do. Let's go.'

With the door of the flat shut behind them, they almost fell on one another. Everything they'd been holding back for what had seemed like an eternity rose up and overcame all conscious thinking. The real feast of the day began on Jane's sitting-room carpet.

He made love devouring, but all the same he knew what to do to her. He squeezed her firmed-up nipples gently but strongly and unbearably; drew warm liquid from her cunt as he gave it that same gentle but determined manipulation. He knew about clits, he knew all her places, he seemed to be clairvoyant, knowing in advance what would make her writhe on the floor helpless with the pain of wanting.

To Paul, her body was slim and firm, her stomach flat, her skin white beyond reality; he could hold the whole of her deliciously cold bare bottom in one hand as he remorselessly fingered her between her thighs. And she was beginning to do to him what he liked, too. He shivered as her fingers slid lightly up and down his back, and even in her apparent abandon she managed to communicate by tongue deep into his ear, saying – what? It didn't matter. It turned out they both liked the other talking dirty.

His body was at the prime for a man, hard and smooth, no gut, oddly hairless, or was it simply a profusion of almost-invisible golden hairs on his chest and thighs, a continuation all over of his natural head-colouring? But he was doing too much for her to think any more of that or do anything other than give way to her own pleasure. Of course it was over too soon, there on the floor. Her long-slumbering body (slumbering even under Humphrey? Compared to this, yes!) had only begun to rouse itself, when Paul spent himself, crying out. She hadn't even started, and she wasn't going to stop now.

A little while later, in a proper bed, the pace slowed down to something more contemplative and playful. Jane came and came again. She didn't know what he would do next. He could be gentle almost to the point of nothingness in his stroking, and then, just as she thought he might lull her off into sleep, he would grab her hard, like one demented whose lust had got out of his control. There were times when he even seemed to fight for possession of her. Humphrey asked, but Paul took with totally un-suppressed greed. And at those times it seemed as if he were inside her up to her head.

After his third time, Paul lay back on his pillow with a sigh of finality. It had taken him three goes to get it out of his system on this woman, and more than he'd had in some time, since that little business with a filing-clerk which he didn't boast about, even to himself. He'd got on to a treadmill of using casual women for their bodies, perhaps much as they were using his cock, and oddly it didn't even satisfy any more on the sexual level. What he'd had today was worth a thousand other encounters. He looked at Jane's face on the pillow beside him, her eyes shut, her breathing calm. The lips smiled as he smoothed back her hair. She turned and their bodies embraced before parting again.

Was he using Jane the way he'd used all the others? He didn't think so. Funnily enough (though no one would ever believe him!) he hadn't had any deliberate intention of seducing her. It was simply a cataclysm which broke over both of them at the same time. That was all there was to it.

'I don't normally approach cases like this,' he said.

'Don't you?' she smiled. 'You certainly get results this way.'

'Perhaps I should do it more often.'

She wrapped herself around him again. 'Only with me,' she said.

Later, when they were getting dressed, he let out the fact that he was going to Amsterdam. She asked, and he told her. Never before would he have betrayed his movements in advance to someone outside the security set-up. 'There, you see what you've made me do?' he asked plaintively. 'What if you were a spy?'

'I'd sell your secret trip to Amsterdam to the Russians,' she said, folding her arms around his neck. 'Only they're our friends now, aren't they? It's all so confusing.' As she was making coffee a sort of atmosphere crept up between them. 'Why are you going to Amsterdam?' she asked, as casually as she could. To Paul it sounded as deliberate as hell.

'In this instance, I think you probably know why.'

'Sarah's death?'

'Something to do with that, yes.'

'Have you got a new lead?'

'I can't talk about the case, darling, you know that. All I'll say is that it may concern Clive, and it may not. There are other people involved.'

'Curiouser and curiouser,' she said, setting the cups on the table.

'I don't think I'm giving much away if I say we don't even know what it is.'

'You don't know what you're investigating?'

'No. Because whatever it is hasn't happened yet.'

'Isn't that tackling it the wrong way round? Reminds me of the White Queen, who cried out in pain before she pricked herself.'

'Yes, it's as crazy as *Alice In Wonderland*–'

'*Through the Looking-Glass*,' corrected Jane. '*Alice Through the Looking-Glass*. I'm a Lewis Carroll freak.'

'Okay, it's as crazy as that. All I can say is that we're taking what you might call preventative action against something that hasn't happened, and we hope to God it never will. No!' He put his finger against his lips as she was about to ask something else. 'When the time comes I'll tell you everything, so long as you don't repeat it.'

'What kind of ninny do you think I am?'

'Sorry, just a habit of thinking. Tight, security-conscious all the time. You understand, don't you? I want to share things with you – honestly, I'd trust you now. But I'm bound by oath–'

'I know that, darling,' she said, kissing him. 'You don't have to spell it out.'

He was beautiful and hard and a sex-maniac and old-fashioned all at the same time, and she loved him. Love? Oh God, how can you know at this stage? You don't really know if quick bonks are his true speciality. Don't love him. Not yet. Be surer.

These appeals to her reason were quite useless.

There had been some snickers of derision when Scottie first began to outline the mission. They were good-natured snickers, because the men had recently found out about the million dollars each at the end of the haul. Each one was going to be set up for life. Scottie had payed out one bit of information after another over a carefully-worked-out period of time. First he told Maxton the cut, and then he told the others. Figac wanted to know if Maxton was getting the same, and if not why shouldn't his own cut be raised, but Scottie dealt firmly with him. If he didn't like the conditions, he knew where he could go. Figac wondered, if he took off, how far he would get alive. It shut him up.

'So we're taking a fifty-year-old tub in the middle of the

Thames River?' remarked Warren Booth; 'nice one, Scottie.' Away from the booze, the natural brightness and sharpness of Warren Booth was taking on a keener edge. He seemed more boyish, too, less heavy, more of the 'Kid'. He was also edgy through lacking the consolations of Piet. Maxton eyed him disapprovingly from time to time. It was the first occasion that he'd ever had such an open poof in an outfit of his. Times were hard.

'It involves a little more than H.M.S. *Belfast*, as I'm now about to show you,' said Scottie. 'Schiele?' He indicated the slide-projector which the German was operating. The room was darkened as the brilliant light reflected from the big, square screen.

With diagrams and snapshots blown up, he showed them. It began to dawn on the men the nature of the job they'd been taken on to carry out. They were hard cases, these men – except perhaps for Booth and Lavitzsky, who were there for their brains. But there were not a few butterflies in stomachs that afternoon.

Scottie sensed their unease. But instead of giving them a cheap pep-talk he went over the elaborate get-away plan slowly and carefully. In the end it seemed virtually fool-proof. They were more reassured. In fact the men were only going through what Scottie himself had gone through when he was first brought into the scheme: a feeling of some awe at the magnitude and craziness of the whole thing.

Only Maxton seemed not to have felt a single compunction. 'It'll show the bastards,' he chuckled. 'By fuck it'll show 'em!'

The Russian was looking fairly miserable – Scottie would have to take him aside later, beef him up with thoughts about the rewards, as well as the challenge of the technical problems. Reassure him that the fighting would be done by others, that his training was solely for self-protection. Meanwhile, Booth cornered Scottie after the break-up of the briefing.

'Scottie, what is this crap? Ransoming London? Their assault forces'll take us out in five minutes!'

'They'd be committing suicide if they tried,' said Scottie, tirelessly reiterating what he'd said earlier. 'Nobody wants a nuclear catastrophe in the middle of London, do they Kid?'

'Do we? We'll be right in the middle of the motherfucker!'

'It won't come to that. Trust me. You trust me, don't you? It's all been worked out. Every detail, down to the last toothpick. You only have to concentrate on what you're going to be there for. We'll handle the rest of it. You'll be okay.'

'Can I see Piet soon? Before we go, anyway? It's just he's done a lot for me and I haven't always been, well, you know, considerate. You know what he means to me.'

'Sorry Kid,' said Scottie, putting a hand on his shoulder. 'No can do. Next time you'll see Piet is after the mission, not before.'

'Christ, it won't do any harm, man!'

Scottie's clasp on his shoulder tightened. 'You don't know if they've found your flat in Amsterdam by now, do you?'

Warren Booth paled. 'Would they have done that?'

'For all you know they might be questioning Piet at this very moment.'

Warren was now looking distressed. 'Maybe I'll never see him again!'

'You'll see him again. You can thank God Piet didn't know where you were going and hasn't had anything with a postmark from you. I don't mean he's not loyal. But they have ways of breaking loyalties.'

'Bastards!'

'Yes, well it may not have come to that yet. There's no reason to suppose anybody knows what's going on yet, but we mustn't take chances.' He quietened Warren down as best he could and sent him off for his evening meal. The Kid would snap out of it when he had to do the job. He may have been a sissy (except when drunk) but he was a survivor.

It was after dark on the 4th of November, in the cul-de-sac near the Rozengracht, when the twelve clambered aboard a small furniture van, together with Steenkerke, who was seeing them off and making sure the trail in the Netherlands was obscured. The mercenaries had back-packs stuffed with equipment and clothes. In twos and threes they were dropped off in side streets near the quay. In twos and threes, at intervals, they dropped down on to the deck of the fishing-boat *Cristina* and disappeared below.

When all were finally on board, the boat slipped its moorings and glided silently out into the harbour – silent but for a gentle put-put not noticeable beyond a few yards.

'Looks calm enough,' said Scottie to Jordaan.

'There's another depression moving in fast,' growled the big man. 'If the forecast is accurate we'll hit it about midnight. Could be strong. You maybe better go down and prepare them for it. You shouldn't be up here anyway if anybody's looking.'

It wasn't exactly the Ritz-on-water below deck in the hold. Cramped and low-ceilinged – it must've been swell for his thirty Asians, thought Scottie. Bastard. Still, we're all bastards in this game. In any game. The men sat round the sides looking disconsolate and bored – Maxton, Figac, Lavitzsky, Booth, Hakayama, Schiele and the others. Nobody had brought any reading-matter – excess baggage – and there was nothing in the bareness of the hold to get excited over except for a drum with a tap which contained drinking-water, and a couple of secured buckets with fitted lids. Apart from Scottie, no one else in the group was a sailor. Great, thought Scottie. They could hear the water thumping against the hull of the *Cristina*: unrhythmic, unpredictable, and they weren't used to it. They tried to relax but they stiffened up instead. Scottie had thought better than to warn them of the approaching storm. Half the business was psychological, after all. And as the thumps began to grow louder and came more frequently, the feeling that they were in a bouncing coffin became irresistible.

Jordaan's forecasters hadn't been far off the mark: the gale hit them bow on just after one o'clock in the morning. At least they were heading into the teeth of the storm and not wallowing at an angle. But it was bad enough. The fishing-boat rose steadily, bow clear of the water, then swooped into the trough with a sickening downward rush. Another steady climb and down again. Another, and another, and another.

Lavitzsky gave way first, before he could reach one of the buckets. For the remainder of the voyage his leavings rolled up and down the floor, inviting companionship. That cunt Jordaan hadn't even provided anything to wipe it up with. Men tried not to look at it, but became sick whether they looked at it or away from it. Soon it didn't matter. Maxton was sick all over his boots. Warren was a deathly green – just his hue was enough to turn anyone's stomach.

Only two didn't give in. Not that Scottie's previous seamanship would have immunised him; no, he was determined by iron will to look as superhuman as he could before the men. He kept as still as a mummy and rolled with the boat.

The only other one, totally impervious, was Figac. He sat, legs crossed and smoking, disdainfully looking away as yet another poor wretch retched. They told him several times not to smoke because his bloody Gauloise made it worse, but he retorted in his unmellifluous French accent that he was keeping the stink at bay and if others chose to be ill it was no concern of his. Maxton looked on him with unfathomable loathing now.

And Scottie had paid out two thousand five hundred guilders a head for this junket. What price secrecy?

At least there's nothing more calculated to distract you from the fear of death than feeling like death.

Three hours went by like this and then something happened that did worry Scottie. He awoke from a half-doze and thought he sensed something different. It was the engine. He could no longer hear it or feel its vibration. One or two others half-noticed too, but they were so drowsy with the exhaustion of sickness that they lay back without concern.

The sailor in Scottie knew something had gone wrong. All that could be heard were wind and waves. Everyone else was being soothed by them now. But the *Cristina* was rocking in different directions. If she drifted broadside-on to the waves there was a risk of her being swamped, of floundering. Every so often another confused wave-pattern tossed her about and threw her on to her beam-ends.

Scottie eased himself up through the hatch, breathing in the salt-laden fresh air. He saw Jordaan and the mate lurching about on the swaying deck, looking over the side now and then, trying to sort out what the problem was. The engine was quite dead; the boat was bobbing about like a cockleshell. 'What's wrong?' Scottie shouted at Jordaan. 'Go on like this much longer and she'll sink!'

Jordaan shouted back: 'It's a rope – fouled the propeller. Must've got washed overboard!'

'Sort of careless, weren't you?' shouted Scottie. Jordaan made a despairing gesture. 'What are you going to do about it?' By now one or two others, unable to bear the hold any longer and oblivious to warnings about being sighted by patrol-boats or whatever, had emerged through the hatch. 'Someone's going to have to go over the side and cut the rope free, aren't they, unless you have a better suggestion?' Scottie said. Jordaan just shook his head and the mate stared like one hypnotised. Plainly the gallant crew weren't prepared to save the situation. 'You maybe got such a thing as a life-jacket on this bucket?' said Scottie contemptuously. Without a word, the skipper went into the wheel-house to fetch it. The boat's sole life-jacket, as it happened. Scottie felt like knocking Jordaan's teeth down his throat – a man not worthy of skippering a plastic duck in a bath. A man prepared to sail the North Sea for profit without any provision for life-saving for those under his care. And for that they would all go under, any second. Even a killer can have contempt for the dirt of the earth.

Scottie took off his jacket and shoes and donned the life-jacket. He tied a knife by a length of cord to his wrist. All this was done with difficulty on the tossing deck – quite how he was going to manage in the tossing sea was another matter. There was nothing else to be done.

He jumped as free of the boat as he could, but the mountainous waves flung him against the hull with vicious force several times, knocking the breath right out of him. One moment he would be completely submerged in the freezing water; the next, gasping air before going under again. God knew how much sea water he might be taking in without knowing it.

He was unaware of the line-up of faces over the rail, staring at him, their only hope of survival – as they now knew.

The lifeline was payed out to help him reach the stern. The stern was pounding the water up and down like a steam-hammer; he would be lucky not to have his brains dashed out. Taking quick advantage of a moment when the stern was wholly out of the water again, Scottie grabbed for the rudder. His hands were bleeding but he was scarcely conscious of that.

There it was. He could barely make out the tangled mass like entrails covering the stilled propeller. Then he and the propeller were under water again. No way of seeing anything – he had to feel his way, knowing that his life had already outstayed its welcome in this sea and that if he didn't do what he had to do in these few seconds he would be dead of the cold – if the water he was trying not to gulp didn't get to him first. Holding on to the propeller with one hand he hacked frantically, his lungs almost bursting. He got some air again as the stern rose high out of the water, before being re-submerged.

Was the bloody thing giving? He couldn't tell. He wasn't thinking any more – just hacking, hacking away like a wild man. Then – at long last – he felt the rope fall around his other hand, felt the propeller again, and knew it to be bare and free. With the last vital energy in his body he tugged feebly at the lifeline and after what seemed like a thousand years of pain he was hauled up over the stern like one of the dead – but still conscious enough to be dazzled by the torchlight shining into his eyes.

Later they said he'd spent a full six minutes in the water. 'I never know a man survive that long before,' said Jordaan in genuine wonderment while Booth and others rubbed him down, applying iodine and bandages from the first-aid kit to his cuts and easing him into the big, smelly and warm, dry clothes that were meant to fit Jordaan.

Jordaan got the *Cristina* moving again, and not before time since the boat had nearly surrendered to the wind and waves. There was a reassuring rumble and rattle and the men around Scottie gave a cheer – for the boat but mainly for him. Scottie had saved all of their lives. It wasn't something they would forget. As reason returned to him, and the last man had squeezed his arm or shoulder in gratitude, Scottie reflected that maybe this new surge of loyalty came as a blessing in disguise. In view of what was to come.

At five o'clock the *Cristina* sailed into the calm of the Blackwater Estuary. On the distant shore was the Bradwell Atomic Power Station. Although Jordaan had made the same run on a number of occasions, time was lost locating the entrance to the Salcott Channel.

Where the men were finally put ashore the frigid mud was knee-deep. They floundered along past tussocks of reeds and coarse grass for what seemed an eternity before they reached the green pasture-land which comes down almost to the high tide mark. Jordaan saw them off with relief: they were a bunch of Jonahs as far as he was concerned, and he was glad enough to be shot of them and able to make his get-away from the Essex coast before first light. The storm had passed, so he looked forward to a calmer crossing home. His sense of ease was only slightly rippled by the thought of the tell-tale labels on the clothes he'd loaned Scottie.

The men of the strike-force flopped down on the grass, exhausted after their long, sickening night, and rubbed their guts. They needed coffee, hot food. Lavitzsky in particular was in a bad way with the shakes. Someone had broken out a blanket and placed it round his quivering shoulders. One of the other mercenaries was cursing because in the rush to get ashore, and bullied by the evil-tempered Jordaan, he had left his duffle-bag on the *Cristina*. He mournfully and silently bade it farewell as he saw the boat become a dull blot past Mersea Island, then head out into the open sea.

Scottie – bruised, battered and shaken himself – was driven by a sense of purpose and an anxiety over any hitches in the arrangements. Fatigue was making him obsessive, coldness and delayed shock a monomaniac. Maxton looked at the luminous dial of his watch: 5.30 a.m. All things considered it was a bloody miracle they hadn't been delayed. It was a bloody miracle they were here at all.

'All right you men,' said Maxton, knowing his leader was beyond rousing them himself, 'get your arses off the pitch.' Groaning, they all more or less stood up. Maxton walked over to the tremulous Lavitzsky. 'You okay?' Lavitzsky managed to nod. 'You'll get coffee later,' said Maxton. 'Right then!' He turned to Scottie. 'All yours, Mr Moore.'

This aplomb got Scottie himself going again. 'This way,' he said, when he'd got his bearings.

Now it was time to see whether their driver had lost his nerve and gone off in the van leaving them stranded. There was enough money among them to get to somewhere, but if they didn't split up (and most of them knew nothing of England at all) twelve guys going around in a bunch like this in the middle of nowhere at 6.00 in the morning was going to be hard to explain to someone whose job it might be to listen. Anyhow, even Scottie was ready to drop into the nearest barn, haystack or ditch. No one was going to make it further than the van. It was supposed to be parked a further half-mile up the lane, to their left.

Lavitzsky stumbled and fell a couple of times and

Scottie detailed Booth to help him along. Booth seemed to have felt a kind of closeness to his fellow intellectual on this expedition. Together the two held up Lavitzsky so that he would make it through that last painful half-mile, step-by-step, coughing and spluttering.

Keeping to the fields they skirted the few houses that make up Salcott and Virley.

Stealing a vehicle would be out of the question. It would bring the law swooping down over the whole area. Scottie's anxiety was playing tricks on him. There's where the van should be – but it wasn't! The trudge round corners and obstacles to get a full view of the lane was interminable. Without that van the whole thing was off. Only his worry kept him on his feet now, staggering onward, onward to that van. He was oblivious to what the rest were doing behind him.

But no fucking missing van is going to stop us. We're gonna do it, do it, no matter what.

Then he saw it, a battered old Commer. Grey, with something painted on its side-panel, looking more abandoned than parked. No sign of life about it, but Scottie knew it was their van. The other men spotted it too and increased their limping pace to get to it. A life-raft in that desolate Essex landscape. This was the first contact with the other side of the organisation. It was there. The whole thing was going to happen.

Scottie happened to know it was their van because of what it said on the side: 'Blackwater Seafood Co.' They were going to pretend to be a consignment of oysters on its way to London.

Heavily, wearily, they climbed up into the back. With only its side-lights on it was edged by the driver – a cheerful cockney who seemed to thrive, whistling, on the early hour of the morning – slowly into the lane. Then, with full headlights on – for it would be dark for some time yet – it gained speed as it took the road leading to Maldon.

And from Maldon, to London.

9

The first lieutenant of H.M.S. *Fyfe* wrote in the log: '12.35 hours. Wind force 4 to 6, 220°. One hour over high water. Depth 20 fathoms. Watch to resume at 14.00 hours.'

He signed the log with a last look round the bridge, and after reading the clipboard of the latest Admiralty signals, reported to the captain that the ship was now secure. H.M.S. *Fyfe* was the first of the small fleet of NATO vessels to drop anchor. Each ship had its own pre-arranged position, taking into account depth and swinging distance. As the fleet came into position, its bows turning into the wind, the ships one by one went through the same manoeuvre as *Fyfe* to anchor.

Bringing up the rear of the fleet, some distance behind, was the American battle-cruiser U.S.S. *Aztec.*

As the vessels of the fleet broke from line astern and took up their anchor stations so did *Aztec*, standing off slightly to the east in deeper water.

U.S.S. *Aztec.* One of the 'Virginia' class of U.S. Navy battle-cruisers. Powered by two General Electric pressurised-water-cooled nuclear reactors D2G, she could voyage for up to ten years without re-fuelling, with a top speed of more than 30 knots. Fully-loaded, 11,300 tons, with a complement of 554, including 40 officers.

Although not officially part of the recent NATO exercise, code-named 'Blanket', *Aztec* was there to observe – and to test her new satellite-based communications network.

Rear Admiral Sebastian Wilkes-Overbury, C.B.E., was flying his flag on H.M.S. *Fyfe*, and it was on board the light cruiser that the debriefing was to take place. Although the gale which had been blowing in the North Sea had moderated, at its worst it had reached Force 8. It remained a tricky operation to bring aboard by helicopter the various captains of the other vessels.

But the debriefing itself went off smoothly, and after it was over Rear Admiral Wilkes-Overbury rose to his feet.

'Thank you, gentlemen. This seems to bring to a close another splendid exercise. We've had a worthwhile exchange of views and operating procedures. As soon as I return to Brussels the formal debriefing here will be passed on to your own defence ministries through the normal channels. I wish all exercises of this kind could run as smoothly as this one has done. H.M.S. *Fyfe* will shortly be returning to port for a major re-fit, and it may be some time before you see her again. I hope, however, that I shall be flying my flag on one of the other Country Class cruisers when next we meet. It has been my pleasure to work with all of you and Captain Littlejohn and his officers hope you will have lunch with them before returning to your own ships.'

Then the rear admiral turned to Captain Weston of the *Aztec*, at forty-three considered young to be commanding such a ship and such a strategic weapons system. 'I am particularly delighted, on behalf of my Lords of the Admiralty, to welcome you, Captain Weston, to these waters for the first time. As you may or may not know, gentlemen, Captain Weston is taking U.S.S. *Aztec* up the Thames to berth alongside H.M.S. *Belfast*. A vivid contrast between old and new, side-by-side in an historic setting. Captain Weston and his men have been invited to form a detachment on Remembrance Day to provide a guard of honour at the Cenotaph. It is the first time such a party of nationals from another country has been requested by Her Majesty to form a detachment.'

The journey to London in the van advertising the non-existent Blackwater Seafood Company may not have been comfortable but it was a distinct improvement on the *Cristina*. Even though they felt every bump of the tarmac, had little air to breathe and almost no light to see by.

After about an hour of this, they could feel the speed of the van reducing gradually, with a lot of stops and starts for traffic-lights. Eventually it stopped altogether and the engine was switched off. The whistling driver banged on the side-panel a couple of times. Welcome to London. The back door opened and the unshaven, blinking men clambered out into a wind-swept morning. It was not quite eight o'clock.

The van stood by a door which had been boarded over. They were in a deserted street flanked by mostly empty and derelict warehouses. All the other doors up the street were boarded over, but at this particular entrance the boards had been taken down. Within seconds they were hustled indoors. The boarding was replaced and padlocked on the outside. The strike-force would be leaving by another door when the time came. They heard the van start up and then cough its way into the distance.

Their hushed voices echoed through the grimy vastness of a ruined but still intact building, with three floors. Scottie led them to a room off the large storage area on the top floor, a former office, which had been prepared with three days of stores for their occupancy. Apparently spices had formerly been stored in this place, and one or two fancied they could detect the odour of cloves somewhere amid the musty smells of damp plaster and decaying wood.

They prised open crates marked 'Fragile, China' to

find the arms, a camp stove, a cylinder of gas, boxes of stores, clean but not new jackets, sweaters, shirts and jeans. There was even a battery-operated razor and a small transistor radio with an ear-plug. Scottie grabbed it off Waleski, who'd turned it on out of curiosity.

'Not in here!' He inserted the ear-plug jack. 'That's the only way we listen in this place, got it?' On second thoughts he decided to keep the radio by him and put it with his own things. The game wasn't going to be given away through the whining tones of rock music or country and western drifting out of a supposedly deserted warehouse.

Most of them wanted to change straight away, and when they'd washed and shaved they didn't look and smell quite so simian-like – though a couple of them would always be simians, no matter what you did with them. When they went aboard H.M.S. *Belfast* they would look reasonably presentable – never mind what they were going to do there.

As well as a business man's suit, shirt, socks and shoes for Scottie there was an anorak and a brief-case containing a clipboard. When he made his exit from the warehouse it would be as someone from a surveyor's office, concerned with the future development of the site once the warehouse had been demolished. And in his nice, sober suit he wouldn't attract attention when, again under the name of John Jarvis Ferguson, he asked for the room previously booked for him which overlooked the Pool.

The Pool.

U.S.S. *Aztec* would be sailing into it in a few hours time.

Paul was no stranger to this sort of thing but even so he was taken a little off-balance by Dutch police methods.

Piet was thrown against the wall of the shabby room

with a discernible thud and roughly frisked. Then his legs gave way from under him and he started to slide down to the floor before being grabbed by two burly blond constables, with automatics drawn from holsters and pointing at him, and stood on his feet. The break-in had been violent: the door was off its hinges and policemen were lumbering around like hungry elephants. Andy looked at Paul with pained despair.

'So much for any little bits of evidence,' he muttered. 'They could've seen at a glance our man wasn't here.'

'Pity we couldn't have handled this ourselves,' said Paul.

'Yeah, well Booth might've been here and put up a fight.'

'Except that he wasn't.'

'No. So – we better get to work on what we've got,' said Andy, eyeing Piet.

Having established that Piet could speak more than adequate English, like so many of his countrymen, the police commissaris in charge of the swoop turned him over to the two foreign agents.

Andy offered Piet to Paul with an oddly courtly gesture. Paul stepped forward. Piet was quaking: he thought perhaps that Paul was about to hit him. Bespectacled and frail, he was cowering. 'Search all you want,' his voice cracked with slight hysteria, 'there's no drugs here!' He turned to the commissaris and spoke rapidly in Dutch, some further protest.

'Speak English!' shouted the commissaris into his ear. The commissaris then looked expectantly at Paul, who wondered if it had been bad form to leave his truncheon at home.

'Where is he?' asked Paul.

'Who are you?' returned Piet.

Paul ignored this unexpected attempt to turn the

conversation round. 'Where is Warren Booth?' he asked again, more precisely.

Piet didn't answer.

'Where is your lover?' asked Andy more provocatively. Paul didn't think that was entirely called-for at this stage.

'I – I don't k-know who you mean,' stuttered Piet. He was a lousy liar.

'We will take you down to the station and there you will remember,' shouted the commissaris, who didn't seem to possess much in the way of modulation.

Paul's instinct was to go for a softer approach. If Piet had a feminine streak, it was as well to remember that toughness, resilience and loyalty were as much feminine as masculine qualities. It might be better to woo. 'It won't be necessary to leave here,' he said, adopting a conciliatory tone, 'if you tell us what we want to know. What we *do* know is that Warren Booth lives here with you. The neighbours have been questioned.'

'Is it about drugs?' asked Piet.

The directness surprised Paul. The boy didn't have the approach of the criminal. In some ways that might make him a harder nut to crack. 'Perhaps you'd tell us about that,' he said.

'We're not—' Andy started to say, but Paul held up his hand.

'I don't take drugs,' Piet said. 'There aren't any drugs here. You can look all you want.'

'You can take any god-damned drugs you like,' muttered Andy impatiently.

'If there aren't any here,' said Paul, 'where are they?'

Piet looked into his eyes. 'You want Warren for drugs? I told him so many times it was wrong – so many times. It ruins your life: have you seen what it is in Amsterdam? He promised me he'd give it up. He promised. I believed him. Now I am not so sure.'

'When did you last see him?' asked Paul.

'About a month ago,' said Piet.

'Do you mean exactly a month ago, or over a month ago, or less than a month ago?' The boy looked puzzled. 'Be a little more specific,' added Paul, hoping he was getting through.

Piet shrugged. 'I don't remember the exact date. Maybe five weeks.'

'He was living here, with you, until five weeks ago?'

'That is correct.' See? What need of truncheons and blows? Piet was going to be the pussy-cat he looked.

'What do you do, Piet?' asked Paul. 'What is your occupation?'

Now it was Piet's turn to look surprised. 'I'm a student. Engineering. Why? Why do you want to know?' Paranoia was creeping back into his voice.

'No reason,' said Paul. 'Don't worry. Just helps fill me in. Why did Warren leave here five weeks ago?'

Piet looked down at the floor and said nothing. 'Excuse me,' said Paul, who took Andy's arm and drew him aside to another corner of the room. 'This won't do. He's clamming up.' Paul indicated the uniformed bruisers standing about. 'All this is entirely unnecessary.'

'It's a fuck-up,' said Andy.

'If he doesn't co-operate, they'll take him down to the station and trump up some sort of charges against him which will bring in lawyers and God knows what. Totally defeat the object. You can see he's not one of this gang. I can see it. Let's get rid of all these fuzz with their guns – it's doing us no good at all.'

The C.I.A. man nodded in agreement. Together they approached the commissaris and as tactfully as they could explained the situation. Piet wasn't the one they were after but they vitally needed his co-operation. They asked for the police presence to be removed, into the street.

'How do you know so much about his innocence?' asked the commissaris too loudly. Paul dearly wished the man knew how to whisper.

'You can always catch up with him later, if there's a problem,' he said soothingly.

The commissaris shrugged and said, somewhat undiplomatically, that it wasn't his business. 'I was only here for the jurisdiction anyway,' he sighed. 'Formality.' Some formality! Curtly he gave the order for his men to withdraw, leaving Paul, Andy and Piet on their own.

With the visible threat of immediate arrest removed, tension eased by several degrees. Piet offered coffee, which they accepted.

'Did you fight with Warren? Is that why he left?' resumed Paul.

'We had many fights,' said Piet. 'Nothing serious to begin with. It was over the drugs. I said drugs killed children. He said he had to make a living, and drugs was all he knew now. It was a little thing between us at first, but...' He made a hopeless gesture.

'Do you have friends who take drugs? No, I'm not asking you to name them. But you've seen plenty of that going on – you must have.'

'Oh yes, I have seen it many times. The addiction. Here in Amsterdam, you know. They call it the drug capital of Europe, don't they?'

'So it's something you must be used to?' persisted Paul. Andy looked up at the ceiling, wondering where all this was leading.

'Yes, I am used to it,' said Piet, quietly.

'But it seemed wrong to you?'

'Yes,' maintained Piet, 'very wrong.'

'And you couldn't handle it?'

'I beg your pardon?'

'You couldn't take Warren's drug dealing any longer?' explained Paul.

'I didn't say he was a drug dealer,' said Piet.

'I'm sorry,' said Paul, 'I thought that's what you were just saying. That he had to make a living at it.'

'Oh, that,' said Piet with a slight laugh, 'he didn't deal on any regular basis. Only now and then when he needed money very badly. He wasn't a drug baron or anything like that. Not Warren.'

'You must have been unhappy when he went away?'

'It was not very nice, yes. But I knew it was at an end, so I had to accept it, didn't I?'

'Did he tell you where he was going? How you could keep in touch?'

'No.'

'So it was a big bust-up?'

'Sorry?'

'I mean you really did break up completely?'

'I suppose so.'

'Otherwise he might have left you a forwarding address, somewhere you could keep in contact with him.'

'Yes.'

'But he didn't?'

'No.'

'So, how did he leave? Did you know he was leaving?'

'No. He just left. I came back from the college one day and he wasn't here. I waited, but he didn't come.'

'So he didn't leave a note behind him?'

'No.'

There was a pause. The three sat drinking coffee. Paul finished his and put his empty cup down on the saucer on the floor next to his foot.

'This is all a load of shit, isn't it?' he said.

Piet blinked. 'What?' The sofa they were all sitting on seemed to vibrate slightly with the rise in tension. 'What do you mean, shit?' The boy was certainly brazening it out.

Paul kept to as reasonable a tone as he could, but this only made what he had to say sound the more deadly. 'I mean that everything you've said so far has been a deliberate attempt to mislead us.'

Andy's interest pricked up.

'*You* introduced the drug business,' continued Paul, 'we hadn't asked you anything about drugs. Then you said your reason for splitting up with Warren was over drugs, even though he wasn't much of a dealer and you yourself are quite used to the drug scene around here. You were together, you were lovers. *Lovers*, right?' Paul almost spat it out.

Piet bristled. 'It is not a crime in Holland!'

'I didn't say it was, Piet. But love's a powerful emotion, isn't it? Love binds people together. You lived with Warren a long time: the neighbours said so. You were devoted to one another. There's too little devotion in the world, isn't there?'

Andy looked across at Paul as if he thought the British agent had a loose screw or two.

'And then one day you come home and Warren isn't here. And he doesn't return. And you just sit back and take it. *Kismet* – fate, eh? You just sit back and accept that he goes away, leaving you no word and doesn't come back. And all because of drugs? Drugs in general?'

'Yeah,' said Andy, 'you're telling us you broke up over a *social issue*?'

'I don't think you broke up at all,' continued Paul. 'I don't think you had an argument over anything and I don't think he left you in some kind of huff. None of this makes any sense. You've been lying to us, Piet.'

'We don't like that, Piet,' said Andy with menace.

Piet shrank back. 'What are you going to do?'

'We're gonna put our cards on the table, Piet,' said Andy. 'We're not from the International Narcotics Bureau. Maybe you didn't get a chance to see our identification?' He flashed his C.I.A. card at Piet. Paul showed him his card as well. Piet nodded a quick acknowledgement, and then sat back, folding his arms. 'We're not talking about drugs, Piet,' added Andy.

'Listen, Piet,' said Paul, reverting to quietness. 'Your friend is mixed up in something a lot worse than drugs. Can you imagine something that's worse than drugs?'

Piet shook his head slowly.

'We think you have an idea,' said Paul, 'or you wouldn't have tried on this drugs smoke-screen of yours. All right, so you made a good effort to protect your friend. It was clever, and it was loyal. But your loyalty is misplaced in the game we're talking about.'

'What game is that?' muttered Piet.

'Don't you know?' asked Andy. Piet shook his head more vigorously.

'We're talking terrorism, Piet,' said Paul.

'*What?*' Piet's body stiffened as if an electric current had been passed through him. 'Terrorism?'

'Killing people,' persisted Paul. 'Lots of people. Lots of innocent people. Women, children...'

Piet got up and wandered about the tiny flat, bereft, his face in his hands. 'No, no!' he cried. Paul went over to him and clapped a hand on his shoulder.

'I think you knew he was involved in something like that.'

Real distress had got through to Piet now. The fences were down at last. He lifted his face from his hands. His cheeks were wet, his eyes glistening. 'I didn't know anything, I swear it! When he went away–'

'What happened when he went away? Who took him away? Who took him away, Piet?'

Piet's legs gave way and he sat down on a rickety chair, which creaked as the two agents stood over him.

'He went away with somebody, didn't he? That's what you've been covering up all along!' snapped Andy.

'Who was it, Piet?'

'You'd better say or you'll be locked up in one of those nice, clean prisons of yours for a long time, kid,' said Andy.

Piet looked as if he were a million miles away. 'Kid...' he said, softly.

'Who took Warren away?'

Piet sighed the sigh of an old man. The jig was up. 'I didn't know it was terrorism – if you say it, I believe you. I didn't know what it was. I thought maybe he was going to join a gang to rob a bank or something like that. Warren didn't tell me anything. I was afraid to ask because it would make him angry with me.'

'Who took him away?' asked Paul for the umpteenth time.

'An American.'

'Young? Old?' asked Andy.

'Middle-aged. Maybe forty.'

'What was his name?' asked Paul. The agents held their breaths.

'Warren called him Scottie.'

'Scottie what?'

'I don't know. Just Scottie.'

'Didn't he ever call him anything else?'

Andy's patience snapped. 'Come off it! The guy had another name, everybody has another name! What was it?'

'He never told me!'

'Didn't you and Warren discuss him when he wasn't there?' asked Paul.

'Yes, but he just laughed all the time and said what a great guy he was. I never heard any other name.'

'Did you hear any mention of this Scottie having been in the American army, or air force, or navy?'

Piet shook his head. 'Never. I would tell you if I had, believe me!'

'And this Scottie took Warren away?' asked Paul.

'Yes.'

'No forwarding address?'

'No. No letters. No telephone calls, nothing. They told me not to expect any contact for a while, maybe two months.'

'He said two months?' asked Andy.

'Yes.' Andy looked meaningly at Paul. 'I swear I haven't any letters here,' insisted Piet. 'You can search if you want! And I don't know where they went. Warren told him I was a student and not involved in any bad business, so I was never told anything. If they made plans it was when I was at the college or somewhere.'

'Maybe Scottie was an old lover, renewing old acquaintance?' ventured Paul.

'No!' exclaimed Piet fiercely. 'Warren said Scottie was straight through and through and I believed him. There wasn't anything like that between them.' He might have added that Warren preferred boys.

'Now I'm afraid you'll have to accompany the police out there down to the station, but–' Paul insisted over Piet's panicking objections '–not for more questioning. We want an identikit on this man Scottie and you're one of the few who can help us put one together.' The P.W.F. professor had been so vague and contradictory about the phoney agent's appearance (except for sun-glasses) that his identikit had been worse than useless. But if his points tallied with Piet's, they would be making progress.

As they were all leaving the flat, Piet stopped them at the door. 'Do you think I will see Warren again?' he asked.

'I shouldn't bet on it, kid,' said Andy.

Although they instructed Piet to contact the police if Warren got in touch with him again, they doubted Piet's good intentions in that regard – quite apart from the fact that they doubted the possibility of Warren's reappearance: before something happened, at any rate. As a precaution, they arranged with the waiting commissaris to have Piet's flat and movements watched until further notice. A few more words with Piet to satisfy themselves as to the American's general physical characteristics (to be getting on with) and they were off.

What worried both Andy and Paul was that things were on the move, no doubt about that.

'Couple of months,' said Andy. 'Five weeks ago he said "a couple of months".'

'Perhaps it was just something to say to keep Piet quiet,' suggested Paul.

'I don't think so. I think it's about the right time-scale even if we are talking a little loosely here.'

They agreed beyond doubt that this Scottie must be the same American who had posed as a C.I.A. agent, and that Andy's theory had been right: someone was collecting nuclear scientists and weapons experts. The prospect was chilling.

Efforts were intensified to turn over the Netherlands for the whereabouts of the hide-out of the gang. A photo of Lavitzsky had long been circulating, and had brought in the usual crop of false sightings. Now to that was added one of Piet's snapshots, blown-up, of Warren Booth (taken away by the police) and at last a more reasonable identikit of the mysterious Scottie.

It was inevitable that the name Scott would turn up time and time again on U.S. services' discharge lists. Along with one or two Scotsboroughs, Scotlands and Scotneys. A sprinkling were deceased, the rest were soon confirmed as wholly resident in America. A run through on Christian names was also tried, with equally negative results.

'Must be a nickname,' said Andy. 'Or an alias.'

'Unless your original info was duff, we must have him on a discharge list somewhere,' said Paul.

'But where?' They didn't have a name.

'I wonder,' said Paul, 'whether he might have been a mercenary at one time or another? Do you have a file anywhere on mercenaries?'

'On known ones, yes, I guess so,' replied Andy. 'Trouble is, people walk off the street to become mercenaries. We can't keep track of everybody.'

Washington faxed through a list of men of known mercenary activity – American nationality, known to have fought in Africa and Central America. No Scotts among them but one thumb-nail profile interested them.

'Who's this Jarvis?' said Andy. 'Did some dirty work in El Salvador at one time. Right sort of age and description. Said to be ex-Navy.'

'What happened to him?'

'Dunno. Vanished into thin air. Said to be a "leader of men" in his way. That's what really interests me about him.'

They ran through the name of Jarvis on the discharges but again turned up nothing. Another alias. Well, what could they have expected?

Paul queried whether or not the Moscow mole might have been mistaken on the nationality? 'Isn't there a chance our Scottie might have been a Canadian?'

'Christ,' said Andy, appalled at the thought of having to run all the same checks through the Canadian armed forces. It took a further day and a half of telephoning and faxing back and forth to Ottawa via Washington, just to learn that no Scott of interest to them had been discharged in Canada in the previous fifteen years.

'Any more bright ideas?' said Andy, standing there in

his shirt-sleeves, hands on hips. 'What about Australia? Or South Africa? Or New Zealand?'

U.S.S. *Aztec* entered Limehouse Reach exactly on schedule, some three miles from London Bridge. Soon on the starboard bow was Cherry Garden Pier, where vessels coming up river would hoist a black ball to ensure that the bascules of Tower Bridge would be raised. More in deference to custom than as a necessary action *Aztec* made the signal: her estimated time of arrival at the Bridge had been known for some days.

The queue of cars, lorries and buses grew by the second as the lights turned from green to red and drivers watched the curious sight ahead of them: a roadway heaving upwards to nearly a vertical position. Some got out of their cars to get a better view of the American warship entering the Pool of London.

Without fuss the ship passed under Tower Bridge. Once it was through, the bascules were lowered and the ruptured artery of City traffic resumed its normal chaotic flow. Slowly *Aztec* edged herself towards the south bank and the starboard side of H.M.S. *Belfast*, where a reception committee was waiting, together with pressmen and television crews and cameras. The battle-cruiser was made fast fore and aft, with springs at bow and stern to keep her steady. Then gangways were placed in position between the two ships. *Aztec* had finally docked in the middle of London.

A silent welcome greeted her from a hotel room overlooking the Pool. 'Here's to you, baby,' said Scottie to *Aztec*, raising a glass of scotch, as he watched her glide under the bridge towards her berth and her doom.

* * *

'How was Norwich?' asked Jane.

'Rather bloody, as it happens,' replied Humphrey. 'If you kill your mother it's called matricide. What is it when you kill your mother-in-law? Felicity and I were getting along fine – well, more or less like civilised human beings, till *she* arrived and started stirring things up. That got Felicity going, of course, and after that it was hopeless. Everything's going to have to be done through solicitors, but there it is. No nice, private and amicable arrangements. Let's not talk about it.' No, let's not, thought Jane.

She hadn't really wanted to come on this drive around Sussex, stopping at various pubs along the way, but she hadn't been able to think of any very convincing way of putting it off.

'Do you want to talk about Clive now?' he asked.

'Yes, why not?' Jane replied.

'You don't seem all that interested?'

Jane stretched and yawned. She shouldn't have had that second half-pint of lager at lunch. It was making her sleepy. Or was it Humphrey who was doing that? 'I'm tired of the whole thing all of a sudden,' she said. 'No I'm not. I'm just tired.'

'You're a lush,' said Humphrey.

'Keep your personal opinions to yourself. All right, what have you dug up so far?'

Humphrey said it wasn't all that much – just the impression Clive gave at the military PR exercise at Upper Heyford Air Base. 'He kept asking questions about this and that,' he said; 'the brass on a number of occasions were singularly reluctant to answer him. Very inquisitive chap, your brother-in-law.'

'Have you any idea where we are?' asked Jane, without much concern.

'Not really. That sign back there said something about a Roman villa.' They had turned off a by-road into a narrow lane which ran through a farmyard and then rose steeply to the crest of the South Downs. 'Yes, I think I do know where we are. I'm pretty sure this is the old Roman road that ran from Chichester to London. I haven't been round here for years.' The lane came to an end in open grassland. A car could go no further. They got out to have a look and enjoy the breeze.

To the north the gently undulating heart of Sussex stretched away towards the North Downs, while to the south, one saw – after walking a few hundred yards along the Downsway – a glimpse of the sea. It was shining, though not especially blue, in the autumn sun.

Jane thought how deceptive the peace of this countryside surrounding them really was. They were going through the motions of an idyllic day. Why only the motions? Why wasn't it idyllic for real?

What makes things real? Jane asked herself silently as she gazed across to the sea. What makes good things in life real? The answer that came to her was: inner peace of mind, not the beauty of surroundings. You could be looking at the most beautiful countryside in the world (and perhaps to some people, this was it) and still be made miserable by the vaguest of premonitions. Premonitions Jane certainly had – but of what? Paul's intrusion into her life? The implications, far more than just personal, of Sarah's death – a mystery that remained, along with the identity of the murderer, unknown? Jane shivered – and not because of the indian summer breeze wafting in from the Channel.

'Something bothering you, darling?' asked Humphrey, putting his arm around her.

'No, I'm all right,' she replied with a small sigh. 'Probably still edgy, to tell the truth.'

'That's understandable,' he said, his hand patting her upper arm.

Poor, understanding Humphrey. She should perhaps have told him what was going on, in all decency. But she still had no idea whether her fling with the security agent had any solid basis. In some ways she dreaded the idea of the case being wrapped up, because her affair with Paul might be wrapped up in the process.

The case. The case of Sarah's death, of Clive Parris's implication. She hadn't told Humphrey about the 'drowning' incident. What she dreaded, she supposed, was the sympathy Humphrey would show, his arms around her and his quiet words in her ear. She couldn't bear the idea of it.

'I still can't help feeling there's something wrong about Clive, I just can't put my finger on it,' said Humphrey, trying to pick up the threads of a faltering conversation. 'Oh well, perhaps one day he'll betray himself.'

If Clive was betraying his country, was she any better – in her way – for betraying her understanding with Humphrey? It was all his fault, for being so tied up with that bitch in Norwich! And anyway, they had no real obligations towards one another. Except love. For Jane still loved Humphrey. It was *that* she couldn't bear. She wasn't a natural two-timer where the emotions were concerned.

The unfortunate Humphrey received no benefit today from her love, however. She seemed to shake him off whenever he came close, and later feigned a headache when the prospect of an evening together came up. Humphrey shrugged it off as a monthly. He was a patient man.

She too kidded herself for a while that she wasn't in a love-making mood, but that illusion was shattered when she found herself in bed that very evening with Paul, who had arrived back from Amsterdam not long after she parted from Humphrey.

They seized on one another again with that hungry desperation. The desperation on Paul's part was for more than love. He was taking out his frustration on Jane, his yearning for action, his overwhelming need to get to grips with the invisible octopus whose tentacles were wrapping round him in his effort to break free and find the truth – or indeed wrapping round a doomed London, for all he knew.

Now things were hotting up he had no business skiving off for a quick one with a mistress. The height of unprofessionalism. For the first time in that professional life he was putting a girl before all other priorities. But she was a priority, too.

Afterwards, he decided to have a good talk to her.

'What about?' For no reason at all they embraced and kissed deeply. For her it was because they were like two lovers before some doom they knew was about to befall. She continued to cling, but he pushed her away, gently and carefully. He told her he wanted her to do something for him, something that had nothing to do with what was now between them.

Jane tensed with excitement. 'What do you want me to do?'

'Hold on and I'll tell you. But first, listen: I don't want you putting yourself in any personal danger. That's because, from the moment I ask you to do something, I take responsibility for your safety.

'Now, so far the only person with some sort of family link with both Sarah and Clive is you. We have absolutely no evidence yet, but I'm convinced her death has a lot to do with what we're investigating. Don't ask me to explain, because I can't. All I can say is that she died in Amsterdam, which is a hell of a coincidence which one day I *will* explain; shortly before that she sent you a note indicating she needed desperately to talk; then there's this business of an attempted drowning of you by Clive because he thinks you're on to something involving him – possibly.

'What I'm leading up to is this. You are in a position to dig around among family skeletons and look for evidence at Baythorne Manor in a way we can't. You can get access to the place, to his and Sarah's things. If your sister left you a note, it's possible she left something else behind too.'

'What would it be?'

'I don't know – that's just it.'

Jane thought for a moment. 'Clive told me I could have anything of Sarah's I wanted. He invited me to go back to Baythorne any time I wished, to claim whatever was there that I might have my eye on. If I could get down and have a look round, preferably when he's not about, so much the better. I get on well with the housekeeper Mrs Banham; it should be all right. If you've got him followed then you should be able to forewarn me somehow if he's about to show up.'

'Whatever you can do, Jane,' murmured Paul.

They made love no more that night. In fact he left shortly after their talk. He didn't know when he could make it again. Somehow Jane knew he wasn't putting it on. It shocked her. The last look he gave her was of a supremely worried man. And Paul didn't seem to be the type to worry easily. What was the matter with him? Why was he so desperate? She didn't feel he would have asked her to take any sort of risks, either, or be involved at all, if what he was up against wasn't so urgent, even critical. If only he could have told her what it was! The worst thing was her sudden thought, then, that even he didn't know.

That night she tossed and turned alone in her bed. She was embroiled in a nightmare – one made up of nasty impressions rather than concrete images. It involved water and her being pulled down into the depths, unable to breathe, unable to scream. When she woke up in a bath of perspiration, the real world she woke up to was still a nightmare – an oppressive nightmare she could not shake off.

Paul was experiencing a different sort of oppression, the oppression of helplessness and bafflement. He had to report to 'C' next day on progress made in Amsterdam, and while it had been considerable compared to what had been turned over during the past weeks and months, it was still far short of what they needed to know if they were to act *now*, to prevent whatever was going to happen from really happening. Would 'C' realise what Paul had long known: that the security service, so long built up in order to face one sort of enemy, was now almost totally at sea when coming up against another?

And events were shortly to render Paul's report to 'C' entirely irrelevant and out of date.

10

Everybody grumbled about something. Figac grumbled about the Cup-A-Soups and the other fast-food junk they had to eat.

'He would say that, wouldn't he?' grumbled Maxton. 'What does he think this is, the Ritz?'

Lavitzsky complained about back-ache from the mattresses. Others had their little hang-ups. It was the gathering tension of men who knew that they had something dangerous to do very shortly, something big, something once-and-for-all. One or two of them might not come out of it alive. Maybe all of them wouldn't come out of it alive.

Fucking ballerinas, Scottie thought to himself, and then was forced to smile at the idea. He thought of a clutch of girls in white tutus in terror backstage at Covent Garden or somewhere, about to come prancing on in 'Swan Lake'. Some contrast with this mob.

Within twenty-four hours of their arrival, the air in their living-quarters was thick with the smell of sweat and the oil they used on the weapons. Figac was persuaded to smoke his malodorous Gauloises apart from anyone else. He'd be running out of those shortly. That would improve his temper no end.

Scottie was glad to be able to get away from the hide-out from time to time in his respectable surveyor guise. But he knew long absences from the men were unwise because it was more crucial than ever now to hold them together, keep up their morale. At first he allowed cards to be played to alleviate tensions, but on returning once found the players gambling for money, feverishly raising the stakes higher and higher. He put a stop to it. He wasn't going to have big debts incurred at this stage – money which could only be paid out later from the ultimate jackpot. That would bring later resentment, later trouble, exposure. Scottie made them play for matchsticks from then on.

He was worried about Lavitzsky and how he would carry out his role in the seizure of *Aztec*. Lavitzsky was his man for the guided missile systems and technology, but he wasn't cut out for much of a fight, and they both knew it. The thing was to keep up his nerve, such as he had. The fact that he was older than all the others by a good ten years didn't help. At least Lavitzsky had assured him that his heart was sound and there'd never been heart-disease in his family, but for how much did that count?

To reassure him Scottie brought Lavitzsky and Schiele together for a mini briefing. He told Schiele that he was detailed to cover Lavitzsky every step of the way on the assault. Schiele grunted, which meant obedience. He was a big, taciturn German who had served six years for armed robbery in a Stuttgart jail, where he'd happened to take up the trade of radio operator. He was to act in this function under Booth, the communications man, when the time came. After the briefing, at which Lavitzsky seemed to be more relieved, Schiele drew Scottie aside.

'What if he panics out of control?' he asked.

'Shoot him,' said Scottie. 'But be fucking sure before you do it. We need the little bastard.' The German grunted again and went back to polishing his automatic.

Scottie was also keeping his eye on Warren Booth, the only one here who was a friend in former times, unless Maxton could be classified as a 'friend'. Booth seemed to have come out of his early withdrawal symptoms over the loss of alcohol. But the presence of his growing campness amongst a group of confined men was a disturbing element. None of these guys was exactly a babe-in-the-woods, but Warren had that teasing, ogling tendency which could get under the skin of the latent, the smouldering ones who could burst out in a rage against him at any moment. Several times Scottie had had to draw Warren aside and tell him to cool it. Warren giggled, abashedly, and said he would, but it always cropped up again. Even the idea of the million dollars and the boys that would bring didn't seem to be sufficient to stop him.

But whether it was because of Scottie's watchfulness, Maxton's square-bashing or the prospect of riches beyond the dreams of avarice, the group seemed on the whole to be in excellent shape. They would have to draw heavily on all they'd learned, practised and hoped for if they were going to be able to handle the pressure of what was to come. The challenge wasn't the assault itself. It lay in what would transpire afterwards. The tension, the waiting, the delicate manoeuvring, pawns in a game that was being played for the highest stakes any operation of this kind had ever gone for.

Striking right at the heart of the West.

Time passed. They stripped and assembled their weapons blindfolded. They went over the plan of attack, made more vivid by their new location almost at the scene of the action to come. They ate, slept, sat around, squatted or sprawled on the old sacks on the floor; they played cards or talked about girls and guns in the light of the gas lamp. They thirsted for real drink, even after their denial all these past weeks. They wished the whole thing was over and they were suddenly whisked off to South America or Morocco or wherever they had focused their dreams.

So far everything was going like clockwork. They were itching to get on with it, to end this unbearable, interminable waiting.

That was just the mood Scottie liked.

The strike-force had been inside the warehouse for two days when the *Aztec* sailed in and docked. Day Three was going to be D-Day. On the morning of that day, at 9.00 a.m., most of the crew of the *Aztec* would depart for several hours of sightseeing and relaxation, leaving aboard a small complement. That's why it was so vital to strike then, with the battle-cruiser at its most vulnerable.

At 10.00 a.m. on D-Day the 'frozen food' boxes to be taken on board *Belfast* would arrive in a van at the back of the warehouse. At 10.30 Scottie and Maxton, who was acting as driver, would take the van on to the quay, from which the containers would be trundled aboard the old cruiser and cached in the place Scottie had previously located.

That was the brilliant idea for concealing the weapons. It could have been something like an updated version of 'The Lavender Hill Mob'.

At 11.30 and for a few minutes afterwards, members of the strike-force, shaved and respectable, would board *Belfast* in ones and twos. They would mix with the real tourists who would be about on the decks by then. Since it was now the beginning of November there would be fewer visitors than in high summer. Scottie hadn't wanted lots of people around, but he wanted just enough of them to act as camouflage. He hoped for a bright morning – or at least one without rain – which would lure enough people out in time. He had heard the forecast on Radio London and it had been good. Anyhow, the U.S. ship moored alongside would be a good bait: it had received a fair amount of publicity.

The evening before D-Day Scottie told the men to get a good night's sleep, and dished out a few mild sedatives when requested, here and there; each man had been thoroughly searched for pills, but Scottie had a stock which he kept, like a charge-nurse in hospital. The more sleep they had now, the quicker their reflexes would be when the time came – less than twelve hours away.

Scottie heard rain on the roof in the night. And drips echoing on distant floors. He fretted that the weather would go on like this into late morning but soon fell asleep again, his own sedative overcoming these endless little petty niggles.

It was easy to sleep in because the place was in permanent semi-darkness. No need to rise before nine anyhow, on this particular morning.

The dull day showed through the dusty, filmy windows and through chinks in the walls and roof. No sound of rain, thank God. It was just after nine o'clock. One by one they stirred, stretched, yawned and went about the business of getting themselves organised. By ten o'clock they were ready, tensed and to varying degrees churning their insides over.

The minute hand on Scottie's watch dragged down to 10.10. He waited for the sound of the van.

Silence.

By 10.19 he wondered if the whole thing was off. Had there been some stupid hitch this side? The men said nothing, as if saying something would be enough to grind the plot to a halt. By 10.21 Scottie's mind was racing along, thinking of ways it could be disbanded without detection. His nerves were at breaking point.

Then they heard it. Scottie looked through a crack in the door and saw a light-blue van draw up. 'What the fucking hell kept you?' he asked of the emerging driver, as much in relief as in anger.

'I'm only twenty minutes late,' said this particularly dozy individual, who wore light-blue overalls with a polar bear emblem over the breast pocket. 'Got held up, didn't I? Some bleeder shed his load all over Tooley Street. Potatoes rolling everywhere like instant mash.'

'Here you are, then,' said Scottie, holding out a wad of notes. 'Okay? Agreed? You can count it if you like.'

The driver seemed to have a practised feel for wads of money and a quick check confirmed the amount. 'I'll be back to collect the van at half-twelve, right?' he said as he stuffed his loot into an inside pocket. He had been told that the frozen food boxes would be filled with oxy-acetylene cutting equipment for a bank job. He handed over the keys and nipped off, fairly sharpish, away to the street.

Maxton got into the driver's seat with the keys Scottie handed to him and backed the van up against the open door of the warehouse. The men then got down to it, unloading the boxes, filling them inside, and re-loading the van with them. This took ten minutes, as had been calculated.

At 10.42 Warren Booth, in jeans, checked shirt and wind-breaker, emerged from the back of the warehouse and walked to the end of the cul-de-sac. He saw that the street was empty, both directions. He spoke into his walkie-talkie.

'Street's all clear. Go for it.'

The van shot away from the building and down the cul-de-sac, into the street. Scottie sat beside Maxton in the front. They were wearing the blue overalls with the polar bear emblem. They were now the Polar Bear Frozen Food Company. As Warren stood on the corner and waved them into the street Maxton said: 'He's not so bad, for one of *them*. Fucking poof!' – and gave a whoop like a war-cry. Scottie himself felt relieved. In his first, though minor, action Booth had performed like a professional villain. He had been the sleepless one, lying on his back and staring up at the darkness of the warehouse beyond the reach of lamp-light. Endlessly staring. That had worried Scottie then – but it didn't now. Anyway, fuck, there was too much else to think about!

In the back of the van were three containers loaded with weapons, grenades and smoke canisters, hidden under a layer of boxes of scampi, Neapolitan ices and frozen peas.

A minute later the van turned into Abbots Lane.

'This is it,' said Scottie.

'You're fucking right,' said Maxton gaily, gripping the wheel like a hungry gorilla, grinning from ear to ear in an uncannily loony way. Scottie had never before seen the dour Yorkshireman in such an elated state. Ahead were about thirty or forty people milling around the gate which led to H.M.S. *Belfast*. Some of them were waving placards. Not a very touristy thing to do, proclaiming 'nuclear-free London' and 'go home, Yanks'.

'Don't run them down, Maxton,' said Scottie.

'Wouldn't I just?' chuckled Maxton, changing down into second. Then a look of alarm spread over his face as he glanced at the wing-mirror. 'Bloody hell, it's a pig's van behind us!'

Scottie squinted at his own wing-mirror and saw them too. Police. A white van was behind them, almost against their rear bumper. Its blue light was flashing but there had been no siren. It couldn't be – not for them. Could it?

No, it wasn't. 'Cool it, Maxy, it's just the anti-nuclear demonstration. Protesting against *Aztec*. I should've known they'd be here. That accounts for pigs. Nothing to do with us.'

'Could have been a bloody trap.'

'Well, it wasn't. Keep moving.'

'I can't. *They're* in the way.' The van had ground to a halt before the crowd of people. The police van came to a halt behind the Polar Bear van; doors opened on both sides and the boys in blue leapt out, led by their inspector.

Their presence created a new focus for protest, and the chant of '*Aztec* out! *Aztec* out!' rose from amongst the group. The police inspector strode past Scottie and Maxton to confront the crowd. 'Who's in charge here?' he shouted.

A man came forward. He looked forty-ish, with glasses and shoulder-length hair redolent of the sixties. '*Aztec* out!' he shouted back at the inspector.

'Right, sir, now we don't want a confrontation here. You're obstructing traffic, and I am empowered to arrest you under the provisions of the Street Acts.'

'We have a legitimate right to protest against nuclear weapons in our country,' said the long-haired man – others were agreeing loudly at his back.

'Yes,' said the inspector, 'but if you're going to do it you'll have to stand back along on the quay. If you and your people stop anyone from boarding or leaving the *Belfast*, or abuse the crews of either of these vessels, I'll have you. Is that understood?' The long-haired man looked down at his feet and nodded. 'Get them moving, then. These gentlemen want to come through in their van.' The bobbies then pushed the protesters back into an orderly line out of the way of traffic. The inspector walked back towards the van and looked in at Maxton, the driver. 'You on official business on the *Belfast*?' he asked.

'Usual delivery,' replied Maxton. He gestured at the crowd. 'Bloody rentamob.'

'Should be all right,' said the inspector, 'they look

harmless enough but I'd appreciate it if you didn't provoke them. Keep your eyes straight ahead and drive through slowly. Follow me, sir.'

'Right inspector – thanks.' Maxton suppressed a chuckle as he put his engine into first and edged through the gate – the inspector walking before the van, waving people aside.

Apart from demonstrators there was a large crowd of visitors waiting to board *Belfast*, larger than usual because of the attraction of *Aztec* alongside. Scottie's prediction on crowds had been right. *Belfast*'s rail was about the closest anyone was ever likely to get to a modern U.S. Navy battle-cruiser.

Belfast was due to open to the public at eleven o'clock.

Over the years the Polar Bear Frozen Food Company had been a familiar sight to the *Belfast* crew. Banquets, dinners and wedding receptions were held in the officers' wardroom, and no one gave Scottie and Maxton more than a glance as the two men – joined by the muscular Schiele from the back of the van – wheeled the refrigerated containers up the gangway on porters' barrows. 'Bill not working today?' asked one of the crew suddenly of Scottie. Scottie shook his head, conscious that his American accent might give the game away. 'Got 'flu,' he muttered, and continued on his way. As they were wheeling the barrows along he whispered to Maxton to do all the talking from then on. It struck him then that if it hadn't been for his muscles Schiele was the last person to have along.

No one was about on the 'Burma Road'. They passed the 'bakery' with its plastic rolls and the 'sick bay' with its plaster dummies. Past the display of mines and underwater gear. Past 'B' turret magazine, into the mess deck for 'A' turret and on to the capstan flat. The clamps had already been removed from the bulkhead door to the paint stores. Within seconds the containers were unloaded and the guns, grenades and smoke canisters safely stowed away out of sight.

Five minutes later the three were trundling the empty boxes back down the gangway to the van. It was all going through like a dick through a used condom, thought Scottie. Without being violently revolutionary, the demonstrators were sufficiently lively to keep the eyes of the police away from the men in the van.

The inspector glanced at Maxton as they drove past. Maxton rolled his eyes upwards and shrugged. He got the betrayal of a slight smile back. 'There's a man whose name is about to go down in history,' Maxton said.

A few minutes later Maxton reversed into the cul-de-sac and they climbed out of the van. Scottie slipped a note under the windscreen wiper: 'Flat battery, gone for replacement', to allay suspicions about an abandoned van. When the proper driver returned they would all be aboard *Belfast* – unbeknown to him.

The countdown to the real action was almost at an end.

They were giving the visitors time to begin circulating on the old ship before joining them, in twos and threes. Back in the warehouse everything was ready. Scottie, Maxton and Schiele slipped out of their overalls, which they pushed into the back of the van's cab. Scottie underwent a complete transformation with only a pair of sunglasses and an anorak. Maxton wore a Frank Sinatra kind of hat which Figac ridiculed somewhat heavily. 'I feel a right charlie in this bloody thing,' Maxton grumbled, reverting to sourpuss Yorkshireman. Schiele had been ordered to shave off his large blond moustache and sideboards, which he did now without protest: *that* had come earlier. Any resemblance between what they looked like now and the three earlier employees of the Polar Bear Frozen Food Company would be purely accidental.

One bonus on the site was a builder's skip in the cul-de-sac, half-full of rubble. Empty tins, food packets and all the other detritus from their stay on the top floor were buried in it. No trace of where they had stayed for two days and three nights would be evident. Not originally planned, it was just one more small ploy to evade any follow-up investigation.

The first lot of the strike-force set off, hands in pockets, at 11.20. At further intervals of three minutes each, they were followed by other groups of two and three.

The old cruiser was trim and the White Ensign flying from her stern stood out stiffly in a strong wind. With the knowledge of the deck-plan almost burned into their brains, the strike-force knew where to make for as soon as they were on board.

Most of the visitors were crowded along the starboard rail, staring at the sleek lines of the *Aztec*, comparing its smooth surface to the much more battle-scarred exterior of the *Belfast*. They looked on with awe as one of the *Belfast* duty crew pointed out a missile launcher on the after-deck of the American.

The strike-force took the rehearsed route past the magazines of 'A' and 'B' turrets into the forward mess deck, passing through the bulkhead door into the capstan flat. Once there, they saw the ladder up which they would have to climb to the main deck when the hatch-cover was opened.

They entered the paint store where the weapons were concealed. One of the mercenaries, an Irishman called Donohue, would remain in the capstan flat itself to enable the bulkhead door to be closed while those inside prepared the weapons.

Figac was on the main deck, sitting on the hatch-cover under the starboard gun of 'A' turret, apparently fiddling with a buggered-up camera but in reality stealthily releasing the clamps which secured the cover under him.

They armed themselves silently in the paint store. Scottie indicated to Schiele that it was time to give Lavitzsky a hand: the Russian was shaking so much that his fingers seemed unable to master the simplest task. 'Keep him well to the back in the attack, and keep him in line – don't let him break,' muttered Scottie.

The attack was set for one o'clock. Dinner hour, when most of the crew of *Belfast* would be in their bar. In a matter of seconds their bulkhead door would be closed and secured, imprisoning them.

At 12.59 the strike-force emerged from the paint store carrying their weapons.

Maxton led the party that was to mount the attack on *Aztec*'s forward gangway. Scottie had re-considered and decided that a parallel attack on the stern gangway was feasible. He was leading this party himself.

With Maxton at the head, they climbed up the ladder. They were to be on deck within thirty-five seconds of mounting the ladder. Maxton banged on the under-side of the hatch-cover with the butt of his automatic.

Immediately it started to open.

With that chink of daylight momentarily blinding them, they all knew their lives had changed forever.

In no time they were scattered all over the deck.

Prodded by Schiele, Lavitzsky stumbled into the light, wondering if someone would shoot him the moment he came through the hatch.

The last man up the ladder, Hakayama, pulled the pin of a smoke grenade and threw it into the capstan flat. Smoke billowed out of the hatch as he climbed through it.

Once they were all on the main deck they ran down the port side and round the main superstructure, pausing for a moment to regroup before moving on to the catapult deck.

'Excuse *me*!' cried a large lady wearing thick glasses when Figac bumped into her from behind. There were audible scowls from several visitors as the strike-force ran among them, pushing their way through. Nobody had had a moment to see who they were, or how armed to the teeth. On the catapult deck they split into the two groups, Maxton's and Scottie's.

This was it. The assault on *Aztec*.

11

A few sailors were standing about on the deck of U.S.S. *Aztec*, a splinter from the skeleton crew left on board after most of the five-hundred-odd men had been sent off on shore leave.

With his contingent behind him Maxton sprinted to the forward gangway connecting *Belfast* with *Aztec*. Reaching for a grenade, he pulled the pin and lobbed the grenade at the sailors. The explosion blew them apart: three were killed - annihilated - instantly; others rolled around in agony. A few on the outside of the circle staggered about, stunned but otherwise unhurt.

Then Maxton and his men crouched down and opened fire on the survivors. They hadn't had a chance.

The screaming began, behind Maxton. It came from within the enveloping smoke of a canister thrown into an admiral's pinnace held in davits on the port side of *Belfast*. The intention had been to sow confusion amongst the visitors, and that was certainly happening. 'Never mind them - over we go!' he shouted, and he and the party ran over the gangway to the other side. Glancing along the deck of *Aztec*, covered here and there in the carnage of bodies and blood, Maxton saw Scottie's group had attacked on the aft gangway.

Within seconds the whole strike-force was on board the American.

The last man on each arm of the attack pulled the pins from grenades dropped by preceding attackers on the middle of the gangways. As the gangways exploded, debris was thrown everywhere over the heads of the crouched attackers. In that instant *Aztec* was transformed into a floating island, with no link to *Belfast* other than its berthing warps.

The first phase had lasted ninety seconds.

As the smoke cleared from the deck of *Belfast*, renewed screaming and pandemonium broke out. There lay the bodies of two of the tourists: a father and twelve-year-old son in jeans and trainers. The son had begged and pleaded to see *Aztec* with her missile launchers on that day of all days. His birthday treat.

The strike-force had the obvious advantage of surprise, and now they must make the most of it. Maxton and his party let rip, scattering bullets on their way into the operations room. Sailors threw up their arms and fell without knowing what had hit them.

Scottie descended with his party to the first platform, the same as a number two deck. They fought their way forward against unarmed men almost to the bows, closing and sealing the hatch-covers as they went along, and thus imprisoning the remnants of crew who were below. One American sailor picked up an axe, the only weapon to hand. He chose his man, springing from behind a ventilator shaft. The blade of the axe was buried with a sickening squelch into the mercenary's back. Figac shot the sailor neatly through the chest.

Maxton kicked open the door of the operations room and sprayed it with bullets before realising no one was there. The radio operator was missing or dead, somewhere on deck.

Scottie joined Maxton, and then took three men out of the operations room by the starboard door to search along that side of the main superstructure. There was plenty of ammunition left, but Maxton told his men to hold their fire and only shoot if they had to. From his position Scottie heard a few, sporadic notes of firing. He returned to the operations room. Maxton had gone to check the hatches. Warren, looking deathly white but otherwise quiet, carried a stumbling Lavitzsky into the operations room; he sat him down heavily in a chair. 'Has he been hit?' asked Scottie. Warren shook his head. Scottie leaned down to the Russian. 'You okay?' Lavitzsky nodded, his eyes closed. 'If you're gonna be sick, don't do it in here,' said Scottie. He then asked Warren if he was all right, and got the same nod. 'She's ours, Kid,' said Scottie. 'This mother-fucker is ours!'

Within a few moments Maxton was back. 'The deck's ours,' he confirmed. 'Anybody left alive on this tub is below decks, and all hatch-covers have been sealed.' His chest was heaving in the elation of attack and joy of killing.

'What've we lost?'

'One dead. Agnelli. Otherwise, just cuts and bruises.'

'Not too bad. That's another million for you guys to share out, isn't it?' Nobody laughed, but nobody threw up, either.

'I don't feel so good,' mumbled Lavitzsky.

'You'll get your sea-legs,' laughed Scottie. He felt light-headed. Life was a joke again. He turned to Maxton. 'Before we come under attack detail one or two with mops and pails to go over those decks and walls. Shove the bodies over the side.'

'Aye, aye boss,' said Maxton, getting into the nautical swing of it. In a few minutes Scottie heard Maxton arguing with a couple of protesting mercenaries over the orders. 'If you want to smell this mess while you're eating your lunch that's your business,' he said. 'Somebody's got to do it! Right? Get your arses out there or you'll join that lot, got it?' They obeyed. You didn't argue with a bulging-eyed, sweaty maniac gripping an automatic rifle, and steeped in blood-letting.

Schiele came into the operations room. 'They've cleared the deck of *Belfast* double-quick. Like a ghost-ship over there.'

'There's a little kid dead,' said Warren Booth, looking out.

'Yeah, well we knew we were going to cause casualties,' said Scottie. 'You don't get yourself a battle-cruiser by saying "Please".'

'I don't see why a little kid has to die, though,' said Warren.

Scottie ignored the remark and concentrated on supervising the securing of the superstructure, battening down for the duration, settling on observation-posts facing all directions, organising internal communications. They were in for a long haul. He looked at his watch. Only six minutes since they'd launched the attack.

In a few minutes more the airspace all around the quay would be filled with helicopters, together with the din of a dozen ambulances and police cars. There was also the river police to consider. When he looked out the porthole Scottie observed two police launches hovering by Tower Bridge. They were probably only now receiving the news.

It was time to get Warren Booth off his jag of newfound bereavement for children and on to the business of communications, with Schiele under him as radio operator. 'I want listening on the police frequencies *now*!' he ordered. As the static and chaotic babble emanating from the vastly superior radio equipment of *Aztec* filled the room Scottie was already making notes and squiggles on a pad.

He was preparing to deliver his first message to the world.

PART TWO

12

The police inspector on the quay was dumbfounded, plain and simple, as he saw the bodies brought away from H.M.S. *Belfast* by his white-faced men. A few, brief minutes before, they had heard grenade explosions, scattered automatic rifle fire; they had seen smoke billowing from the ship like a vision from World War II. At first they thought it was a gas explosion or some other accident, but before long they knew it was foul play – major foul play. The bodies now confirmed that. He was sickened by the little form of the twelve-year-old boy, carried past him on the stretcher. What the hell was this?

Then the realisation hit him between the eyes. They were after the *Aztec*.

The first priority was to clear *Belfast* completely and as quickly as they could. The inspector organised as good a rescue operation as possible and then got on to the radio.

He could almost feel all hell breaking loose at the other end when he mentioned *Aztec*. He was ordered to do nothing, absolutely nothing, that might endanger innocent people or his men. To stay away from *Aztec* and clear the area. Reinforcements and ambulances were on the way.

Managing to find binoculars, the inspector positioned himself to see what had happened to *Aztec*'s gangways. They had been blown up. And as the smoke from the engagement lifted he could see that the decks were to all appearances utterly deserted.

There'd been nothing like this since the Iranian Embassy siege – only this looked as if it might be worse. The visitors to *Belfast*, dazed and shell-shocked, were being herded away along the quay as his men tried to find out from them what had happened. There were no coherent replies. The most anyone could say was that some bunch of men loaded with weapons had swooped among them and then there had been smoke, screams, shooting and panic.

How had they arrived there? Had they lain concealed on board *Belfast* all night? How would that have been possible? Fear now struck the inspector at the pit of his stomach. If the gang hadn't sneaked aboard the previous night, was it possible that they had done so right under his nose? That he had actually been watching them do it? His mind raced over the possibilities. He recalled the frozen food van – but they had departed in the same way as they had come in. He'd even spoken to the driver on both occasions. Still, it might be something. He made a note to have a check made on the frozen food company.

It looked as if whoever it was had indeed taken possession of *Aztec*. So what were they going to do with her?

Within ten minutes, Abbots Lane and the adjoining streets were filled with fire-engines, ambulances and police cars.

How many casualties there might be on *Aztec* was impossible to say. With the clearing of the smoke the decks revealed no bodies, only some smears of blood on the walls. But now the worst was known about *Belfast*. Five bodies were counted, including two of the *Belfast* crew hit while trying to pull people away from the starboard rail. Three other visitors had been injured by grenade fragments, not seriously. Discounting loss of life on the *Aztec* the death-toll was mercifully low, though that didn't lessen the tragedy.

As visitors and demonstrators were gradually cleared off the quay, the inspector took another moment to scan the *Aztec* and then the river. There were two police launches in position by Tower Bridge. Surely they weren't going to send them out against this mob? This was a job for the S.A.S., if anyone. Well, the launches didn't appear to be moving.

With the speed of lightning orders were being fired by radio to all quarters. Tower Wharf was closed to the public. Groups of police and army officers from the garrison in the fortress peered at the silent and seemingly deserted *Aztec*. Within the fortress the Jewel Room underneath Waterloo Barracks was cleared of visitors and the massive doors closed. Shipping was halted all along the river.

After that, there didn't seem to be anything else that could be done except to size up the situation and wait for developments.

Armed police arrived at the quay with shields and automatic weapons, and, crouched down, they quickly boarded the *Belfast*. The voice of an inspector through a loud hailer rang out harshly, the sound of it bouncing off the metallic hulls of the two ships. But he was under strict instructions to say nothing provocative at this stage. The concern was for the wounded and dying among the American crew. 'If you persist in holding the ship, please send out all wounded from the company. Will you allow medical personnel aboard? Repeat: Will you allow medical personnel aboard? Please indicate!'

Answer came there none. Several times the message was repeated, while sharpshooters' eyes ached trying to find viable targets, without success. But in view of the possibility of hostages, no firing was to commence except under order. There was not even a warning shot from *Aztec* to tell the police to go away. After an hour or so, the police withdrew to a safer distance, off *Belfast*.

Word was getting through to the higher-ups in the establishment and to news agencies that the *Aztec* had been mysteriously seized. The few news flashes that first appeared, or were heard, gave out only very confused and garbled stories. More news was promised for later.

At three o'clock in the afternoon, approximately one-and-three-quarter hours after the seizure of the U.S. warship, a signal was picked up by the Emergencies Officer on the Mayday frequency at the Air Traffic Control, Uxbridge:

> Advise Prime Minister that U.S.S. *Aztec* is no longer under control of United States authority. In order to avoid progressive destruction of London by nuclear guided missiles or damage to ship's reactors, the sum of 100 million American dollars in gold, with safe conduct from U.K. is demanded. This message will be repeated three times.

The transmission concluded with the announcement that the communications system of U.S.S. *Astec* would be open to receive for two minutes' past each quarter hour. And then came the warning:

> Any attempt to recapture the ship, whether by outside forces or by any of the crew still on board the *Aztec*, will lead to immediate disaster. That crew is now contained below decks.

At the Air Traffic Control office the duty watch was alerted by the Emergencies Officer and the signal from *Aztec* re-run on the voice data recorder. When keyed into the data transmission system it was displayed on the large video screen for all in the room to see.

Before further action was taken, New Scotland Yard

was contacted. Yes, shortly after 1.00 p.m. there had been an incident involving the cruiser *Belfast* and the visiting U.S. battle-cruiser *Aztec*. There had been casualties and Scotland Yard was liaising with the Port of London Authority. So, rumours from news flashes had been right. And the signal must be genuine. The Duty Controller had been called in and now picked up the receiver of a red telephone which gave him a direct line to the head of the Civil Aviation Authority. He said it was an emergency and asked for the Director-General. 'Sir, it's Bowman here, Air Traffic Control, Uxbridge. It looks as if we have a major emergency on our hands. One of my Duty Watch recorded this transmission about ten minutes ago.' Bowman ran the tape and the recording was played down the phone. The Met had confirmed the situation on the ground, added Bowman.

'Leave this one with me,' ordered the Director-General. 'No release or acknowledgement to anyone, is that understood?'

The Director-General then rang the Home Secretary. He was told that the Home Secretary was in emergency session with the Met Police Commissioner. In a moment, he came through. 'Yes? Alan? What is it?'

'Duty Watch at Uxbridge received a signal on the Mayday frequency, which goes like this.' He related the text. 'I checked with Scotland Yard before ringing you to make sure it was genuine.'

'It's genuine, all right,' said the Home Secretary, Jim Dodson. 'Thanks for that, Alan, it makes everything that much more gruesomely clear. Whatever you do, restrict circulation for the moment. I'm getting on to the P.M. You'd better make yourself ready for a meeting.' With that, Dodson rang off.

The Prime Minister was at Chequers, entertaining the new Romanian president, her guest during his State Visit.

She was not best pleased. 'Was no attempt made to regain control of the ship immediately?' she asked.

'It was a surprise attack, Prime Minister, all over within the space of five minutes. Nearly all the *Aztec* crew had shore leave. *They* must've known that. And with all the tourists about we were lucky not to have more casualties than we got.'

'How many casualties?' she asked.

'Five.'

'Cowards!' Dodson presumed she meant the terrorists, hiding behind innocent women and children to gain their objective. She went on: 'Are you saying the ship was inadequately guarded in the first place?'

Dodson sighed. 'That is really an M.O.D. matter, Prime Minister.'

'Well, we're all in it now, aren't we? Can these terrorists get to the missiles?'

'We don't know that yet. We don't even know what *Aztec*'s present armament is – there's been no time to find out. But if they can penetrate her reactors we may be in for some trouble.'

'Information on this must be turned over as soon as possible. We are returning immediately to Downing Street. At five o'clock I want to see you, George, Basil, Sir Peter Kenton and whoever we can find from the Chiefs of Staff and the security services.' In other words, she would be forming an emergency committee of operations, headed by herself. 'We're not letting them get away with it, Jim,' she said, and rang off.

While the Prime Minister and her immediate *entourage* – minus the bemused Romanian president – flew from Chequers to Downing Street by helicopter, a police motor-cyclist with braying siren brought a recording of the demand received at Uxbridge. The P.M. sat forward in her chair as she listened, upon her arrival, examining at the same time a report compiled for her by the Met Commissioner Sir Peter Kenton.

She thought it a fairly educated-sounding American voice. Expressionless, but it meant business. So did she.

She spoke to the Chairman of the B.B.C. In view of the fact that news flashes had already been put out (which she deplored), a statement was going to have to be made. There was to be a complete embargo on further flashes, however, until after the five o'clock meeting. To what she sensed was a slight caveat in the responding voice of the B.B.C. Chairman, she said: 'I hope I don't have to go through with you at this moment the list of the powers I am invoking?' All tentative resistance to gagging ceased.

The various cabinet ministers with relevant responsibilities were summoned to Downing Street, together with their aides, the defence chiefs and high-ranking police officers. Each man, blameless in himself, expected blame to be dished out. No one was wrong on that score.

'Disgraceful,' said the P.M., 'that this should have been allowed to happen. You will all be held to account in your various ways. It is estimated that one dozen men boarded and took *Aztec*. A dozen men? How could that happen? I'd like to hear what the Defence Secretary has to say.' Basil Pennington, the plump Defence Secretary, paled and appeared to grow visibly smaller. But before he could open his papers the Prime Minister carried on speaking, unrestrainedly berating the man. 'When all this is over you'll have to go if you can't give a good account of yourself! Parliament will want your head and who'll be able to stop them? Me? We might all go down over this!' The senior cabinet members were discomfited at hearing themselves being blasted with politics in the presence of the non-cabinet personnel within the group, but the P.M. was clearly in a rage which overlooked such feelings and niceties. Poor Basil Pennington, as minister in charge of the department with direct responsibility, came in for much of the flak. For a while he saw himself back in Bedfordshire cultivating his cabbages. But not yet, as he realised. For the time being the government had to show total unanimity before all else. Then the Prime Minister had a go at each one in turn, not forgetting the Commissioner of her beloved police force, who was berated for not turning out enough men to begin with. 'It doesn't take clairvoyance to see that the arrival of a nuclear-powered foreign warship in the Pool of London requires a special detail. Why was this detail not provided?'

'With respect, Prime Minister,' Sir Peter began, and everyone looked to the one person in the room prepared to stand up for himself. Apart from being a popular Commissioner with the public and the force, he was probably the gutsiest man in the room, after the P.M. herself. He also had no political skin to lose. 'We did have men in the area, principally to guard against anti-nuclear demonstrators. They were of course unarmed and we knew of no reason why they should be otherwise. In any case the responsibility for guarding the actual vessel rests with the United States Navy, ma'am, not us.'

At least Sir Peter Kenton halted the steamroller of recrimination. The Prime Minister was clearly frustrated – as much over her own helplessness as the failings of her ministers. 'I want that ship retaken. I don't care how. I cannot hold the Press back for more than a couple of hours. All traffic has stopped on the Thames and everyone's aware something dreadful's happened. Without decisive action our credibility will be blown to the winds!'

An aide from the Defence Department tiptoed into the room and handed a piece of paper to Basil Pennington at the table. 'Prime Minister, if I might intervene? Much depends on the state of the *Aztec*'s armament and the ability of the terrorists to get hold of and utilise it,' said the Defence Secretary. 'I have here a medical report on the present state of Captain Weston, commanding officer of *Aztec*, who of course was ashore. I'm afraid he's gone into shock, possibly had a slight stroke, which was entirely unforeseen given his relative youth. He cannot be medically-cleared yet to give us precise and detailed information. His executive officer will not speak to anyone without clearance from the United States Navy in Washington.'

'I shall speak to the President about that,' said the P.M. 'Which I must do before he rings me,' she added, turning to her secretary.

'But,' persisted Basil Pennington, 'there is no question of our boarding the ship so long as the group in possession is capable of a missile attack – for all we know with nuclear warheads. Perhaps even now we're within their sights. They might be able to blow Big Ben off the face of the earth!'

'They ought to know what'll happen to *them* if they do,' snapped the P.M.

'But you risk full-scale melt-down if you blow up the vessel,' persisted Pennington. 'Full-scale melt-down in the middle of London?' His plump features pinkened. 'I will not continue to be a member of any government that contemplates such a possibility!'

Everyone turned to see how the P.M. would react to this outburst.

She leaned forward, smiled, and touched Basil Pennington's arm. 'Tempers are running a little high today, Basil,' she said in her huskiest voice. 'Of *course* there's no question of your resigning. I regret my earlier words. But something must be done. You *do* see that?' Basil's fire was drawn. He looked down at his fleshy hands, nervously fumbling with a blotter.

'Sir Peter?' The Prime Minister returned to business, but she now spoke with an almost serene sweetness, as if she might be asking if he took sugar. 'I take it the ship is now completely cut off?'

'Yes, ma'am. We've sealed her off. No one can get to her or away. Whoever they are, they're stuck there.'

'Well, at least we can do that. I want plans drawn up for the re-boarding of the ship, ready to be put into action as soon as word is given. I shouldn't think they'd want to blow themselves up, by the way?'

'We don't know who they are, yet,' said Jim Dodson. 'When we've had profile assessments we'll have more understanding of what group they're working for and what sort of men they are. At the present time we have utterly no idea. They could be religious fanatics.'

'With a taste for 100 million dollars,' commented the P.M. drily.

'That could be for some financing project, not personal gain,' replied Dodson.

'All this is speculation until we have something more definite to go on,' said the P.M.

'What about the demand?' asked Dodson.

'What about it?'

'Are you going to reply? The message is addressed to you, really.'

'I haven't yet decided what to do about that. We will have to stall. I know the risk, but we will have to. The implications of giving in to terrorism are so wide-reaching that we must do nothing precipitate, whatever hold they appear to have over us. It works both ways, you know. They may have the hold, but we have the gold.'

This little catch-phrase seemed to go down well. The meeting took on a slightly more cheerful aspect.

The Press Secretary, Barry Rogers, put forward a formula for a news item. This was to the effect that a small group of fanatics were staging a sit-in demonstration in one part of the American warship, and that although there had been initial casualties, there was no immediate danger to the public. The formula was accepted, apart from the deletion of 'fanatics' ('it presumes too much on our part,' suggested Pennington) and the deletion of the mention of no danger ('we never mentioned anything about danger in the first place,' said the P.M.).

The question of bringing the Opposition parties into the emergency was opened up. 'The Leader of the Opposition and the leaders of the other parties have been asked to a meeting with me this evening at eight o'clock,' said the Prime Minister. 'It is imperative that we seek a meeting of minds on this issue and speak with one voice. Parliament will plainly weigh-in later, as I said to you before. How we comport ourselves now will determine what they say then.'

With that, the meeting broke up. The Prime Minister decided it was time to speak to the Queen. The two spoke at some length by phone, from Downing Street to Windsor Castle. To the monarch, the P.M. was absolutely direct. It was potentially the worst crisis to hit London since 1940, or since the V-1 raids of 1944, at any rate. There was the outside possibility that a new government might have to be formed: the monarch would be kept in close touch with all developments. The Prime Minister met with a flat refusal when she suggested the Queen might remove to a more distant and safer location. The Queen declared that if anything were to unleash public panic, that might be it. She herself was even considering moving in closer, to Buckingham Palace, particularly if political and other matters intensified. Not noted for getting on together particularly amiably, the two seemed to draw nearer to one another in the crisis. Perhaps because each had respect for the other's courage, if nothing else.

The Prime Minister decided she would speak to the American President after her meeting of joint leaders of all the parties represented in the House.

This meeting proved a little stormier than the previous ones with colleagues and monarch.

It all arose from the P.M.'s suggestion that the matter not be brought before the House at the present time. 'When I said "present time" I meant the *immediate* present – until the situation becomes clearer,' she said, her voice rising against a tide of mutterings about 'muzzling democracy'.

'When do you suggest we make you once more accountable?' asked the Leader of the Opposition acidly.

The Prime Minister outfaced the jibe. 'I am always accountable,' she said. 'I have never been anything else. I was going to go on to suggest that if you and your nominees join me in the emergency committee we might be able to fight this thing together. We are about to become embroiled in what may turn out to be highly complex negotiations with these monsters, upon which the safety of our country rests. I cannot allow, nor can you, these negotiations to be openly debated in the Chamber. Judge me afterwards, if you will, but let us deal with the problem first.'

The Opposition Leader begged leave to consult with his Shadow Cabinet members before committing himself to any further action. After some discussion, they returned to the table and announced that they would accept membership of the committee.

'We are not yet ready to create anything like a National Government,' said the Prime Minister. 'It hasn't by any means been ascertained that the danger is sufficiently great for the elected government of this country not to continue making decisions on behalf of the people. It would therefore be constitutionally inappropriate for you to have a role other than as advisers and monitors of the situation,' she said, to more howls for her blood. The Leader of the Opposition, however, chose not to renew his earlier acidity. He sensed that time was marching on, and he told his troops so. He also said that a monitoring position was advantageous: they would be able to keep fully informed for the later Commons debate, and he agreed that constitutionally he and his colleagues had not yet been elected to act. Privately, later, he said a non-active role absolved his party from any mistakes made by the committee in their manoeuvres. The P.M.'s attempt to pull a fast one could well backfire.

With all that settled, and all these uncongenial politicians sent on their way, the Prime Minister got down to the business of what she was going to say to Washington.

Of course these particular set piece meetings were not all that took place during those first frenzied hours. Streams of people filed in and out, people high and low, informing the Prime Minister of this, informing the Prime Minister of that. She was beginning to feel like a punch-bag.

For immediate safety a Control Room was set up, deep beneath the Home Office, supervised by the Home Secretary Jim Dodson himself. It was here that the Prime Minister set up her command post for the duration.

'We're flying out naval experts to you at this very moment,' said the U.S. President over the hot line to the Prime Minister, by way of some slight mollification for the fact that *Aztec* was, indeed, armed with nuclear warheads, as he had just revealed to her.

For a moment she felt all the remaining strength she'd had up to then drain out of her body.

'Prime Minister?'

'I'm here, Mr President.' She recovered herself.

'It may not be as critical as it sounds. The warheads aren't actually on the missiles, they're stowed below. It would take a hell of an operation to arm them.'

'But it could be done?'

'Yes, I'm sorry, but it could be done. Anyway, your people will get a better idea of what they might be able to do when they see the *Aztec*'s plans.'

'What about the reactors? Can they be penetrated?'

'Take a hell of a lot of fire-power to puncture those things,' replied the President. 'My experts tell me that of course anything can be punctured if you have the right-sized slingshot for it. They could have that.'

So, at least two means of sending everyone to hell were available.

'You do realise we're totally unprotected here,' said the P.M.

'I am very, very sorry about it,' said the President.

'The guarding of that ship was your responsibility,' she continued. 'You leave me no option but to protest in the strongest possible terms at the extreme negligence involved.'

'We're still looking into that,' he replied circumspectly.

'A *dozen men*, Mr President, a *dozen men* hijacked your battle-cruiser! I believe three grenades were used,' she added cattily.

'We're sick about it here.'

'I should hope some heads are going to roll – perhaps your Defence and Navy Secretaries' for a start!'

'You can rest assured that appropriate action will be taken when there's been a full investigation. We'll be wanting to question the commanding officer Captain Weston, when he's able, over those guarding arrangements. But it strikes me you may be able to deal with the situation. Any number of ways. Wear 'em down, for a start. Exploit their differences and their tensions. And you can even accede to their demands if you have to. Have you considered actually paying over the 100 million?'

'It's under consideration.' It was the Prime Minister's turn to be circumspect.

'Well, it's an option,' said the President.

'Mr President, I hope you are aware of the implications if I give in to this extortion? Of course if you look at it one way, it's the easiest problem in the world. They want 100 million – you give them 100 million, and they go away. But they come back, Mr President: they come back as other groups, hijacking other things, demanding other forms of extortion. Why stop at 100 million? Why not go on and on until they have us all under their heel?'

'Remember what happens, though, if you don't consider the option. You could lose London. We lose some of our boys on board that ship – and I hope you're bearing them in mind, by the way – but you'll lose London. Who was it said, "Paris is worth a mass"?'

'You don't have to tell me what I would lose, Mr President,' said the Prime Minister. As if to soften her stance, she added: 'And I am truly concerned about the plight of your men on board the *Aztec*.'

There were other hot line calls. There was a fevered and confused conversation with the President of France, agitated over his own intelligence reports of the Thames situation and wondering aloud if nuclear attack or radiation would endanger life across the other side of *Le Manche*. 'There is no immediate threat to countries on the other side of the English Channel,' retorted the Prime Minister with more vociferousness than logic, deliberately invoking the British name for the slender body of water dividing the two nations of the *Entente Cordiale*. The presence on the line of an interpreter, who kept getting in the way just as the two leaders were making themselves half-understood to one another, didn't help.

There were more politely-exchanged and briefer conversations with the prime ministers of the Netherlands and Belgium, the two countries most likely to be affected, particularly by radiation. The Prime Minister reassured them, too, mentally crossing her fingers as she did so. An entirely unsolicited call came from the President of the Soviet Union, offering to put his own intelligence network at the disposal of Britain in the tracking down of the miscreants. This was the first sensible word she'd had internationally of the lot– and it reminded her that she was overdue for an Intelligence briefing. The Soviet President suggested the possibility that the plot might have originated in the Middle East and that perhaps pressure should be put on those governments to be candid. The Prime Minister had not had time to consider a Middle Eastern plot but it became in her mind a likelihood more and more plausible. She thanked the Soviet President and said she would keep him in touch with developments.

The Prime Minister of Ireland rang, ostensibly fearful of reports of possible westward drift of fall-out in the event of a nuclear attack on the south-east of England. The British Prime Minister, already besieged from so many other quarters, didn't even speak to him but put him on to the soothing Sir George Rayner, Foreign Secretary. The message came back that Irish Intelligence would be instrumental in helping if an I.R.A. connection were established. As reported by Sir George, the Irish Prime Minister was plainly afraid that it might *be* the I.R.A., and that a major catastrophe in London, with thousands of lives lost, would cause a terrible backlash against both the Irish Republic and the millions of Irish people living in England. The British Prime Minister so hated the man in Dublin that she wouldn't have spoken to him directly even if she'd had the opportunity – for fear of creating a diplomatic rupture between the two countries that would outlast this crisis and any other.

Yes, it was high time for a meeting with Control...

The assault on *Aztec* had of course taken 'C''s department entirely by surprise. Too late he learned from Paul Finningham that a gang had been assembled in Holland and appeared to be poised for some large-scale operation in Britain. Ports and airports were even now on alert, but now *Aztec* had been taken. 'If only we'd had a little more time,' he wailed to Paul prior to departing for Whitehall, 'even one more day!' Paul was feeling none too happy himself.

'Do you mean to tell me you knew nothing about this until my secretary telephoned your office?' asked the Prime Minister of her Intelligence chief in shocked disbelief. 'If *you* don't know what's going on then God help this country! Do you know where the first information on the hijack came from? From the C.A.A.! Perhaps I should transfer Intelligence operations to them! Nor do I enjoy receiving my Intelligence reports from the French! I gave you my full authority to track down these killers. I gave it to you as long ago as September. I don't recall that we have had any sort of briefing to speak of since that time.'

'There was nothing to brief you on,' said the wretched 'C', with a futile gesture of his wrinkled old hands. 'Believe me, Prime Minister, we have been ceaselessly chasing up every lead, in full co-operation with the C.I.A. and other agencies. We are at the very verge of discovery as to the identity of the ringleaders.'

'With whom we now have to negotiate it seems. And

negotiate without having an iota of knowledge about any of them whatever!'

'Fortunately, that's not altogether so,' persisted 'C'. 'We know of the existence, if not the exact identity as yet, of an ex-U.S. Army or Navy officer who is probably the ringleader and whose voice is probably the one on that tape. We know of two others, another American and a Russian, who are without doubt members of the same group. They appear to have a background in communications systems and nuclear weapons technology.'

'That's comforting, I must say,' sneered the P.M. 'What about the others?'

'We don't know yet, but information is trickling through all the time. Our collation of available material suggests they are not I.R.A., P.L.O., Black September, Red Brigade or any of the better-known terrorist groups. We don't believe the attack was Islam-inspired, although a Middle Eastern government may be behind it.'

'Which one?'

'C' held his silence. The Middle Eastern angle was pure surmise.

'So, you think you've established what they are not. What *are* they?'

'We think, as the message suggests, and as backed up by our investigations so far, that the motives are almost entirely mercenary.'

'Mercenary?' The Prime Minister was quiet for a moment, subdued at last. 'Mercenary. Does that mean they are rational?'

'We're putting our psychologists on to this even now,' said 'C'. 'When we can gain adequate profiles and identities, particularly that of the apparent American leader, it should be possible to give a complete reading on motive and mental outlook.'

'How long will that take?'

'Not long, once we have some kind of answer on the identification of this voice, which will link up with our other information on this person.'

'You will work round the clock on it. The responsibility for my briefing behind whatever negotiations we have to carry out will be entirely yours. Mercenaries. Yes. There's a weak link there somewhere. Mercenaries are men who fight for money, and only for money, when it comes down to it. But money isn't everything, is it?'

'No, Prime Minister.'

'Money doesn't make one do things against life and limb, not when the chips are down. They're not kamikazies – I'm sure of it! Yes, they've gone this far for the sake of 100 million dollars. But will they die for it? Actually die?'

'They may prefer death to lifelong imprisonment,' ventured 'C'.

'Or, equally, they may not,' said the P.M. softly.

'Prime Minister, I beg you not to take this idea too far. We simply don't yet know enough to hazard a scenario. On the face of it, yes, the objectives are mercenary, but who is to say what lies behind the action of leading, what to all intents and purposes is, as crazy and as grandiose an action as this one?'

'Well put, but what option does your reasoning leave me with at this present moment? Stalling, presumably, until you or somebody can come up with the key.'

'Prime Minister, I assure you from the bottom of my heart that we will leave no stone unturned until you have the information you require.'

'Make it as soon as you can. These people appear to require some sort of response before too long, and if they don't get it the consequences might well render all we have been discussing entirely academic.'

* * *

The question of a state of emergency came up. The Prime Minister argued that while all possible precautions should be taken, and the news media restrained, a state of emergency was premature until more was understood about the precise nature of the action. The question was tabled. War plans were floated, kites were flown: ideas such as floodlighting the two warships, or creating some irritant, such as constant noise, or helicopters buzzing overhead. The P.M., belligerent and running to form, was strongly in favour of provocative action, but found herself overwhelmingly outnumbered. The danger - not least to the remnant of *Aztec*'s crew imprisoned below decks - was one of provocation and too great a risk, in view of nuclear possibilities.

Sir Peter Kenton returned to Whitehall with his latest report, which in effect was nothing to report: the situation hadn't changed. There was no sign of life on board.

'Perhaps they've murdered each other,' said Jim Dodson, none too hopefully.

The P.M. had directed a request for a repetition of the original message to be sent to *Aztec* - a classic stalling manoeuvre. No response was picked up.

'They're waiting for an offer,' put in Clive Parris, who had been summoned along with other junior ministers. That seemed evident. How long would they wait?

Whatever ideas came up - an attack by Jaguars or P111's - flailed against the rock of the one answer: the *Aztec*'s nuclear capability and power, as well as the fate of the imprisoned Americans.

Contingency plans came in thick and fast.

There was the idea that the S.A.S. should board *Aztec* and use gas to immobilise the terrorists. But, again, the gang were in a position to do maximum damage to both the ship and to London if attacked directly. The Defence team came up with another proposal: frogmen might bore a hole below the water-line large enough to admit a small task force, entering the hull and closing bulkheads after them to seal off the immediate area. A company specialising in oil-rig rescue operations was contacted for advice and the loan of underwater cutting equipment and plasma-arc torches.

This idea was tabled for the time being, because of objections from the Admiralty, on grounds that the U.S. Navy would scarcely countenance the very real possibility of one of its finest and most modern battle-cruisers being sunk in the middle of the Thames. 'Excuse me, but may we have permission to cut a large hole in one of your battleships?' No, that wouldn't do at all. Better to pay over 100 million in gold blocks than sink 100 million in warship. The Defence experts insisted that the plan guaranteed the absolute safety of the battle-cruiser; the Admiralty wouldn't budge. Should the P.M. override the Admiralty? She might then have to consider how she was going to save the Special Relationship with the United States.

One small problem – far away from the concerns of Whitehall – had arisen with regard to the main bulk of the crew of the *Aztec* who had been given shore leave to see the sights and whose return to the ship was inevitable. More than a dozen large coaches were sent to the perimeter at Tooley Street to pick them up as they arrived, bewildered and in some cases argumentative, to take them to barracks such as Knightsbridge and Wellington, where they would spend an indefinite number of nights. One or two had heard of the disturbance and had turned up at the U.S. Embassy in Grosvenor Square instead.

Not far from where the Prime Minister sat in almost constant session, deep below the Home Office, was the Emergency Control Room. The atmosphere there was strangely calm. Although no one could possibly have foreseen the threat of nuclear action taking the form it had done, the Department was designed for such an emergency. Seated in the centre of a horseshoe-shaped console the Communications Controller from time to time raised his eyes up to those around him. He saw the full-time staff, now augmented by Military Police liaison officers. Although there was no outward sign of acknowledgement between individuals as they went about their duties, each had a specified role to play in this labyrinth of communications.

With its dozens of glowing lights, some steady, some flashing, in red, green, yellow, the Emergency Control Room was the core of a sophisticated communications network which linked the whole United Kingdom. The Home Counties' emergency organisations were on standby. If one particular large red light glowed it would mean the end of London.

The Prime Minister knew she had somehow to find time the following morning to visit the bereaved families and wounded victims of the assault on *Aztec*. She briefly and almost unconsciously rehearsed the face she would use for meeting the woman who had lost both son and husband in the affray.

Falling asleep at three in the morning after twelve of the most traumatic hours in her long career proved, strangely, to be no problem at all for her.

13

It now devolved on how long the attackers would be prepared to wait before they received a message of some substance replying to their demands. And upon what their true capacity for destruction really was.

Taking advantage of the silence from the *Aztec*, the government at least sought to gain the initiative in the propaganda war. Concerned to avert panic, a state of emergency was not called even though theoretically they were indeed in the midst of one. In news bulletins and reports, superbly orchestrated by Barry Rogers, the Press Secretary ('the only real genius in the administration,' as he was sometimes called), the band was referred to as a small group of fanatics, holed up in one section of the warship only, with no access to its more lethal areas (the danger element had finally been brought in, with the approval of a reluctant Prime Minister). No mention was made of any ransom demand – as far as the public was concerned, any demand was still being waited for. Also discreetly held back was the fact that the ship's nuclear reactors, though far too thickly cladded for any conventional penetration could – theoretically, at close-range – be pierced by say a Carl Gustav Recoilless Anti-Tank Gun. That gun could penetrate armour-plating of a thickness up to 1200mm, and *Aztec*'s reactor plating was rated at about 750. The M.o.D. experts could not agree on the likelihood or not of the gang actually possessing such a weapon. These guns were used by the Swedish, Czechoslovakian and a dozen other armies; there wasn't really any reason why they couldn't be found here. Surviving visitors from that fatal day on the *Belfast* were questioned over and over again, but although some did speak of rather bulky weapons they thought they had glimpsed, no one could be sure of what they were. Why should they? They were only tourists after all.

The Prime Minister had reason to be quietly grateful for the existence of the fifty-or-so men believed to be holed up below decks on *Aztec*. With stores and supplies they were not in any immediate danger, but they provided her with a public excuse as to why the ship should not be rushed: to the public some of them, at any rate, might be hostages. This neatly got the P.M. off the hook, publicly, over her uncharacteristic reluctance to do anything forceful.

In the constantly running emergency committee meeting, evacuation of London was considered: and ruled out for the time being as economically crippling. Besides, so run down were the public services (as compared to their scale in 1939 – the last real evacuation of the capital) that the possibility of the roads choked with private cars – probably at a total standstill for hours – would simply give rise to panic and anarchy. With the advent of wholesale private transport, a long-term trend enthusiastically endorsed by the present government, London was actually less mobile now than it ever was before World War II. Nevertheless, contingency evacuation plans were compiled based on expert evaluations.

Evacuation would only become a serious possibility if the public discovered what was really going on, and this was something the government was determined should not happen. Or that it should be delayed for as long as possible.

But supposing the attackers themselves should decide to 'go public'? So far they had broadcast only on emergency channels. What was to prevent them from proclaiming their demand openly, and announcing to the whole world what cards they actually held?

'We'll fight that battle when it comes,' said the Prime Minister. 'It is not yet in their particular interest for this to become more widely known. And we are building up our own messages to the people all the time on this matter. We should be able to counter anything spread by them.'

'Except that we will be telling lies, while they will be telling the truth,' grumbled old Lord Carnock, the former Lord Chancellor and now the P.M.'s increasingly cranky back room *guru*. 'And truth will out in the end.'

'Perhaps other developments will have taken place by then,' said the P.M., her tone softening a little in deference to the man who had once master-minded successful General Election campaigns.

For the time being, however, an operation resembling a pincer movement was put together between the P.M. herself and Barry Rogers. While Rogers relentlessly regaled the Press with stories and rumours about the possible identity of the fanatical faction clinging on to a small part of the warship together with its hostages, the Prime Minister was applying more strong-arm tactics in the back room with the newspaper proprietors and editors, the Chairmen of the B.B.C. and I.B.A., and one or two leading journalists. Together with her Home Secretary and Attorney-General, she outlined a battery of already existing laws and regulations that would be invoked should certain aspects of this crisis (which she did not spell out in detail) be reported. There was to be no mention of the extent of the hold over the ship by the attackers. There was to be no mention of the ship's nuclear power or the potential for utilising its weapons system against London. There was to be no mention of any transactions taking place, or thought to be taking place, between the attackers and the government. An embargo was placed on contact with the ship's senior officers and even with the men in the barracks. The P.M. had been informed that formal D-Notice procedure was inappropriate to the circumstances, which were utterly without precedent. To meet them, she asked instead for a code of practice to be drawn up between government and media. Offered plenty of copy by the beguiling Barry Rogers on the one hand, and threatened with criminal actions in the courts on the other, the chairmen, proprietors and editors agreed and signed the code. It was a black day for freedom of the Press, muttered one on the way out. But what else could they have done? Governments are powerful in emergencies.

Then there was a major problem which brought in the Chancellor of the Exchequer: the extremely sensitive antenna poking up from the City, which had its own way of finding out anything even slightly amiss with the world. The P.M. was much in conclave with the Chancellor and the Governor of the Bank of England, establishing measures that might have to be brought in to relieve the City as quietly as possible of any collywobbles. Should the crisis be prolonged, it was considered that fiscal measures might have to be introduced to have a more soothing effect on markets and uneasy stockbrokers than bland assurances. The Treasury would also be keeping a sharp eye on property prices: any possible plummet, particularly in the threatened region, would be an indicator of alarm. A crash on the Stock Market itself was a real possibility – another arm-twister, by the way, for the media people.

There was also the sensitive issue of the gold transfer. Fortunately the American president had offered to underwrite the 100-million-dollar ransom, as recompense for the failings of his navy. This was still under consideration – apart from being a windfall it might also mask sudden movements of money within British government Treasury operations, which would be necessary if the gold had to be derived from British government sources. The P.M. didn't like to face the issue. At this point she was still determined not to pay. But reluctantly she admitted it was necessary to have a fall-back position: one offered only by the presence of the gold itself.

What was happening, step by step, was that the British government was elaborating a gigantic hoax, on a scale infinitely greater than that of the subversive machinations of the hijackers. Was this the price that would have to be paid for maintaining the rule of law and order against terrorism? In other words, for law and order itself to be subverted by its own guardians? In a very short space of time, the country's Parliament had been excluded, its media gagged and its financial markets duped.

Despite all these elaborate measures, and as hours began to turn into days, a peculiar situation was developing. A feeling was arising, a feeling of growing estrangement between government and people. Life went on. People commuted as usual, watched television, drank and argued in pubs, went shopping. Other signs were detectable, however, of unease. More and more people were keeping extraordinarily mum about something. These included ambulance men, firemen, coppers on the beat, and administrators and members of the committees which co-ordinated their efforts – all sworn to secrecy with regard to the parts they would play in contingency operations. It was this atmosphere of secrecy that was cloaking public life. More than one sensitive soul began to feel that all the newspapers, television and radio were carrying out one great charade: that life going on as usual was, somehow, a charade.

But the government's efforts were aided in one respect: the British people maintained a propensity for turning away from the unthinkable. The destruction of London, the irradiation of the entire south-east of England, though the thought of it must have crept into the subconscious of more than one mind no matter how uninformed, was firmly pushed to the back. It couldn't happen, so it wouldn't. Perhaps it was the experience of seeing so many disaster movies and videos that neutralised fears. Cities like London and New York had been 'destroyed' so often on the screen that such a scenario was already old-hat, out of date. These films had exorcised fear, drawn its teeth, like the rituals of a primitive tribe inuring its members to danger from war or hunting. Yes, the sheer enormity of the possible scale of disaster was a factor on the Prime Minister's side. This, even more than the hoaxing operations, aided the government's cause. Even in the very midst of their growing unease – and perhaps because of it – the people *wanted* to believe the comfortable line that the government was doling out to them.

Jane, of course, had been watching the T.V. news with avidity like everyone else. The peculiar drama being played out on the Thames had hooked her as it had most of the general public. Like others she felt frustration when the news switched to some other item. The broadcasters kept promising more up-to-date news as it came in, but when the pictures of the battle-cruiser loomed once more, no real news was forthcoming. One oddity was that the usual on-the-spot reporter, clutching microphone to chest with the scene of the action behind him or her, was absent. As a journalist herself Jane saw that something about the coverage was remote, not quite right.

Humphrey Cathcart insisted on coming round to her

flat immediately. There was none of the usual polite request or invitation-angling about it. No, he couldn't tell Jane why on the phone.

He was hardly out of his coat and into the armchair with a whisky in his hand when he blurted out: 'That Barry Rogers is full of shit!'

'What do you expect from a smoothy like him?' said Jane, amused that a high-flyer like Rogers was now frustrating the best attempts of honest newshounds like Humphrey to earn honest livings.

'This *Aztec* business. It's a total fabrication. I've never seen anything like it, even with this government.' He took a large swallow.

'You mean it isn't going on?'

'It's going on, all right. My editor's just got back from Whitehall. Very select little gathering – Chairman of the B.B.C. and I.B.A., Lord Newburg, people like that. Bob wouldn't tell me at first but I got it out of him. Jane, it's bloody dynamite. That warship's got nuclear reactors and missiles on board.'

'But they said there wasn't any danger.'

'Don't listen to what "they" say. That's just Barry Rogers doing the job he's paid for. The government's scared. And I mean fucking scared.'

Humphrey wasn't normally a hard-core swearer. Something heavy sank to the pit of Jane's stomach.

'And it's no load of crazies on that tub, either. It's a highly professional gang of mercenaries who know exactly what they're at and what they want. And what they want is 100 million dollars in gold!'

'Or–'

'London gets it. Maybe the whole south-east.'

'But – but do you know what you're saying?'

'I've only got Bob's word to go on, apart from what feels like a very strange clam-up everywhere you go these days. I tried to get down to *Aztec* myself. They won't let you within miles of it. No reporters past Tooley Street. Nobody whatsoever.'

'There haven't been any reporters on television. Just pictures of the ship and a voice-over.'

'That's it. Now listen, Jane. You've got to get out. I mean really far out – away from London. Don't mess about. Just do it. Before the crush. Thank God Felicity and the boys are far enough away – I hope. I have to warn you, darling, because anything might happen.' Without thinking Humphrey had leant forward and was gripping her shoulders.

'Humphrey, don't panic for God's sake! I'll be all right.' But Jane's voice held little conviction. Humphrey's hands slid down her arms in release.

'I'm not panicking for me, Jane. Sooner or later this story is going to blow and I'm going to be in on it whatever happens to me. But you're young, you've got a real future. Christ – don't you see? They're holding the whole of London to ransom! And if they don't get what they want – wham! And can you see that bitch in Downing Street giving in to them? Get out, get out while you still can!'

Humphrey was behaving more wildly than Jane had ever seen him. She found she was calming herself by calming him.

'But these terrorists can't think they'll get away with it? An American battleship? What do they plan to do? Sail it away? With a crew of ten or whatever they are?'

'They're probably gambling on a safe-conduct by helicopter to some airfield or other,' replied Humphrey. 'Could I have another one of these?' He held out his glass, almost a command.

'Don't go too heavy on this stuff,' she said, pouring a stiffer one.

'I've never been more sober. They didn't tell Bob or

the others any details on the weapons systems of these battle-cruisers. So nobody – maybe not even them – knows if the terrorists can get at the missiles or not. They usually come up on a hoist but whether they can be operated from deck level, nobody is prepared to say. If they took bombs on board with them, of course, then that's it. Hiroshima Mon Amour.'

'But there's the crew locked up down below. Couldn't they switch off the electricity or the power or whatever to stop the missiles from being fired?'

'Nice one darling, but it's not that simple,' said Humphrey. 'There are emergency generators all over the place which could come on automatically. They're for use if the main supply is cut off by a hit. But all this is beside the point, Jane!'

She wanted to be alone now, to think things out. She sent him away with promises that she would keep her lip buttoned, pack her bags and let him know where she could be reached – when she knew herself.

In fact she had been preparing in her mind to leave London as soon as work would permit – at least for a day or two, to go to Baythorne Manor, at Paul's behest. But crisis or no crisis, she couldn't just walk off, like that. She was a career-woman in a tough, demanding job; the work was piling up and she had already taken off too much time here, there and everywhere.

It had not yet occurred to her that the crisis on the Thames was anything to do with her brother-in-law, Clive Parris, and indirectly herself. If it had, she might have made excuses and departed to Baythorne Manor with more expedition.

Crisis had given Clive Parris fuel for an unusual display of petulance.

'I'm sorry,' he said at the door of his London town house, 'I don't care who you are, I can't see anyone now. I'm expected at Whitehall for an urgent meeting with the Prime Minister.'

Evidently showing the minister one's identification wasn't enough. 'Do I have to explain my business on the doorstep, sir?' asked Paul Finningham.

'I don't have time to hear your business,' said Parris, who then started pushing the door to. Paul's foot got in the way. Parris pushed at it two or three times. Resignedly, he opened the door wide again. 'Look, I don't want to argue with you. You know who I am and presumably you know what's going on. No power in the land can stop me from seeing the P.M. So I suggest you come back another time. Ring my secretary.'

'That won't be necessary,' said Paul. 'The Prime Minister's office has already been told that there is likely to be some delay in your arrival. Not too long, I hope sir.'

'How dare you? Who do you think you are? Gestapo?' Well, the door was still open. Clive Parris was pinkening, darkly.

'Sir, we know the gravity of the situation. That's why we're here. If you'll let us in we'd like to play you a tape.' Paul's sidekick on this occasion, Mort Ridlake, stepped forward from the shadows. He was a tall, gaunt specimen of his breed whose high cheek-bones and long chin cast a more-than-slightly sinister air. He made no attempt to conceal a small cassette-player in his hands.

'Tape? What tape?'

'A tape of the ransom demand,' said Paul.

'Is that all? I've heard it,' said Parris.

'We'd like you to listen to it again.'

'What's the point?'

'We'd like you to hear it again, sir.'

There was a pause. Clive Parris had run out of puff. With a massive shrug he opened the door wider to let in the two agents, conducting them to his front sitting-room. It was dark and he switched on the lights, motioning them to sit down. He was a little disconcerted when they remained standing. 'After you, sir,' said Paul, with all the politeness of a very formal arrest. Heaving a sigh Parris sat down and without further preliminaries Mort Ridlake switched on the tape. The crackly voice of the American blared out of the cheap little speaker.

'I expect you've heard it on better-quality equipment,' said Paul after it was finished. 'Sorry about that.'

'Well?' asked Clive. 'What about it?'

'Can you give me the name of the person speaking on that tape?' asked Paul Finningham.

Instead of answering, Clive's jaw dropped open slightly. 'What makes you think I know who is speaking?' he asked.

'Mr Parris, for some time my department has been carrying out certain enquiries in connection with the *Aztec* capture. It's possible we might have got to the root of it without disturbing you, but recent events have forced us to speed up the investigation, which the Prime Minister has given top priority to. She was consulted before we came here to question you.'

'I – I don't believe you,' said Clive Parris, blustering. He began to perspire and looked as if his whole world was opening up beneath his feet. 'On what grounds do you make these insinuations?'

'I don't believe any insinuations have been made, Minister. But as for the enquiry, we think it may involve the question of the unfortunate death of your wife in Amsterdam.'

'What's that got to do with it? I've been over that time and time again with the police.'

'We have reason to think the voice here belongs to someone we also traced to Amsterdam. Someone who goes by the name of "Scottie" or "Scott".'

'What's in a name?' said Clive, attempting a poor show of lightness, 'Scott – could be his first, last or middle. So you think he might have been my wife's murderer? How am I supposed to know him?'

'I didn't say we'd established him as her killer, and I'm not saying you know him.'

'What else could you be implying?'

'On what grounds do you say that this is the voice of your wife's murderer, sir?'

Clive Parris stood up and began wandering about. 'I said no such thing; you're putting words into my mouth. I expect you're good at that.'

'Mr Parris, do you know who he is?'

'No, of course I don't. How could I? The idea's preposterous – I'd have identified him as soon as I heard the tape if I had known. I've a good mind to complain to Downing Street about this harassment.'

Paul didn't bother to tell him that it might be unwise to take the issue further. The implications for Clive's future political career were none of his business. When 'C' had informed the Prime Minister that the questioning of Clive Parris was vital to the *Aztec* enquiry alarm bells rang in her head. Paling at the thought of consequences she cared not to think through at that time, she merely cautioned 'C' to be discreet and to keep her informed of developments. She hoped that an arrest was not imminent. 'C' told her that they were a very long way from that.

Paul looked hard at Clive Parris while Mort Ridlake quietly put the cassette-player back into his pocket. If only he could have lasered his way into that brain to find out what was hidden there!

Parris had sat down opposite Paul now. He seemed to have regained some of his composure.

'Do you have any more questions?'

'Only the one, sir.'

'Well, I know a good many Americans, but I don't recognise that voice. I find it extraordinary you should see some link between these terrorists and my wife's death. I don't suppose you'll tell me what you think that is?' Paul remained silent. 'No, I thought not,' continued Parris. 'All sorts of strange things can happen in a city like Amsterdam, can't they? They must have at least one murder a day. Drugs, that sort of thing.'

'Are you suggesting your wife's murder might have been drug-related, sir?'

Clive Parris gave a slight shrug. 'Possibly there was a drugs-crazed element. My wife was a spirited woman. She might well have put up a struggle with some maniac. Or perhaps she died because she had nothing on her worth robbing.'

'I believe you suggested the possibility of robbery when you spoke to the police originally,' said Paul.

'Yes I did, as a matter of fact.'

'If you're in a hurry to get back to Downing Street, we won't detain you any longer,' said Paul, rising.

Clive Parris jumped up as if this were his cue. 'I suppose so, if you're finished.' He was friendly now, positively jovial. They even shook hands in farewell on the doorstep. In fact, he and the agents were leaving the house at the same time.

As Paul watched him drive down the street in his purring Porsche, one thought bored through his mind.

The man was a lying bastard.

14

Scottie received one message for clarification of his original signal. He received a further one. Both of these he ignored. He knew them to be standard stalling devices. At this stage silence was the most ominous reply, the one calculated to get finger-nails bitten. The last thing he wanted to put across was that he was in a hurry to reach a quick agreement.

He kept his observers hawk-eyed. So far there had been no attempt to rush the ship, though the early occasion, when the gang saw police swarming over the *Belfast* and then loud-hailing them, had him wondering for a moment: would they be so stupid?

Of course they would have been absolutely right to rush the ship then, if at all, for his defences weren't yet in place, nor his ability to use any of the *Aztec*'s destructive power. But they had faltered and stopped short of that, probably in the fear of reprisals against his sailor hostages. Strictly speaking, Scottie didn't have any hostages; he had men imprisoned below decks, but the two parties were cut off from one another. This was distinctly advantageous. It meant that there was none of the distraction involved in keeping live hostages in their midst; at the same time the outside world would feel that the gang had the power of life and death over the sailors, which of course in one way they had.

The news coming from the ship's radio on the broadcasting frequencies was good. Sufficient concern and plenty of coverage, if of a superficial kind. The stories evoked quite a few laughs – over the nature of the 'fanatics', particularly; and a fair number of protests when they were told how harmless the 'sit-in' occupation was. 'If it's all that harmless,' cried Maxton, 'why the fuck don't they invade the bloody ship?' Scottie wondered how long the public would believe these stories. When the time was ripe, and the news had run out of stories and credibility, he might well choose to do a little broadcasting himself – just to put everyone in the picture.

The French and other foreign stations were a little more sensational (Figac was, of course, the expert here). Here in Britain the good old B.B.C. kept everything to dignified proportions, granted the outright lies and fabrications being perpetrated in the name of public information. Even Scottie was a bit surprised at the extent to which a government could lie. It pleased him: the bigger the whoppers the more he knew he had them on the run. But it also chilled him a little: a government prepared to go in for that much distortion would stoop to any number of other 'dirty tricks' too. That was why everything had had to be planned and calculated, 'down to the last toothpick'. You would not be able to trust the bastards one inch.

He was also surprised – and pleased – that no one had apparently yet tumbled to his own identity, though reports had spoken of a man named Scottie or Scott who might or might not be the ringleader. Still, it was only a matter of time before they found out who he was, even though he'd been covering his tracks around the world for years.

Morale within the gang was high. A kind of peace had descended now that the strike-force was settled in for the duration. But the vigilance could not be relaxed, and watches were set up along strict hours with more than a touch of old-fashioned naval discipline. Maxton sent Figac and a small party on a tour of the hatches from time to time, to 'make sure none of that lot down there come popping up like t'devil through t'trapdoor at a pantomime.' Maxton enjoyed stamping about in his new-found role of Master-At-Arms. Never mind the tension, the waiting and watching. He was thoroughly enjoying himself.

Scottie Moore was waiting for Lavitzsky and Booth to sort out the systems so that his next message – when he finally decided to send one – would have some real force behind it. He didn't want to pressurise these hothouse flowers too heavily while they figured out what to do from the training manual, studied the diagrams, put two and two together. But it didn't hurt to let them know he was around, and to saunter to the operations room to see how things were going.

Aztec had two missile rocket launchers, one on the foredeck and the other at the stern. In the operations room the two systems were quite independent of one another. On a normal voyage, the director of operations would sit in the centre with separate controls on either side of him. On a previous visit, Scottie had seen Lavitzsky admiring the radar cabinet as if it were his prize orchid. 'There must be a large dish aerial and high frequencies, together with mono-pulse operations,' he was mumbling to himself. 'And two small microwave dish antennae for missile command transmission...'

At first Scottie had wondered whether Warren Booth, working alongside the Russian, would crack under the pressure – denied the inoculation of alcohol. He needn't have worried. Warren's face retained its pallor but he was obviously fascinated with the technology confronting him. He actually smiled for the first time since the attack when Scottie looked in now.

'How's it going, Kid?' asked Scottie, softly. He didn't want to break Lavitzsky's concentration.

'Shouldn't be long,' replied Warren. 'Scottie, I think we've just about got it cracked.'

'Glad to hear it, Kid.'

'What's happening out there?'

'Nothing compared to what's going on in here. If you're not giving me bullshit–'

'Would I do that?' said Warren, with a smile and outstretched arms.

'Well, if you're not, this could be the breakthrough. How long before we can launch?'

Warren's smile vanished; his arms went down. 'You're not going to do it, Scottie?'

'No, Kid, I'm not going to do it. Not unless I have to. For all our protection.'

'But once that happens they'll fire everything they've got at us!'

'You leave the strategy to me, Kid,' said Scottie. 'It's a war of nerves, not of weapons. But we need the weapons to fight the war. In case you'd forgotten why you're here.'

'I hadn't forgotten.' The corners of Warren's mouth turned down, the same expression he'd had when glimpsing the body of the small child on *Belfast*'s deck. Scottie put an arm around his shoulder.

'I know how you feel about the kid,' he said. 'I feel the same way. Do you think I wanted a little boy like that to get hurt? He was unlucky. So are about a million kids starving in Africa. See? You have to put these things in proportion.' Warren looked down; Scottie couldn't see if his brand of logic was getting through or not. 'We'll be away from here by this time day after tomorrow,' he continued. 'With 100 million in gold. No way can they stop us now, Kid. I think we'll get this system set up for conventional warheads. That might allow for a little demonstration.'

'Demonstration? You're crazy, Scottie!'

At that moment Warren's voice was all but drowned

out by the roar of a helicopter, hovering not far above the ship. At first these 'copters had kept their distance; now they were becoming bolder by the hour, intrusive.

Scottie rolled his eyes upwards, then down at Warren again, and grinned. He left the room.

'So it seems you got precisely nowhere with him,' said 'C', whose hands gripped the blotter of his desk as if to keep him upright in his chair. 'The P.M. is demanding a report on Parris as soon as we have anything – a report to which she is fully entitled, by the way, we having alarmed her to this extent.'

'I needed to see him face-to-face,' said Paul. 'I know he's lying.'

'Is that the most you can say? She'll love that. "One of our agents has a feeling that Parris is lying". And I can just hear her reply: "Is that all you have to show for six weeks of investigation? Crowned with dragging one of my ministers through the mud?" '

Paul sought to steer the conversation along more constructive lines. 'What's happened about the Polar Bear Frozen Food Company?' he asked. 'Have the police got anywhere yet?'

'They've arrested one of their drivers,' said 'C'. 'Claims he knows nothing – just a supplier to mysterious contacts, thought it was a bank robbery. The police have given him the third-degree and he's scared enough, but all he's been able to divulge is a description of this blessed American. No name, of course. Nothing as simple as that! So, another dead-end, it seems. Paul, unless we come up with this man's identity, and whatever organisation is backing him and his gang, we're finished. All of us – you, me, a few others. You don't think the P.M. is going down without dragging us with her?'

'I couldn't care less about that,' said Paul angrily.

'Well, you may not. You may not. Some of us happen to care about the credibility of the Service!'

'There's only one thing I care about,' said Paul, 'and you should know what that is.'

'How long do you think they'll go on giving you and me the power to do anything about it?' declared 'C'. 'Find that ringleader's identity, Paul. Find it *now*! We must know who we're dealing with. Sooner or later – and sooner rather than later at this rate – we've got to start negotiating with him. We have to know who he is, his background, his psychology, everything. *Intelligence*, Paul. It's called *Intelligence*. Our department. Nobody else's. Ours.'

Paul caught Jane Illingworth in the act of packing to go to Baythorne.

'At last,' he said.

'What do you mean "at last"? I haven't had a chance to leave London till now. There is such a thing as work'

'To tell the truth, I'm just glad you are going.'

'You're the second person to say that,' said Jane as she folded a skirt.

Paul looked up. 'What? Who else has been saying anything?'

Too late, Jane had let the cat out of the bag. She found herself forced to tell Paul about Humphrey and his warning. There wasn't any point in saying that her relationship with Humphrey had nothing to do with Paul, or to start going into some long-winded explanation. Strangely, Paul didn't seem in the mood to go into it, either. And suddenly the penny dropped.

'This business about Clive is all about what's going on in the Thames, isn't it? That's what you've been investigating all along! The thing you said you didn't know was going to happen!'

Paul stood in the middle of the room, staring straight in front of him, as if he was about to have a seizure.

'What is it?' cried Jane, now thoroughly terrified. 'Paul, what is it?'

'My God,' said Paul, and then he had to sit down. 'I got it. From the horse's mouth!'

'What?'

'From Clive himself! To me. And I've been so preoccupied chasing my own bloody tail I didn't even take it in. "Could be his first, last, or middle."'

'I haven't a clue what you're talking about.'

'No, of course you haven't. Don't worry,' said Paul, standing up. 'You'll be safe enough at Baythorne. We've still got our eye on Parris – if you're worried about his returning there we'll give you plenty of warning. I have to go. I have to make an urgent call.'

'Do you want to use my phone?'

'It's to Amsterdam. Do you mind? I'll see you reimbursed.'

Jane laughed at the idea of worrying about a few pence at a time like this. Paul, talking into the receiver, was so avid to speak to someone called Andy Hartford in Amsterdam that he seemed oblivious as to whether she was about or not.

'Andy? That you? Thank God.'

'Things hotting up over there?' asked Andy at the other end.

'The Thames is boiling, all right.'

'Well, you still got your job or you wouldn't be ringing,' said Andy drily.

'Hanging in there,' said Paul. 'Listen, Andy. We've made a balls-up. Over checking your ex-services lists. Stupid. As amateurish as Watergate.'

'Sounds bad.'

'The name Scott – remember? It came up. Well look, it's neither a Christian name nor a surname. It's a middle name. That's why it didn't come up on the computers, or if it did we weren't looking for it.'

'I guess so,' said Andy. 'It could've slipped through that way. I still think "Scott's" a nickname or an alias.'

'It doesn't matter what you think. We're desperate over here. Just run another check on the dischargees.'

'I'll get right back to you on it,' said Andy.

'I'll be at my own number in half an hour,' said Paul.

'It'll take a little longer than that, but we'll talk.' Andy rang off.

Paul gave Jane a hurried kiss and flew out of the flat.

'We got him,' said Andy on the line from Amsterdam. 'Nailed him right down. Profile fits – everything down to the last filling.'

'Who is he?' asked Paul excitedly.

'Lieutenant Abel Jeffrey Scott Moore.'

'Aha!'

'Ex-Lieutenant. U.S. Navy. Forty-three years old, born Schenectady, New York; naval tradition in the family, fourth generation to enter U.S. Naval Academy at Annapolis. Graduated, no particular distinction, good at sport. Brought before the Board for cheating at exams, but they couldn't make the charge stick. Received commission, not a spectacular service record. Then court-martialled – get this – court-martialled for hazarding his ship in Chesapeake Bay through negligence. Received a severe reprimand, resigned his commission, walked out on his wife and daughter, and disappeared.'

'How long ago did he disappear?'

'Five years. Believed he may have been a mercenary in various theatres of war since then. The F.B.I. think he may be the same as that Jarvis character in El Salvador we were talking about.'

'Why do *you* go for him, Andy?' Paul had to be sure.

'Right age. Experience in handling warships. Looks like a chip on his shoulder all his life. And no sign of him since. Anybody pursuing a legitimate line should have turned up before now, don't you think?'

'Maybe he's dead.'

'So? Where's the record? All right, so they don't keep records in the steamy jungles of Central America. But some disappearance would have been notified somewhere along the line. My money's on him, anyhow. He's the hottest so far. Could be called Scottie. All the right background. What more do you want?'

'Fax the details over here as soon as you can.' Paul was about to hang up. 'And thanks, Andy. Let's hope it's in the nick of time.'

'Stay cool, pal.'

Paul then got straight on to 'C' with this new information.

Further confirmation arrived which made it certain. Moore's deserted wife was quickly traced by the F.B.I. They played her the voice-tape sent to Uxbridge. She identified the voice as being that of her missing husband.

Now she was being flown to Britain – reportedly in a fair old state of shock – by the U.S. Air Force.

The F.B.I. coughed up supplementary information. After he left the U.S. Navy Abel Scott Moore drifted to New York City. He stayed in the same rooming house as Warren Booth, the down-and-out ex-communications expert from Neptune, believed to be on board *Aztec*.

With that, the last pieces of the jigsaw fitted into place. Now the enemy was known.

* * *

There was just enough wind blowing along the Thames from west to east to send tiny waves against the hulls of the two warships. That and the dismal sound of the ensign at the stern of the deserted *Belfast* slapping against the staff were the only noises coming from the vessels. In the light of dawn they were hardly distinguishable.

Downstream, Tower Bridge stood out, gaunt and soaring, silhouetted against a sickly yellow sky which was streaked with pink clouds – pink above but jet-black underneath. It had been raining and there was the promise of more to come. The Met. Office was making no predictions as to whether the cloud-belt would clear south-east England and the London area before the start of the Remembrance Service at the Cenotaph at eleven o'clock.

Soon barriers would be set in place along Whitehall on either side of Lutyens' memorial. And some time after that the crowds would start to form behind those barriers.

It was going ahead. The government had fallen into its own propaganda trap. Having – with the connivance of the opposition – kept all real information as to the extent of the true danger in the Thames from the people, there was no way in which it could suddenly cancel a ceremony of national prominence such as this one. The Prime Minister was positively defiant about it. To cancel a Remembrance Day ceremony was itself a criminal act, an act of compliance with terrorism.

Some people in the know were wondering privately who was madder – the gang holding the warship in the Thames or the Prime Minister? Aloud, they objected that to expose thousands of people, not to speak of the nation's ruling political establishment and the Royal Family itself, to such immediate danger was nothing short of folly. To which the Prime Minister replied that if what they knew about the range of the ship's missiles were true, there would be just as much danger if the ceremony was held in Epping Forest, Shepherds Bush or Luton. But cancelled it would not be.

Moreover she had two important supporters: the Leader of the Opposition, not to be outdone in the courage-stakes, was of the same mind as herself, and so was the Queen. The Prime Minister did indeed make one more attempt to plead with Her Majesty to let someone else stand in on this occasion, but the Royal rebuttal was unanswerable. Why should she and her family be more shielded than any marching veteran? In any case, a Remembrance Day ceremony without the Monarch was like a chicken without a head.

Without any doubt in her mind, but taking a deep breath all the same, the Prime Minister had announced the decision to proceed with the ceremony as planned.

Waleski came to rouse Scottie. Waleski was a blond young man who came from the land he had once known as Rhodesia. His family had farmed there for three generations until they were wiped out in a massacre. He had been away in training as a boy-cadet at the time.

'Time to get up, Mr Moore. Situation meeting.'

'Right,' said Scottie, yawning. He stretched and got out of his cot. It was the first real sleep he'd had since taking *Aztec*, and after a little grogginess, he felt fine. In fact his mind was suddenly and wonderfully clear.

'They didn't say anything about not having the Remembrance Day ceremony at the Cenotaph,' said Waleski. 'According to the news, they seem to be going ahead with it.'

'Oh they are, are they?'

When Scottie got to the operations room Schiele handed him a slip of paper. It had just come in on the ship's radio.

Request further detailed information on demands.

It was terse but it was enough. They had stopped repeating requests for clarification in parrot-like fashion. They had moved the game one stage forward.

They were ready to talk.

Scottie gave a whoop which startled everyone. 'We're in business! Now, what's the launch situation?'

'Ready to go into operational mode,' said Lavitzsky.

'Well, don't look so cheerful about it, you guys!' said Scottie. Everything was starting to come together. The realisation of all his plans.

'I'm sorry. I have been up all night on it,' said the Russian, gesturing limply.

'Me too,' said Warren Booth.

'You've done *great*, you know that?' said Scottie, half-hugging Lavitzsky from behind. Lavitzsky was like a sack of potatoes. But he managed a smile. 'Look, you and Warren go and get some rest. Operational when I call.' The two experts didn't need any more prompting and left the room. Scottie turned to Maxton. 'Any sign of frogman activity?'

Maxton shook his head. 'We're keeping our eyes peeled,' he said.

'Good. But I don't expect it to happen. They'd have to climb over the rail and we'd pick 'em off then.'

'What if they cut a hole in the ship down the side?' asked Maxton.

'What, and sink her?'

'They've got watertight compartments down there, haven't they?'

'So they get in – then what? They're still below decks, like the others. They still got to come up through the hatches – hell, even they've thought of that one. They won't try it unless things get desperate. What about sharpshooters?' Scottie turned to Hakayama.

The Japanese had seen service in terrorist assaults on Tokyo's Narita Airport, and in Sri Lanka and Africa. When he wasn't likely to be picked off as a target he wore a white headband that made him look like a latter day *samurai* warrior, which is perhaps what he thought he was. 'We been scanning the whole area with the infra-red binoculars,' he reported. 'Can't see anyone so far.'

'They're there,' said Scottie. 'You know it and I know it. They're there all the time, just waiting for a head to show.'

The first of the day's helicopters was roaring in the distance. Scottie went to the porthole to take a look at it. There it was, some way off beyond Tower Bridge. Like the others had been, it was the small sort, probably used by the police normally for traffic surveillance.

Surveillance.

By now the street lamps on Tower Bridge and London Bridge were paling to nothing against the sun's light spreading across the whole sky, catching the windows of the stacked-up ice-cube trays of the City. There had been no lights on Tower Wharf all night, presumably to make it easier for the marksmen during their long, cold vigil.

Scottie chuckled. They'll just have to wait a little longer. Maybe a lot longer.

The helicopter, flying without lights, moved in an arc, above and behind the Tower. Then it hovered again over the river beyond Tower Bridge.

And Scottie suddenly realised what it was doing. He called for Lavitzsky and the others to make ready. They didn't have long.

* * *

Gathered at the Cenotaph on that fitfully sunny Remembrance Sunday were Royalty, the Prime Minister, members of the Cabinet, leaders of the opposition parties, High Commissioners of Commonwealth countries, heads of the armed forces, more notables and a crowd of onlookers. What intermittent light there was glinted on the instruments of the Guards' band. Out of the Home Office building came the choristers of the Chapel Royal in their red and white surplices, followed by the Bishop of London. The entire ceremony was under-way as planned, except for the quiet omission of the detachment of American sailors from U.S.S. *Aztec*. The solemn tones of Elgar's *Nimrod*, Chopin and the *Last Post* fell gently on the vast, silent gathering.

The wreaths were laid. And then, to mark the anniversary of the eleventh hour of the eleventh day of the eleventh month of the year in which 'the monstrous anger of the guns' had died away in Flanders and northern France, Big Ben sounded the chime.

The helicopter was drawing nearer to *Aztec*. They were photographing it, charting the means by which the dish-aerials and the command apparatus might be taken out in a single, swooping operation by some of their brethren in rather more formidable craft.

They meant to disarm *Aztec* without causing too much serious damage to the hull.

Scottie saw it all in a flash. They must've got permission from the U.S. president.

So *that* was their game!

* * *

The resonance of the last of the eleven chimes of Big Ben died away. The Two Minute Silence commenced, and the only sound to be heard now was the rustling of leaves from the plane trees, curled like the talons of birds, blowing along the roadway in the wind.

The Prime Minister closed her eyes in silent prayer.

In the midst of that strange peace, there was a distant explosion.

'Bull's eye!' yelled Scottie Moore. 'Fuck me, we got it!'

Hit by a missile with a conventional warhead from *Aztec*, the small helicopter with its doomed crew – or what was left of it after the lot had turned into a flaming, crackling ball – fell into the Thames. With the impact on the water came a huge hiss of steam and what sounded like a death-rattle as it sank below the waves.

'Right in the middle of their Two Minute Fucking Silence!' shouted Scottie. 'Maybe now they'll start talking turkey!'

'Maybe now they'll sink us,' whispered Warren Booth, who had joined him at the porthole. 'Scottie, what have we done?'

'No going back now, Kid. It'll stop our aerials from getting knocked out, anyhow – and stop anybody else from getting too close, I guess,' he added, drily.

Perhaps the ghost of a thought of the desecration of Remembrance Day passed through the mind of ex-Sergeant Maxton, if only because he'd stood through so many Remembrance Sunday ceremonies himself. But whatever came to him just then quickly passed. Scottie was right. There was no going back now.

The frenzied preparation hadn't left anyone on the *Aztec* time to think about what was happening. Now it had happened. It was going to be a new ball game from now on. Unconsciously the gang observed its own Two Minute Silence.

Scottie let it all sink in, before he spoke again: 'Good work. They know our capability. There won't be any more fucking around. They're not going to try and board us, because they don't know what we'll do next. They're not going to try to disarm us with a little light bombardment because they know we can hit back. They're not going to try to blow us up because of the boys down below. We're sitting pretty, as long as we keep our nerves and don't do anything stupid. Don't stop keeping your eyes peeled the whole fucking time. And let me handle the negotiations. That's what I'm here for. You do your jobs and I'll do mine. We're okay for rations for a long time to come yet. The boys below are okay for theirs, so we don't have to worry too much about them. I'll run through the transfer drill with you again soon. And we've got a little technology to help us after we vacate the ship, don't we, Warren?' Warren Booth nodded, looking down at his feet.

'I know what you're thinking, and you're right. If they could get their hands on us, any of us, they'd string us up on the nearest lamp-post, doesn't matter how bloody British and decent they think they are.'

Warren spoke up. 'Is that what you intended? To raise the stakes, to make them hate us, so we'd all fall into line?'

'I hope you're not going to get out of line, Kid. Just remember one thing: you've got real blood on your hands now.'

'We all have.'

'Yes, that's right. We all have. Share and share alike.' He grinned.

* * *

Those gathered at the Cenotaph who had more inkling of what was going on knew it hadn't been a sonic boom, as most of the crowd seemed to think. There was a perceptible tautening of the Stiff Upper Lip.

Was a mushroom cloud about to loom next?

Flinching at the noise, the Queen stood her ground thereafter like a monument. The aide holding his piece of paper fluttering in the breeze perspired, wondering whether to rush out to the Prime Minister there and then. He was restrained by someone who told him the ceremony was on national television. On no account could the image of solid Britain be shattered during those solemn moments. The aide was only allowed to go out when the processions had started. Camera crews were instructed to avert their lenses from the Prime Minister and the government party for the rest of the proceedings, and the commentators for both T.V. and radio were similarly restricted.

'So what happens next, Scottie?' asked Warren. His tone was half rebellious and half curious.

The pale eyes turned and regarded him, almost glittering. Since the shooting-down of the helicopter something new had come into Scottie's manner. What? Omnipotence? Megalomania?

'You wait and see. You ain't seen nothin' yet.'

'I need a drink,' said Warren. 'I *really* need one, no kidding.'

'All this excitement going on, and the man needs alcohol?'

'I will not stand idly by and watch while they blow up our helicopters and our capital city!' shouted the P.M. down the telephone.

'You must not, repeat not, assert more drastic action against *Aztec*!' Thus came back, across the Atlantic, the steady, southern-tinged voice of the American president.

'Mr President, I have a people to defend and a House of Commons to face.'

'I am aware of your political problems, Prime Minister, and you must protect your people the best way you can. We will continue to give you every assistance. I have personally authorised the gold shipment to you, as you know. I'm doing everything I can for you to get this thing scaled down.'

She had been prominent on the world scene for more than a decade. She had been running her country when he had been nothing more than a Federal agency director.

And now he was virtually ordering her to pay.

Already she could tell how he was manoeuvring: blamed initially for the errors of his navy in the inadequate guarding of a warship subsequently lost to a humiliating twelve men, the American president was getting ready to groom himself as the peacemaker who had settled the problem without violence. While she would be made out as the irresponsible warmonger. This situation would never have arisen with his predecessor!

The point was this: was she to give into terrorists just so he could pull his political chestnuts out of the fire?

'You know that our concern for the future of London is uppermost in our minds,' said the president. In a pig's eye. His predecessor would have meant it. This man was entirely hollow, through and through.

'Mr President,' she began, a trifle wearily, 'there is much preliminary work to be done before we can talk directly to these people. I am not going to sell our country down the river – at the very least let me scrutinise every single possible option before doing something that future generations will construe as that?'

'Your caution is laudable – so long as you can hold back public feeling in the meantime.' Was he, perhaps, worried that if she provoked a major crisis he would go down with her, possibly through impeachment? 'But sooner or later you will have to reach a settlement with them – whatever you're able to do afterwards. My analysts tell me that they hold virtually all the cards.'

'They don't hold the gold, Mr President, and it is the gold that they want.'

'How long are you prepared to let them wait for it? How long are they prepared to wait?'

'Before doing what?'

'Blowing you and themselves to kingdom come, maybe,' said the president. 'I must say from this side it looks a strong possibility.'

'I don't think you are in a pos–'

'All I want is your assurance that you will not do anything drastic that would destabilise the situation,' he said, interrupting her. 'Do I have that assurance?'

At last she was paying the real price for having upheld the Special Relationship for so long. She was paying the price for hitching Britain so firmly to America's coat-tails. What she had been virtually ordered to do went against everything she stood for – went against the very *grain* of her personality. 'You have that assurance, Mr President,' she said, her voice seeming to come from somewhere else. She hung up. She had been told what to do by a president who was not worthy of a junior portfolio in her cabinet.

After the helicopter incident it was no longer possible to deny the lethal capability of U.S.S. *Aztec* in these hands. What couldn't be masked, either, was the evident ruthlessness of the gang. Only the nuclear aspect continued to be played down – but the implications would soon be running rife, with rumour and counter-rumour abounding.

An operation long-planned was now put into effect. The immediate vicinity on either side of the Thames, the Tower, Tower Bridge, all the flats, hotels and workplaces were evacuated. All the streets were cleared and barred.

Eyes looked towards the Palace of Westminster and the Whitehall ministries – so easily within range of *Aztec*'s missiles.

The House of Lords packed up altogether for the duration. The House of Commons voted itself off television and went into secret session at an undisclosed underground location not far away. There, the whole matter was debated openly for the first time. The Leader of the Opposition rallied the troops to stand behind the Prime Minister in this hour of crisis. While this proposition was accepted in general, there were a number of queries and ideas put forward for the solving of the crisis, dividing opinion more or less between the position of hawk and the position of dove. The Leader of the Opposition was quite aware that a certain provisional support now would earn him and his party credit, without necessarily tying his hands later when the time came for more ruthless dissection of the government's handling of the situation. The Deputy Prime Minister relayed his thanks on the government's behalf and sent also the P.M.'s apologies to the House for her absence, for understandable reasons. She would give a full account of herself at the Dispatch Box when the situation let up. Parliament resolved to sit in continuous session as the drama unfolded.

The Prime Minister and her advisers ruled out the possibility of a missile attack, or any other kind, while the subject of 100 million dollars in gold was on the table. The idea was to keep it on the table as long as possible, until all alternatives to giving in had been thoroughly explored.

What was worrying was the possibility that another target might be selected – Big Ben, perhaps? – for *Aztec*'s missiles, should the government be perceived by the terrorists to be dragging its feet. It was finally agreed to follow up any reply to the most recent request for clarification of the demands with a statement which made it sound as if dialogue was being pursued.

It would be difficult at this stage to say who was more in control of the situation, the Prime Minister – or Scottie Moore.

15

The waiting round the radio was growing intolerable. Scottie was sure they would be coming through again at the specified time. But that time passed, so they had to wait for the next one.

Just when the minute was almost over, and Scottie had given up hope of contact, there was a crackling over the loudspeaker.

His heart rose to his throat. This was it. The other side were coming through.

'Calling U.S.S. *Aztec. Aztec,* please acknowledge.'

It was a very ordinary impersonal sort of voice with the naval overtones of southern England. Scottie had half expected to hear the Lady herself and was slightly disappointed. Never mind. He'd bring her to the microphone soon enough. He'd bring her to her knees.

'Acknowledge,' he said to Schiele, who did so. It was their first acknowledgement of any signal so far. And it would come through to the authorities in guttural German tones – let them make what they liked of that!

The voice responded. 'I am authorised to speak to you on behalf of Her Majesty's Government. First we would like to know the situation regarding victims of the recent assault. We would like to request safe conduct to bring them out, on humanitarian grounds.'

Scottie seized the microphone from Schiele's hand. 'There are no wounded or sick aboard this vessel,' he replied. 'All is well here. Next question.'

Taken a little aback by this, the voice hesitated before

pressing on. But press on it did. 'Would you be prepared, under strict guarantees according to law, to cease all hostile action and give yourselves up?'

Scottie smiled. 'What guarantees are you referring to?'

'Procedures according to law. Right to a defence, trial by jury.'

'We'll get that anyway, I hope,' said Scottie, who then burst out laughing. 'I'm sorry. You fellas are marking time. Let's get on with it. Have you got the gold?'

'With reference to your request, the matter is receiving active consideration.'

Who was this nincompoop? 'It wasn't a fucking request, and I want to know where it is and when we're going to get it.'

'I cannot make any statement on that issue.'

'Well, then. Who can? I want to talk to the Prime Minister.'

'I will relay your reply to the appropriate–'

'I don't care what the fuck you do. Maybe you'd like to know that we have Big Ben in our sights. That is our next target at eighteen hundred hours this evening if your Prime Minister is not on the line to me at least one hour before then.'

'Would you repeat that, sir?'

'No, I won't repeat it. You've recorded this anyway. Just get her on.'

'Sir–'

'That's all I have to say. Out.'

'They've killed already. They've nothing to lose – and we'll lose Big Ben.' So spoke Cyril Hartnell, Deputy Prime Minister and long-time political dog'sbody, with appropriate savvy. 'The devastation of a symbolic loss of this kind outweighs other considerations. You must speak to them.'

'I'll speak to them all right,' said the Prime Minister. 'And I'll tell them what I think of them, too!'

'You'd better do no such thing,' said the Deputy P.M., a prim, non-smoking teetotal character who spoke crisply when he was of a mind, and without fear or favour - fortunate for him that his views generally coincided with hers. A rare breed of politician with little or no tact, a survivor, perhaps, of earlier days. 'The man is unstable - listen to the tape! Any provocation will blow us sky-high.'

'You want me to be mealy-mouthed, Cyril - perhaps you ought to do it. You know what I mean,' she said, waving her hand impatiently. 'You're much more of a diplomat than I am, in these sorts of situations at any rate. Perhaps you ought to speak to him.'

'They have asked for you, and I think, under the circumstances–'

'Yes, of course. Now for goodness' sake, will someone get me some briefing on him?'

Life blew up in the face of Alice Moore, seized by a squad of big men in grey suits who flashed F.B.I. cards at her and her daughter Cheryl (whom she'd just picked up from school), rushed off in a whooping of sirens to some great building, bundled into a room where a tape recorder played her the voice of the man she'd not seen, let alone slept with, in more than five years. She didn't know what that voice made her feel now. Yes, yes, it was Scottie, of course it was Scottie. But there was so much she wanted to know, the questions came flooding into her brain...

Where were they taking her? Could she make sure Cheryl was looked after? She had to get Marlene in, to keep an eye on everything. On the air-trip (when would she get back? She was supposed to go to work in the morning!) she sat with a matronly U.S.A.F. officer who held her hand and told her everything would be all right.

Why was she needed in England? Did Scottie need her? He hadn't needed her all this time. She'd never been out of the United States. They told her it was quite cold and damp this time of year in England so she had packed an extra cardigan.

The plane didn't even land at London or any big airport but at some very flat base in the middle of nowhere. She didn't think ordinary international travel was much like this: she was whisked off the airplane as soon as it landed and was hurried into a police car with a motorcycle escort. They screamed their way all that distance to what she supposed was London, England. Every screech of the tyres made her heart thump.

Then more bundling in and out of rooms, more courteous attendance by uniformed women, though these ones didn't call her 'Honey', like the big one on the plane. Because they weren't Americans now. Then she was sat down in a room without any windows and a group of men came in, headed by one man who looked worried – not worried for her sake, she hoped. He seemed to be trying to hide his worry as he asked her question after question. She didn't want to bring up the past – where was Scottie now? What was going on? The man was patient, even though he was sweating and his blond hair glistened with perspiration. But she seemed to have lost the power of speech, or maybe she just couldn't say the words that were forming in her mouth and then disintegrating in her mind. She wanted to say the right words for him, she wanted to say what he wanted her to say. It was all so sudden, she managed to tell him. If you could talk to me tomorrow I'd be a lot better.

'We don't have until tomorrow, Mrs Moore. Mind if I

call you Alice? You can call me Paul.' Well, that was nice, but she didn't know him really, and these English always seemed so formal even when they were trying to be friendly. If only he'd sit down, be more level. She wished she didn't look such a mess – she must do, she hadn't seen a mirror in five hours and had forgotten to pack her own in the rush.

'Could you sit down? I'd be happier if you sat down,' she said. She felt like such a stupid broad. He sat down straight away though, as if ordered to.

'You said he drank? You mean he was an alcoholic?'

No, we weren't like that. We had good times. Now they call it alcoholism. We were never like that, never what they make out nowadays. She shook her somewhat mousy, brown locks. 'No, I didn't mean that: alcoholism. He just went out drinking. They all did, on the base.'

'So he didn't have a drink problem?'

'I don't think so. I don't even know what a drink problem is.'

'Something I have to ask you, Alice. Did you sleep together throughout your marriage? Were there any sexual problems between you?'

It was these sorts of funny questions, one after the other – so personal, impossible simply to rip answers from the tangled mass of memories, the memories half forgotten because one tried so damned hard to forget.

'It was – all right. Most of the time. Not towards the end. Does this really matter to you? – Well, before he left me; he didn't seem to want to do it any more.'

'Was he seeing other women?'

'You never know, do you? I don't think so. He must have done, I guess, or he wouldn't have left, would he?'

'Were you unhappy about that, when he left?'

She began to cry.

'I'm sorry, Alice. I know you're going through a great

deal. We'll try and make it as easy for you as possible. We're trying to build up some kind of complete picture of your husband, a psychological profile. That's why we need your help so much, you see.'

'What's he done?' she asked. 'Nobody's told me really what he's done!'

'It's pretty bad I'm afraid, Alice.' Then the man told her what it was and yes, it sounded pretty bad. A funny way of putting it. It was like the end of the world.

And it was the last act of her marriage to Scottie. That was the thing, the really bad thing, that had been pursuing her on this dash across the Atlantic. The last act. She'd hoped and prayed that last act would never be. Because in her mind and heart she'd never been unmarried to Scottie. And now it was going to end after all.

'Did he beat you, Alice?' Paul's voice was soft. Yes, he beat her. He liked doing it, and she must have asked for it. She didn't remember asking him for it but he said she did so she must have. He didn't ever beat her too hard. She got a black eye once, but that was the worst thing that happened.

She nodded.

'How often did he beat you? Was it bad?'

'I don't want to talk about it, okay? Yes, he did sometimes – that's our business. I don't want to talk about it.' Scottie had needed her. He had needed her more than love itself could offer. That's why she always thought he would come back. After five years, even, he would come back. Or six. Or ten. One day. Jack was a mailman who had started calling, and they went out for a few beers now and then and finally he'd made the proposal, but she said she was still married and Scottie was coming back to her soon. She didn't see Jack after that. It was kind of sad, but there it was. Her life was in a deep-freezer, waiting for Scottie. But Scottie didn't come, and now this man with that funny English way of talking was telling her that he never would again.

'I didn't get that much out of her,' reported Paul to 'C', anxiously getting ready to go off to the Prime Minister. 'But out of what she said about this and that we've put together a profile of sorts. He is violent, though he has no clinical history of psychosis. He comes over as psychopathic, from what that poor thing's told us and what we've gleaned from other sources. He obviously has a power over people. He ruled her and even though he left her she still loves him and wants him back. I suspect he has a kind of charisma that draws certain susceptibles to him. Like the homosexual Warren Booths for example.'

'You mean they're having a homosexual relationship?'

'I don't know. I doubt it. It doesn't sound to me as if this Scottie Moore was able to have a very close relationship with anyone, male or female.'

'So in short, what do I tell the P.M.?'

'Her man's dangerous, willing to resort to violence, has a psychopathic tendency that will probably not respond to authoritarianism in any form, a chip on his shoulder and a mind of his own.'

'Politics?'

'No politics. I'm almost certain this man is entirely out for himself.'

'Will he do it, Paul? Will he blow us all up?'

'My feeling is yes, he could. If driven to it, he could. I said he's dangerous, and that means taking no unnecessary chances with him. He must be treated with kid-gloves. That's my opinion, considering the cards he holds at the moment.'

'C' raised his eyebrows as he left the room. 'We shall have to see what *she* makes out of *that*!'

Alice Moore was dumped into a four-star hotel with a

guard at her door. Her blue Sears nightie didn't exactly match the coverings of the bed with its scrolled carvings. She sank deep into the bed and cried up the five years of unhappiness – because they'd been for nothing at all.

At Baythorne Manor the trees were bare and the roses pruned. Everything awaited the onset of winter. Mrs Banham was living on her own of course, so it made a pleasant change to be cooking for someone else, especially Miss Jane, whom she preferred (it had to be said, no disrespect) to the girl's late sister. Jane had the same breeding but less of the airs and graces, though Mrs Banham had to scold her for not telephoning earlier so that she would have had time to prepare what she called a proper lunch.

'It will just take a little longer, but it doesn't matter, dear. Now go out in the garden for a while and get some fresh air till it's ready!' Jane allowed herself to be shooed out of doors in a way she wouldn't have tolerated from anyone else. She would hunt through Sarah's things after lunch.

From the garden she went through the gate in the wall into the churchyard to visit Sarah's grave. There it was, neat and well-kept. But no fond memories overcame Jane. Instead she shivered in that damp, forlorn place, she shivered in fear. Fear at the sense of some black, malignant organisation that was somehow centred here in the middle of these peaceful surroundings, like a spider in the middle of a gossamer web. She knew it now from Paul, so it was true. Something in this peaceful place was even now giving off the stench of evil.

Over lunch she asked Mrs Banham, as casually as she could, if the housekeeper was expecting her employer to put in an appearance within the next few days. 'Not at this time of year, Miss Jane. We don't normally see him now till Christmas. He's either off to his constituency or on government business. And what with this terrible to-do in London I don't suppose we'll see him even if he was to take a small break – which I don't suppose they'd let him do now, would they?'

This allayed Jane's fears a bit, but she still wondered if Clive might come back unexpectedly for one reason or another. Often she would glance down the valley at the long, winding drive to the Manor, imagining his car on its way, almost willing it. She had her story lined up: an acceptance of Clive's earlier invitation, a wish not to bother him, a need for rest. What was good enough for Mrs Banham was good enough for him.

Jane had discovered earlier that Sarah and Clive had slept in separate bedrooms. What a life. Sarah was too young for such middle-aged arrangements.

Sarah's own bedroom was as she'd left it, as if Clive had just shut the door and left everything to remain as it was. It was a sepulchre of soft, rosy-pink fabrics, with an unmistakable scent of Sarah's still in the air. Jane opened the bulging wardrobes of Sarah's clothes; she looked over the dressing-table covered in cosmetics. A person's little, trivial things can make her live again. Jane wept quiet tears.

She pulled herself together. Ostensibly her purpose was to claim possession of keepsakes and articles of clothing, as Clive had invited her to do. Sarah's good jewellery was either in the bank or under lock and key in a safe somewhere else in the house. But there were pieces of costume jewellery, small ornaments, mostly inherited from their parents, from an altogether humbler genteel world than that of Baythorne Manor. Jane was pleased to see that Sarah had still kept these cheap and cheerful pieces of her childhood in her bedroom.

What was missing? Looking at these little china ornaments and other leftovers from the family past had jogged Jane's memory. Something teased her, something tried to make her remember a piece of her girlhood and of Sarah's.

Of course! The little box!

One time when they were small their daddy had brought back presents from his trip to Hong Kong. They included a beautiful box for Sarah. It was about seven by six inches and carved in low relief with ivory dragons, and – magic! – it contained a Secret Compartment. Jane was given something just as nice, an exquisite china doll; but she always envied Sarah her box with the Secret Compartment. And Sarah had always taken it quite seriously. She indeed concealed things there: love-notes, photos of certain boys, love-tokens. Jane was quite sure Sarah had taken it with her when she left home to be married – she would never have been parted from it.

Where was it now? Not perhaps of great value in itself, Sarah would still never have thrown it away. Yet despite the fact that a mangy old teddy still lay on her pillow, and a wispy corn dolly stood none-too-securely on the mantelpiece, there was no box. These things were trivial compared with the box.

Jane decided to risk asking Mrs Banham about it. Mrs Banham looked perplexed and said she *had* remembered seeing the box but didn't know where it was now, if it wasn't in the late mistress's bedroom. She suggested the loft. 'Mind yourself, Miss Jane. It's rather dusty up there and there are one or two low beams.'

Perspiring now because she was on a quest, Jane climbed the narrow ladder leading into the loft. Fortunately the loft was illuminated, if somewhat dimly, by a single naked bulb.

For more than an hour Jane rummaged through boxes

of old toys and rusty appliances, magazines and clothes, the dust getting up her nose, her fingers turning grimy and sticky. And then she found it.

The Chinese box was unaccountably buried under a massive pile of old disused velvet curtains in a large chest with a humped lid. Nearly at the bottom. Why she had even thought to look in there she could hardly imagine. But then she'd looked everywhere else.

Why would anyone want to bury the box in there? It definitely smacked of concealment. Jane pulled it out. It was still quite lovely, as she'd remembered it. The ivory was a little yellowed but otherwise it looked as new as when Sarah had squealingly opened it.

In the box itself there was only an amber necklace. The secret compartment was contained in the lid, which was about an inch deep. But how did it open? Jane had never been allowed to open it. Indeed it was more than ten years since she had seen it. One of the panels pushed up at the side of the lid. Then one could slide the carved panel which formed the lid itself right out: this revealed the compartment, about three-quarters of an inch deep. Taking out the amber necklace Jane held the box up to her ear and tilted it from side to side. There was something in the compartment. She could hear it sliding about.

She couldn't suppress a shiver, though it was quite likely to contain nothing more than some ardent pleas from a long-lost teenage lover. Would Clive have been jealous of that? Jane giggled at the thought of Sarah hiding such juvenile passions from her staid husband. But it left her puzzled. Why had the box been hidden? If it had been merely discarded amongst the old toys and magazines, it would have made more sense, though even that seemed unlikely.

Was there something hidden in there of a more recent origin?

With a bit of pressing here and there, and the use of her finger-nails, Jane went to work on the secret compartment. At last it yielded its little panel.

What Jane pulled out was the stiff print of a photograph, a snapshot. There was with it a brief note, typewritten on half a sheet of paper.

The snapshot was a little fuzzy, a Polaroid.

It was probably a hotel room. There, sitting up in a bed, wide-eyed from the light-flash, was Sarah naked as a jaybird. With his arm around her was an equally naked man who didn't look much like Clive Parris. He was swarthy, heavily moustached and hairy, perhaps in his late thirties. His thick, meaty penis was uncovered, betraying at the moment a healthy tumescence. Sarah looked English-rose-like beside him, her small breasts firm, her thighs slightly open. It could have been a shot from an under-the-counter video.

Goggle-eyed, Jane turned to the note. 'Remember that your husband may recieve a copy of this at any time.' Blackmail! 'Receive' had been spelt incorrectly. It wasn't anything in itself, but that plus the Latin or Mediterranean look of the man in the bed suggested something foreign involved in the blackmail of her late sister.

Somebody had set Sarah up. And got her hook, line and sinker.

'Jane?'

It was Clive Parris's voice at the bottom of the ladder. He had returned to Baythorne.

16

The military prevailed upon the Prime Minister to allow them to try to ascertain from Scottie Moore just what he had at his disposal before she spoke to the man. The Defence Secretary Basil Pennington was determined that his P.M. should know the kind of power she was dealing with – in order that she shouldn't become precipitate.

Scottie explained patiently and obligingly to the military experts that he had a Carl Gustav Anti-Tank Recoilless Gun which would be trained at close quarters on the ship's reactor, or one of them, in the event of *Aztec* being rushed. He also explained that he had both conventional and nuclear warheads to fire directly at the centre of the nation. He had a number of options, therefore, which they should bear in mind. If there were delays, he would pick off conventional targets, one by one, until the demand for 100 million dollars in gold was met, plus the safe conduct. If the demand wasn't met and there was an all-out attack on him, there would be nuclear catastrophe in London. It would affect south-east England and possibly France, Belgium, Holland and parts of Scandinavia.

No, they weren't kidding, and by now they had nothing to lose.

All this was relayed to the Prime Minister by nervous officials. Technical matters were checked and confirmed. Analysis of Moore's threats strongly indicated that there was no bluff involved – the loss of the police helicopter and crew said as much. And Big Ben was still maintained as the next target.

The deadline was drawing nearer and there was no longer the possibility of delay. The Prime Minister went to the microphone. Old stagers like Pennington and Hartnell bit their lips in fear. This was no time for House of Commons dispatch-box hell-raising.

They had not reckoned on her Grandmotherly Mode.

It wasn't brought out very often. Usually it was reserved for hospital bedsides.

'Do you mean to say you intend doing this to us, Mr Moore?' she asked, gently, her voice down a few tones from her usual pitch.

It was the first time he had heard his surname mentioned. So, they knew who he was. Bound to, weren't they?

'I wouldn't be here otherwise,' he replied in his first words to the British Prime Minister.

'You must be an unhappy man, I think, to want to cause this destruction. Surely that cannot be your intention?'

'My intention is to obtain 100 million dollars in gold and a safe conduct for my men and me out of your country,' he said, crisply. 'And it would be better if you didn't stall over concern for my happiness.'

'But I am concerned,' she persisted, 'if your unhappiness brings about the destruction you say it will.' She was trying to spook him.

'Can we get to the point?'

'Your wife is very unhappy, too.'

'What's my wife got to do with it? Have you got her there? Bastards. Well, she won't make any difference if that's what you're thinking. What did you want to bring her in for? Alice couldn't say boo to a goose!'

The Prime Minister was silent. She decided to withdraw the wife gambit. Scottie continued:

'Are you intending to put obstacles in my way instead of doing what I've asked you to do?'

'Nothing of the kind,' replied the P.M. soothingly. 'We are ready to do anything and everything that you wish.'

'Do you mean that?'

'When you tell us exactly what you want.'

'You know damned well what I want!' he shouted. 'You're just stalling. This is a waste of time. Get off the air and let me do the countdown on Big Ben!'

'You have that in your power,' said the P.M. quickly, her voice rising. 'And we don't want you to do it. We beg you not to. Yes, we beg. Does that make you feel any better?' There was a pause. 'Now, you must give us patience. Your demands are surely very complicated and require organisation.'

'They require gold. Where is it?'

'One hundred million dollars in gold is a good deal to raise in a short space of time. The time is taken by the conversion into gold bars. About ten tonnes, I believe. But where do you want it? What do you want done with it?'

Was she talking turkey at last? Was it really going to be as easy as this? Scottie concentrated now as he spelled out what he had been saving up for only the Prime Minister to hear.

'I take it you are recording all this, so I won't repeat myself. You have an air force base for R.A.F. transporters, a place called Lyneham in Wiltshire. I want the gold put on a Hercules transporter – I know they can lift that much all right, plus a complement of eleven men and crew – for a destination which I will reveal after the plane is airborne. I want helicopter transport for all of us out of here to R.A.F. Lyneham, where we will board the Hercules with the 100 million already stowed and then get out of your hair. Those with us on board the helicopter will act as our hostages. I want twelve hostages altogether. I hope all that is clear because that's what it's got to be. You know the alternative.'

There was silence in the air. The Prime Minister – and all behind her – were taking it in.

'Well?' demanded Scottie impatiently. 'Do you agree to this or not?'

Another pause. Scottie held his breath. Then it came:

'Yes. We agree to your terms. Unreservedly.'

There was a suppressed whoop in the operations room. Scottie shushed them up and continued: 'Then it only remains for me to add one thing. I have already computed the length of time needed to fly a helicopter from *Aztec* to Lyneham. It will take your experts more than that to search the length and breadth of this battle-cruiser. You'd be surprised how many little nooks and crannies there are to hide small devices. We have done this. They will detonate from a radio-control box which I shall be carrying with me on my way out of this country. The range of my control on the *Aztec* is approximately 100 miles. You will not be sure where we have hidden all the devices until the Hercules with the gold is entirely out of your airspace. Naturally we will also have hostages with us, but this other is in the nature of extra insurance. I hope I've made myself clear, ma'am?'

'Oh yes, Mr Moore. You've made yourself extremely clear.'

'So let's get down to time-scale, shall we?'

'Before we do that,' said the Prime Minister, 'I have a condition of my own.'

'I don't think you are in any position to lay down conditions,' sneered Scottie.

'Please be serious for a moment! My government would be grateful if you refrained from making any public pronouncements of your own or revealing anything of our deliberations here. In the name of humanity we ask this, Mr Moore. You cannot be without some civilised scruples. You have an honourable background and family tradition in the American Navy. You would not want to foment mass panic, I feel sure.'

'I hadn't given the matter of mass panic much thought,' replied Scottie.

The Prime Minister's tone was even. 'Then I suggest you do, Mr Moore. If our people are needlessly panicked into widespread stampeding and fear, this government will consider itself at war with you. I believe it was one of your generals who said "War is hell". If you make it hell for us, you may rest assured we will most certainly make it hell for you.'

There wasn't much by way of come-back to this. Scottie grunted. The Prime Minister kept at him:

'Do you agree to *my* terms, Mr Moore?'

'Yeah, sure, whatever turns you on. Now I want to talk time with you. You'd better bear in mind that I won't allow delays to the timetable for any reason you may give.'

Between them – and with the Prime Minister quickly referring to experts by her side every step of the way – a timetable was agreed for the delivery of the gold to a Hercules at Lyneham, followed by the pick-up by helicopter from *Aztec*'s deck. Other, exact details were spelt out, one by one.

Looking drawn and ill, the Prime Minister emerged from her ordeal to gushing praise: 'Well done, ma'am!' 'Superb handling!' 'Statesmanship!' etc. She lingered in the room long enough to issue orders to put into effect what she and Scottie Moore had agreed.

'I've bought time, George,' she said to the Foreign Secretary on her way out. He noticed tears glistening in her eyes. 'We'll do everything we can to stop him, Prime Minister,' he called out after her – as if he knew what he was talking about.

'Keep me informed of initiatives,' were her parting words.

When, finally, she was alone, her tears so long dammed up burst forth.

They were tears of fury, impotent fury, coming on the heels of delayed shock and tension. She, who had fought her way to the top in politics without giving way on a single matter of principle, had caved in to one man, of the breed she hated more than any other: terrorist. Criminal. No one had ever got the better of her, until now.

But what else could she have done?

Fleets of helicopters and scores of frogmen and S.A.S. crack troops were standing by, ready at her signal to attack, board and disarm the hijackers. She had only to give the word. How she had longed to give the word!

In the end, she couldn't. A missile might go off, it might contain a nuclear warhead. What if the Palace of Westminster were destroyed? What if a million people died? What if there were a nuclear melt-down and scores of millions died? Her entire government, even the bullish Jim Dodson, had lined up against such a solution. The President of the United States was against her.

And all so a hooligan like Scottie Moore could have his gold for the taking.

There aren't many nuances to a decision. Tell that to *Guardian* leader-writers. When a decision is taken there are no ifs and buts. You do either one thing, or something else. She had made the decision to accede to Moore's demands. The consequences were incalculable. Britain, the whole free world, would never be safe again. And she, of all people, had allowed that to happen.

It was all very well to say that one was buying time. Buying it for what? What could possibly be done now?

Jane heard his steps up the ladder. Slowly. Perhaps he'd never been up his own loft before.

She had only enough time to slip the box back inside the chest and close the lid before Clive Parris's silvery head appeared through the loft hatch. 'What are you doing up here?' it asked.

Then the whole of him climbed into the loft. He was very tall, up here. Ducking his head once or twice, he walked towards her, staring at her.

Jane went for being as stupid as she felt. 'I didn't realise you were coming down to Baythorne,' said she, vacuously.

'Obviously not,' said Parris. He stood over her. 'It's only an hour up the M1.'

'I was going through some of Sarah's things,' said Jane truthfully. She began to pick up courage. 'You said I could any time.'

'Mrs Banham told me you were up in the loft when I rang along the way,' said Parris. 'I thought I might be able to give you a hand to find anything you wanted.'

'That's all right, Clive.'

'Have you found what you wanted?'

'I didn't want anything in particular, really,' replied Jane, rising from her knees. She slightly exaggerated a look round. 'I don't think there's anything up here after all, so perhaps we ought to go down now.' She wished she could still her pumping heart.

'Why were you searching just here? There's nothing of Sarah's here.'

Jane shrugged.

'Or were you doing a bit of snooping?'

'It's hard not to come across old things that are interesting,' Jane rattled on, trying to defuse the situation. 'Magazines and things like that. I must've spent at least half an hour going through that pile of old *Illustrated London News*'s over there.' Her little laugh sounded hollow and awful to her ears.

Clive's eyes searched all round her face as if he were trying to penetrate to the truth. In the long shadows cast by the single lightbulb he looked cadaverous and ugly. 'Could we go down now?' Jane asked in a small voice draining down her throat.

'Not yet.' He stood in her way.

This was Clive Parris, the man who had never done anything wrong, who had gone through life without a hair out of place.

'What – what is it, Clive?'

He looked past her and down at the chest.

'I was about to have a look in there,' she said brightly.

'There's nothing of Sarah's in that one,' said Clive. 'It's one of my family's old chests.'

'Oh. Thanks for telling me. I shan't bother, then.'

'Or have you had a look already?'

Had he hidden the box himself? It seemed like it. Jane decided to brazen it out. 'Of course not! Do you think I'm lying?'

'The latches look undone.'

'They were like that. Perhaps Mrs Banham was putting something away and forgot to latch it up again.'

'Yes, that's possible,' said Clive surprisingly. Was he letting her off the hook?

'I'd like to go down now, Clive,' she said for the third time.

He seemed to snap out of something, giving a quick shake of his head. 'Of course,' he said, and stood aside for her to pass. Jane moved past him: she wasn't going to look a gift-horse in the mouth.

But walking towards the hatch, with Clive behind her, she wasn't so sure about the idea.

When she reached the edge of the hatch and the top of the ladder leading to the floor below, she was about to turn to ask him to go first when she felt his hands suddenly grip her shoulders. Her heart leapt to her mouth. Now, unbelievably, as in a nightmare, he was whispering rapidly into her ear. It was almost as if a lover were breathing into it – but this certainly wasn't love.

'You were lying to me, Jane. You've been into that chest and I know you've found something there, haven't you? You put it back when I came up here, didn't you?' The grip became harder, bruising – like when he'd gripped her in the river. 'You thought I'd killed her from the beginning – I knew that when you came to Amsterdam. No doubt she went running to you about one thing or another and when she died you believed all sorts of things. You were using the excuse of going through her belongings to find evidence against me – that's why you came back to Baythorne. You never liked me, did you? None of your family ever liked me. Well, I'll tell you one thing: Sarah was glad to be shot of you, the whole lot of you!'

Tears welled up in Jane's eyes. 'That's not true!' she cried in a strangulated voice. Then her voice found itself as she found the words, and damn the consequences! 'Sarah was never the same after she married you! And if she was so happy why did she send me a note from Amsterdam, saying she wanted to talk to me so desperately about something?'

His eyes bulged almost out of their sockets. 'She wrote to you? Then?' His grip didn't slacken.

'You're mad!' Jane shrieked. All at once she knew she would die now. Balanced precariously before the open hatch with her back to the ladder, all Clive had to do was push her and make it out as accidental. 'Stop it! Stop it!' she screamed as he bent her backwards over the hatch.

Suddenly the colour drained out of his face; his eyes went vacant and dull. Unfortunately for Jane his grip slackened, her body slipped through his hands. She jack-knifed and fell through the hatch, snatching at his trouser-legs vainly. But it was too late.

How had she earned the right to come out of this?

Swimming in front of her half-open eyes was an image of Paul, close to her, saying something softly. What was he saying?

'It's okay, Jane, it's going to be okay.' Slowly, feeling and sensation came back to her. She found her head throbbing and didn't dare feel where the source of the pain was.

She was sunk deep into a sofa, prone and limp, all strength gone. But with a feeling of great warmth. It was a pleasant room, with mouldings on the ceiling. She might have been in heaven, her version of heaven at any rate, with her lover by her side. Except for the pain in her head and an aching in her neck and shoulders.

She was in the comfortable sitting-room at Baythorne. The low-key lamps were on. It was already dark outside.

Paul smiled. One big hand was holding both of hers. The other was behind her head. 'Back in the land of the living?' Suddenly she felt nauseous and started retching. 'Easy, easy,' he said. 'Mrs Banham?' The taut, worried face of the normally cheerful housekeeper loomed up, and the edge of a glass of water was placed against Jane's lips. It was cool, just right. 'How's that?' Paul asked.

'I'm all right now. Paul? What's happened? Why are you—?'

'We got here in time, that's the main thing. We're whizzes at first-aid, too. No bones broken!'

In a few minutes Jane was sitting up, sipping at a scalding cup of the herbal tea she'd asked for. Paul sat with her, his bedside manner gone with her recovery. In fact he was running his fingers through his hair and sitting bent over his knees. 'I shouldn't have let it go this far, it's my fault. It's just that we had so little to go on!'

'Is he – still here?'

Paul jerked a thumb in the direction of the library. 'We're holding him in there for the time being. Don't worry: he can't harm you now. We've been tailing him – you knew that. Well, he left Town so quickly that he caught one of our operatives on the hop. Anyhow he just managed to catch up with him and followed him up the M1. After he was able to get through to me I got a police escort out of London and made it up here hell-for-leather. I kept in radio contact with our operative, so I knew where Clive was heading.'

'Has he told you anything?'

'Not yet. He says he won't talk without a solicitor present. We're waiting for one now.'

'But how did I– I mean, what happened after–?'

'Like I said, just in the nick of time.' Clive had suddenly gone dull-eyed and lost his grip on her because he had seen Paul below the hatch, over her shoulder, at the bottom of the ladder. They had arrived stealthily at Baythorne. No crunch of car tyres in the drive. No sounds in the house. Not being policemen, they didn't observe the formalities of proper entry. While Mrs Banham was in the pantry they had staged a break-in. Only at the critical moment had they reached the loft.

'What he did, or tried to do to you is at least compromising. We may or may not be able to bring an attempted murder charge under the circumstances but at least it shows he was up to something. If you've recovered I'd like you to tell me what led up to it.'

'Don't you know about the box?' asked Jane.

'What box?'

So, nothing had been said about the Chinese box. Of course! There wasn't any reason for anyone to know about it up to now! Clive hadn't even known if she knew about it, which was why he kept humming and hawing around the chest; so as not to betray its existence there if she *didn't* know about it!

'There's something I found I think you'd better see,' said Jane.

17

Basil Pennington, Sir George Rayner and Cyril Hartnell were in for a shock.

To their dismay they found they had not won over the Prime Minister to outright capitulation.

'But you've promised him now, you've given him assurances!' protested Sir George.

'One is not bound to keep promises to criminals,' said the P.M. Evidently she had recharged her batteries in the hours of rest after her bruising confrontation with Scottie Moore. 'I am not going to hand over the gold. Already I hear the police are receiving complaints of hoax calls. The copy-cats are on the loose.'

'But these deliberations are top security!'

'That doesn't stop people knowing what's going on, George.'

'What are you going to do when the agreed twenty-four-hour deadline for delivery is up?' he asked.

'I'm putting it off for another twenty-four hours while we continue to investigate the problem of seizing the *Aztec*.'

'But the longer they're stuck in there the more unassailable they are!'

'And the more prey to psychological deterioration.'

'They've got their finger on the button, Prime Minister.'

'Give me another twenty-four hours, George – just another twenty-four hours to exhaust every possibility. The stakes are too high to give in, just like that'

'And if the position is the same after another twenty-four hours? What then, Prime Minister?'

'Then they'll have their gold and you can die in bed with your boots off,' she said, bitterly.

There was bitterness on board *Aztec* when the delay was announced to the gang over the radio. Scottie refused to acknowledge the signal at all. He was white with suppressed rage.

'So. So, so, so…' His fingers kept tapping the radio-desk, relentlessly, compulsively. 'So, so, so, so…'

'So what are you going to do now, Scottie? Nuke London? Blow us all up?' Warren Booth was letting fly at last. 'She's called your bluff, hasn't she? And here we were thinking the gold was in the bag! Christ, how stupid could we be?'

'Can it, Warren,' said Scottie, low and dangerous.

'How long are we supposed to sit it out in here, then? This place stinks! It stinks of sweat and it stinks of *pigs*!' he shouted at Maxton, who was sprawled over a chair, exhausted from a sleepless vigil. Maxton opened one eye.

'Shut your gob, poof,' he said.

Warren suddenly seized the Yorkshireman out of his chair with both hands. He caught Maxton by surprise, but it didn't last long. With the deftness of a man whose whole life is combat, Maxton grabbed Warren Booth's arm and twisted it round behind him. Booth yelled out in pain. The more he yelled, the higher Maxton yanked his arm. At any second he would break it.

'That's enough, Maxy,' said Scottie. 'I said that's *enough*!' Maxton let go of Booth with a grunt.

'Yeah, you stick up for him,' he muttered. 'You're all alike.'

Scottie sprang from his chair and pushed Maxton against the wall. 'Keep smart, Maxton. I'm warning you. You break now, I'm gonna have to break *you*, like I always said I could. If we crack now the whole thing's up the spout – you got the brains to see that?'

'Brains were never his strong suit,' said Booth.

Scottie released Maxton and walked over to Booth, who was sitting on the floor after his deliverance from the ex-sergeant.

'Don't mind me, Scottie,' said Booth, as Scottie Moore gently pulled him off the floor.

Scottie threw a punch deep into Warren's gut. Booth crumpled and went down. He rolled round and round, clutching his abdomen and crying. Maxton couldn't resist a little twitch of pleasure at the corners of his mouth. Maybe Scottie Moore wasn't a twat after all.

Booth wouldn't get up. He continued to lie there, sobbing.

Scottie got down on the floor with him and whispered into his ear: 'It's for your own good, Kid.' Booth had done his job like the best of them. He couldn't help it if he wasn't made of iron. Who was, when it came down to it? He sent Warren off to bed with a sedative. As Warren Booth dragged himself out of the room, Scottie Moore turned once again to Maxton.

'You're a mother-fucking cowshit-for-brains,' he said.

'You've no call to say that to me,' growled Maxton.

'I'll say it again! Cowshit-for-brains! Mother-fucker! What are you going to do about it?' Scottie sprang out his knife, waved it in Maxton's face, tossed it from hand to hand as he advanced on the ex-sergeant. 'Come on, come on, go for me! Go for me, Maxy! You want to fuck everything up? Okay! Let's go for it! Fuck everything up!'

Maxton gasped in fear. 'You're crazy.' He backed away.

'Come on, Maxy! It's time to cut each other up, isn't it? That's what you like, that's what you've always liked. That's why you're here! It's your destiny, Maxy!'

There was a wild look now in his light, glittery eyes.

Maxton was rooted to the spot. The bloke was crazy all right. The tip of Scottie's blade caressed his throat. Maxton started to shake. Scottie brought his own perspiring face right up close to Maxton's, as if he was about to kiss him on the mouth. He grinned.

'No hard feelings,' he said, backing away and putting the knife down. 'Sit down,' he said. Maxton slumped down on his chair.

'You're right. I am crazy. There's something loose in my head. Or maybe not all there. You know? Out to lunch? Be as well for you to remember that. I got prime ministers licking my ass: it *makes* you crazy, you know. It goes to a guy's head. But I was always like that, deep down. Do you know that's how we've got as far as we've got? Because we're all nuts in our different ways, and I'm the nuttiest! You may not know it, but it's the crazies who end up ruling the world. That prime minister's crazy in her own way: she's daring to defy *me*! Do you think she got where she got to by having all her marbles in the right place? Face it, Maxton, you're in the hands of crazy people, and maybe you always have been. Maybe we all have been.

'Anyway, I got no feelings about slitting holes in a crummy ex-sergeant of the fucking infantry, I'll tell you that much. I got no feelings about blowing this ship, or blowing London. Or blowing the world. Does that frighten you? It should. You see, I got no fear of death. I don't care, Maxy. Like Rhett Butler! "Frankly my dear, I don't give a damn!" Well, neither do I. I don't give a damn, I just don't give a damn!'

'But I'm all you got from here on in, aren't I? Without me, where do you think you're going to get to? Out there? Out to Morocco or wherever you're thinking of going? Fuck that. You won't get across that deck. You need me, and you know it...'

Maxton was trembling with shock and fear. He was afraid of Scottie Moore, perhaps he'd always been a little afraid of him, ever since Moore had trounced him, in El Salvador. But the fear was of something else, deeper. It seemed that more things lurked in the pit of hell than simple brutality. There were banshees who shrieked in the dark corners of certain brains, spirits of havoc and death. It was the banshees who frightened Maxton now because they were dancing around the room, a room with Scottie Moore in the centre of it.

Scottie sat down on his swivel chair and put his feet up on the desk. He broke out a cigar, lit it, and ordered a missile to be prepared for firing.

'Where?' asked an open-mouthed Lavitzsky.

'Anywhere.'

The headquarters of the Imperial Lion Insurance Company in the City of London had the misfortune to receive the blow. Its top three floors, out of the seven, were virtually demolished. Great shards of glass from the curtain-walling littered the narrow street below.

Fortunately the missile was launched after working hours when that part of the City is almost deserted. There were injuries sustained by passers-by from falling debris – serious ones – but thankfully no deaths. Between nine and five it would have been a very different story. None of the M.o.D. analysts could come up with a feasible theory for the attack, except to say that the missile must have been aimed at random. It was hard cheese for the Imperial Lion Insurance Company. Fortunately, their building was insured.

Up to now a few people, sniffing the wind, had quietly pulled out of London, careful to leave a note for the milkman.

It began to be an avalanche.

Streets were choked with hooting cars, vans, lorries, some piled high with bedding and belongings, trying to go any which way so long as it was Out. People saw their neighbours packing up the family Toyota and decided they knew something – so they left, too. Pubs and shops were closing down. Reports came in of looting, first in Barking and in Rotherhithe, later in Kensington and elsewhere.

The more the government appealed, the more panicky people became.

The government declared a state of emergency in London and the south-east. The whole paraphernalia of a Civil Defence once thought never to be needed came into operation.

Reception centres were opened in the outlying districts, on the borders with Hertfordshire, Oxfordshire, in Essex, Kent, Sussex, all around Greater London. Fields were requisitioned for tents, parking-space, soup-kitchens. Those who had relatives outside the south-east headed for shelter with those – without being told. Heathrow and Gatwick were a nightmare of foreign nationals bribing anyone within hearing for a quick flight, and ticket touts were soon in business.

Within London itself, armed patrols were set up to deal with looting, but it was a losing battle: there were just too many streets, too many shops, too many warehouses. Hospitals and other institutions were evacuated. Gradually, London settled into the eerie state of being a ghost town. Essential services were maintained, and many people simply stayed on. But they were afraid to venture out: it is interesting how menacing an empty city can be.

Apart from the careering around the streets of official and armoured cars and motorcycle escorts, the occasional crash of plate glass, the baying of the odd drunk and the marching boots of a patrol here and there, the shrieks of starlings and the cooing of pigeons became the dominant sounds of London.

Deep beneath Whitehall, however, activity continued at a furious pace. The stillness of the ministries above ground was deceptive. In cavernous rooms underneath them lights flashed, telephones were answered, fax machines stuttered, signals came and went, people came and went.

The armed forces were in position all around the Pool of London, waiting for the command. *Aztec* lay at anchor, mistress of a dead landscape. But thousands of pairs of eyes were watching her, round the clock.

Scottie announced on the radio that the missile attack had been 'symbolic'. He said that he accepted the revised schedule, but that if he and his men were not taken off to Lyneham exactly on the dot he would stage a break-out, armed with the radio-box that would detonate high explosives all over the ship.

News came through from Lyneham that the gold had been loaded on to a Hercules transporter which was standing by, fully fuelled for a range up to 2,400 miles, ready to take the terrorists to any destination they asked for.

The moment of decision for the Prime Minister had come.

Immaculately coiffured as usual, she arrived at the underground conference room dead on time. She was followed by her Deputy Prime Minister, her Foreign Secretary and her Defence Secretary, all of whom looked – in contrast to her – completely washed-out. They had been in continuous secret session with her for the previous seven hours. But it soon became apparent that tiredness alone didn't explain their woebegone looks.

The Prime Minister spoke.

'I have decided, after all due deliberation, consideration and calculation,' she began, slowly, with only the slightest quaver in her voice betraying her state of tension, 'to take action against *Aztec*.'

Pennington threw up his hands, silently. It had all been said, all talked out. He had failed to dissuade her at the final moment, as had his colleagues.

'It is intolerable that these criminals – and I could think of much, much worse words for them – should be seen to get away with the enormity of that which they have perpetrated. If they do, we will never see peace again in our time. The Libyas, the Irans, the Black September groups, the I.R.A.s, the P.L.O.s of present and of future times will rise up and conquer. Were we at war with a foreign power we would do no less than what we propose to do now, whatever the sacrifice. I realise the depth of that sacrifice, but for too long there has been nothing but talk of risks and dangers. Of course there are risks. Of course there are dangers. Is it any less so in a war against terrorism than in a war against a foreign power?

'We have reached a point where we could, if we chose, meet all their demands fully. I can assure you that I have the backing of the Loyal Opposition and of the Sovereign herself for what I have decided to do. I have decided that an attack will be mounted on U.S.S. *Aztec*. All forces are in place. We have been hoping and praying for the deliverance of the remnants of her gallant crew still imprisoned on board. But, as I told the American president this morning – and I am pleased to say that he has reached the position of concurrence with my view – even their lives may now have to be sacrificed, in the most noble traditions of their fighting service, so that the world may be free once and for all from terror.

'The decks are cleared. London is to all intents and

purposes evacuated: her people, we hope, in relative safety. We ourselves will remain at our post, where our duty lies.'

Scottie looked at his watch. He had ordered every man to be ready. He had previously announced the break-out.

Now he had an even better idea. He got out the map of southern England. Soon he would be speaking to Lavitzsky and Warren Booth, and instructing Schiele to get on the radio again.

An aide had called Jim Dodson from the meeting. He returned with a slip of paper. 'Prime Minister, some news just in from Uxbridge,' he said. The whole room fell silent. 'Uxbridge' meant Scottie Moore. He showed the paper to the P.M.

She blanched and sat back in her chair. 'Are you serious?' She asked. 'I mean is he serious? Can they have co-ordinates for firing on Bradwell?'

'I'm afraid it is quite possible, Prime Minister,' he said. 'The catastrophe of that would, of course, be incalculable.'

Now Jim Dodson was a fairly tough customer, the Prime Minister's favourite in the whole cabinet. But even he seemed to be behaving with more than usual coolness given the shocking turn of events. 'Prime Minister, two people are waiting outside this meeting who have just arrived. They would be grateful if you would hear them out before authorising the launch of the attack on *Aztec*. One of them you know. I anticipate their remarks by saying that an alternative plan has been worked out. A plan which I believe will be 100 per cent effective.'

Impatiently the Prime Minister waved the two men into

the room. One of them turned out to be her old *bête noire*, 'C'. As soon as she saw him she visibly bristled, but held herself down as he proceeded in his lugubrious way.

'C' had been cagey in gaining the ear of Jim Dodson, the beloved cabinet hawk, as the means of having quick access to the Prime Ministerial presence at that critical time.

'Prime Minister,' said 'C', as he interlaced the fingers of his delicate old hands opposite her at the long table, 'I would like to introduce one of our senior agents, Mr Paul Finningham, who has what we believe to be the key to solving the dilemma thrust upon you. We now know who is behind this terrorist attack, and we believe we have found the means of defeating it.'

The room was as still as the grave while 'C' outlined the substance of Paul's investigation and the way in which this pointed to a new plan of action. As he spoke, the Prime Minister leaned forward in her chair, allowing her mouth to drop open at some of the information revealed, absorbed and intent when the rudiments of the plan were spelt out.

It was left to Paul Finningham to describe the plan in detail. He was concise and direct in a manner approved of by the Prime Minister. When he was finished, there were – apart from one or two questions – no arguments or even discussion.

The plan set out by Paul Finningham was overwhelmingly agreed.

'They're not coming!' shouted Lavitzsky. 'They're not coming!'

'Too early to say yet,' said Scottie. But he looked at his watch all the same.

The little Russian was now practically gibbering in

terror. 'I'm not a soldier like you! Leave me here. Please leave me here! Don't take me with you! I won't be any good to you out there!'

'I can't do that, can I?' said Scottie. 'You know there we're heading. It'll take them about two seconds to get it out of you. Sorry, buddy – you're coming with us all the way!'

'They'll follow us to the ends of the earth,' murmured Booth, listlessly.

'Spare me the poetry, Kid. I know who I'm working for. We're getting changes of identity, new papers, new places to go. And some nice gold bars thrown in. Keep smart and nobody will ever find you.'

'If the helicopter gets here,' said Booth.

It was now seven minutes to the deadline.

'Well, we'll just have to go for the nuclear power-station,' said Scottie. 'You make a promise, you've gotta keep it.'

'That really will push them over the edge,' said Booth. 'They won't have anything to lose then.'

'At least we'll go down fighting, eh Maxy?' Maxton nodded, oblivious now to the taunting memory of Scottie's claim to insanity.

Soon it was five minutes.

Not a sound. Scottie eyed the missile control console. He would do the nuclear power-station and *then* try for the break-out if it came to it.

One minute to go.

And then they heard it. Echoing across the still waters, the distant roar of a twin-rotor Belvedere. It was a sweet sound. There was a rush to the portholes as it grew louder. There it was, flying down the Thames, silhouetted against a pale sky.

'Wow, baby!' shouted Scottie, backed by other cheers.

'She's done it!' shouted Booth. 'The old bitch has caved in!'

They were on their way.

The Belvedere came in to land on the after-deck of *Aztec*.

Schiele operated the radio as Scottie responded to the incoming voice of the pilot. The pilot was directed as to where to land in relation to the outer door they were leaving by. As per detailed previous instructions, a specified contingent of unarmed hostages – taken from men of the R.A.F. – were to line up on both sides, forming a human moving, masking corridor between the door and the entry-point of the Belvedere. Scottie's men were to emerge bunched together in tight formation, weapons ready and aimed. These instructions were repeated over the radio now.

No sharpshooter would get a shot at any of them. For good measure, Scottie threw in a reminder about the radio-box he would be carrying at all times, with his finger on the button. He had said that so long as *Aztec* was in sight from the departing helicopter with them in it, any spotted attempt to board her would be met by a reprisal: the loss of two hostages from the Belvedere. Scottie meant to keep the search for the devices at bay for as long as he could. Extending the view of *Aztec* with binoculars would prolong the delay.

No one ventured from *Aztec*'s superstructure until the helicopter had set down, engines running, and the human corridor had been formed of about a dozen nervous and wind-blown men, immediately outside the door.

Hakayama opened the door for Scottie. He stepped forward, and held high the radio-box he was carrying. Then, as ordered, the gang formed close ranks and came out, quickly making their way, slightly crouched, to the waiting chopper. They might almost have been going furtively down a guard of honour.

They climbed aboard and were followed by the hostage

contingent, held at gunpoint as they returned to the Belvedere. The door was shut and the helicopter slowly took off.

The *Aztec* was free of her captors.

18

In the hour of his deliverance, Warren Booth was now experiencing the tremors of fear.

It didn't matter that Maxton, Figac, Hakayama, Schiele, Waleski, Donohue and the others had their automatic weapons trained firmly on every uniformed hostage in the Belvedere, just as Scottie Moore was up front, his pistol pointed at the skipper's head, monitoring radio traffic between ground and craft, clutching his radio-box.

It didn't help because Warren Booth just didn't believe any of it. It was all too good to be true, becoming a gold millionaire after pulling the biggest job of the century. He didn't believe in Lyneham or a Hercules transporter laden with fabulous riches. It was all a put-up job. In reality they were being ferried to a prison camp, where they would be rounded up in a jeep and taken off to be shot – once separated from their hostages.

He thought about being blindfolded in front of a firing-squad and wondered what the advantage was. He had heard of men refusing blindfolds and being considered very brave guys. As he looked at the serious fates of the young hostages he fantasised that he and his cohorts were *their* prisoners instead of the other way round. It had to be, it was inevitable. He wished Scottie weren't so far off at that moment, that he were accessible so that Booth could communicate his fears. It might make all the difference if Scottie knew what Booth knew.

The weight of Lavitzsky's head against his shoulder was beginning to irritate him. The Russian had drooped and, amazingly, was now fast asleep. Thank God Scottie had relieved him of the requirement to carry a gun!

What had developed between the two men over the past traumatic days, as well as the previous arduous weeks of training, was a caring attitude to one another: fellow scientists, the only two in this mob to pass for intellectuals, and both of them non-combatants (except, in his earlier life, Booth when drunk). Their long discussions into the night on the technical complexities of the battle-cruiser's weapons and communications systems inevitably created a bond which couldn't be shared with anyone else, not even with Scottie who – as a former naval officer – had a workman's knowledge of his tools, but no more.

During the tense hours they had sustained one another. Booth looked down at the little man with the dark bags under his eyes and thinning hair – he could be a shoe salesman waiting for his pension. The thought made Booth smile, so that his crazy fears were pushed away, at least a bit. The little man had done his stuff, all right. Helped bring down a helicopter and scared the shit out of London, England.

Once, at two in the morning on *Aztec*, Anatoly had leaned back against the wall and rubbed his eyes with forefinger and thumb. 'I'm sorry,' he said. 'I have been speaking English for eight hours now. It takes much sometimes to find the words, the technical ones.' It had never occurred to Warren that talking English could exhaust anyone. And fussy, small Anatoly had kept it up uncomplainingly, often over matters so abstruse that even Warren found difficulty remembering the right words sometimes.

Would the man ever see his wife again that he had talked about so much? Warren doubted it. At best Anatoly would find himself shacked up in some flea-bitten *hacienda* in Bolivia or somewhere, with a tub of lard of an old squaw – he seemed to like the type. Ugh! Give me the sacred cleft any day, thought Warren, his shakes subsiding in drowsy, sensuous half-thoughts brought on by the din and vibration of the Belvedere's engines. As he relaxed he got a hard-on and wondered if any of the youngsters staring into space opposite him would blush to see it. Or – fantasy of fantasies – get a hard-on himself?

The radio up front crackled into life.

The Belvedere was in communication with R.A.F. Lyneham control tower. Scottie allowed himself a glance down through the thinning cloud which parted to reveal the sprawl of buildings, undistinguished except for a whirling radar grid and a wind-sock or two. The first phase was nearly over.

Impatiently he looked out for the Hercules. As he gave instructions to the pilot, and the Belvedere slowly descended, the old-fashioned, squat goose of a huge airplane came into view.

As per stipulations, there was no sign of loading activity around the craft; no maintenance, fuelling, anything. Also according to plan was the fact that the airplane was parked at least five hundred, if not a thousand yards from the nearest building. He didn't propose that they should be picked off from a control tower or whatever while making the transfer from Belvedere to Hercules. The plane was to be loaded and ready to go upon their arrival. And there it was. Like ordering a taxi.

'That's it,' said Scottie, holding his elation at bay, 'nice and easy.' He waited until all the engines had wound down and been switched off. 'Wow. We're just going to sit here for a moment, take in the lie of the land. No panic.'

He could see neat coils of nylon rope lined up on the tarmac. His instructions had been fulfilled to the letter.

'Right,' said Scottie. 'Now we're going to vacate, real calm.' He waved his pistol at the cabin crew. 'You guys first.' They extricated themselves from their seats. Their appearance at the door signalled to Maxton, down in the body of the craft, to order evacuation.

This was a complicated manoeuvre. First a small group of hostages descended and formed a circle outside the Belvedere. Then, a detachment of the terrorists. Then, more hostages, followed by the remainder of the terrorists. Scottie with his box, pushing the skipper out in front of him, came last. They were now all down on the tarmac.

Helicopters appeared on the scene, creating a din, not quite over them, a little to one side. Scottie wasn't worried. He had his box, and as long as the hostages were deployed strategically – never too far from his men and never too close – it should be all right until they were tied up inside the Hercules. It was essential to get this phase over as soon as possible. Standing and free, men are dangerous even without weapons. Somebody always wants to be a hero, or gain promotion.

The three priorities were the marching of the hostages onto the Hercules and their binding, the gaining of command of the Hercules itself and its crew – who should be waiting on board – and the counting of the gold before take-off.

But first, something else.

'Anybody wants a piss, do it now,' he ordered. He wasn't going to have the whole thing screwed up by little trips to the bathroom, with all the security risks involved in those. 'You want to crap, you'll have to hold on. Anyway, you don't want to crap, you're all constipated.' So, before anyone got into the Hercules, there was the spectacle played out on the tarmac of small groups of men, under guard, wandering off a discreet distance to pee. 'Remember what your moms told you about long journeys,' said Scottie, his first intimation of what lay in store.

Such is the stuff of historic occasions.

Bladders emptied (for those lucky enough to be able to do it on command), all were zipped up and ready.

The men were then ordered into the plane, gathering up their own lengths of rope as they went. Their value as users of arms and legs was past. From now on they were pieces of meat, but valuable, like prime beef. Their presence on the Hercules might add to the weight but it was also the chief insurance against the possibility of the lumbering plane being shot down, especially past the Channel and over Europe.

Inside stood the neatly piled gold bars. Ten tonnes of them. With a nod of the head Scottie drew out two from his group to count them. And to make sure there weren't any tricks, like concrete or something in the middle. The two had been briefed on what to look for and how to evaluate. They weren't to slaver at the mouth. They were to check for tricks, every step of the way.

'Don't look at it, boys,' said Scottie. 'Only lumps of metal to you until we get to where we're going.'

While the counting was going on the hostages were tied up and put into crouched positions along the walls of the fuselage not taken up by the cargo. Docile as mud.

Scottie wasn't too sure he liked this. Not so much as a jostle. Not a scowl on the lips. They behaved like automatons, these hostages. Hand-picked men, they must've been, and they were like dummies.

'I can't help but feel they're getting away with it,' murmured the Prime Minister as she watched closed-circuit TV pictures of the R.A.F. Hercules lumbering to an agonisingly slow take-off from the Lyneham tarmac. 'Terrorists. Criminals.'

Already she was aware that she faced new political battles. All of the previous cover-up of the emergency would now come out. She would be blamed for everything that had gone wrong: the helicopter disaster, the loss of the insurance building. She would be accused of having arrogated dictatorial powers to herself. The Leader of the Opposition was no longer by her side. No doubt he was working already on the Parliamentary speech that would spearhead the attack. Well, the people would judge. Countless lives had been saved. Anglo-American relations were intact. Law and order had been preserved. But at what price? Would she be remembered, *she* of all people, as the Prime Minister who had capitulated to criminals?

It all depended on what happened next.

The Finningham Plan in retrospect she saw as a last, desperate throw to save the country from the real possibility of attack on a nuclear power-station. The question was, would it work?

'It'll work, Prime Minister, it'll work,' said Basil Pennington. Coming from him, the remark was less than reassuring.

The originator of the plan was not, however, sitting with the Prime Minister and her party watching television.

Paul Finningham was on board the Hercules.

Dressed in the uniform of the flight-crew, he had flown to Lyneham by jet, long in advance of the arrival of Scottie's party. Now, he was crammed into the corner with the navigator, hoping he wasn't spotted as a supernumerary.

The pilot, Graham Ritchie, had no idea where he was going. Now, with the Hercules airborne, Scottie Moore told him. 'Cyrenaican Peoples' Republic,' he said. 'Souke Airport. Plot a course. And that little piece of information stays inside this cockpit, understand?'

'You're the boss,' said Ritchie without emotion. 'You know we'll have to fly over French airspace. I'll have to alert French Air Traffic Control.'

'Do what you have to do. Someone'll be here listening the whole time, remember.'

'Things would be a lot easier, chum,' said Ritchie, 'if you didn't point that thing at me the whole way.'

'Don't worry about it. Let's just get some of the way first.' He leaned out the door. 'Maxton?' And turned back to the pilot. 'We've got compasses with us, so if this crate starts veering any direction other than generally south, I'm going to know about it and I'm going to want to know why.' Maxton arrived and Scottie told him to stay with the pilot and watch the cabin crew. He went back to a seat he'd earmarked for himself for the long trip.

Paul breathed a sigh of relief. Confirmation that Cyrenaica was the destination. Scottie intended to take his millions in gold to Souke Airport, in the weird and wonderful world of the Cyrenaican Peoples' Republic under President Zamisces.

Cyrenaica had for years been a peaceful North African backwater under the corrupt government of the ineffable Bey of Souke. It withstood the revolutionary surges which brought radical socialist, Muslim governments to neighbouring Algeria and Libya. Then, about fifteen years before the present affair, the Bey was over-thrown by Colonel Zamisces and his merry men. Unlamented, the Bey retired to sumptuous seclusion in Switzerland and Zamisces proceeded to create a one-party, indeed one-man totalitarian state with help from the Soviet Union and Colonel Gaddafi.

Having achieved a measure of semi-colonial prosperity under the Bey, with the strings-attached help of the former French colonial masters, Cyrenaica was transformed under Zamisces. Unfortunately the country possessed no oil with which to feather-bed his dynamic intentions. Foreign investment fled from the land, leaving it utterly dependent on the charity of the Soviet Union and the dubious help of Colonel Gaddafi, who would have dearly liked to swallow it up. Poverty was desperate even by North African standards. The population was a time bomb: fifty per cent of it under the age of fourteen.

Zamisces simply increased his grip on the country. Ten years after his assumption of power he found himself leading the Albania of Africa: poor, ideologically rigid, isolated from the West, isolated from pan-Arab developments, and growing increasingly estranged from its up-till-now reliable lifeline, the Soviet Union, which was having problems of its own.

Zamisces had painted himself into a corner. He couldn't appeal for Western aid – he had already reneged on deals in the past. He couldn't look to Gaddafi for more support for fear of Libyan absorption, and he could no longer rely forever on payments from Moscow.

Meanwhile, the crowds on the streets were becoming more and more restive and secret police activity was intensified. Those fourteen-year-olds were beginning to grow up.

And so Zamisces, with a combination of megalomania which was a result of believing the myth he had created in order to deceive the people, and fear for the future of his own Swiss bank-account, hit upon a plan. It might not save his government in the long run, but it should save his skin.

* * *

Maxton stood over Ritchie while the latter communicated with French Air Traffic Control. The ex-sergeant was listening to every word.

'Permission to fly over French airspace has already been granted,' said the voice at the other end.

Paul stiffened. The fools, were they giving the game away? From his corner he watched Maxton intently.

Maxton didn't move, didn't seem to understand what he'd heard. The pilot completed his communication and the radio was switched off. Paul held his breath.

Then Maxton turned and shouted over his shoulder: 'Boss!'

In an instant Scottie's head poked through the doorway. 'What is it?'

'They've already had clearance to fly over France.'

Scottie took a step towards the pilot, black box under one arm, pistol brandished in the other hand. 'Okay, so somebody gave you clearance before you even took off – what is this? How come you got clearance already? What's going on?'

'Perhaps I can explain,' said Paul, who rose slowly from his seat. Scottie whirled round on him, waggling his pistol. 'You, stay where you are! Who the hell are you? You're not in the crew!'

'I was sent to supervise operations,' said Paul evenly. 'To see everything goes according to plan.'

'So why are you dressed up like a crewman?'

'We thought you might object otherwise if I came along.'

'Yeah, well I object now. So maybe you'd like to leave – by the door?' He turned to Maxton. 'You keep a watch over this bunch and give us another shout if there's anything, like you did then. You,' he said to Paul, waving his pistol again, 'you come with me.'

Paul went through the doorway into the main area

inside the fuselage, feeling cold steel against his back. Was he going to be pushed out, there and then? He felt strangely cool. If he was going down, he'd take at least two of them with him.

But Scottie didn't try to push him out the door. Instead he told him to sit across the aisle from him, and sat down himself. 'All right. First let's find out who you are.'

'I work for government security,' said Paul. 'I was detailed to make sure everything went ahead according to your plan, see to it that all the gold went into the right hands, that sort of thing.'

'Don't you think we could be trusted to make sure of that ourselves?'

'Well, you never know,' said Paul, stretching his silly-ass Englishman act to the limit. 'The odd bar might go missing or unaccounted for. They're worth £95,000 apiece, you know.'

'You don't say? Christ, you don't even trust your own people! So, what's this with the air traffic clearance?'

'Quite simple,' said Paul, tossing it off. 'My government assumed you'd want to fly over France and so made the appropriate arrangements.' He was consciously modelling himself on one of the permanent under-secretaries of his department.

'Why did you assume that? Maybe I'd have wanted to fly to Ireland. Or maybe Russia. Or maybe South America via the Azores. Why France, 'specially?'

The success of the whole plan now rested on the impression Paul gave.

'We discounted Ireland,' he said. 'We didn't think the Irish would offer you sanctuary. Can you blame them? As for Russia – well, they're out of this sort of game these days, aren't they? South America was a possibility, but you don't need clearance for the Atlantic anyway. We hardly thought you were going to Norway, or the North

Pole. So what else is there but a route over France? It's France for all points south. Do give us credit for knowing our geography!' Paul hoped he wasn't overdoing the prissy campness. If he wasn't to appear too brave and hand-picked for a daring assignment, he must go the other way, look like the fool who didn't know what he'd let himself in for.

Once Scottie got an inkling that the government already knew Cyrenaica to be the destination, anything could happen. He could order the plane down anywhere, off-load the gold anywhere, blow up the plane, the crew and the hostages in some deserted area – and nobody would know where he was or be able to do anything about it until he got clean away with the gold. Having brought a major NATO country to its knees in the process.

Scottie Moore was silent.

Schiele came up from behind and spoke to Scottie. 'We still got a helicopter escort. Half a dozen, I counted. R.A.F.'

'Still with us, eh?' Scottie looked down, out of the window. The Hercules was still over the Channel, but approaching the French coastline. 'We should lose 'em any minute,' he said. 'Unless they're going all the way.'

'They were under instruction to escort you to the French coast,' said Paul. 'Then you're on your own.' He hoped to God the R.A.F. wouldn't try anything heroic as a last fling.

'You better be right,' said Scottie. 'I'm still within range for *Aztec*, and your guys won't have found *every* device on board her by now, I don't think.' He held up his box. 'I'll still be in range for some time yet.'

Paul looked at the box. It could have been totally empty, a complete bluff, a toy. But was it? And even if it was for real, could they be within range now? It didn't seem conceivable. But he wasn't going to argue the point.

Schiele was looking out one of the windows. 'They're falling back now,' he said.

'Good,' said Scottie. 'But keep watching. And keep your eye on your compass.' Schiele returned to the back. 'I hold all the cards; there isn't any point in trying anything now. You guys never give up, do you?'

'I'm only here to look after the gold,' said Paul.

'Don't give me that pigshit. You're a top agent. They wouldn't send up a clerk on a job like this. So what's the angle?'

Paul sat back in his seat and tried to relax or give the impression of relaxing. He dropped his camp act. 'Okay, you're right,' he said. 'I'm an agent. They wouldn't let anybody else up here with you lot. But there's no plan, or anything. How could there be? Like you say – you hold all the cards.'

'This thing does work, you know,' said Scottie after a moment, holding up the box. His pale eyes had taken on their dangerous glitter. 'Maybe you don't believe me?'

'I believe you,' said Paul. If he'd been sitting next to this man on an ordinary commercial flight, would he have sized him up as a killer?

Paul saw Scottie's thumb slide over the button. The button that could signal a detonation or two in the Pool of London. 'I kind of hate to waste this,' said Scottie. 'One push and it's all gone. London, maybe England. Maybe other places as well.'

Paul thought it was more than likely that all the conceivable hiding-places in the superstructure would have been located by now, if indeed they were still within range.

Scottie looked at him and seemed to read his thoughts. 'You *don't* believe me! The man who blew up London! I'd go down in history, you know that?' The thumb continued to slide over and over the button on the box. 'Devised by experts, this little baby. Couple of hundred miles range. We're just about out of that now. Maybe it stretches to three hundred miles. They couldn't be all that specific.'

'I'd go for the nice, easy life if I were you,' said Paul. 'No hassles, nobody after you. You'll have all that money. What's your cut?'

'That's my business.'

'Well, whatever it is it must be plenty to be getting on with.'

'So, you think I retire to a little place in the country, is that it? Wise up. Where do you think I'm supposed to go after this?'

You might have thought of that before embarking on this caper, thought Paul.

'They'll be looking for me all over when this is finished. Because I got your Prime Minister to kiss my ass, right? They don't like kissing ass, none of them. They don't forgive that. They don't forgive you for being too smart for them. That's the worst crime of all. Not killing people, oh no! Being too smart. *That's* the crime of the century! So, why not go all the way? Why not do what I said I'd do? If they get me in the end and I haven't done it, then there won't have seemed much point, will there?'

'You've got the whole world to play in,' said Paul. 'Christ, people disappear in a little country like Britain every day and nobody finds them.'

'That's because nobody's looking,' said Scottie. The thumb slid over and over the button.

Paul was trying to keep him talking. 'They'll forget about you in time. Like Lord Lucan.'

'Who's he?'

'Chap who murdered his wife's nanny. He disappeared.

There was an almighty hunt for him, all over the world. People claimed to have seen him in Australia, Europe, everywhere. He never showed. It was assumed he was dead and everybody eventually forgot about him. It'll happen to you, too. Keep on the move for a while, but in time, with your money – which Lord Lucan didn't have, by the way – you'll submerge. No one'll find you. And they'll forget. That's the main thing. But they won't forget if you use that.'

Scottie grinned. 'You talk too much,' he said.

Then, suddenly, he tossed the box into Paul's lap.

'There you are. Souvenir. It was a near thing, though. I almost did it. Now it's your turn.'

'What?'

'You do it. Go on. Push the button. Just for laughs. It may still work.'

Paul looked at the button on the box. It didn't look so harmless now. In fact the box itself was a lot heavier than he had thought. 'You know I can't do it.'

The barrel of the automatic pressed against the side of Paul's head. 'You know you can,' said Scottie. 'Why do you think I haven't pushed you out the door before now? I was saving you up for this. It's your big moment, boy. The guy who *really* blew London!'

Paul froze. There might still be a chance if he could stall until he felt sure the plane was really out of range. The two sat there for a moment. Then Scottie shouted: 'Schiele!'

Schiele came forward.

'Take one of those hostages – doesn't matter which one – and push him out,' said Scottie.

Schiele never questioned a command, no matter how brutal. He grunted and turned away, down to the hostages at the rear of the Hercules. 'One life against London. What about that? What's your name? I don't believe I caught it. I don't like talking to a guy without knowing his name.'

'Paul.'

'Paul. Nice name, like the Apostle.' Paul heard the sounds of a struggle and a cry from a man at the rear above the engines' din. He closed his eyes and pushed the button hard down on the box.

'There, that wasn't so bad, was it?' said Scottie. He shouted back to Schiele to call off the execution. The pressure of the barrel against Paul's head was gone. Paul rubbed the spot and wondered what he had just done.

'You've started something back in London, I guess,' chuckled Scottie, 'or not as the case may be. Like I said, I don't know if it's out of range or not. We'll have to wait and see, won't we?'

Paul thought of Jane and wondered if she would be all right. Suddenly he wanted her desperately, her mouth, her arms, her body...

'Well, Paul, now that's over I've had enough of your company. You want to leave us now?' He grinned, and the eyes still glittered.

This was it. Paul again swore to himself he'd take two men with him.

'Go back to Schiele. He'll tie you up for the rest of the trip.' It seemed that Scottie wasn't interested in killing after all, only in a little shut-eye.

They tied him tightly, binding his wrists. He was shoved down to sit, ignominiously cross-legged, with the other hostages near the rear of the creaking, rattling old airplane.

It would take many hours for the plane to reach Souke Airport. There was time to think, think things through.

The extraordinary thing was that Zamisces had been entirely overlooked. There were no *bona fide* Western agents working inside Cyrenaica, no inkling that he might be the source. All sorts of scenarios had been devised to link Gaddafi, or the P.L.O., or the mullahs of Iran to the crime – but all fanciful and without solid Intelligence substance. Thus valuable weeks had been lost in the run-up to the *Aztec* takeover because of mistaken and half-baked assumptions.

Maxton was relieved by Figac in the crew's cabin. Even the pilot Ritchie had a kip. Scottie dozed intermittently, his previously precious radio-box tossed aside; the drone of the plane's four engines was lulling, when you got used to it. A funny old thing to be carrying out the *coup* of the century in, but the only aircraft with the big pay-load he knew would be easily available. Soon they'd be at Souke. God-forsaken, fly-blown gnat's-ass of a place.

He knew Zamisces, for all his retainers and silk suits, was as big a crook as he was, only bigger since he'd be getting away with more. Eighty million bucks for himself and his wife and concubines. Scottie was under no illusion that Cyrenaica would be a safe haven for long. Zamisces would have to work quickly if he was to get out before concerted pressure by the whole world was put on the country to return the gold. If Reagan could strafe Gaddafi with impunity the British would clobber Zamisces. But he'd be out of it before then – and so would the gang. They'd stay long enough for their meeting at the airport with Zamisces to divide the spoils, get their papers together, and then arrange to disperse to the four corners of the world. Zamisces' ambassador (who, like the rest of his people, all but for the inner circle, knew nothing of the plot) would be instructed to stall diplomatically for as long as possible in London before the British government finally lost patience and sent out the F111s.

The whole project had been paid for out of the dwindling Cyrenaican treasury. Three, four million pounds had been spent on initial outlay. As the outgoing money didn't belong to Zamisces, but the incoming gold would, a clear and cool 100 per cent profit had been made!

Oh well, at least he was robbing a rich country instead of his own people. For *that* you got American aid, if you were also fighting guerillas.

Yes, thought Scottie; you have to keep these things in perspective.

19

They were here.

'Souke Airport Control to Hercules. You are clear to land, Hercules.'

Figac woke Scottie. 'Okay,' mumbled Scottie, stretching and trying to get his bones realigned after an uncomfortable night. 'Get back to the pilot, then. They can still try anything, even at this stage.' He rubbed his hands together. 'Last phase!' He looked out both sides. It was still dark out. No lights indicated the presence of any other aircraft in the skies. He got up and walked to the rear of the plane. 'This is it, boys,' he said, 'we've made it to Souke.'

Perhaps it was sheer fatigue, but there was no verbal response to the announcement of the end of their adventure. Scottie ruffled the hair of the half-awake Warren Booth. 'All right, Kid?' he asked, smiling.

'You bet,' murmured Warren. Then he opened his eyes wide, as if to force them open, stretched, and gave a sudden loud whoop.

It was this which woke Paul. Sleep had almost forced its way upon him, determined as he was to keep vigilant. He wanted to stretch and rub his eyes. Funny, the things you can't do when your hands are tied behind you.

The engines altered the pitch of their noise and the fuselage began to tilt downwards. Scottie decided to move into the cockpit to oversee the landing. Once there, he looked out and could see the lights of the runway, dead ahead.

The plane bumped its tyres along the runway a few times and eventually came to a stop. The last detail of the flight plan was that it should not park too near the airport buildings. The lights of the control tower and one or two others could be made out, perhaps a thousand yards away.

Scottie ordered everyone to keep still. The Hercules engines were cut off, silent.

The quiet that followed was uncanny. Scottie could make out no movement outside the craft, but then they were a long way from anywhere. He decided to get things organised for the removal of the gold.

The great hatch at the back of the Hercules was opened and came down. So as to get them out of the way of the transfer, Scottie then ordered the hostages to be removed from the plane and stood to one side on the tarmac, under guard. The crew also came out.

Lorries could be heard in the distance. Straining his eyes in the direction of the airport, Scottie could make out three. They drove slowly, their old engines whining, slowly in the direction of the Hercules and the waiting men. As they came more into view, Scottie could make out that they were old army lorries, painted in camouflage. Gears grinding as they changed down to stop, two of the lorries disgorged about a dozen men each, leaping out of the back, gripping rifles. They were not soldiers, or at least they were not in uniform. Scottie knew what they were: members of Zamisces' secret police, the military wing. This was a covert operation, to be kept from the knowledge of his own people – naturally, therefore, the regular army was not involved.

The third lorry was empty. This was the one to which the gold was to be transferred. Its cab door opened and the man who was obviously in charge of the contingent dropped down to the tarmac and came over to where

Scottie stood. He smiled a row of pearly teeth under a black, swooping moustache. In French he explained to Scottie that the president was waiting back at the airport; that the gold was to be placed onto the lorry and removed, with his gang, to a location not far from the airport where all the necessary arrangements would be made.

Scottie asked him who was to unload the gold. The moustachioed man indicated the hostages with a toss of his head.

Scottie ordered the hostages' wrists, including those of Paul Finningham among them, to be untied. While that was being done, the empty lorry was turned round and reversed towards the Hercules.

Scottie didn't like the sound of the 'necessary arrangements'. He didn't like it at all. A thought struck him. As the moustachioed man was about to issue an order, Scottie touched his shoulder and asked him what was to happen to the Hercules after the gold was removed.

The man shrugged. 'They can fly back where they came from,' he said.

Scottie thought he had it. On its way back over the Mediterranean, after being re-fuelled at Souke, and flown by its original British crew, the Hercules would be shot out of the sky by the Cyrenaican Air Force (an easy-enough target for that ramshackle outfit!) on grounds of 'infringing Cyrenaican airspace'.

Meanwhile, Zamisces would have Scottie and his men 'disappeared'. The implication being, of course, that the plane had sunk, all hands lost, in the middle of the sea (exact or even inexact spot unknown) with the gold on board. Zamisces would not only have all the gold for himself; he wouldn't even be fingered by Britain and the international community for having master-minded the plot to capture it. It was certainly a neat idea.

'Our cut of the gold stays on the airplane,' said Scottie to the moustachioed officer.

'All of the gold is to be removed!' protested the man. 'Those are my strict instructions from the President!'

'Plans have changed, then,' said Scottie. 'We'll keep our share of the gold on board and then fly the plane somewhere else to unload it ourselves. Got it?'

'No, no, that will not be permitted!' shouted the man. 'All of the gold is to be removed and you are to come to meet the President!'

'Tell him to come out here and meet us,' said Scottie. 'In fact it might be a good idea if he came along too, for the ride.'

'You cannot order our leader in this way!' blustered the man, his moustache twitching. 'You are to do as I say!'

And Scottie knew he had been right. After the biggest job of all time, the biggest double-cross. It was what his intuition had been telling him from the moment he saw that President Zamisces hadn't come out personally to welcome him, which Scottie had understood to be the original 'arrangement'.

'None of that gold leaves the plane,' shouted Scottie to all and sundry, 'until we've sorted this thing out!'

'They're in a spot of bother,' whispered Paul to the R.A.F. hostage next to him. 'Shouldn't be long now.'

Scottie ordered the flight crew back into the aircraft. He was plainly having the Hercules ready to fly out again.

He had been strung along all this time by Zamisces' insinuation that the gold was his last throw as president. In reality Zamisces had no such idea. He would have the gold *and* keep the presidency!

The moustachioed man gave a barking order and two dozen rifles were cocked. Scottie shouted to his men to get down.

'For Christ's sake get down!' rasped Paul to the man next to him, shoving him down on the tarmac.

Distantly could be heard the sound of approaching helicopters. Both Scottie and the moustachioed man looked up, startled. The Cyrenaican screamed at his men to take cover close to the lorries. Scottie shouted to his contingent to make for the Hercules.

'Now!' shouted Paul. He and the hostages sprang at the gang, distracted as they were by the helicopters and the sudden turn of events. Nobody was to regain the Hercules at any cost.

Brilliant spotlights glared down then from the roaring sources. The Cyrenaicans raised their rifles to fire but were blinded by the light. Whiplashes of bullets sent some of them flying – others ran off to get out of the circles of light.

The hostages, 'dummies' till then, came into their own. In the *mêlée* Paul found himself grappling with Donohue. The Irishman had him pinned down to the tarmac, while Paul struggled to push off the automatic rifle whose length was pressing against his wind-pipe. With superhuman effort, Paul raised the rifle, inch by painful inch, until he had the leverage to push Donohue back, whereupon he gave him a decisive crack on the jaw with a left hook that sent the Irishman reeling, his automatic flying from his hands. Paul scrambled to grab it.

Blindly he looked round for Scottie. There was too much confusion to see. Hakayama was beating hell out of one poor 'hostage' with the frenzy of a madman – before his back arched inwardly and he threw his head up in a yell of pain: he had been shot in the back. Maxton was swinging his rifle round and round a circle of 'hostages' who were trying to go for him – until one brave man made a diving tackle for the ex-sergeant's legs and brought him down, rugby-style. Maxton's head cracked on the concrete.

Warren Booth ran screaming into the darkness at the edge of the light: there he was caught by gun-fire and swivelled round again into the light, his hands at his face, blood gushing through his fingers. He was dead before he reached the ground.

There was no sign now of any living Cyrenaicans, though there were plenty of dead ones lying here and there. The rest had flown into the dying night – to be caught by the gun-fire of men emerging from landed helicopters in the distance, helicopters whose roundels could be dimly made out in the new-born morning.

Lavitzsky lay flat on his stomach, his head buried in his arms.

The sporadic firing in the distance ceased as the harsh voice from a loud hailer blared out from the dark: 'Give yourselves up! I repeat, throw down your weapons and give yourselves up!'

Just then, the engines of the Hercules began to roar into life. After a few huge revs, the craft slowly began to move, its hatch-door dragging along the concrete. With a cry, Figac leapt on to it. Paul leapt on to Figac, and as the Frenchman tried to claw his way up the bouncing ramp, Paul dug his own hands into the man's belt, then up and around his shoulders and neck. Twisting round, the Frenchman tried to push him off, back on to the tarmac as the Hercules began to gather speed. Others had made a grab for the ramp and Paul had no idea whose side they were on. Gradually he worked his way up the Frenchman's back until he reached Figac's gripping fingers, trying to dislodge them. The grip loosened and Paul rolled himself and Figac over so that the Frenchman was now lying and kicking precariously on top of Paul. With one great upward shift of the knee – Paul thought he heard his knee-joint crack – Paul sent Figac flying before rolling back to get a grip for himself. He had a chance to see that one who had grabbed the ramp along with him was an R.A.F. man, kicking someone else who had done the same – Schiele – off the ramp with his boots. Schiele fell back and in an instant could be seen lying on the tarmac, his body growing ever smaller with the movement of the plane.

Paul crawled up the ramp little by little, and then lurched into the fuselage. If the hatch-cover wasn't raised the gold would soon slide out and scatter over North Africa, once the Hercules was airborne.

The door into the cockpit was swinging wildly in the juddering plane. Through the doorway Paul could see the back of Scottie Moore, forcing Graham Ritchie and his co-pilot to fly the plane at gunpoint.

He wanted very much to shoot Scottie in the back.

Quickly he looked round to see the R.A.F. man with him, who also had a weapon. As one man, they both crouched and Paul shouted out: 'Scottie!'

Scottie Moore wheeled about, his face contorted with hatred as he stared down the gun-barrels of two automatic weapons trained at him. He had almost let off his own gun turning round – almost. Was it because for a split second he thought it was one of his own calling to him from behind?

Whatever it was, the hesitation was vital. He would be shot before he could shoot them. And there were two at his back who would surely go for him from behind when they looked round and saw what was up.

Then, something odd. The hatred seemed to drain from Scottie's face. The lines around the strong, pale-blue eyes softened and crinkled. He grinned.

'Nice one,' he said. 'But there's more than one way to go.'

The smile took on a strained, tightened look, and suddenly the eyes clamped shut. The pistol fell from Scottie's hands as he clutched his stomach and slumped forward to the floor.

Paul and the R.A.F. man waited a few seconds, in case it was a trick. But the pistol had well and truly bounced out of grabbing distance. 'Stop the plane!' shouted Paul. 'Stop the plane!'

A little later, he stumbled down the fuselage towards the gaping hatchway. Approaching the craft from behind were four low-flying helicopters which settled themselves down. An officer leapt down and ran up the ramp. 'Is he in there? The ringleader?' Paul waved, weakly, and indicated an affirmative. The officer turned and shouted a command, and four other men with machine-guns jumped out of their helicopter and ran up the ramp, brushing past Paul.

He turned and looked at the massive, solid pile of gold-bars, glittering inscrutably in the rays of the rising sun. 'We fought for you,' he said aloud to 100 million dollars in gold. But maybe they had fought for something else, too.

As Paul walked back past the gold, he approached a little circle of men around the doorway to the cockpit. On the floor in the centre of it lay Scottie Moore, exactly in the position where he had fallen.

'Cyanide,' said the officer, shrugging – a little sadly, perhaps, having hoped to capture his man alive.

There was the ghost of a death-grin on Scottie's face.

Well, at least London was still in one piece.

Paul had expected 'C' to be pleased. Instead, the old man was fussing and fretting – more like his usual old self, in fact.

'I don't see that you had to expose yourself to danger like that,' he said, making a gruff show of shuffling papers on his desk. 'You might have been killed. You should have left the commando tactics to the S.A.S.!'

'It was *my* plan and I had to see it through,' said Paul, smiling.

'Nonsense, you were just trying to prove you were still twenty-one years of age. Well, you're not and I won't have a man of your experience gallivanting about like that again.'

In the old man's opinion, the whole thing had been hare-brained and over-dependent on almost split-second timing. The civil servant in him recoiled against Wild West stuff. But it had worked. Perhaps it was the only thing that could have worked. As they were leaving for their debriefing with the Prime Minister and Cabinet, 'C' put his arm around Paul at the door of his office and hugged him. Gratitude was, at last, expressed.

20

Long before the combined operation of Mediterranean Fleet and S.A.S. on Souke Airport, in fact back to the time when Scottie – on board *Aztec* – was negotiating with the Prime Minister, her junior Minister for Nuclear Energy, Clive Parris M.P., was once again being interrogated.

By Paul Finningham with Mort Ridlake and officers of Special Branch at Baythorne Manor.

Paul held up the photograph of Sarah in bed with the man. 'Who is he, sir?' he asked.

The M.P. sighed and bowed his silver-topped head.

'Do we talk now or what?'

Aubrey Bilston, Parris's solicitor, started to interject. Clive Parris waved him aside. 'You have rights, Clive,' he was told by Bilston.

'I will not impede these men in doing their duty,' said Clive. His defiance had drastically altered when he saw the picture.

'Who is this man?' repeated Paul Finningham.

'His name is Akim Mahmoud. It's a long story.'

'We'd like to hear it, sir. From the beginning, if you would.'

Bilston settled back, with a worried look, ready to spring if he saw his client get into trouble. Clive Parris turned to him: 'Aubrey, leave it to me. I know what I'm doing. Right. Where is the beginning? Perhaps it all goes back to the day Sarah and I were married. That's when it really began. But you don't want to hear all about that.'

'Whatever is relevant to the case, Mr Parris,' said Paul.

'I don't suppose I could have a cigarette off someone? I haven't smoked in years – gave it up, like everybody else. Suddenly I feel I want to smoke.' Paul nodded to Mort Ridlake, who still kept up the habit. Ridlake stepped forward and offered Clive a Silk Cut and a light from his lighter. Exhaling deeply, Clive sat back in the armchair.

'My family never thought I was up to much. Even my own mother was condescending. I suppose I've spent my whole life trying to prove something – prove to *them* – that I would get somewhere, on my own. That's why I worked so hard, to achieve things my own way. To show *them*. I didn't have time for things like romance and marriage – well, until I found I had to. My party likes its candidates married, you know. The wife matters as much to the voters as the man himself. So, I looked for a wife and I found her. But something happened that I didn't expect: I fell in love with her. Can you believe I fell in love with her *after* we were engaged? It's true.

'But it was too late. I was years older than her. And it didn't dawn on me until much later that it wasn't because of hard work that I hadn't pursued women before – plenty of my colleagues work as hard as I do and still manage to go for a bit on the side. It was basically because I was under-sexed. Certainly compared to Sarah I was under-sexed.

'Do you know what it's like, lying in bed in a sweat next to your own wife, terrified that tonight she's going to want it, and you damned well knowing you haven't got it? Her, tossing and turning – waiting? It's the dark night of the soul, I can tell you. Time goes by and she doesn't wait any more. Actually, when you work up the gumption she rejects you. That's women I suppose, but it wasn't her fault. Sarah was a warm, animal woman. She had a right to expect what she had thought was to be hers. She had everything material that anyone could have wanted, but she couldn't get from our marriage what the poorest woman in the country can hope for.

'She did her best to cope – by God, she did! She set out to become the very picture of the dedicated politician's wife. She could open fêtes and cut ribbons with the best of them. I owed a lot of my political success at the beginning to her.

'She couldn't keep it up, of course. She developed a kind of rigidity, a sort of going-through-the-motions. After I became a minister she told me she wasn't going to go in for so much of the socialising and politicking any more. It bored her. The people bored her. I was well-enough established to deal with most of it myself. I was shocked. She seemed to be suggesting that we lead more or less separate lives. I racked my brains to come up with some way of bringing us back closer together, of sharing. I wanted her more than ever.

'I don't think she ever deceived me in those years. She held off from other men. There were certainly plenty around – there always are – waiting for the chance to go for the unfulfilled wife.'

Paul remembered his own impressions on the plane to Schipol and inwardly congratulated himself on his instincts.

'I think it was because she was proud. Too bright and proud to become someone else's bit on the side. Perhaps things would have turned out better if she had been. Of course I can say that now: the idea would've been intolerable to me at the time if I'd had any inkling of such a thing.

'Well, enough of my marital troubles. Now to business.

'A few months after I became Nuclear Minister, Sarah and I paid an official visit to Cyrenaica.'

Cyrenaica? Now we were getting to it. Paul sat forward in his seat.

'You've probably got all that on file. But then I've been to lots of countries, haven't I? Nothing particularly remarkable about my going to Cyrenaica.

'Zamisces was in one of his pro-Western bargaining moods at the time and of course nuclear power was a vital issue in a country without oil. In our foolish optimism we thought we might be able to see off the French, who had been so entrenched there, by undercutting their tenders for a possible power-station. We got the V.I.P. treatment. They can certainly be lavish, you know. Sometimes I think the poorer the country the more lavish they are. Of course in the end it didn't amount to a hill of beans. Zamisces went on to nationalise his energy programme, with Soviet help, and that was the end of that.

'But something took root in Sarah. She'd never visited a Third World country before and she was appalled at the poverty. She became completely involved in helping the Cyrenaican people, getting involved in appeals over here, and so on.

'Of course they set out to charm her, and they're the world experts at that. For all her sophistication Sarah was a fairly conventionally-brought-up English rose. I don't think she'd ever come up against real Mediterranean charm before.

'I don't think Akim Mahmoud was an agent – not then, anyway. He was just one of many diplomats she met at various functions. I learned later that he's married with four children. I think they both walked into a trap, give the fellow his due.

'When did it begin? Well, certainly long after our return to England, at any rate. After Akim Mahmoud was posted as military attaché to the Cyrenaican Embassy in London. The only thing "military" he was ever involved in was the operation to go to work on Sarah! As she was a frequent visitor to the embassy at this time it wasn't too difficult for their paths to cross.

'You see, Zamisces had her squarely in mind for something. Something so rotten, so evil... Anyhow, she was placed just right, being married to me. Through her I was to be roped in as well.'

'Clive–' warned Aubrey Bilston.

'I have to tell it, Aubrey: I have to tell it in my own way!' The solicitor's anguish was clear to all but he had no power to influence his client.

Paul continued thoughtfully, 'It was a classic set-up, the simplicity of the blackmail has to be complimented and Sarah fell for it like an over-ripe apple off a tree. Akim was the lover she had clearly wanted in her husband, instead she had found solace in what started out as an uncomplicated and straightforward affair.'

Clive took up the story, 'As their relationship grew Akim pleaded for her help to obtain classified information which came through my hands – clearly gentlemen – a spy for Cyrenaica. My wife was torn between her loyalty to me and her basic physical desires fulfilled by a man who was passionate in everything he did. He had his opportunity one last time for a night in a hotel and I was abroad that week. It started with him being apologetic and grovelling with such passion that she succumbed, agreeing to help him. They ended up in bed: him and her with the prearranged photographer skulking in the background.

'It was almost eerie the way Sarah began to take a renewed interest in my affairs. It was a build-up. They didn't tell her what to go for then. Perhaps they didn't even know themselves. But they saw her as a means for finding certain things out when they had wind of a plan.

'In the end she came to me with it. Perhaps it was a cry for help. She couldn't stand the pressure of the blackmail any more. Yes, perhaps I should have told all then. But how could I? How could I drag Sarah through the mud – my own wife? Of course it would have destroyed me politically: my wife sleeping with foreign agents. But *why* had she slept with a foreign agent in the first place? Because she wasn't sleeping with me. How could I heap it all on her, when it was basically my fault, my inadequacy? And now, in any case, I think I loved her more than ever – strange, that.

'I think that's when she really began to despise me. She had turned to me for deliverance, and as she saw it I was too spineless to do anything. She saw my protestations about public disgrace as an attempt to save my own skin. So with grim and cynical determination, she went to work with them. I became bitter with her, too. That's why I kept that photograph. I thought: "To hell with it. If I get into trouble at least I'll have the proof as to how it all started!" Foolishly I kept it. I should have thrown it away, though of course they could always come up with another one.

'Someone must've gone to Zamisces with a wild scheme for extorting gold from Britain. Whatever the circumstances, he was hooked on the idea. Sarah became some sort of co-ordinating agent for Cyrenaican espionage activity in this country, under the cover of her charitable work. Don't ask me the details – I only know because from time to time she would ask me questions, questions I was occasionally to winkle out of my M.o.D. contacts.'

'There's also your involvement with arms-sales,' said Paul. 'Did she know about that, too?'

'Don't answer that question, Clive,' said Bilston. 'This has already gone far too far.'

Clive Parris ignored both Paul's question and Bilston's interjection. 'It was through me that Sarah learned of the schedule of U.S.S. *Aztec* long in advance of its arrival in London.'

'Did you volunteer that to her?' asked Paul.

'No. She had already got wind of it from somewhere and asked me for confirmation and details. By that time we were in it too far for me to refuse. Of course later it became public knowledge. The vital thing was for it to be known about sufficiently in advance for Zamisces to activate a plan.'

'How involved were you in that plan?' Paul asked.

'I wasn't involved at all,' said Clive.

'Not even with the arms supplied to the terrorists?'

'I'm warning you! I won't have this line of questioning!' cried Aubrey Bilston.

'I'll go so far as to say that I told Sarah certain details of something that were a little in advance of public knowledge at the time. It was entirely about a courtesy-visit to be paid to the Pool of London. Really rather a dull piece of news to most people, I'd have thought.'

'Let's move on to Amsterdam,' said Paul.

'As you know I had to go to Amsterdam for an E.E.C. conference at ministerial level on nuclear energy. When Sarah heard about it – or rather, a few days after I told her I was going – she came to me and insisted that she come along. I was a bit surprised because she'd given up accompanying me on these junkets long ago. Then I thought darker thoughts, but I didn't ask any questions.' He looked down at his lap. 'I wish to God I had now.' He looked up, his eyes shining with the suggestion of tears. 'I now believe she had been summoned to Amsterdam, having reported my impending visit to her masters, for some kind of "conference" of her own with the plotters. I have heard that the headquarters for the operation was in Holland, so I think it must be so. I thought it *might* be then, too.

'One evening I was arriving back late to the Hotel Erasmus from a meeting when I saw Sarah leave, seemingly in a hurry. I decided to follow her. Her taxi and mine took us all around the houses. I had some crazy impulse that if I could track down her people and have it out with them I might be able to extricate us both from this mess. I had a minder, of course, but I told him I was off to pick up a present for her – their shops are open all hours, you know – which I hadn't had a chance to do in the daytime. I said I wouldn't be a few minutes and he could just as easily wait at the hotel. That's how I shook him. I don't suppose the chap has had the courage yet to admit to anyone that he wasn't doing his duty – I suppose he'll be sacked now. I made it worse for him by offering him a bribe later, which he accepted.

'All that's by-the-by. Presently we drew up outside the big cathedral there, the *Nieuwe Kerk*, they call it: the name's engraved on my memory. I saw Sarah go inside, and dismissed my taxi. After she'd been in there some while, I thought perhaps I should take the plunge and confront whoever it was there and then.

'Suddenly she came out, with a man. It was dark and I couldn't see him too clearly, but I heard him speaking to her. It was the voice of Scottie Moore, the one who led the assault on *Aztec*. It seemed to be a friendly conversation – as friendly as Sarah could ever be with these people. He even had his arm around her in a pally sense. They got into a car with a driver and sped off into the night. I was stuck without a taxi and couldn't find one. It was the last time I saw Sarah alive.

'I now know that it was simply a plot to get rid of her. The plan was under way and she was expendable. Worse, she was in a position to blow the whistle if it came to it. I think they felt her conscience and sense of duty might prevail when things got rough for England – as they are now.'

'So you have no actual proof that Scottie Moore murdered her?'

'How could I have? Unless you're thinking I have an inside source of my own. I can assure you I have not. But it all fits and it must be so!'

'Why didn't you report what you had seen to the police?' asked Paul.

'Believe me, I was on the verge of doing it several times. But I was afraid and confused – afraid for my own skin by then. And I didn't want Sarah's name dragged through it all now. I wanted her decently buried and remembered for what she had been – not for what she turned out to be. I delayed, and of course the longer I delayed the harder it became. With events tumbling over each other as they've been doing the past few days I've felt even more driven into a corner.'

'It only put you under more suspicion, your silence,' said Paul.

Clive Parris shrugged. 'Well, my involvement would have to be proven, wouldn't it? And since I wasn't really involved, there was nothing to prove. Only the Cyrenaicans knew about the link with Sarah, and of course they would keep quiet for their own reasons.'

'Jane Illingworth became suspicious, didn't she?' asked Paul. 'Perhaps you'd like to tell us what happened on the river here at Baythorne the night of your wife's funeral?'

Parris looked up, stunned. 'The little bitch!' he said.

'Clive–' shouted Bilston.

'So she's been spreading something round about that? Well, I can assure you it is totally without substance.'

'What is?'

'You won't trap me that way. You're about to tell me she thinks I was trying to drown her. Well, the truth is nothing like so melodramatic! We went swimming, I had a sudden attack of cramp, she tried to pull me out of the water and I was too heavy for her – and that's all there is to it!'

'She has said to us that you were extremely evasive when she was questioning you about the murder in Amsterdam. Did she suspect you thought she was on to something?'

'That is quite an impossible question for my client to answer,' said Bilston. 'Really!'

'Of course I was evasive – haven't I just told you why?' said Parris.

Paul read out to Clive Parris the content of the note from Sarah that Jane had received. 'Did you know Jane had received such a note?'

'I've had no knowledge of this until you read it to me just now,' said Clive. 'As for the note itself, I can only imagine Sarah was desperate by then to unburden herself to somebody – perhaps going to her sister with the cry for help she'd originally confronted me with.'

'Which brings us to the incident in the loft with Jane Illingworth,' said Paul.

'No comment,' said Aubrey Bilston. Paul looked back at Clive Parris.

But Clive Parris had nothing further to say.

Had he made an attempt on Jane's life once, or twice, or never? That would be a matter for the courts to decide.

All-in-all, Clive Parris had turned in a professional performance. He had salvaged what he could of his life, and perhaps done better than that. His lawyer had allowed him to speak freely all the time he was implicating Sarah and playing down his own role in the affair. Obviously, confronted with the hidden photograph, he had to admit to something. And so he admitted to being a dupe, in thrall to his lovely wife. It would lose him his career, and even give him time to do in one of the more comfortable of Her Majesty's prisons. After which he could retire to Baythorne, or go abroad.

But it wasn't that simple, for Clive Parris wasn't out of the woods yet. There was the arms-link that would be investigated, and two charges of attempted murder to face.

He obviously understood this, white-faced Clive, as the senior officer of Special Branch arrested him on these charges and one of espionage, informing him of his rights. The criminal investigation would begin now that the security investigation was over – so far as Clive Parris was concerned.

So. The frightened woman in the glamorous yellow dress on Flight BA430 to Schipol had been the moving spirit, not the pawn.

How Paul was going to explain this to her sister Jane he didn't care to consider at the moment. In any case, more urgent matters were on the agenda.

For Clive had told them the source of the plot. 'C' would have to get straight to the Prime Minister with the information.

And the plan that would save London came into being.

21

'We have a little bone to pick with you, Georgi,' said Andy Hartford to the old K.G.B. agent.

The chat so far had been amiable, and Georgi's broad, wicked smile didn't then desert him. 'Oh yes? And what is that?' His vodka twinkled in his chubby hands.

The last round of the Ransom Affair was being played out in another anonymous hotel room in Amsterdam. With the same three players as at the beginning: Paul Finningham, Andy Hartford and Georgi Arbatov.

'Go ahead, Paul my friend,' said Andy, who settled back in his armchair and raised the bourbon to his lips. He was going to enjoy this.

Paul Finningham's demeanour was somewhat grimmer. *Détente* or no *détente,* the K.G.B. hadn't been playing the game.

'We've been having some interesting conversations with a man called Anatoly Lavitzsky,' said Paul for openers.

Georgi started. 'The man is a liar, and a known criminal,' he barked.

'Be that as it may,' persisted Paul, 'he told us an unusually absorbing story.'

'I shouldn't believe all the stories you hear.'

'Why are you so anxious to discredit him? I haven't even begun!' said Paul.

The Russian shrugged. 'Carry on,' he said, as if he thought the whole matter trivial.

'Lavitzsky has told us that you recruited him shortly after he was brought into the *Aztec* plot by the terrorists.'

'I said he was a liar.'

'We believe him. He described you perfectly. Apparently two days after he joined Steenkerke's training-camp – and I take it you know who Steenkerke is, so I won't go into details – you collared him while he was taking a walk in the woods by himself. You told him he would be absolved of all crimes committed against the Soviet state and would be allowed freely back into the bosom of his family in return for his becoming your mole among the terrorists.'

Georgi was still trying to look the picture of innocence. Wide-eyed, he asked: 'And why should we want him to do that?'

'I should've thought the answer to that was obvious,' said Paul.

Andy Hartford crashed in: 'It was an ideal way for you to get details on the latest weapons and communications systems aboard U.S.S. *Aztec*!' he exclaimed. 'Come off it, Georgi, we weren't born yesterday.'

'Which naturally leads us to the question of how the K.G.B. knew about Steenkerke's set-up in the first place – and the plot to capture *Aztec*,' continued Paul. 'Now that Zamisces has killed himself we happen to know that the leak of his so-called top secret plot came directly from your bugging devices in his office.'

'The Cyrenaican Provisional Government has been very co-operative,' added Andy.

'And you know what it all means,' said Paul.

The Russian was growing sullen. 'No. I don't know what it all means, and I resent your manner.'

'It means you were somewhat less than straight with us when we appealed for information from you in the first place,' said Paul. 'You professed total ignorance. We have proof now that this was far from being so, that you knew everything that was going on. You let us flounder around while the whole of London was exposed to the possibility of catastrophe – a catastrophe of which you were forewarned!'

'You didn't know you were in for this, did you?' teased Andy. 'You thought Lavitzsky had "died of wounds" received at Souke Airport? Just a little rumour, pal. Which we put out after we listened to what he had been telling us. Mr Lavitzsky is completely unwounded and sound in wind and limb!'

'I do not have to listen to this any more!' growled Georgi, now reverting entirely to Brezhnev Man. He banged his empty glass down on the table. 'I do not have to answer to *you*!'

'No,' replied Paul in dead earnest. 'But you may have to answer to your own President. He assured our Prime Minister of the full resources – the *full* resources – of Soviet Intelligence to bring these terrorists to book. Soviet Intelligence means you.'

'So where was the help?' asked Andy.

'The Prime Minister is awaiting our report prior to sending your President a message of the strongest possible rebuke. Is that going to come as a surprise to him?'

Georgi Arbatov rose from his chair heavily and made for the door. Before opening it, he turned and faced the two Western agents. 'You don't seem to have been following events in our country too closely, which I find surprising in those who are supposed to spend their lives doing nothing else,' he said. 'The President is not all of Russia. The days of Personality Cults are long past. Everything is no longer as you have come to expect. Perhaps it will become clearer to you as time goes by.' And with that, Georgi Arbatov was gone from the room.

Paul and Andy sat together in silence for some time afterwards.

'I don't like the sound of that,' said Andy at last. 'I don't like the sound of any of that.'

'Are you thinking what I'm thinking?' asked Paul.

'The K.G.B. going freelance?' said Andy.

'The state within a state,' murmured Paul. 'Well, we always knew that, but–'

'But now the Communist Party's up shit creek, who's taking control of the *apparatchiks*?' asked Andy. 'Ninety thousand people in that outfit – Ceausescu's *Securitate* with bells on!'

'And Georgi's right in there,' said Paul. 'Like he always was.'

'Doesn't bear thinking about, does it, "old boy"?' said Andy.

'I do wish you wouldn't try on the Englishisms,' said Paul. 'You aren't much good at it.'

'Somebody's got to prop up your identity,' said Andy.

Lavitzsky seemed to have maintained his genius for escape. He was the only one in the *Aztec* plot to get clean away with it.

Scottie Moore, Warren Booth, Maxton, Figac and Hakayama were dead. The others, recovering from various wounds, received life sentences – in the literal sense – which they now serve in a number of Her Majesty's top security prisons.

And Lavitzsky escaped with nothing more than a bad state of nerves.

Whatever Paul and Andy thought about the cunning and callousness of the K.G.B., its plan had spectacularly failed – on this occasion.

Lavitzsky was to have been 'rescued' by K.G.B. officers inside Cyrenaica once the gold had been unloaded and he had his cut. Zamisces had agreed that he was the one member of the gang who was to be spared the slaughter that was on the cards.

Of courses Lavitzsky had to operate on his own while the occupation of the battle-cruiser on the Thames was actually going on: the K.G.B. had no control over his fate then. If he were captured by the British in London they would work through diplomatic channels to have him returned to the U.S.S.R. But Lavitzsky, not being a brave man, had a fit of the collywobbles prior to the departure of the Belvedere helicopter. For a moment his mind was seized by the danger involved in the so-called 'safe' conduct out of the U.K. and the hazards of the trip to Cyrenaica. No matter. He was hauled along by Scottie to Cyrenaica – a Scottie who was entirely unsuspecting of Lavitzsky's true role.

What the K.G.B. hadn't bargained for was Paul's plan for the seizure of Souke Airport and the rescue of the gold right inside the country of its destination. The shooting on the tarmac had exposed their man to real, unforeseen danger – which they, waiting helplessly at the airport buildings, could do nothing about. On the tarmac Lavitzsky merely froze like a rabbit, to be carted back to Britain by courtesy of the S.A.S. and the Royal Navy.

In the original plan, Lavitzsky was to be debriefed by his Soviet masters upon arrival at Cyrenaica, expected to off-load the gold-dust of his findings on the latest in American naval technology. After this, he was to be flown back to Russia with his gold, and – reunited with his wife – given a new identity to live more or less wherever he wanted. His cut meant that the Soviets didn't even have to pay him for their information!

Well, it didn't quite work out that way, but there was a further chapter to the Lavitzsky story.

He escaped from British clutches, for the Americans wanted badly to debrief him. At their strong insistence through diplomatic channels he was shunted off to Washington for further lengthy questioning sessions as to the extent of his knowledge about the workings of U.S.S. *Aztec.* After all, the man might just be acquitted by a British court and free to wander about with all his information!

It was at this point that Lavitzsky pleaded with them on humanitarian grounds. Apart from the fact that the Soviets might just gain his extradition from Britain (and thus gain the secret info as well), he claimed that he could expect no justice in Britain, such being the feeling there after what had happened in London. The two ideas were mutually exclusive, but each was powerful in its own way. He told the Americans that he had been a true defector, that he had been forced to join the plot under duress from both the terrorists and the K.G.B. He had had no choice in the matter. Nor had he handed any information over to the Soviets, as it turned out. Technically, therefore, as well as morally, he was free of the charge of espionage.

Incredibly to Paul, the Americans accepted his defector story, along with everything else.

The upshot is that Lavitzsky was given immunity from prosecution, a new life and a new identity in the United States. The Soviet authorities were prevailed upon to grant his wife a passport so that she could join him in America. Mr and Mrs Lavitzsky, and three of their younger children, all Alias Something-Else-sky, now reside contentedly in the suburbs of a middle-western American city, where they have been warmly accepted by the neighbours. Mrs Lavitzsky is a pillar of the local Orthodox Church, and Mr Lavitzsky (or whatever-he-is) sells tyres. Someone drops in from Washington to see them from time to time – Uncle David – but otherwise their lives are calm and unruffled, just the kind of uneventful and materially fulfilled life suitable for Anatoly's nerves.

At one time his story was much sought after, but Uncle

David and Washington put an embargo on any publication. Lavitzsky complied readily with the ruling. He knows which side his bread is buttered.

Andy could never again look Paul in the face when the subject came up.

An ex-Prime Minister now prunes roses in her garden and gently guides guests to their places at her dinner parties.

She was forced to relinquish both high office and the leadership of her party after the exposure of the Clive Parris affair. So, her fate was not, after all, decided upon the weighty questions of her handling of the greatest domestic crisis ever to hit Great Britain. It was decided upon what happened in a bed in a two-star hotel. The mud stuck, stuck everywhere. She'd been in power a long time. She had grown complacent, lost control over the behaviour of a junior minister who had lied to the country and to the House. A grand political career came ignominiously to an end. Where had we heard this before?

A General Election was called, and the opposition party, already riding high in the polls, got in. But many old-timers in politics quietly wondered whether the new Prime Minister (yes, a man) would have shown the same strength of mind under the strain of those desperate hours as she had done.

And they had reason to wonder, and to care, because as Britain and Europe approached the millennium, terrorism was destined to become a permanent nightmare reality.

Scottie's gang had not achieved its purpose. No gold was lost, no capital city blown up or saturated in radiation.

But the gang *had* got the gold out of the country. Point Number One. Point Number Two: they *had* brought the government of a NATO power to its knees and had been instrumental in kicking it out of office. Not bad for a dozen men, some might reason. Would a few more men, and a few more resources, and even a better plan, have done the trick?

More than one 'all-powerful' nation had cause for fear, and more than one secret society cause for hope.

'He tried to drown me! He tried to attack me, Paul, he nearly killed me! And now you're saying I imagined the whole bloody thing?'

'It has to be for the courts to decide, you know that,' persisted Paul.

'But what have *you* decided?'

He sighed. After avoiding the subject for as long as they could, it was coming out on this particular evening. It was going to be a bumpy night, as Bette Davis said.

'It's important to me, Paul.'

'I know that. But Jane, what can I say? To me he's pathetic. A hollow man, the kind that looks glib and plausible in public and turns out to be jelly inside.'

'That's not hollow.'

'Okay, allow me to mix metaphors. I don't know what I think about Clive, darling. As I said, it's for the courts to decide, not me.'

'And what about Sarah? I suppose you believe all his rubbish about her, too?'

'The new Cyrenaican regime has opened the files on the case. From what's coming out it points very strongly to her, Jane.' He wanted to touch her. He put his arm on her shoulder but she shook him off. He got up and walked about. 'Well? What do you want me to say? That your sister was a saint?'

'She was *my sister*!'

Paul flared. 'Yes, and she led the terrorists right to the heart of London! Some sister *she* turned out to be!'

She rushed from the room without speaking and slammed the door. In a moment Paul heard her sobbing, from the other side of the closed door of her bedroom. He wanted to go in, but the gulf was too great.

He was the man who had brought her sister to a kind of posthumous justice. And she couldn't forgive him for that. It's what it came to.

Later, after she had recovered herself, he said: 'I won't stay if you don't want me to,' meaning 'the night'.

'I think that would be best,' she said tightly, not looking at his eyes.

Truth to tell, Jane was thinking at that moment about Humphrey. Humphrey had come through with the best coverage, overall, of the whole affair and was likely to be nominated as Reporter of the Year. He might even be able to forget about little contempt of court troubles after that triumph. But Humphrey had the grace not to allow his elation to get the better of him, for he knew Jane was going through a kind of second mourning. The second being for the death of an illusion.

It was Humphrey who'd come round, Humphrey who offered quiet support and a drink, Humphrey who stoutly maintained Sarah's essential innocence. Meaningless words, coming from him: he was the reporter who'd cracked the story wide open and knew every facet of it (he was commissioned to write a book). If anyone knew the dirt on Sarah, it was him, and in time it would all be preserved forever in his prose, as it had already appeared in his articles. But Jane wasn't reading the articles. What was important was that Humphrey was giving her comfort and moral support at the time she needed it, just at the time she was having to come to terms with Sarah's betrayal of her country.

And the old question returned: was Jane betraying Humphrey? Was she traitor to his hopes and dreams for them both?

Felicity had stood in the way: stood in the way for what had seemed an eternity. But that was over, now. The divorce was through and a settlement on custody and other matters mutually agreed. Humphrey was truly free at last, and he loved it. He brought over some champagne to celebrate. On an evening of a day when Paul had been to see her, in the afternoon. It couldn't go on like this.

The crisis which they had all lived through seemed to have affected Humphrey for the better. In his own words, 'it made me think through just where I should be going and who I should be sharing my life with, once and for all.' But something about that crisis also made Humphrey suddenly grow up into the kind of man Jane wanted to marry, it was as if he had matured overnight.

'In fact, I think it would be better if we didn't see each other for a while,' said Jane to Paul – still not able to look him in the eye.

Paul seemed about to erupt with a protestation, but then it died in his throat. His hands released her shoulders.

'Let me think things out,' she added, to soften the blow. He had heard it before: the kiss-off.

'Yes, of course,' said Paul, tight-lipped. Well, it had to be faced. He was on one side and she was on the other. He was Law, she was Private Citizen. Through this case they had come together – a frenzied and wild coming-together. And because of the case they were soon going to part, never to meet again. Jane had once feared that with the end of the case there would also be the end of her affair with Paul. It had turned out to be true. But she was no longer afraid.

Back to the office bike, he thought – bitterly and not without a touch of self-pity – out on the landing of Jane's bare, cold hallway. So much for the glamorous life of the secret agent. Whose days might be numbered, by the way, unless Georgi and his cohorts managed to come up with something else to throw into the international brew.

But he would survive. Well, yes, he did survive. The occasional pangs for Jane kept recurring for at least a further six months. But it took only six months.

He got over it, all right. But sometimes it made him wonder if it wasn't he, rather than Clive Parris, who was the true 'hollow man'.

The news came through at nine o'clock on the B.B.C., just as Jane and Humphrey were finishing off a dinner celebrating their first month together. For some silly reason they had left the set on, burbling away while they were engrossed in their meal and in one another. They were celebrating their first month with all due pomp and extravagance – time for such frivolous 'anniversaries'. Something caught her ear as she was pouring them both a liqueur.

'Clive Parris, the former Minister for Nuclear Energy in the last government, was today found hanged in his cell at Woodley Remand Centre. Mr Parris, who was 55, was due to stand trial for espionage and attempted murder in connection with the so-called Ransom for London Affair, which came to light...'

Jane sat down on a footstool by Humphrey's leg. Humphrey had to take his glass from her hand.

'I'm not surprised,' said Humphrey. 'He was a sad case all right.'

It seemed Clive had managed to knot his sheets together, tying them to the upper bar of his cell window.

A note was found, but its contents were not yet available to the public.

Jane was relieved and even cheered by the thought that she was not going to have to go through the ordeal in court as prime prosecution witness. The case, so far as the attempted murder charges were concerned, was tricky and she dreaded the cross-examination by a leading Q.C. Now it was to be no more, and it made her positively light-headed.

Later, in bed, she found her cheerfulness had made her sad. Sad for Clive, now that he was no longer her adversary. No one should be cheerful at the thought of an unhappy death like that. Here they were, having called him a cold fish so often, and he had fallen from his high perch because of his love for Sarah. Yes, for all his weaknesses, his passion for her was the ruling emotion of his life, meaning far more to him than any ambition or lust for power. Perhaps more than life itself.

Jane found it in her heart to weep a little for him.

Clive Parris was the last victim in the train of events that almost destroyed a metropolis and a country.

And so, with his death, that particular story came to a close.